INTO *Her* FANTASIES

THE CIMARRON SERIES: BOOK THREE

ANGEL PAYNE

INTO *Her* FANTASIES

THE CIMARRON SERIES: BOOK THREE

ANGEL PAYNE

WATERHOUSE PRESS

For Thomas. The road on this one wasn't always easy, and I couldn't have done it without you. I love you so much. Thank you for being my prince of perfection, and for making my wildest fantasies come true.

CHAPTER ONE

"Here's to the adventures of Lucy and the prince!"

"*To Lucy!*"

The rally cry, fifteen voices strong, made it official. My face was surely as red as my strawberry margarita. My giant, delicious strawberry margarita. So delicious, I threw down an extra tip for Gervase, my favorite Velvet Margarita bartender.

"*Viva!* To Lucy and her *príncipe!*" he shouted, skirting the bar to sweep me into a gallant tango.

I laughed but blushed harder. *Uh-oh.* Out came the cell phone video cams, belonging to the majority of my friends and family, gathered tonight in my favorite Los Angeles bar to see me off on said "adventure" with said "principe." To be more specific: Prince Shiraz Cimarron of the Island of Arcadia, one of the world's most mysterious chunks of land, overseen by the most fascinating royal family since the Tudors. Of the whole family, Shiraz was the most intriguing—or so the western media claimed. To them, he was one hell of a fascinating subject: pretty but pragmatic, serious and secretive, an outer shell of calm hiding a cutthroat businessman on the inside...

And, at the age of twenty-five, had not had a single serious romantic relationship.

The press had indulged in *a lot* of fun with that one— and still were. A glance at the video monitor over the bar, broadcasting one of Gervase's favorite celebrity gossip shows, proved as much. The audio feed wasn't necessary to follow along, since the image montage was accompanied by headlines which blended mesmerizing and mortifying into a rare art form.

His Highness of Hotness—Hiding a Hidden Harem?

Shirtless Shiraz—but where are the Bikini Babes?

Single and Cimarron: Blessing or Curse?

Prince of Playboys...or not?

Cimarron CEO: Nasty and Naughty or Virgin in Hiding?

Sheez.

I blushed on the guy's behalf. Almost felt sorry for him.

Almost.

To be honest, it was hard to feel anything but lust when treated to a nonstop parade of Shiraz Cimarron's magnificence. Was I proud of swimming in such a shallow first impression puddle? Of course not. But it was the truth, as blatant and bold as the man's beauty itself. When confronted with both, sometimes all a woman could do was...

Stare.

God, *yes.*

The third Cimarron in line to the Arcadian throne was a work of art, plain and simple. Piercing blue eyes. Greek god lips. Strong, jutted jaw. A lean but sculpted body, likely developed from running and swimming in the constant sunshine on his island. His skin was the color of Moroccan sand, his elegant face framed by hair like midnight over that exotic land. Gazing at him was like marveling at a natural wonder; his picture should've been shuffled into the screensaver image packets between Moab cliffs and Tahitian Rainbows.

Yeah, he was that stunning.

That sinful. That unreal.

Seriously.

Unreal.

I didn't just live in LA. I'd grown up here, in the land where illusion was reality and vice versa. I'd waited in coffee lines, stood at airport security, and picked up my dry cleaning beside pasty, bad-tempered people who'd been touted to the whole world as sex on sticks. Camera angles and editing tricks could turn Broom-Hilda into a Victoria's Secret goddess—

Which meant maybe that unreal Arcadian prince was really a doughy little yokel and photo filters had done the rest.

That was it. My safety valve. The sane way to approach this little "jaunt" out to Arcadia. Recasting the stud as doughy dud meant my head could stay on straight—and focus on the bigger picture here.

The *much* bigger picture.

Like landing the contract to coordinate the hugest wedding event of the year. The Cimarron royal wedding day.

The event, a double ceremony to bind Shiraz's two older brothers to the American women with whom they'd fallen in love, would be more than the biggest coup for the wedding planning company into which I'd poured myself for the last eighteen months.

It would mean that company was officially half mine.

But for now, that company had only one president's name on the door.

Ezra Lowe.

Yeah, the same Ezra throwing me the weird once-over from down the bar. Even a couple of twice-overs.

Damn it, Ezra.

What the hell was he up to? Those glances weren't flirty, but Ez had *something* on his mind...something making him laser his baby blues right into me.

I had to get to the bottom of this.

And probably, if my bladder had any say in the matter, before I got to the bottom of my next drink.

Uggghhh.

At least Father Gravity and Mother Tequila played nice, allowing me a graceful twirl to wrap up the celebration spin with Gervase. I landed in the perfect position to sweep a saucy bow to the crowd. "And now, the principe's new wench must pee."

Everybody laughed—except Mom. She rolled eyes so closely matching my own in color, their tiny gold flecks were apparent even in the bar's dim light. "Lucina Louise. Must you be so crude?"

"Antonia Marie"—yeah, the first name, middle name hookup was our snarky subtext for affection—"must you be your daughter's damn shadow?"

"Only when I'm her designated driver." She smirked and folded her arms.

My *mother*.

Smirked at *me*.

In a damn bar.

"Okay, okay. Break it up, hussies."

Damn it. Ezra needed to be renamed the happy hour ninja. Five seconds of distraction, and the man had slipped all the way over here without detection. No way not to notice him now. His strong fingers curled over Mom's shoulders, his Charlie Hunnam scruff resting atop her poofy-styled head. Sometimes I wondered if the man's looks had gotten matched to the wrong destiny. With that lumberjack jaw and cascading Thor hair, he should've been a pussy-chasing demon with a guitar or a Harley...or both—not a bisexual Jewish wedding planner with a natural talent for crazy centerpieces, perfect photo ops, and awful phallic jokes.

Not that I had a chance to hear a single phallic funny now, thanks-no-thanks to Mom. "Who you calling hussy?" she bantered, adding a girlish giggle.

"*You.*" Ezra smacked a kiss to her cheek. "Hussy."

"Gahhhh." I slashed a hand through the air. "*Stop.*"

"*Pssshhh,*" Mom snickered.

"I love it when we make her do that," Ez chuckled.

Pinched glower. "Excuse me. You two are already making me want to puke, and I'm only down by one Gervase special."

"Lucina Maria. Did I raise you in a barn?"

I stopped. Damn near pivoted back around, the Uber app open on my phone, to flash at her. Maybe it was time her grand mission came to an end. It had been three months since she'd married Ben, giving her more than enough time to make up for her scarcity in my teens, and it had been pedal-to-the-metal on the mommy-daughter time since then. But hanging at the bar for my Farewell-to-Fantasy-Island party, even in the name of letting me get as plowed as I wanted? It was time to land the helicopter.

I marched away to the bathroom. Thank the Good Virgin, the human helicopter didn't follow.

She let Ezra do the dirty work instead.

Even more funny? I wasn't surprised by the stunt in the least. I was, however, torqued as hell—especially as the man pushed the door shut and then locked it.

"Are you kidding?"

He braced his ass against the portal. "We need to talk."

"No." Another adamant talk-to-the-hand. "You need to leave, and I need to pee."

He gestured at the stalls with a King Arthur sweep. "Have at it."

My bladder screamed too loud for an argument. Off to the races I went.

As I took care of business, his determined steps battled each other for echo factor. Once he confirmed we were alone, he did the butt brace thing on the lip of the vanity counter, or so I guessed from the vicinity of his sigh. "So..."

"So...what?" I countered while flushing. Getting scooched all the way back into my jacket wasn't such a slam dunk. By the time I was done, my bra strap was twisted four times over and my panties were crunched to the left of my cooch, but I was beyond caring. The better part of Gervase Special *Numero Dos* was still waiting for me out on the bar.

"So you're ready to rock this thing in Arcadia, right?"

Breath of weird relief. So this was what the looks were about.

Wait a second.

This was what the looks were about?

I stomped out of the stall on the heels of that thought, letting him see my full glare because of it. "Gee. Thanks for the vote of confidence."

Ezra plowed a hand through his hair. The move lent him more of the King Arthur vibe—though it was more the stressed-post-wars guy, not the congenial-spot-in-Camelot one. "Do you really not get it by now? *Oy gevalt*, Luce. I've got more confidence in *you* than *me* right now."

"Only because you let your passport lapse."

"That has nothing to do with it, and you know it."

Wry side-eye. "That so?"

"You think I'm making this shit up?" He scowled. "You schmooze with these royals like you belong with them, darling. We both said as much after the video conference call."

"Guess all those princess movies as a kid *did* stick."

"Whatever it was, I'm grateful." He followed my path over to the sink. "You're our best chance of landing this, Luce."

"Okay, okay." I chuckled. "Chill, sparky."

"Yeah." He whooshed out a breath. "Chill. Good suggestion."

"So what's the problem?" I examined myself while washing my hands. Noticed, with tequila-induced clarity, that my brows needed plucking, my chestnut asymmetrical bob was split end city, and the acne cream fairy seriously needed to visit my pimply princess forehead. *Lovely.* Twenty-four years old, and I still had to check for acne.

Stress for another time—especially because deciphering Ez consumed a lot of brain space right now. I stared at him as he stared at his fingers, now drumming incessantly on the counter, with abnormal focus.

Finally, he mumbled, "There's no *problem*..."

"Which was why you locked me in here and then straight-up jabbed if I was 'ready' to rock—" Hard jolt. Straight to the chest. Sudden, horrid understanding. "Shit. What the hell, Ez?"

His jaw visibly clenched. "What the hell what?"

"You're...scared." I tossed the hand towel into the bin, using the move to face off to him. "Why are you scared?"

"I'm not scared."

"Nah. Nope. No more flying there, Superman. Out with

it." I wiggled my fingers inward. "The Kryptonite. Out with it. Now."

He glared—well, tried—one last time before pacing back toward the door, fingers now laced behind his head.

Like a prisoner ready to confess.

Shit. Shit. Shit.

With his back to me, he blurted at last, "We lost the Ramone wedding."

"We—"

Shock choked the rest of it into silence. Like *that* was going to make it any less real. Or horrific. Kii Ramone's pageant of a wedding was Expectation Inc.'s crown jewel, our finest contract to date. Kii was a triple-threat star at the top of every Hollywood A List, meaning every wedding planning team in the Southland had battled for the chance to orchestrate her special day. Ezra and I labored for weeks on Expectation's proposal, appealing to the woman's Polynesian roots and sense of family, doing so on a wing and a prayer. Neither of us had a stellar point of reference on the subject of family.

But we'd left Kii's place with homemade poi and a stack of signed CDs. A realization I vigorously sank my teeth into. "But...she gave us CDs. And poi. And the verbal okay to start ordering flowers. When we won the Crystal Award for the LeHavre engagement party, *she* sent *us* flowers!"

"I know."

"Then why?" It was just a rasp from me this time as I braced both hands on the counter. "What the hell?"

Kaboom.

The stall door Ez had smacked swung hard into the bathroom wall. I was still so shocked, I barely flinched. "Who?" I finally whispered. "Who got it?"

Ezra's weighted huff said everything—and nothing. "She decided to go with a team directly out of Honolulu. She said they *really* understood the *ohana* thing."

"Family." I managed the translation despite the acid in my gut.

"Bingo," Ez muttered.

We stood together, heads bent in silent defeat, for several minutes. *Family.* There were few subjects about which both Ez and I were way out of our league, and that was one of them. Not a damn thing we could've done, nor a bullet we could've dodged.

Finally, I mumbled, "At least LTK didn't land it."

No need for translation on that one. LTK, aka Love's True Kiss, were the New York-based dynamos who'd snatched a dozen gigs from Ezra and me over the last year, including the coup of the Santelle-Court wedding. The dressed-down but uber-elegant party had landed them the covers of every major event-planning magazine, officially turning them into our cross-country rivals—though Ezra preferred the term blood-sucking enemies-on-high.

After a few more minutes, I reopened my eyes. Rubbed my temples. "Well, this is a real shit fest."

Kaboom.

Another Ezra special. Damn, those stall doors were sturdy. I almost giggled at the thought—well, that and the odd comfort inundating me. Ez was punching things—which meant he still wanted to fight. Only once had I ever seen him at less than full warrior mode. It had been when he found his real dad through an adoption connection service, and the alcoholic shithead hadn't wanted anything to do with him.

That was the trouble with planning fairy tales for a living.

Life itself rarely reciprocated. Ez had learned that one the hard way. I'd been there to help him through that darkness, but I didn't want to revisit anytime soon.

Just to be sure we really weren't going there, I slid out a wry smirk. Added a slow drawl. "Feel better?"

Ez pulled in a sharp breath. "No."

"Imagine that."

"Fine," he snapped. "Go ahead. Crucify me."

"What? Why?"

"Because this is going to ruin me. Ruin *us*. You gave a year and a half of your life to me, and I squandered it for fucking nothing." He dropped his face into his hands. "So go ahead. Do it. Call me the hugest douche on the planet. Diarrhea in the cat box. Mold in the shower. Spittle on the—"

"Gah!" I held up both hands. The man and subtle had never shared the same byline, but my appetite had been murdered for at least the next two days. "Baby Jesus in a car seat," I muttered, yanking out my phone as a reminder text pinged in. Time to check in for my flight tomorrow night. "As soon as I handle this, I'm dialing the Radio Emo fan line for your ass. Isn't the 'Wallowing Pit of Dark Dedications Hour' starting about now?"

He glared. "Says the girl who probably still has Radio Emo on speed dial?"

I arched a brow. Correction: arched it and then mentally peeled it off and hurled it at him. "Below the belt."

"Calling it like I see it, Betty Stepford."

Okay, *now* he was a douche. Using the nickname I still hated, his favorite during the six months I'd tried fitting into Ryan's vanilla mold, was salt in a yuck-deep wound. And since Ryan was ancient history as of six months ago, *douche* said it perfectly.

"I'm sorry." He shook his head. "I'm not in my right mind."

I reached up, rubbing his back. "Neither of us are, sparky. But I still love you."

He pulled me into a fierce hug. "I love you too, most un-Stepford one I know."

"Damn straight—which is why I'm going to get on that plane tomorrow, fly to the Mediterranean, and save your douchebag ass."

"You mean *our* ass?"

I jerked back. Severed the air with my gasp. "*Our—*" I stammered, succumbing to the double-take. "So the partnership's still on the table?"

"Honey bunches, you get Shiraz Cimarron to put ink on this deal, and I'll have half the *world* waiting when you get back."

I jogged my chin up like Scarlett O'Hara, donning the curtains to get her freaking plantation back. "Then consider this contract a win."

The confidence overflowed. Ezra grabbed me up into a fresh hug. "There's my girl."

I beamed a brash grin. "She was never far, baby."

He stepped away. Leaned against the counter with a relaxed pose but an all-business gaze. "So...you've done all the homework on Shiraz Cimarron?"

"You mean all the gossip web pages and photo collages you sent over?"

"Girlfriend, that part wasn't studying."

"Oh?"

"That part was *fun*."

"Yeah?" I let the smirk turn skeptical. "This isn't about

having *fun* with the guy, bucky. I want his name on a contract and a deposit check, period."

His arms dropped. So did all traces of his smile. "As long as we're turning fun into the pariah here..."

Groan. "What now?"

He exhaled, now adding his big brotherly mode to the mix. *Uh-oh.* "Luce...you know to go carefully with this guy, right?"

"With who?" Incredulous—but nervous—laugh. "You mean pretty prince boy?"

"Pretty prince boy." The echo came with his careful enunciation. I never liked that shit, especially when his regard was equally somber. "That's really the angle you're taking, Miss Fava?"

Miss Fava.

Shit just got real.

And the *bigger* shit in the room knew it—which explained why he stiffened like a slap was coming. I considered it but checked myself. Ez would love easing his guilt with a little effortless penance, clarifying why he dug in on treating me like a four-year-old. That was usually the direct line to my wrath, but no way was I rewarding Ezra's exploitation of it by assuaging his guilt.

"Tell you what, Ez. Since you seem to be the new Cimarron expert on the block, why don't *you* just take over from here?"

He huffed, again all serious big brother. "Did I say that?"

And yeah, my snort was all petulant little sister. *Yuck.* "Didn't have to," I retorted. "You implied—"

"Nothing." His gaze softened while his jaw hardened. "Just some real concern, okay? As your boss *and* friend, I want to be sure you have your eyes wide open about Shiraz Cimarron."

The weirdness in his face wasn't my eventual undoing.

It was the gentle vigilance in his voice, like where a real big brother would take things, that finally melted me. "Don't worry, Ez. I'm a big girl, remember? And under the crown, or whatever the hell he wears on top of all that great hair, he *is* just a man."

He yanked away with a grimace. "Damn it, Luce. That's exactly what I'm talking about."

"Exactly what...*what*?"

A new snort. "He's a *man*, not just the title. There are... nuances to him. And you know me; I'm a big fan of nuance, but in this case..." He frowned deeper. "There's a lot of shit here I can't put together." He shook his head, letting out a motorcycle rumble of a sound. "Fuck. The man is so damn private."

"All right, untwist your panties." I smoothed both hands on the air. "Obviously, there's a lot we *do* know. Work backward from there."

"Don't you think I've tried?" His eyes developed blue shards. His jaw turned to granite. Sheez, the man *could* look hetero and intimidating when he wanted. "But all we've got is a happy royal upbringing in the Palais Arcadia, a gap year turned down in favor of four years at Aalto U in Finland, followed by a direct flight home and then straight to work as CEO of the Island of Arcadia."

"Which was three years ago," I supplied.

"Which was three years ago," he confirmed.

"And...?"

"And what?"

I took a turn at the frown. "And what else?"

"You think there's *more*?" He folded his arms. Swished his head. So much for hetero. And my patience.

"Oh, come on." My hands hitched to my hips. "Three years

of nothing but work and sleep? Uh-uh. Not flying, either. The man has to have hobbies, interests." Images from Gervase's gossip show blazed again through my mind. "Shit that requires him to be shirtless. With bikini babes."

"Who are apparently just friends."

I *pssshh*ed. "Because you have court spies in Arcadia?"

"Not a one," Ez returned. "Only verified reports that those 'babes' were companions only, knowing no more or less about him than his male buddies."

"Verified reports *how*?" My eyebrows were getting a great workout today. "Is someone paying off his security detail to talk? Does he *have* a security detail? If not, are people following the man around? And who are *they*? Verified journalists or free-wheeling hacks?"

And again with the teeter-totter smirk. "Want to start talking nuances now?"

"Shit," I muttered.

"Another good way of putting it."

More of the TV headlines returned to mind—with a fresh, shocking implication. "So...nobody even knows if the guy's actually punched his V card?"

"Ding, ding, ding."

"And pretty princey himself won't confirm or deny it either?"

"Remember the part about how he likes his privacy?"

I pivoted. Faced the sink. Eyeballed the blinking red motion detector for the faucet, wondering why my pulse had suddenly upticked to match its beat. What the hell? The status of Shiraz Cimarron's virginity—or, more likely, just how far from "virginal" he'd gotten by now—was of no concern to me. *None.* That included all thoughts of how and with whom the man chose to get naked.

And now I'd gone and done it.

Just thinking of the man getting naked...

Wow.

Not. Going. There.

"Well, he can keep his privacy." My reflection scowled at Ezra's. Using the secondhand delivery system made it easier to connect with the message. Or maybe the words just felt damn good to declare. "I'm flying there to connect with his brain, not his dick, and only long enough to impress the shit out of him with our proposal."

Ez also used the mirror as his messenger, rocking out a skeptical glare. "Hope you're damn serious about that, missy— especially when that boy's fine, fierce, potentially undipped wick is right in front of you."

I did it. Went ahead and rolled my eyes. "You want to give me a *little* credit?"

"A little," he conceded. "But I've seen your libido in action, Lucina Louise—action you haven't enjoyed in a while."

I let my head drop. Batted both eyes in coy exaggeration. "I'm bringing all my favorite appliances along for the trip, darling. Extra batteries too."

He returned the grin. "Well, *e*xcellent!"

We sealed the deal like usual. Hip bump and then a hug. As soon as that was done, in our considerably clearer air, I ventured, "So aside from knowing this proposal better than my own name, what else should I do to prep for Shiraz of the Nuances?"

Though that made Ez's lips twitch, he was quick with the serious comeback. "Brutal truth?"

"Is there any other kind?"

He sucked back a big breath. "Dial back Miz Kinky Sass. Turn *on* Miss Prissy Tea Time. One thing we definitely *do* know about him? He's a straight shooter when it comes to corporate prowess. I mean, the man's daily planner probably has target goals instead of action plans, and he scores bulls-eyes on every one of them."

"Sheez."

"Bet your sweet ass, sheez."

"So what are we talking here?" I turned, meeting him eye-to-eye again. "Quick run to Costume Castle for a Mary Poppins cos play, or do I break out my nanna's Dior?"

Nanna, God rest her, had possessed impeccable fashion taste. I loved her stuff so much, she'd left a few pieces to me in her will, including a flawless black Dior, circa mid-50s, with layers of crinoline and a deep V-neck. I loved finding excuses to wear it.

"No!"

And apparently, this wouldn't be one of those times.

"This guy is your CEO nightmare on crack," Ezra went on. "Wear your pinstripe skirt suit. And nude hose. And for God's sake, secretary shoes."

I scowled. Deeply. "What the hell are secretary shoes?"

"Do you have any flats?"

"I have stilettos, wedges, platforms, boots—do boots count as flats?"

"Not *your* kind of boots."

"Then no *bueno* on the flats."

"So borrow some from your mom. And wear your hair back. *All* the way."

I grabbed a hock of my split ends. "Hello? Layers?"

"Hello? Bobby pins? And darling, *one* earring in each ear.

Pearls are best. I know you have those."

Fighting him on that one was futile. He'd been there the day Mom moved into Ben's place for good, and she'd found Nanna's wedding earrings. Ez had held us both as we'd bawled after Mom gave them to me, saying she knew Nanna would want me to have them.

I watched as the memory struck him, just as it did me—underlining the truth that bloomed, warm and full, between us.

That despite executive meetings in the ladies' room, we were a damn fine team. Despite all the ups and downs, twists and turns, dysfunctions and malfunctions of life in LA-LA Land, we'd managed to forge something rare in this strange place.

A true friendship.

Proved very clearly by my next thought.

If I looked at Ez right now, even refusing to fly to Arcadia so I could roll out Expectation's dog-and-pony for some stick-up-his-ass prince, he'd not love me an inch less. We'd hug and then begin tomorrow from ground zero. We'd find other weddings to produce—and before they came through, rent ourselves as kid party clowns if need be.

We'd find a way. We always did.

Which was why *I'd* find a way to get through this bullshit with Shiraz Cimarron. I'd do it in a stupid skirt suit and boring shoes, and I'd hit the hell out of this home run for our team and our future.

How long could the whole process take, anyway? Couple of days? Perhaps a week? I could do anything for a week, even in flats. Once Ezra had his new passport, he'd make the actual follow-up trips to Arcadia for planning the wedding, likely flying me back solely for execution on the big day itself. By then I'd have exchanged the flats for boots. Or roller skates. Or both.

One week.

An eye's blink in the whole span of my life. Barely enough for a few memories, let alone massive life landscape changes.

Yeah, I had this shit.

By this time next week, Shiraz Cimarron would be just a pretty face in my rearview—viewed through the shades I'd have to wear because of my bright, blinding future.

CHAPTER TWO

"Holy shit."

The words ricocheted back at me from the mosaicked walls of the Palais Arcadia rotunda, bringing the horrifying recognition I'd spoken them out loud. Okay, whispered. At least it wasn't a moronic gasp. *Those* I gulped back—between numerous mental floggings.

How the hell had I thought internet "research" was a proper substitute for all this? How could I have bitched, for a second, that the Cimarrons' insistence on flying me here was a waste of money? Most importantly, how did I assume Ez and I could conceive a ceremony and reception to match this grandeur?

The beauty continued as I followed a petite court page with a sleek French twist down several more hallways. Every tiled masterpiece was more intricate than its predecessor, shifting in theme from ocean and rainforests to the gold, red, and cobalt of the Arcadian crest. In spots where the walls gave way to archways, I snatched glimpses of balconies with elegant wrought-iron furniture, overlooking lush gardens and unspoiled shoreline. Beyond those beaches and cliffs, the Mediterranean was beautiful beyond description. The waves, like liquefied blue orchids, were dazzled with diamonds of sunlight and edged with lacy foam. It was splendor to the point of pain, but looking away wasn't an option—as I learned while waiting for the page to swipe a fob over a digital panel embedded into a wall.

I looked away from the view long enough to gape at the state-of-the-art lock. The moment was like the scene in *Somewhere in Time*, with Christopher Reeve jarred back to real life by pulling out a modern penny. I was equally jolted as we left the enchanted castle, entering offices that could've been transplanted from any modern corporate park.

All traces of the old-world majesty were gone. Our footsteps were muted by industrial carpeting instead of echoing on marble hallways. A collection of secretary cubicles stretched in front of us, decorated with kid pictures and puppy calendars. Their occupants chattered merrily. I was a little surprised, happily so, to see the international assortment of complexions and body types. From curvy redheads to ballerina blondes to wild Beyoncé locks, there were men and women to represent the look. Everyone was dressed in modern white pantsuits, accented with red and gold brocade scarves for the ladies and matching ties for the men.

My fascination was returned a hundred-fold. Though conversations didn't come to screeching stops, I discerned fascinated whispers as I kept up with the page. Weirdness. While I was used to such behavior, it was usually because of gossip about the bride I trailed, not me. What were these people thinking of the American main attraction now?

Not that I had a lot of time to ponder those answers. Keeping pace with the assistant was turning into my workout for the week...maybe the month. *Ruthless pace, thy name is a court page in flats.*

Inwardly, I hissed at those flats.

Note to self. Leave out that part during the debrief with Ezra.

We entered another part of the offices, where the cubicles were replaced by actual offices lining a modern hallway. Through one open door I glimpsed an eye-popper of a modern conference room, outfitted with speakerphone consoles, wide AV screens, and even the latest in two-way hologram projectors.

"Sheez-ussss."

The page glanced over her shoulder. "Miss Fava? Is anything wrong?"

I lifted a perky smile. "Nope. Right as rain."

"Oh! I love that expression too!"

"I'll bet you do," I mumbled.

"Excuse me?"

"Uhhh...mmm...I said, what a coincidence...boo?"

So I'd never win a rap battle. Thank God the girl looked more set on guiding me deeper into the office labyrinth than throwing down some one-liners—though we didn't get much farther on that quest either, once a couple of women emerged from the next conference room, curious smiles on their faces.

I recognized them at once, as damn well I should have. A brunette and a blonde, one rocking a cute ponytail and the other with a chin-length blunt cut. Both looked me nearly eye-to-eye because of the killer-cute heels on their feet. *Heels. What the fuck?*

On the other hand, they weren't the ones needing to make an impression here—proved by the goose egg diamonds on their ring fingers.

"I heard a Southern California accent," the blonde claimed in a sing-song.

Her companion went for an eye roll. "I'd spank you, but you'd like it, sister."

The blonde scowled. "What the hell?"

"Californians don't have accents." She directed a wider smile my way. "They do, however, know how to greet one of their own." And in seconds, had me locked in a sunshiney hug. "Hi there. Welcome to Arcadia. You're Lucina Fava, right?"

"Guess you're hoping I am." As I'd hoped, the quip met with her approving chuckle. "It's lovely to meet you, Your Majesty Camellia."

"*Just* Camellia," she insisted, stepping back to let her "sister" shift forward, extending a hand with more formality. "Or Cam, please. I'm not officially 'Majesty' of anything until after the wedding. And this is Brooke Valen-Cimarron, already the sister of my heart, soon to be my real sister-in-law."

Yeah, I knew that too but tried to shake the petite blonde's hand with a blend of formality and friendliness. "And I'm here to propose ideas about you both doing that in beauty and style."

"Oh, we know." Brooke tilted an impish smile. "And believe me, the fact that you're here says *a lot* about what we thought of your proposal."

I looked at the ceiling for a second, praying for the strength not to leap all the way through it. "That's incredible to hear." Swung my gaze over to include Camellia in the *kumbaya* of its gratitude. "The competition's been fierce on this one." Nervous laugh. "But duh, you both already know that. And I really did just use 'duh' in a complete sentence." Forget the laugh; fast-forward to the blush. "And now I'm really babbling like an idiot, because that's what I do when I'm nervous as hell, and—"

"You too, huh?" Brooke interjected, though Camellia joined her own giggle to the mix as well.

"We get it, Lucy. Really, we do." Her body did a squirmy

thing, as if she wanted to hug me again but chose a more "queenly" response. "But you wouldn't be here if we didn't love your ideas and weren't impressed by Expectation's credentials—though as you might guess in situations like this, we aren't the only ones in on the decision."

"Of course." I blurted it automatically but studied her with fresh intensity. Did I accept her words at face value, or was she being kind, trying to hide that they'd learned about us losing the Kii Ramone gig? That tidbit hadn't gone public yet, but celebrities talked, just like all their "help" did. If someone from Arcadia had spoken to Kii recently...

Brooke pushed into my rumination with a snort. "She's just trying to be delicate, Lucy."

My heart thudded into my throat. "Delicate? About what?"

"What she *means* is, if we two alone had the choice, Expectation would have bagged this thing already."

"Oh." I struggled to keep my exhalation casual. "Wow. Okay. Cool."

"Regrettably, though, we don't." Brooke punctuated with a girl growl, when Camellia really did smack her backside. "Whaaat, damn it? She has a right to know!"

"Know what?" I rushed the words to avoid stabbing too much insecurity into them. Like I needed to remind myself of *that* little factoid.

"Nothing you won't be able to handle." Camellia scrambled to squeeze my arm, though it didn't carry the reassurance she clearly intended.

What the hell was that? What was I supposed to handle, other than meeting with their fashion spread hunk of a brother-in-law? Was she talking normal political bullshit "handle" or zombie apocalypse "handle"?

"These things are rarely just a simple signature on a contract," she went on. "You know that, right?"

"Sure. Right." I hoped that sounded better than it felt, especially because the page started guiding me away. The golden rule of wedding planning was to keep the bride—in this case, *brides*—on one's side as much as possible, but I'd gotten here early so a *prince* wouldn't be waiting on me. "It was awesome to meet you both," I blurted, blushing *again* like a damn teenager. "Errm— I mean, it was a true pleasure, and—"

"Awww, shaddup." Brooke invoked enough Daffy Duck to crack the three of us *and* the page up. She sweetened the deal by hauling me into another full hug. "It was awesome to meet you too, girl."

After that bath of bridal warm and fuzzy, it was rough to keep following the page down the hall, but I steeled my nerves for whatever lie ahead. I could do this, damn it. I'd rehearsed this presentation so thoroughly I'd be able to present the whole thing to Congress if needed.

Around a bend and past one more boardroom, and then we stepped into a high-domed atrium filled entirely by natural sunlight. The effect was nothing short of the word that emerged before I could help it.

"Wow."

The page lifted a knowing smile as I peered around, taking in the bounty of tropical palms and flowers surrounding a mosaic set into the floor. The sparkling glass pieces emulated the eddies of a lagoon, with a quaint stone bridge arching gently over the "water." At the other side rested a wide reception desk overseen by a woman with the face of a fairy and the hair of Morticia Addams. Not a lot of people could rock that combination, but on her it seemed right—to the point I was intimidated once more.

Yay me.

Sheez and fucking rice. I didn't do intimidated.

Intimidated was for people who hadn't been told their daddy was shot trying to catch a bad guy. Who hadn't had to pack up a house by themselves because Mom was in the other room sobbing about it. Who hadn't gone to bed listening to Mom cry harder, after the department ruled he'd acted "outside the law" chasing that bad guy. And who hadn't started working at thirteen, hoping even a part-time job would make it possible for Mom to quit the shittier of *her* two jobs—the one with the greasy boss who used phrases like "three's really not a crowd" and "I like eating candy two at a time."

Yeah. *Intimidated* hadn't been part of my vocabulary for years. I wasn't about to let it in now.

It worsened as Fairy Morticia stepped around her big marble desk, extending a hand as if I were the damn president coming to visit. "Miss Fava. Greetings." She leaned in like I was the most riveting person she'd ever met. "Were your travels pleasant?"

"Yes, thank you." Total lie. The turbulence had been so insane I'd spouted *Hail Mary*s for the first time in years, but no way was that getting shared. I was certain Morticia would march to heaven on my behalf, to have a few words with the big guy about the winter weather patterns over the Atlantic.

"Excellent," she replied, backing off on the lemur stare. Good thing, because her voice was actually the craziest part about her. It really was a mix of Morticia and Tinkerbell, though it was as soothing as her handshake. "My name is Crista Noble. I am Prince Shiraz's main assistant, and I am here to take care of you in any capacity during your stay in Arcadia."

I lifted a teasing smile. "*Main* assistant? What happened to Park and Central?"

The page girl giggled. Crista didn't. Though if Shiraz Cimarron was half the workaholic *everyone* painted him to be, I doubted Crista got out much. Not that there was "much" to get out to. Sancti might be large enough for an actual Main Street, but I doubted there was a Park Avenue or Central Boulevard to go with it.

"Sorry," I muttered. "Not even...a little funny."

"Well." Crista's lips quirked a little. "Perhaps...a little."

I rejoiced at not having to jam Crista into the Stepford Assistant file. "I'm early," I continued with a bigger smile. "Maybe I'll just take a second to run to the ladies—"

"Crista."

The interruption was as fake as it was sweet. Glass disguised as candy. Its source, a woman who'd emerged from the arched doorway behind Crista, exuded the same impression. She was a few inches shorter than me, with an hourglass figure enhanced in all the right ways by a dark-pink sweater and black pencil skirt. But for all the softness of her outfit, her eyes were lined in sharp kohl and her cheeks contoured in severe blush, making it difficult to appreciate her God-given beauty.

"*Crista.*" It was a full demand this time.

Crista and the page locked gazes. I sensed some serious subterfuge eye rolls on both their parts. "Yes, Miss Stratiss?"

"Ambyr." The woman stepped forward, brushing a strand of her dark, sex goddess hair away. "Remember, darling? It is simply Ambyr, since we shall be working so closely together on the wedding."

The wedding?

I breathed deeply, calling logic to my aid. Nobody had a lock on this thing yet, even this slice of peppermint candy. Nothing confirmed that better than the smile Crista clearly plastered to her lips while turning to the woman. "What can I do for you, Miss Stratiss?"

If the snip threw her off, Miss Ambyr Stratiss didn't show it. Instead she pivoted to face *me*, swooping an assessing stare down to the tips of my basic black flats. My head responded at once—*stand down, baby girl; fleas like her just want under your skin*—but damn it, my head was never a match for my instinct.

Fleas are only eliminated if they bleed.

"I shall need these assembled into a proper binder." Ambyr quirked her pale-lipsticked mouth at me while swooshing the stack of papers into Crista's chest. In my peripheral, I recognized wedding color boards and image sheets similar to a fourth-grade science fair project. "There are six categories, color-coded. The binder tabs should correspond. After it is all comprised, make a matching binder for His Highness Shiraz."

Crista took the papers with a resigned sigh, as if knowing an argument would get her nowhere. Once she did, Ambyr adjusted the stylish cream tote on her shoulder, cocked her head the same direction, and traveled her gaze over my face and hair.

Finally, with another little hitch of her mouth, she issued, "*Karsivoir en Arcadia*, Miss…"

"Fava." I extended a hand. She offered hers in return, princess style, manicured fingernails dropped forward. Before I hooked around and forced her to go palm-to-palm, I locked her in with my gaze. "Lucina Fava, from Expectation Inc."

"Ahhh." She jerked her hand away as soon as I let up on the pressure. "Yes, of course. One of the two American firms bidding on the wedding." Her manicured eyebrows rose and then lowered. "You are from the team out of California?"

"Yes." I forced pleasantness into it. While physically nothing like Dolores Umbridge, she gave me the same hivey feeling as that fictional bitch on wheels. "Near Los Angeles."

"Ahhh, yes. The Crystal Award winners. The wedding designers to the stars."

"Yes on the first, no on the second." Light laugh. "Not yet, at least. But it has a nice ring to it."

"Hmm. I suppose it does." Yep. Umbridge. Which technically wasn't fair—I'd just met the woman—though there was something unnerving about a person with a peach silk voice and emerald-hard eyes. "Though you are still a smaller organization than Love's True Kiss, yes?"

Screw unnerving. Infuriating was the new word— especially as she curled one side of her mouth as if to add, *I know even more tidbits about you, but I'm storing the ammunition.*

She'd landed the first round, that was for damn sure— though Ez and I had hopes LTK had gotten a little lax since landing the Court-Santelle gig and had slacked on their proposal.

Hopes. And more than a few prayers.

Prayers I repeated while studying Ambyr's face a little harder. Who *was* this priss who had me reinforcing my mental fences with electric wire?

"That's true," I finally conceded, finishing with a self-deprecating smile. "But Love's True Kiss has also been around longer than us—which is perfectly fine, if clients want something less innovative for their big day."

It wasn't an argument I pulled out often—*innovative* was often the exact opposite of what people wanted in their wedding day—but the glint in Ambyr's eyes proved I'd aimed my own guns right. "Well played, Miss Fava," she murmured, turning Umbridge into Cleoptra inside two seconds. "Too bad you will not have more time in Arcadia." She swished a toe back and forth on the tile, making me notice her expensive shoes. Pointy toes. Completely flat. "I think I would have liked you."

She turned, but I stopped her by clearing my throat. "Sorry," I drawled as she swiveled her gaze back over. "What planning company did you say *you're* with?"

Her lips twitched. She raked the hard green gaze over me again. "Because I did *not* say."

In the three seconds it took me to rein in my *what the hell*, the woman pivoted, tossed a winsome look at Crista, and then made her way toward the bridge, finishing with a breezy, "Tell my sweet prince I shall see him this evening."

My sweet prince?

"Because you did not tell him a thousand times yourself?" Crista muttered as Ambyr strolled out of sight. Another soft snicker from the page. I remained guarded, though that was tough when Crista tacked on, "*Salpu merde.*"

I cocked my head. "Do I want to know what that means?"

"Probably not," the page answered. "But it rhymes with *wilthy witch.*"

I pressed my lips to keep from fully snickering—though the humor wasn't such a hit with Crista. "Now I need to fit *this* project into the day somehow." She sent a baleful stare at the pile of papers still clutched against her chest. Ambyr had left her with no other choice about preventing the sheaf from spilling everywhere. No way could I let her continue to struggle, so I grabbed about half the load and slid it onto her desk. "*Merderim,*" she murmured, dropping back into her chair.

I directed a sympathetic smile down at her. "Likely none of my business, but what *is* all this?" Besides the dream wedding scrapbook of an eight-year-old.

The secretary looked ready to laugh. Then cry. "Is it not obvious?" Swept a hand at the haphazard pile. "Miss Stratiss's approach for the royal wedding day."

"Approach?" The page, lowering into a U-shaped chair, thrusted a pout. "You mean her royal party wet dream?"

Crista snickered.

I couldn't get over the feeling of being throat punched.

"I don't understand," I stammered. "Is she another bidder on the event?" And if so, why hadn't Ez and I been filled in, after being told the selection had been narrowed to two companies? We'd suspected the news about Love's First Kiss—if we were in a toe-to-toe bidding war, it was usually with them—but Ambyr and her art fair project were an unexpected twist.

"Miss Fava, *désonnum*. My deepest apologies." Crista held up one of Ambyr's pages. Was that actually a piece of colored construction paper? "This is not Miss Stratiss's 'bid' on the wedding." As she plopped the paper down, her forehead furrowed. "It is..."

"Her treatise for true love?" the page prompted.

"Her manifesto for matrimony?" Crista giggled at her own take on the theme.

"Her swag of sensuality?"

"Her...foof before the fucking?"

They both slammed hands to their mouths like mortified nuns.

"Hey, it's all right." I kicked up one side of my mouth. "If you can't say it you can't do it, right?" I made a ta-da with my hands, freezing the smile until they recognized the line. Come on, *everyone* knew *Risky Business*. Annnd maybe not. It was probably a blessing in disguise, especially because I still wasn't set straight about Ambyr's...what? Creative arts display? Wannabe coffee table book? Helpful suggestions?

"So what the heck is all this?" I picked up another page and was immediately sorry for it. Dying doves bright pink for the conclusion of the ceremony? An eight-course reception dinner on Plexiglass platforms over the ocean, lighted in the same hue? "Is Ambyr a local vendor?"

Of course. That had to be it. Ambyr owned local supply stores and was hoping for a big score once the overall coordination bid was awarded to Expectation—because I refused to think any differently. In that case, bitch on wheels or not, I was glad the woman had stopped by. Local suppliers would be our saviors for this. I'd just have to talk her out of the pink birds idea...

"No." Crista answered my question with a tight, careful expression. "Miss Stratiss is not a vendor."

Damn it.

I managed to keep *that* one silent. Barely.

"This is Ambyr's version of a few...guidelines," she followed up.

"Guidelines?"

"Yes. For either you or the representative from Love's True Kiss."

"Why?"

A skirmish flickered across the woman's features. Clearly she wasn't sure how much to reveal to me—if anything at all. I kept my own expression neutral and friendly—and, hopefully, trustworthy.

Crista leaned forward. A *very* good sign. Finally, she murmured, "The queen mother and king father, Xaria and Ardent, have voiced their desire that the wedding be a triple ceremony."

"A *triple*..." I probably looked as knocked-for-six as I felt. A swift recovery was helped by the thousand details lining up in my head.

After two hundred years of self-separation from the modern world, Arcadia was still struggling for a place on the international stage.

The Cimarrons' ability to get there had been hit hard lately, courtesy of a sadistic terrorist named Rune Kavill. After kidnapping Princess Brooke, he was captured, but he escaped prison and added insult to injury by orchestrating the explosion that blew the Grand Sancti Bridge in half. With one of the island's icons in ruins, Arcadia's economy and national spirit had hit a massive snag.

Weddings injected joy into a kingdom and stability into a global image.

Two weddings would accomplish that with double speed.

Three weddings would make this country the talk of the globe for weeks. And the darling of international banks for weeks after *that*.

Three weddings...of three sons.

"Of course." No more bafflement. Exactly the opposite. My new stare down to Crista said as much. "A triple ceremony, With Shiraz as the third groom." I paused for just two seconds before barreling on, "Only the man has no bride."

The furrows had vanished from Crista's forehead. Favoring Morticia over Tinkerbell, she murmured, "Not anyone close."

I pulled in a deep breath as full comprehension set in.

"Except for Ambyr Stratiss."

Ding ding ding. Crista's tight smile relayed that much before she explained, "She and His Highness met in the Arcadian version of—how do you say it?—high school? Yes? After that, as our country began opening up to the outside world, her father was sent to Finland a few times for business training at Aalto, and she accompanied him."

"At His Highness's request?" I had no idea why that concept gave me the squeebs.

"Oh, *no.*"

Or why the vehemence of her answer felt so nice.

Squeebs aside, perhaps Miss Noble had just given me insight as to why the world's jury was out on the prince's sexual experience—or lack of it. Had he truly been "studying" all those years, if Ambyr Stratiss was jetting over for secret booty calls? And if that was the case, did she take those assignations as her God-given right to become his bride now?

Sheeeeez.

God help Shiraz Cimarron.

It resounded in my head like gongs—until the tolls were interrupted by the big arched door opening again and a man appeared in the portal.

No. Not a man.

A freaking god.

The moment was literally like something from a movie—though hell if I could remember which one. Not like it mattered, since I barely remembered my own name. For that matter, did I have a pulse? Or limbs? Even those weren't conscious thoughts, more like meaningless wonderings far beyond the wild race of my bloodstream, pushing a deafening din into my ears.

Yet the next second, the world went still again.

So still, I couldn't even breathe in it. Couldn't feel or comprehend anything, except him. *Everything about him...*

The luxurious rustle of his suit. The way he pushed air from a straight, narrow nose that flared just enough at the bottom. The way he advanced, steady and sure, moving like some computer-created creature of power and mystery—and then the gleam of sunlight from above as he stopped, igniting the ocean-blue depths into pure cyan fire.

Perfection.

Perfection.

Dear freaking God, *perfection.*

Yep. That about did it for describing Shiraz Cimarron.

In more ways than Ez's photos or the gossip tabloids could ever show.

Photos, even videos, couldn't encompass this. *All of this.* The command of his stature. The force of his presence. The blend of his smooth yet rugged beauty. The effortless intensity with which he wielded it all, as if he already sensed even the air's gratitude for touching him and then swore its fealty wouldn't be in vain.

As soon as our stares met, his posture straightened. How tall *was* he? And did *that* even matter? The man could've been three-foot-three and filled that pinstripe suit with the same muscled grace. His substance was that potent, that lethal to any carbon-based life form within twenty feet of him. One quick glance at Crista and the court page, who'd both gone all shuffling feet and batting eyes, proved the theory clearly enough.

Lucky wenches. At least they could still move. I stood

like a dorky doe in the headlights, all too aware my stare had bugged-out, my mouth was an awful O, and I swayed like a willow in a hot, hormonal hurricane.

God help Shiraz Cimarron?

No.

God help *me*.

CHAPTER THREE

"Crista." Sheez. Even his voice was flawless. And yeah, I could tell after one word. The exotic flair of his accent flowed like aural velvet, a baritone mixed with a growl, masculine magic flowing from lips so sensual, they nearly belonged on a woman. "Has Ms. Stratiss departed?"

"Yes, Your Highness."

He exhaled. "Good. Then before Miss Fava arrives, I need to look over the ledgers for—"

His next breath entered him audibly.

As he turned his head, fully looking at me.

No. Through me.

Seriously, I had to have a giant hole in the back of my head now. Undoubtedly, brilliant blue light spilled from it, taking every synapse in my brain along for the dump. That wasn't right, either. The hole had to be in the front, because all those neurons and memories and thoughts and dreams were now funneled at him...surrendering to him...completely and utterly willing about it.

What the hell?

No. He didn't get to do this. Nobody did. Not anymore.

Get a grip. Get composed. Get clear.

I timed my breaths to the words, forcing my mouth to stay shut until it was time for wow-the-client roll call.

You've got this.

You've got this.

I'd rehearsed this presentation so many times, I could do it in my sleep. This man...prince...reality-bending force of nature—whatever the hell he was—wasn't going to take that from me. The big-girl panties would have to be lined with lead for the next hour.

"Surprise," I told him with fake cheer. "Miss Fava, at your service." I pushed out my hand once more. "Don't you hate it when those damn Americans are annoyingly early?"

Shut. Up.

Shut. Up.

I rambled when I was nervous. I also made lame attempts to become the new siren of sleek and snarky. Massive fail on both fronts, judging by the man's expression. He was nowhere near smitten by my sleek, nor captivated by my snark.

Well, shit.

What the hell *was* he close to?

Reading people was an invaluable trait in what I did—and I was good at it—but right now, he'd rendered me a babe in the emotional forest. *His* forest, in which he alone knew the way. I could do nothing but stumble along, following his lead. In certain circumstances, that might be an epic turn-on.

In *this* case?

No way.

Or so I tried telling myself.

"I am far from annoyed, Miss Fava."

Deeper into the forest, lured by that exotic, velvet voice. Into the shadows, both mysterious and glamorous, of his alluring energy...

I shivered. Fought the chill by trying to be funny again. "Oh, give me time, Your Highness."

He let his hand slip from mine.

New tremors. Visible now. Thankfully, he didn't notice. His stare was fixed to the empty space between us, his features pursing. He seemed troubled. Or confused. Or both.

Did that mean he'd felt it too? The energy between our palms, the awareness between our fingers? Had he felt them, noticed them—or was this how he affected everyone he met? Wouldn't be a surprise, though it'd force me to chomp crow after throwing shade at the reporters who'd been here for junkets and returned with wet spots for the remaining Cimarron bachelor.

Holy shit. It all made so much sense now.

He made sense now.

What the hell did *that* mean?

I had no idea—only to admit that somehow, even as aroused as I was, I felt...

In the right place.

At the right time.

Standing in front of the right man.

Who gazed back at me with unprecedented, unflinching knowingness. As if his instincts acknowledged the exact same thing.

Trouble.

Trouble.

In giant, lethal vats of the stuff.

It wasn't just his beauty. Hell, I came from the land of gorgeous men. They made me lattes in the morning and margaritas at happy hour. Loaded up on sprouts next to me in the produce section. Had their own gyms on the beaches. None of them made me feel like this. Reminding myself to breathe with every inch they moved. Doubting my ability to walk a straight line after being beckoned into their office. Forcing myself not to fixate on their impossibly long, elegant fingers...

Somehow, I managed breathing *and* walking. At once. Whoa.

My success was fleeting.

Even the man's office turned me on. Probably because it seemed so much like him. Old-world class met modern-day strength in the form of a large, semicircle desk crafted in dark wood, embellished at the front with an art deco version of the Arcadian crest. The chair behind the desk was basic and functional, though the five chairs facing the front of it were expensive pieces of dark-brown leather. The floor was polished travertine tile, covered mostly by a plush ivory rug.

Just gazing at it all made me throb a little more.

Hell.

And wonder what my naked body would feel like against all of it.

Double hell.

Especially that rug...

Blasting insanity into my mind. Beautiful, incredible insanity.

A vision of me, sinking to my knees in that plushness. In front of him. Leaning close to his sinewy thighs as I unbuckled his belt. Unzipped his expensive slacks. Sighed against the flesh beneath as he gave me illicit commands in that decadent accent and then fed his hard flesh into my eager mouth...

Was there such a thing as *triple hell?*

There was now.

"Well." The voice from my little fantasy, now just inches behind me, nearly plummeted me to my ass. Yes, even in Mom's basic flats. "Shall we get to it?"

Gulp.

Hard.

Again.

Was he trying to drive me crazy? That had to be it. Mind fucker. Fantasy maker. I hated and wanted him for both.

He made nothing easier by pressing his big hand into the sweet spot at the small of my back. Yeah, *that* sweet spot. The halfway point between innocent and illicit. Of course he knew exactly where to find it and then push hard enough to make me yearn for him to travel lower. Much lower.

I persevered until he guided me toward a huge, plush leather couch, and then my thoughts exploded. My mind filled with a vision of us making out on those cushions. How would he taste? How would he taste me in return? Slow and sensual? Hot and dirty? Maybe both. God, I could only pray.

Holy shit.

It was time to pray, all right.

For the thoughts of a nun.

I perched at the edge of the cushion, grateful the leather was as firm as it appeared. The hard surface helped me pretend my thoughts hadn't turned into a horny hothouse. I even went for the virginal-hands-in-lap thing, though closing my knees only made a lot of things much worse—very fast. *Do* not *think about your throbbing clit. Do* not *think about anything else throbbing either.*

I whipped my laptop out of my satchel. It was never the action I liked opening with, especially during a first-time meeting with a client. A wedding was one of the most intimate acts of a person's life, whether they were an academic, an acrobat, or an Academy award winner. The journey toward making those dreams come true began with conversation and eye contact, not tapping on a keyboard.

But there was nothing normal about this client.

This *client*.

The only way I'd save myself—and Expectation's chance for this gig—would be remembering that.

As in, tattooing it on my brain.

I closed my eyes for two seconds, mentally inking the words across my forehead. *Yes*. Perfect. Hard-dialing Shiraz Cimarron into the client zone was like the friend zone only better. Number one, that was exactly where he belonged. Number two—

Screw number two. Whatever the hell it had been.

The moment I reopened my gaze, he wiped it away. The client zone tattoo? Yeah, that too—along with virginal hands, clamped knees, and attempting to ha-ha-ha my way out of this, all obliterated as he consumed my sights again, his big body lowering to the couch too.

His mien was the polar opposite of mine. Not *completely* opposite. He was on a high alert of his own. I felt that attention like pinpricks on the air, despite his outward air of smooth indolence, hooded eyes, and lazy leisure. And getting an accurate read on him through the contradiction? Might as well toss that notion out the window. Funny, because jumping through the panes behind his desk seemed a fantastic option right now. Though the dark wood shutters were only half-cracked, they exposed enough ocean, cliffs, and palm fronds for me to crave a chaise, a book, a cocktail, and several hours of peace.

He was nowhere on that list.

Nor would he be.

I pulled in a deep breath. Forced the calm down my limbs, ordering it to loosen my nerves. The man—the *client*—

across the couch remained the same. He was a giant body of relaxation armed with a thousand darts of attention. He hadn't even brought his phone over. His suit jacket was gone, slung across one of the chairs by the desk. When had he shirked his tie too?

Thank God he hadn't done the rolled-up shirtsleeves thing on top of it. I bet his forearms were dusted by hair that'd turn my composure inside out. It would probably match the thick, luxurious waves on his head. The umber-onyx mess was another subject of fascination for the press—at least the female members of it—and now I understood why. In person, it literally caused sweaty palms and itchy fingers from just the thought of tangling in the strands. It was that perfect length too: somewhere between a corporate lawyer crop and a guitar god mane, tickling the curve between his neck and shoulder, catching the light so some of it turned a deep cinnamon hue...

"Miss Fava?"

"Hmmm?"

"Are you ready to discuss the proposal?"

"Cinnamon."

"Excuse me?"

Mortification, party of one.

"Sorry," I stammered—a word I'd be repeating over and over to Ez in a few hours, if I didn't get my shit together. "Jet lag. It's the middle of the night for New York right now." And thank God for that. If I blew this, there were still a few hours before Ezra rolled out of bed. Surely that would be enough time to form an excuse other than *I was so fixated on his hair, I blew the presentation.*

"Of course." His tone soothed but his gaze narrowed. Just like that, I was back in what-the-hell-does-he-mean mode. I didn't feel judged or scrutinized, not in the traditional sense of the words, but he was definitely...

Watching.

Waiting.

Searching.

For what?

And in the end, did the answer matter?

Because all I could anticipate "answering" for Shiraz Cimarron was the logistical hassle of this wedding.

With an efficient tap, I woke up my smart pad. "Well, then. Shall we—" *Get to it? No. Not there again.* "Shall we begin?"

"I am all yours."

Not in half the ways I could dream, buddy.

I only had myself to be pissed at for that one—so it was up to me to rectify. I cleared my throat. Stated serenely, "Ezra told me you viewed the preliminary proposal video we sent, along with the virtual color boards, the load-in and breakdown schedules, and our client list. I'm happy to address any questions you might have about any of it."

Extended pause—long enough to fray my nerves. If a Cimarron had questions, they weren't likely going to be the standard. *Stay sharp. Focus. You've got this. You know this, inside and out.*

"The video was well-done and thorough." He hitched an elbow over the back of the couch, accenting the breadth of his shoulders. "I understand that since then, Expectation has been honored by the industry, as well."

"Yes. The Crystal Award." I smiled and meant it. "For creativity and excellence in planning a specific event."

"Mr. Lowe told me that event was your brainchild."

I shook my head. "We work as a team, Your Highness. No

idea belongs fully to either of us."

He leaned forward. "But many of the ideas in *this* proposal are yours too."

Funny squirm. And jolting comprehension. Why had Ez disclosed that to Cimarron? Never mind that it was the truth; Ezra rarely cared about that when presenting our joint ideas to clients...

Unless taking a different path would secure the business.
You schmooze with these royals better than I do...

He hadn't been blowing sunshine up my ass. He actually believed I could do this.

But did Shiraz Cimarron?

I had to look up, to learn for myself. To force our gazes into alignment and then pry without hesitation, "Why are you even interested in that?"

No pause this time. Only his answer, with the same resolve, like silk-covered steel. "Because I am interested in you."

Shit, shit, shit.

I was *so* getting that T-shirt.

My senses backed the decision. My lungs hung on to another shaky breath, hoarding air until my pulse ached at the bottom of my throat. I needed to look away. I could have stared at him another hour. Maybe I did.

"Why?" I finally got out.

He glanced across the room, considering that. Thank God. A moment of recovery time. Being the focus of his attention was like standing in a shaft of sunlight piercing that same thick forest. It was intense and wonderful—and blinding.

At last he explained, "Because all the ideas in the proposal do not add up to the woman who just walked in here."

I shifted a little. Back into the sun. "Oh? And what kind of woman were you anticipating?"

His breath left him in a careful measure. His features darkened by a new degree, though certainly not in anger—but not undressing me with his eyes, either. This was different. In many ways, scarier. His regard stripped off more than my clothes. He was going deeper. Into my head, my thoughts...my sex.

Shit, shit, shit.

That T-shirt better come in the cute, boob-enhancing style.

"Not a woman who took the time to research the history of our family and our kingdom and then weave them into romantic symbolism for a wedding ceremony."

Scoffing laugh. "It's not rocket science when the country's seal is a dove with sunbeam wings."

He nodded deferentially. "True—but proposing a sun*rise* wedding, instead of sunset, was unique."

"But bright-pink doves are also unique."

His stare flared. "Excuse me?"

"Never mind."

Thankfully, he heeded. "How did you conceive the commencement of the ceremony? The hawk circling the room and then taking the scroll from the high minister's hand?"

"Well, the hawk comes directly from your family's crest. The animal's natural majesty seemed a perfect way to symbolize the unions about to be forged. A herald of the past, grasping and then taking flight with the hope of the future." I leaned forward, excited about relaying the aspect we hadn't included in the preliminary proposal. "If you *really* like the idea—"

"I do."

That silk-on-steel tone again. He wasn't making this easy, but excitement was on my side now.

"Well, we could have the hawk displayed on a perch in the reception hall. After your brother gives the king's blessing to the meal, the hawk could return the scroll to *him*—before he turns and gives it to his new bride, symbolizing how he needs her as his partner and queen, with their love guiding the future of the kingdom."

The corners of his lips lifted. Not quite a smile. Something, I sensed, representing deeper emotions—but when he said nothing to elucidate it, I finally prompted, "What?"

"You have just—how do you say it?—provided fuel for my fire." The smile cracked free as he circled a finger in the direction of my head. "All those fairy tale notions, from the picture of pragmatism before me."

It seemed like a compliment, but I didn't want to take it as one. Not by a long shot. Of all the impressions I wished this man would walk away with, "pragmatic" did *not* top the damn list. But "idealistic" didn't, either.

What *did* I want from Shiraz Cimarron? And did that answer even get a vote?

Adulting. In some dictionary, maybe a few, the description *had* to read: *Not getting everything you want. Not even half.*

"Some people get their fairy tales, Your Highness." I hitched a dorky shrug. "People who are *not* me."

His gaze narrowed—again making me feel shoved under the emotional x-ray. "But you are not sad about it."

Again, a compliment-not-compliment. "Should I be?"

"You are evading my question."

"You didn't ask a question. Though once you get the question mark on it, perhaps you should ask yourself the same question." I straightened a little, spearing him with a steady gaze. "Do *you* believe in fairy tales, Your Highness?"

His angular lips continued their quixotic smile, though the look vanished from every corner of his gaze. "I have no time or space for towers, dragons, and glass slippers."

"Which is why you asked about all the symbolism in my proposal?"

Now I *was* fueling fires—and he showed me just how hot. With one push, he swung his elbow from the cushion to his knee, looming his whole torso forward. The result was a little surreal. Though his face was lower than mine, his stare was more consuming than before.

"Fairy tales are just fantasies," he murmured. "Symbolism stands for reality." He pushed in even closer. Oh *hell*, until I could smell him, expensive and European, bergamot crushed with blackberries. "And reality is where I must live."

Just a quiet murmur—but it felt like a fist to my chest. I tightened my grip on the smart pad, fighting the longing to reach for him...to comfort the loneliness in his voice and the resignation weighing his shoulders...

No.

I had to grab the opening he'd inadvertently given me.

"Reality," I echoed. "All right, then. Long as we're going there, let's do it."

His brows scrunched in. "Do...what?"

Big-girl time. Line up the shot. "Better question for you than me, Your Highness."

"I do not understand."

I stood. "It's time to get real with me, Your Highness," I clarified. "Am I proposing on a triple Cimarron wedding now, instead of a double?"

CHAPTER FOUR

Direct is best.

It was a favorite credo for Ez and me. In our business, subtleties and subtext often became exaggerations, especially if a bridezilla was on the loose. No stalking lizard here, but I assumed a "numbers guy" like the prince would appreciate the mode.

I was so wrong.

I had time to glimpse the tension of his jaw and the fire in his eyes before he stalked across the room. Three seconds later, he halted at the window behind his desk.

Clack.

I jolted as he parted the shutters, slamming them to the window frame and then keeping his arms extended. His delts were lines of sculpted perfection beneath his white shirt. At the open end of his sleeves, his forearms were equally muscled—and dusted by dark hair worth fixating on. A lot. As in, the blowjob-on-the-rug scene was right there again, making me imagine what those hairs would feel like against my cheek as he guided my mouth to the tip of his cock...

Dear freaking God.

Pull. Your. Shit. Together.

And what shit was that, besides the normal? *This is your norm, Luce. Remember?*

Right. Only my unique brand of naughty was usually for a guy returning my bedroom thoughts with bedroom eyes from across a crowded bar, not a client in perfectly-fitted Prada, making me this horny just from gazing at his *forearms*.

"You proposed on a double wedding, Miss Fava."

And apparently, one able to instantly dunk his velvet voice into a gallon of stiff starch too.

Perhaps a cue well worth taking.

"So that's *all* we're discussing?" I returned—though instantly slapped myself for it. Sheez and crackers, why did I care whether the man had a ring in his pocket for Ambyr Stratiss? They were completely wrong for each other—even after thirty seconds with her and ten minutes with him, I could see *that* much—but the requirements of *his* station didn't have a thing to do with what *I* thought or felt.

"Yes." Barely a beat went by before his retort. "No," he muttered a second later, followed by something in guttural Arcadian as he pushed from the window with a fluid motion. But the supreme control of his body couldn't mask the tension in his energy. If this was an old-school sci-fi flick and he had a perceptible aura, it'd be smoky red from all his frustration. "I... I do not know." He tapped both sets of long fingers atop his desk.

I wrestled for how to answer that. Part of me longed to lob a pillow from the couch at him. Time was money, and I'd crossed a major ocean and seven time zones getting my ass here. "I do not know" wasn't an acceptable answer at this point.

But there was another part of me here.

The part that felt his conflict, right along with him.

Because nobody, not even a royal prince with wicked business acumen, wanted to marry a person they had no feelings for.

But maybe jetlag had really fucked with my radar on

this one. Maybe he *was* into her. Maybe he'd been relieved by Ambyr's departure so he could focus on work instead of bonking her on the cool, curvy desk. Good explanation for her smug exit and his tousled hair.

And just like that, I went inner voyeur on his ass. Envisioned the two of them going at it, on top of his neat file stacks, next to his gleaming pens...

No.

Just no, no, and *no.*

"Gah," I pushed through clenched teeth. Had to openly confront my envy, likely shared by half the women on this island, when thinking of that woman with Shiraz's mane in her fingers, name on her lips, and body between her legs...

"Gah?"

"Just an expression," I managed, throwing up a dismissive hand. The move was as much for my benefit as his. It was time to face several simple but shitty truths.

One: something—all right, *many* things—about Shiraz Cimarron flipped my damn switches.

Two: it was up to me to slam them back off.

Three: yes, *all* of them.

Wasn't like it was going to be hard, right? The switches had been there a long damn time, and I was extremely used to powering down the "less acceptable" side of myself by now. Or so I liked to keep telling myself.

"An expression meaning what?"

"Many things," I volleyed to his quiet question. "And nothing. Sometimes, things are just better said without real words."

"Things like what?"

I bared teeth in teasing exasperation. The man hardly

ANGEL PAYNE

reacted. At last, he lifted both hands to the back of his cushy chair. Period. Not a blink, flinch, or twitch after that.

"Anyone ever call you a dog with a bone?" I finally groused.

"More than once." Still no falter—though he did grip the chair tighter. Sweet God, he had breathtaking fingers. They'd even be creepy long, if they didn't bely such latent strength. And sensuality. And the ability to use both quite well...

Switches. Off.

"So what did the 'gah' represent this time?"

Yeah. Dog with a damn bone.

"Confusion," I confessed. "Maybe frustration." *Probably* frustration, if my raging hormones had anything to say about it. What the hell was in the secret sauce of this man's presence that had fried my libido this hard, this fast? He was so perfect even now, with his stance visibly tensing and his features crunching to a grimace.

"Hmmph," he grunted. "That does not sound like a very constructive word, then."

"Says *you*," I flung back. "It's very constructive. And versatile. As a matter of fact, it's my go-to for celebration as much as frustration."

"And I have not given you cause for much celebration yet."

Well...hell. He had to go and do it again. Flip my game plan completely on its side. Who the hell was I kidding? The game plan had been shredded the moment I walked in here. His quiet, commanding concern just aided in the shred.

Not. Acceptable.

I needed him to be the uptight asshat I'd drawn out so clearly in LA. While we were at it, where was the doughy dude who wasn't *more* beautiful than his gossip rag pictures? And the prince who was too royal to be worried about a "commoner" like me?

Flip. The. Switches.

"Well then, let's talk about a celebration." Inner fist pump. *There* was the switch flipper I knew and loved. Long as I had the ball rolling, I nudged a little harder. "That starts with being straight-up with me. Your Highness, will you or will you not be proposing to Ambyr Stratiss?"

CHAPTER FIVE

A long minute of silence bridged into two.

I was the only one in the room who noticed.

The prince was lost to his own thoughts, even while yanking out his big chair and plummeting into it. He leaned back at a slant, comprising one of the most graceful slumps I'd ever witnessed. The man had a pirate's game, a ninja's grace, and a dark, etched beauty that was strictly his own. The thick, tumbling hair. The majestic, oceanic gaze. That unstoppable, unmerciful jawline.

He drummed his fingers again, drawing my attention to the two photos—his only personal items—on the desk. The images, in matching black frames, looked recent. In one, Shiraz laughed on a beach with his three siblings. They were barefoot but dressed in formal Arcadian wear, their red and black outfits a perfect blend with the sunset's bronze glow. The other photo was a formal portrait of the queen mother and king father. Ardent stood behind Xaria, a hand on her shoulder, and she reached up to cover his hand with hers.

With eyes fixed on that image, he finally murmured, "My parents' marriage was one step short of being prearranged."

His wistful tone yanked my stare back to the high couple's photo. "Really?"

He glanced up, a soft tease in his eyes. "Your research about our land did not cover the practice of the Distinct, I take it?"

Deep frown. "The what?"

He rose again. Strolled back around to my side of the desk. "The Distinct date back to Arcadia's earliest days."

"What the hell is it?"

"You mean they."

"Huh?"

"You mean *who* are *they.*"

I lowered into one of the chairs facing the desk. Let out a slow, "Okay..."

"The prince in line to next inherit the throne was required to be married by the time he was thirty, whether he'd ascended to full rule or not," he explained. "Blood lines needed to flow, despite the country's political climate. A selection of the kingdom's finest maidens was compiled for him to select from. The final fifteen were culled from an extensive review and vetting process. All of the women, then known as the Distinct, were then invited to the palais for a period of time so the prince could make the final decision and proposal for himself."

I instinctively slid a hand over my belly—as it turned over in three different ways. Was he kidding?

The serious set of his face provided my answer.

"Right," I snapped. "So they brought him—what—a freaking catalog of women to pick from?"

Shiraz's lips twisted. "Not exactly."

"But not *not* exactly."

"It is complicated."

"You think?" I flung. "So what happened if anyone arrived broken? Maybe a few cracks from shipping and handling? Was he allowed to return her for store credit or something?"

His gaze narrowed. "What?"

"Or maybe they just sent a replacement over. That'd be

easier, right?"

This wasn't keeping the switches off. I knew that and still couldn't help myself. What was *wrong* with me? *Me*, who'd been diligent about my research of Arcadian values, traditions, and ceremonies—

Mostly related to *weddings, vows*, and *marriage*.

All the shit that took place *after* the courtship and proposal.

Because the happy-ever-after was the part worth focusing on, right? Who wanted to deal with the mess of what it took to get there? One look back at my own dating history was a great answer for that one—so who the hell was I to mock the Arcadians' ways? Vetting brides for a royal wasn't totally horrendous, even in the modern world. Wasn't that what the tabloid press was for?

"The process was in place to prevent uncomfortable snags." Shiraz's sincere answer didn't assuage my chagrin. His new proximity kept the *rest* of my switches flipped on. "A committee of three, comprised of two High Council members and one representative of the royal family, were appointed as initial agents of the process. They interviewed thousands of young women across the island, seeking those they felt would be comparable in talent and disposition to the incoming monarch."

"And they cleared only the exceptional applicants."

"That was the idea."

The irony in his tone hit a second before the context of his words. I seized the recognition, glad to think of something besides him inching a little closer...closing in on me again. His big body and powerful presence were so damn intoxicating. And hypnotizing. And utterly, thoroughly breath-stealing...

"Whoa. Wait," I said it slowly, as a new realization stabbed. "If that's the tradition, why is Evrest marrying an American?"

The story of his older brother, who'd fallen ass over elbows for Camellia Saxon when she came to Arcadia with a film crew two years ago, was the stuff I *hadn't* had to research. Their fairy tale love was an international legend by now, inspiring everything from fan fiction to boy band songs to a couple of high-end perfume lines.

All facts that fled my head—and helpless senses—as the prince next to me became the man *next* to me. Leaning in until he filled nearly all my vision...

Ohhhh, shit.

My gaze dropped down the straight line of his nose. Stopped at the lush curves of his mouth.

Ohhhh, *shit.*

The mouth, now parting with sensual surety.

"Things are changing in Arcadia."

I stabbed my mind at his words. Clung to them as my lifelines toward a response other than *Your Highness, prithee might I have the honor of ripping your clothes off?*

"So they just didn't do that screening process thing for Evrest?"

"Oh, they did it." For some reason, that snapped him back to his original distance. I sighed in gratitude. It *was* gratitude, wasn't it? "A pair of my father's finest advisors, Fortin Santelle and Jaymes Hester, were joined by my cousin, Tytan, to comb the country. They returned with fifteen beautiful Arcadian women, all ready to win my brother's heart."

I leaned a hip against the desk, sarcasm already wooing my composure. Figured I was allowed this time, since the ending of the tale was obvious. Prince stud didn't help, emulating my posture and balance—and looking more worthy of a magazine cover than ever. In this moment, I voted for *Inc.*, the corporate hunks edition. Or maybe *Too Beautiful for My Own Damn Good* monthly. There was one of those, right?

"And how'd that work out for everyone?" I finally quipped.

"Hmmm." The syllable screamed at deadpan, one of my favorite looks on a man since it hinted at other things going on in his head. On his chiseled features, it became an art form. *Help.* My second base thoughts officially tried to steal third. "Considering Fortin's being investigated for conspiracy against the kingdom, my cousin is more obnoxious than ever, and the most notable candidate of Ev's Distinct is still at large because she tried killing Camellia—"

"Holy shit."

"I am not certain what is 'holy' about it, but if you insist..."

God, how I yearned to pick up his riff and run with it. Somehow, I kept my mind honed on the subject. "Those are some pretty huge details left out of the global narrative on the story."

His head dipped. Not a nod. A full tilt, deep enough that the ends of his hair played at the V in his shirt. "It is all contained in the Arcadian security forces' records, which are on file in our halls of public records, but Evrest and Camellia did not feel the need to call international attention to it all." His eyes sharpened, newly serious. "My brother's goal is not to garner the world's pity. It is to earn the world's confidence. He has taken a stand about doing that with the love and strength of a worthy woman by his side." He paused as if his words had come as a revelation. Took a full breath through his nose. "It was not simple to do that without bringing Chianna's violence to light, especially when the Pura used the issue to rise to prominence."

"The Pura." Okay, I knew this one. "They're that semiradical fringe faction, right? The ones who think Evrest and the current High Council are guiding the kingdom to ruin?"

"Among other things, yes."

"What other things?"

"You want the printable ones or the wild ones?"

"I'm not a reporter, Your Highness." Tiny smirk. "I don't care about printable."

His own lips quirked. "To start, they claim my brother *surely* sat at the right hand of Hell's Overlord before being born—*if* he was even born."

Snort. "Do they think he just spawned? Or...what... hatched?"

He chuckled. The sound was rich and sincere, and I liked it. "Interesting theory."

Oh, this was fun. "What else?"

"Well, Camellia Saxon is certainly a succubus, created in the same vile place, which makes her not only Ev's sister as well as his betrothed but a soul sucker brought into this realm for the sole purpose of stealing all his spiritual essence. When she finishes with that, she shall, of course, move on to the rest of his kingdom, dragging us all down into the underworld with her."

I finally laughed too. Fully. And dared anyone not to do the same when presented with that kind of a story. As soon as my head aligned back into place, I side-eyed him, spurting residual giggles. "Do I dare ask what they feel about Brooke Valen?"

His head cocked to the other side. I'd expected a lot of

reactions when bringing up the woman, an American who'd grown up on Arcadia, but his open brood wasn't one of them. "Brooke is...how would you say it in America...a delicate subject?"

"Okay." I extended both syllables. *Delicate* didn't enter my mind when thinking of Brooke, the American senator's daughter who'd trained with Arcadia's security forces for years before their leader, Prince Samsyn, fell hard and fast for her. Their legal wedding had been a rushed affair in the mountains to the northeast, but now the pair wanted a romantic ceremony, so a double wedding with Evrest and Camellia had materialized.

"Let me guess," I finally ventured. "Brooke is a people's princess because she's lived here so long and laid down her life for the country." *There* was a story they hadn't screened from the world. Probably impossible. The drama of how Brooke took a bullet for the youngest Cimarron royal, Princess Jayd, had made global headlines last April. "In normal circumstances, that would make her the ideal bride for Samsyn."

"Under normal circumstances, yes."

My shoulders dipped beneath the weight of understanding. "But Evrest had proposed to an American."

His shoulders stiffened. "But Evrest proposed to an American too."

"And the Pura expected Samsyn to fix that."

His jaw went taut. "They expected him to do *something*."

"And when Samsyn sealed the deal with *another* American, people's princess or not—"

"Shit got real."

My head snapped up. Hearing the vernacular of my language on *his* lips was like telling me to resist one of

Gervase's margaritas back home. Somehow I did it—with Shiraz's accidental help. The somber intent in his eyes was still there, reminding me of the rest of his story.

The scary parts.

"That was when the Pura aligned with Rune Kavill?" I had to force out the asshole's name. When Shiraz nodded tightly, I sighed heavily. "Damn. The terrorist even all the other terrorists hate."

It was the truth. Kavill was the worst kind of outlaw. No higher purpose or religious mandate had called him to a life of violence. He inflicted destruction because he liked it. He got off on the high, the monetary power, perhaps even the vengeance for abuses suffered during his childhood—or so the psychobabble experts liked to proclaim. Nobody could be certain because Kavill had concealed all connections to his real identity.

In the meantime, the sicko aligned with "partners" like the Pura of Arcadia, who found new ways to let him wreak chaos over the good King Evrest was trying to accomplish for his land. As a result, his ultimate goal was reached: to make Arcadians tense, angry, and afraid.

Just like the burden I saw in this man's azure eyes. The weight wasn't just on Shiraz's mind. It tore at his spirit. Was it stupid to assume such a thing? Maybe—though from that moment of a stare, I knew that about him. I just...knew. I could see it about him, inside him—that though he'd likely never sit on the throne of this country, he took its leadership as seriously as both his older brothers.

With the same gravity he infused in his next words.

"So." His dark eyebrows hitched, expectant. "Do you have your answer now, Miss Fava?"

"My answer?" The words drifted out of me. His eyes...I got lost in them all over again. Every new stare I likened to diving into an Arcadian lagoon, where hidden crevices and caves awaited discovery. "My answer about what?"

For a moment, he seemed amused. "About what I plan to do with Ambyr Stratiss."

Time to get out of the lagoon.

No. Time to think about going home, to the middle of the desert, where I could bake my senses back into clay. I'd harden them in the kiln clearly labeled *Do Not Touch.*

No matter how badly I'd thought of doing exactly that... everywhere.

Letting him do the same to me...more than everywhere.

He's. The. Client.

Do.

Not.

Touch.

I shoved to my feet. Marched back to the table, my sensible fucking flats making dull fucking thuds on the carpet, to retrieve my laptop. The device still showed the opening slide of Expectation's proposal, which I tapped to close and suck it back down into the folder on the home page. The screen saver was an image of the Arcadian coast, elegant white cliffs parted by a waterfall resembling draped silk strands. I'd left nothing to chance, wanting to prove our dedication to this project in any way I could. Now the image only made my teeth grind and my sex clench, thinking of how close that azure water came to matching the prince of perfection's gaze.

Another note to self. Priority. Change screen saver back to Henry Cavill the second you get back to your room.

"What are you doing?"

I almost laughed at the incredulity of his demand. "At the risk of making this a meme, Your Highness, I think we're done here."

"Done?"

My laugh expanded as I zipped up my satchel. "Done? It's a word that means complete or finished. Perfect for wrapping it up when everyone knows the event will be orchestrated by the woman about to score the prince's engagement ring."

As I straightened, he approached. There was enough time to steel myself against his perfect scent—yeah, I'd noticed how perfectly the currant and bergamot of Creed Aventus fit the man—as well as lock my stare to his neck. Meeting his eyes would be the death of me right now. In more ways than just the figurative.

With a pair of harsh scuffs, he halted. I fought the need to scream. The distance was too close for professionalism, no matter what cultural filter through which it was screened. A glimpse at his bottom lip—that was as high as I looked—said he knew it too. But hell if I'd give him any satisfaction by backing up.

"Done." He was more final about it this time—as if he didn't want to let it go. His challenge hung in the air like a whole plate of glass, daring me to break it.

To get to what?

To him?

But then what?

Would we give in to this draw for a minute, an hour, a night? It didn't change the reality of the situation, confirmed so completely by Ambyr's confidence and then Crista's explanation. The deal probably had his parents' seal of approval too. Soon, likely sooner than I imagined, he'd be stepping on a new stage of his life, planning to marry another woman. Even if every set piece there was a fake front, it wasn't a winning ticket for me to even think of approaching the theater.

And *there* was the buzzkill I needed.

I sucked it up. Stepped backward. Made my head lift the extra inches to directly meet Shiraz Cimarron's gaze. *God...his gaze...*

This was the last time my breath would snag from those stunning blue depths. On a better note, the final time my body would ache, craving to be clutched by the rest of him too.

"I think"—determined breath out—"that's a pretty good place to leave it."

I'd rarely meant anything more.

Nor meant anything less.

And made the mistake of letting both show through on my face—a weakness instantly seized by the man mere inches away.

His hand dropped. Skimmed against mine.

"Lucina."

My skin tingled.

My sex clenched.

"Your *Highness*."

He flinched as I gritted it.

I jerked as he closed fingers around my wrist.

I twisted against his grip. But not before letting his heat permeate into me for a couple of seconds.

Two of the best seconds of my life.

Followed by four of the worst.

The four it took me to summon four determined syllables to my lips.

"Now we're *really* done."

CHAPTER SIX

"So the Prince of Earthly Perfection didn't let you feel up his codpiece before you left?"

Damn it, Ezra.

I glared at my laptop camera while swallowing a mouthful of rich Arcadian nectar—the same gulp the shithead had timed his cute comment to. No way was I giving him the satisfaction of spewing a drop. Besides, I'd already changed into my beloved *Hamilton* sleep shirt, purchased at the Richard Rodgers in New York after waiting three hours for tickets. *Nothing* got spilled on this shirt.

As soon as the fruity alcohol was down, I let my most annoying giggle fly, again right into the camera. "You're a goof—and now, apparently, a lush as well."

In the video call frame dominating my monitor, Ez toasted me with his fresh martini. Two olives dangled from the glass's brim, speared with penis-shaped cocktail picks. "Hey, it's happy hour somewhere in the world."

"Like here?"

"That works."

Actually, it was well past happy hour in Arcadia. The curtain of stars over the ocean, dancing between moonlit clouds, was an epic reminder of the fact. I gazed out into the firmament—I wasn't into Biblical descriptions, but this one was true—and struggled not to let it knock me off my chair. Wasn't like I teetered in dorky third-rate patio furniture either.

The Cimarrons knew how to treat their guests with style. Even here in the palais's guest wing, the rooms were like beachfront apartments, complete with patios outfitted with the same stuff as five-star resorts.

"It's so beautiful here, Ez." I swiveled the laptop outward. "Can you see this sky? The clouds...they even have shades of *purple*..."

"Shit."

I yanked the screen back around. "Shit...what?"

He didn't answer for a long moment, tapping and clicking like a hacker who'd gotten into the Pentagon's mainframe. "Purple skies? That means heavy rain, honey. Maybe even a hurricane."

"Saint Paul wept." I gave in to a full eye roll. "Are you serious? I know all about rain, Ez." Sort of. "I'm not going to melt if a little water falls from the sky."

"But they don't call them hurricanes in the Mediterranean," he went on, continuing with the click-and-type. "And when I was tracking the weather for the region this morning, there *was* a blip off to your west..."

"Whoa. Back up, bucky. You were tracking the weather for the Mediterranean?"

"Duh." A fast *pssshh*. "As a favor to your mom. Like I do for all your trips."

"Oh, my God."

"Come *on*. You totally know this, right?"

Groan. Head plant into a hand. "If she's GPS'ing my phone too, I don't want to know about it."

He hadn't heard me. His deeper glower said so, directed at the other stuff he'd been pulling up on his computer. "Uhhh, Luce?" he uttered slowly. "You packed protein bars, right?

Like you always do for a trip? How many do you have left?"

"All right," I ordered. "*Stop*. This is getting as bad as your cavalcade of apologies."

That refocused him. "Which I *meant*, damn it. Every single one."

"All of which were ridiculous." As he pulled in a breath for a retort, I flashed up a firm hand. "It's *over*, Ez. Does it suck that I had to fly all the way here to find that out? Of course. But sometimes, things happen for good reasons. Ambyr Stratiss was the wild card none of us was informed about." And, if I was honest, probably a blessing in disguise. Though Ez didn't have to know the fine print about it, even a "working relationship" with Shiraz Cimarron would've been stickier than juggling gummy bears. "If Love's First Kiss still wants this gig after looking at her *idea book*," I went on, "then God freakin' speed to them. We'll watch the train wreck and be thankful it isn't ours."

Ezra sighed. Grabbed a penis and teethed the olive off its tip. "Fine. You're right."

Cheeky grin. "Of course I am."

"Still doesn't stop me from being sorry. Again."

"Gaaaahhh,"

"I'm a Jewish queen, darling. Guilt is my fifth food group."

"I thought that was Twix bars."

"You're right. Okay, guilt is sixth."

"You might be scooting it to seven if you could taste this nectar stuff." I giggled, grateful for the excuse to let out some nerves. "Damn, these Arcadians make good shit." I swished, sipped, and sniffed the fruit drink again. Wait. Was that supposed to be swish, sniff, sip? And did that even apply to this stuff? And wasn't spit somewhere in there too? Oh hell no.

ANGEL PAYNE

This stuff was too good.

"Hmmph," Ez countered. "That supposed to make everything all better? A bottle of comped booze, after you dropped everything and flew halfway across the world, only to find out the gig has already been taken by one of the *brides*?"

"*Shit*." Sharp lean forward. "You want to cut that quiche in half, mister? That's not public knowledge yet."

"Quiche, schmeesh." He stabbed a finger at the camera. "Those royal-boy putzes could do with a little egg on their fancy faces. Once it's smashed in good, we'll make them lick it off each other. And we'll watch."

I slammed my glass down. "I'm not sure whether to be horrified or intrigued."

"Why not both?"

Another long laugh. "Done!" Broke out into applause. "Oh, I like feisty Ez way better than guilt complex Ez."

He waggled tawny brows. "How about horny and curious Ez?"

"Huh?"

"Think a little guilt would make me forget the codpiece question?"

Groan. Yet another laugh. "Freaking hell."

"Come oooonnn." He pushed his begging knuckles at his camera, turning them into weird, pale flesh mounds on my end. "I'm living vicariously through you, okay? I've been a good boy lately. Haven't even glanced at any boys."

I narrowed my stare. "Not even any girls?"

He narrowed his. "I'm not a saint, Luce."

"Because you don't even believe in saints?"

"Beside the fucking point?" He shifted, shoulders hunching, as he pushed closer to his camera. "Admit it, woman.

73

I see it, deep in those Bambi brown eyes of yours. You *looked*, didn't you? You looked long as you damn well could at Shiraz Cimarron's family jewels, in those moments when *he* wasn't looking..."

"Shut. Up." But my quirking lips undermined the words, inciting his victory whoop.

"*Aha!* I'm right!"

He was. But if he thought I was *ever* going to go there with him, the smarty-pants had an ice water bath coming to him.

"The finer points of His Highness's physique are not a subject you get to know about when I'm talking to you from a Wi-Fi network called Palais One."

He curled a small grin. "So there *were* finer points?"

"Hmmm." I ran a finger along the rim of my glass. It was a cross between a standard wine goblet and a champagne flute, resulting in a little finger-and-glass song that was strangely melodic. "Maybe. Just a few."

More than a few. Oh God. So many more.

But he wasn't going to see that, even after I didn't have the Wi-Fi as an excuse. As long as I kept the Bambi peepers averted, I'd make good on that vow—for now. And later? I had a whole night's sleep and then a day's worth of travel to develop the answer to that.

Who the hell was I kidding?

Answer? *What* answer?

There was no "answer" but one.

I had to wash that man right outta my hair, damn it.

And my memories.

And my fantasies.

All the decadent, dangerous fantasies he'd been filling since I left his office this afternoon...

Decadent because I allowed them to consume nearly every sense I possessed. Smelling him again, dark fruits and spicy skin. Touching him again, strength and energy and force. Hearing him again, baritone growl dropped to an intimate tone.

And in seeing him again, inviting the danger.

Because in my mind's eye, he was still as perfect as the last moment I'd seen him...in that last, hesitating second before I'd left his office.

I'd succeeded in stepping away from him, even turning and making it nearly all the way to the door, before stopping to consider the silliness of my melodramatic exit.

I should've let the theatrics stand.

Not that the professional replacement made it to my lips. My only chance to pull off a bad-ass combo of Scarlett O'Hara and Olivia Pope, torched by the blue blaze of his gaze, the towering inferno of his stance, the burning force of his attention.

Oh, *God.*

His *attention.*

Another movie moment, surely one I must have imagined. An unfulfilled thing from my teen dreams, where the hottest guy in school suddenly notices the girl with pink hair and braces in the corner. Only now it was worse, because the teen dream came with grown-up desires. I'd instantly envisioned all that heat and fury directed over me...and then into me. I was nude for him. Pinned by him. Opened for him. Pounded by him...

Pound.

"Luce?"

Pound.

"Luce!"

Pound.

"What?" I snapped it, unwilling to admit I'd tuned out in favor of a naked Shiraz Cimarron fantasy.

"You tell *me* what."

"Huh?"

It fell from me just as another pound echoed through the room—coming from the door across the room, leading to the palais's interior hallway.

"Did you order room service or something?" Ez pried.

Twisted lips. "It's a palais, Ez, not a hotel."

He matched every inch of my bratty. "Then who's at your door?"

Before rising, I flung him a middle finger. Our version of "BRB" was more fun than the usual. Besides, the knocks had stopped. Whoever it was had likely realized they'd gone to the wrong room and—

As soon as I pulled open the door, my breath was a new brushfire in my throat.

No. Worse.

Or better, depending on how I chose to look at the situation.

Right now, I couldn't *not* look.

Holy, deep-fried shit. Shiraz Cimarron rocked the hell out of a suit and tie but blazed new definition into jeans and a black T-shirt. As in dark-angel-in-mortal-clothes time. As in dear-God-give-me-back-my-tongue time.

As in, I wasn't about to get back my voice anytime soon, so I hoped he still had *his*.

For a moment, that seemed an impossibility too. He was half-turned from the door, as if he'd decided against pounding on the portal a fifth time—turning his first full look at me into a bumbling experience for us both.

Bumbling...and too damn hot.

How else could I interpret the scorching sweep of his stare down over my legs, even studying the neon-yellow flowers on my bright-blue toes? What was I supposed to think as he slowly, *slowly* climbed that study back up, an undeniable visual caress, nipping its way into every curve of my body before locking again on my face? And what the hell was I supposed to do in return, besides scope him out just as shamelessly?

"*Bon aksam.*"

And what the hell was I supposed to *say*?

"Uhhh...hi." *Smooth, Luce.* "I mean, bon aksam...back at you. I mean, good evening." *Groan.* Thank God the sound wasn't literal, though it seemed to be the only verbal diarrhea I could restrain. "What're you... *Why* are you—"

"I need to talk." He looked stunned again, as if what tumbled out wasn't what he'd planned, before composing himself and barreling forward. Two steps into the room, he about-faced and stomped back over to the portal. "I mean, *we* should talk. I—" Did a flush actually steal up the line of his jaw? "May I come in...please?" More words that were obviously strange for him. "I shall not take long."

"Uhhh. Sure." I stepped back, tamping another insane urge to giggle. "Yeah, come in." More efforts not to giggle—making me remember Ezra, waiting in the Skype chat out on the patio. "*Shit.*"

Shiraz spun around, eyes bugged like I'd pantsed him. It was kind of adorable. "What?"

"Sorry," I muttered. "One sec. Really. Hold on."

By that point, I'd gotten back to the patio—and, as I

expected, Ezra's eagerly grinning face. "Holy shitballs," he hissed. "Is it him? Has Princey Perfection come to visit your *beaudoir, mademoiselle?*"

I'd never glared with more meaning. "I'll reconnect with you later, Ez."

"Wait! Come on."

"*Later.*"

"Wait! No! Not without letting me glance at the royal jewels!"

I slammed the device shut. He'd get the idea. We could pick things up later, like during my trip to the airport in the morning. It'd be about two a.m. in Los Angeles. *Perfect.*

I scooped up the laptop, glad for something to do with my nervous hands, especially because Shiraz was back to his usual demeanor. Completely controlled. Quietly concentrated.

Utterly gorgeous.

His focus cycled around the room, taking in the surroundings like he'd never been to this wing before. I wondered if that were the truth, until he spoke again.

"Do you like the accommodations?" He leaned against the back of the couch while stabbing his focus back into me. "These suites have been newly refurbished."

I looked around too. The room, only illuminated by recessed lighting, was still a panorama of Mediterranean luxury. Gold fixtures and marble-topped tables were mixed perfectly with furniture in rich woods, upholstered in luxurious tapestries. Across the room, cloudlike curtains slung back to reveal the grand production of a bed in the next room.

"They're awesome." I picked at invisible lint on the hem of my T-shirt. "I feel like Sara Crewe on Christmas morning."

His dark brows pushed together. "Who?"

"Character from an old movie," I explained during my trek to the wide work desk. *"The Little Princess.* Nineteen thirty-nine. Shirley Temple. The ninety-five remake isn't worth discussing. It's about a little girl forced to work for her boarding school after her father is assumed dead in the war. She and her scullery maid friend wake up on Christmas morning to find their dumpy attic turned into a luxurious palace. At first, they think they're dreaming."

"Is that how you feel?" he returned. "Like this is a dream?"

I sat at the desk. After plugging my laptop into the charging port, I quipped, "Pretty much from the moment I got here."

He barely moved. Even his eyebrows stayed where they were. "A good dream or a bad dream?"

I shrugged. "Little of both, if you want the truth."

His answer came faster than I expected. "Truth is not something I 'want,' Miss Fava." His shoulders squared. "It is something I require."

"Then why are we talking about dreams at all?"

Again with the barely moving thing. "Dreams cannot be truth, as well?"

I was glad to be sitting. Gave me a perfect excuse to glance down, fiddling with the laptop's cord, so he wouldn't see the smartass "truth" tempting the corners of my lips. "Depends on who you ask," I murmured. And that *was* the truth. This was his taco stand. If the prince wanted all the salsa jars filled with "truth," I was happy to oblige for the next twelve or so hours. After that, I was done with *Señor* Cimarron's hot sauce forever.

He shifted, pushing away from the couch. I swallowed, battling not to notice. Not as easy as it sounded, especially as the air glued itself to him like groupies on a rock star, and he inhabited that outfit better than most million-dollar models.

His stride, sure and elegant, would've silenced a whole room at Fashion Week—another nearly impossible feat. I knew. I'd been to Fashion Week.

And now, wished I was there again.

And not for the bling-and-beyond goodie bags *or* the free shoes.

For the crowd.

An extra hundred people in the room suddenly seemed like a damn good idea, if only for the sake of veering his course a little. Maybe a lot. He continued to remind me of a muscled musician—on his way to smash a guitar to pieces.

I wetted my lips. Wondered if my lungs would pulverize my ribs. Fought to keep my heart from climbing into my throat—but more than that, to keep that incessant throb from resonating in the folds between my legs.

I failed on every account.

Especially as he rounded the desk, pulled out the chair, and then swiveled it around, pointing me directly toward him. Locked me further into place by gripping the furniture's arms with both hands. Tighter still, as he leaned in...filling every molecule of air around me.

"Hey." It sounded pissed, but that was because of my fear—and arousal. Like I was going to break all *that* out for him. "What the hell are you—"

"Truth." He growled it this time, grinding on it twice as hard as before. "I require it, Lucina."

I concealed a shiver. Barely. "I understand. Now back off."

He didn't move. Let his nostrils flare as his gaze went heavy, studying me from forehead to chin. "Do you want me to...back off?"

Shit, shit, shit.

There he went again, slathering my California slang in his exotic accent, until I could barely remember the point I'd been trying to make. But damn it, I sure as hell remembered *his*.

The truth.

He'd demanded it.

And, whack-a-doodle as it sounded, would probably know if I futzed even the tiniest detail on the "getting it" part. I didn't know how I recognized that. I simply did.

It'd be kind of hot—maybe more than "kind of"—in a man I stood half a chance of being pursued by. But this was a damn prince of a whole kingdom, a whole separate *world*, determined to become that country's new hero by proposing to another woman.

And there was fate's little favor for the day.

"Yes," I pushed out, even meeting him eye-to-eye about it. "I mean it. You *need* to back the hell off. Now."

CHAPTER SEVEN

Why wasn't I more relieved when he did exactly what I'd asked?

Okay, had demanded. In my bossiest, huffiest tone—and in case I hadn't forgotten, with words I *did* mean—and now yearned to suck back into my lungs so he wouldn't rise, silken as a curl of smoke, to walk away.

And all I had left to drool over was the V of his back, etched flawlessly by the black cotton, as he moved past the first sitting chair. Around the edge of the couch.

Shit. He really *was* going to leave.

At the last moment, on the farthest side of the couch, he sat again. Hitched an elbow to the armrest and lifted his hand, which became the instant cradle for his forehead. His fingers kneaded in, their tips as taut as his expression.

Turning me into an equally bunched ball of feelings.

Conflicted ones.

Part of me squirmed, a little contrite. I'd cranked up the snark, when he was clearly troubled about something. He'd even come all the way to the guest wing, to my room, to talk about it. But hold the phone. *My* room? To talk about *what*? Our business with each other—all three seconds of it—was over.

But I couldn't ignore the stiffness in his shoulders. The taut kneadings of his fingers. The fist his other hand had become.

"Okay." I forced myself to rise, just to have something to do other than sit and gawk at him. *One foot in front of the other, Luce. It's called walking. You remember it, right?* The small in-room bar felt like a good direction. Maybe I'd find more nectar there. "You going to need some gargle juice for this hot topic?"

His head lifted a little. His gaze narrowed a lot. "Some what?"

"Sweet sauce." I nodded at the alcove. "Hard stuff? Maybe some basic nectar?"

"No." He looked like I'd asked him to swallow explosives. "Merderim, but no."

I canted my head, acknowledging a new realization. "You don't like letting go of control, do you?"

His posture didn't change, but his aura sure did. The change in his energy was nearly a visual force, as if the air groupies around him had tensed, waiting on his next breath. If he took one, I didn't discern it. His tight swallow, consuming the length of his neck, was a different story. Noticed every second of that—wondering when I'd become a "neck woman." Just thinking of tucking my face against it and then licking my way along the muscled column until his growl rumbled beneath my lips...

Oh, my God.

"There is nothing wrong with self-discipline."

His commitment to that was understandable. From where he stood, both his brothers had shirked *their* self-discipline, choosing their hearts—and perhaps a few other things—over their country. In Shiraz's world, where black was black, white was white, and numbers became sums that were either right or wrong, those decisions didn't compute. After Evrest changed a major law to have Camellia, the palais was breached by Pura rebels. After Samsyn went public about his love for Brooke, the Grand Sancti Bridge was blown apart. In his mind, the lunatics were taking over the asylum—and it was up to him to appease them again.

Somewhere in that logic, I actually found the reason he'd come slumming in the guest wing. But how to broach that little sticky?

I started by submitting, "Nope. Nothing wrong with discipline at all—unless it becomes your middle name."

He lifted his head fully. Regarded me with extra caution. "I am perfectly happy with my middle name."

"Really?" I pushed out a little *hmmph*. "Could've fooled me."

He rose once more. Though his movements again belied the strength of a quarterback, they were as tense as one—at the damn Super Bowl. "I am not trying to *fool* you."

"No?" I scooted from behind the bar, striding back toward the terrace. The bottle I'd been sent came with two of those cool flutes, along with a plate of cheese, crackers, and plump local olives. "Then come out here and join me for some nectar."

Soft snarl. "I already said—"

"Yeah, I know." I had his glass poured and extended. "But I seriously need you to cut the cologne ad antics, sexy as they are, and be real with me."

"Sexy." He backed the stupefied stutter with a little scowl. "I am not trying to be...sexy."

"Which only makes that shit sexier."

"That...shit?"

"*Shiraz.*" I reached for his hand, still weirdly clenched, and pulled out his long, tanned digits until they formed around the glass. "Just take a freaking sip, okay?"

He blinked. Several times. I did the same, hoping it spurred me to breathe. *Bull, meet china shop.* Ez actually called me "Ferdinanda" because of it, but always in affection—though his emotional shop was lined in leather, satin, and feathers. Not the case with Shiraz Cimarron. This man had blue fire in his eyes, burnished bricks beneath his jaw, and sheet-metal walls around his heart—and right now, I'd knocked new fissures into all three.

Just by meshing our fingers.

Sheez.

I was in big, fat, fucking trouble again.

And I wanted more.

More of the heat permeating me from his skin. More of the heat radiating from those eyes. And definitely, oh *definitely*, more of the milliseconds in which his shields cracked, giving glimpses of a man—a person—who was more than columns, lines, perfection and duty.

More.

What would happen if I decided to go for it? If I leaned in just a little...pressed forward by just an inch...followed the invisible tractor beam of his pull, and just joined the atmosphere groupies in needing to touch more of him...

More...

Thank God one of us was still thinking.

Without another millisecond to spare, he pulled his hand away by raising it. With a deft nip, wetted his lips with the nectar.

"Mmmm." Just like that, the steel doors were back up. He glanced at the remaining pink liquid in his glass as if regarding a calculator printout. "Yes. That is refreshing."

My dire case of awkward dissolved beneath a laugh.

"*Refreshing?* You want some cool jazz sounds to go with that, Mr. DJ?" I hooked a thumb at the beach. "We already have the soothing wave soundtrack."

He stared back, openly perplexed—or so it appeared. Whatever the hell it was, he softened again—not a lot, just enough—to the point his gorgeous turned back into devastating.

Damn it. I needed his steel slabs back in place. I needed *my* walls back in place. Trouble was, I'd taken out half the nectar by myself already, so those barriers were half in ruins—and no part of my brain volunteered for cleanup. It was an even more hopeless cause as he angled his head down, his focus sharpening from blue fire into midnight smoke...curling into my senses with the same allure.

"You do not find the nectar refreshing?"

"I find it damn delicious," I quipped. With the same snazzy speed, an idea hit. "Hey." I peered up with new interest, grateful for the excuse of true curiosity. "Are there different kinds of nectar, like varietals of wine?"

"Of course." Questions sparked across his face, but he said nothing else.

"Hmmm."

"Hmmm?"

I turned my gaze toward the sea. It was mostly dark, though the moon glow and starlight formed intriguing liquid shadows along the waves. "Just an interesting idea for the wedding. What about a nectar tasting menu for the wedding reception? You could pair it to Arcadian food specialties. It'd be cool, since you're likely to have a number of world dignitaries and celebrities there, and most will be visiting the island for the first time."

He still didn't say anything, though I felt the force of his contemplation. When the weight of that passed and he still didn't speak, I hazarded another look over.

The man was grinning at me like a loon.

A gorgeous loon, with the moonglow playing on his inky hair and a new, silvery light in his eyes...

And a force of concentration stabbing through me...

filling all the fibers of me...

even down there.

Especially down there.

I swallowed. Hard. Finally mumbled out, "Or maybe not." Shrug. "It was just an idea."

"A brilliant one."

His praise turned my blood into champagne bubbles. I counteracted the effect by turning the shrug into a sassy shoulder shake. "Well, cool. You...ummm...can steal it. Well, Ambyr can. You can tell her about it. Hey, you can even make it your idea. It'll score you extra points—not that you need any more, Mr. Prince-of-Her-Dreams."

I played up the teasing tone, but it didn't dent in his new solemnity. "Am I?" he finally countered, delving a stare into his nectar. "The 'prince of her dreams'?"

"*Pssshh.*" There was no stopping it. "Tell me you don't have *those* blinders on." When that earned me an incredulous glance, I cut loose a new laugh. "Yikes. You *do* have those blinders on."

His quizzical look persisted. It didn't change even as a night breeze ruffled dark waves against his face, even snagging them into his long eyelashes. Finally, he confessed softly, "I am aware that Ambyr carries an affection for me. But—"

"Affection?"

"Is that not the American word for it?"

"I'm familiar with the word," I insisted. "It's just not applicable here."

"Not applicable?"

"*Affection* is daisies, lemonade, and walks on the beach." I teeter-tottered my head. "Or if you were courting her in LA: parking tokens, Starbucks—and walks on the beach." I laughed lightly again, spreading my hands. "But even if you two were in the middle of the Sahara, 'affection' isn't the place you're in with Ambyr Stratiss."

After I finished, his gaze eagerly roamed my face. His scrutiny only lasted a couple of moments—the ones I needed to verify so much.

"Then what 'place' am I 'in' with her?"

I weighed what to say next, at last deciding on my instinct's first choice. "This was why you came here to talk, wasn't it? Because you need some advice about Ambyr?"

Once more, he moved very little.

Until he lifted his glass of nectar again—and downed the whole thing.

So much for wondering if he'd give a definitive reply.

So much for wondering if all of Ezra's claims were true, also. The man looked like sex on a stick but had no idea how the "stick" really worked. Maybe so much of his life had been defined by the boundaries of royal life, even dating and women were supposed to be in tidy boxes. But he couldn't figure out the box for this and was lost. And pissed.

"And what the bloody hell if I do?"

Yep. Pissed said it right.

A situation I *so* could have had some fun with—except that I saw beneath the anger to the uncertainty and uneasiness. The totally blind leap he'd taken in coming to me about this.

The lost beggar beneath the assured prince.

He confirmed the impression by slamming his empty glass down. He returned inside with stomps tremoring the floorboards. I followed at a more measured pace before joining him on the couch. This time, we both sat toward the middle of the big leather expanse.

Another long moment passed. I let it go on, sensing it was necessary. The man could protest all he wanted about this shit being just a business decision for the country, but if he really was a virgin, this was a bigger step than he wanted to admit. I didn't have the heart to make it any more difficult.

"Your Highness." I almost reached for him again. *Not a great idea, missy, and you know damn well why.* Didn't stop me from revising it to, "Shiraz..."

His head tugged up. "What?"

And now that I had his attention, I wasn't sure what to do with it.

Stick to the plan. That's what you do.

Wise. Really wise. No matter how strongly my body screamed to betray the mission...

"You know that Ambyr's all-in for this, right? A proposal," I clarified, answering the new knit in his forehead. "She'll agree as soon as you ask. She'd be a fool not to."

It was my foolproof encouragement voice, the one I usually had to save for skittish brides—which made his fresh frown an unexpected twist.

"A proposal," he finally echoed. "All right." But nothing backed that up. His left knee jiggled a little. His right hand drummed atop the other. He stared into the corners of the room as if expecting something to materialize from the rafters. A guardian angel? An avenging demon? I couldn't figure it out.

"Isn't that why you're here?" I queried gently. "For ideas about how to propose?"

He swung his head back around. Practically impaled me with his gaze. "Do you have any?"

I smiled again. I'd never meant a sentiment more. The dichotomy between the bustling businessman prince I'd met this afternoon and this awkward, earnest suitor, all but fidgeting from one end of the couch to the other... I was kind of enchanted. And yeah, might as well admit it, jealous as hell of Ambyr Stratiss. I hoped the woman knew what a rarity she had in him.

"To be honest," I finally said, "I don't. I'm sorry. By the time our company is contacted, the proposal part is usually finished."

"Of course." Shiraz rubbed both hands against his knees now. "I suppose that would be the case."

I pulled in a long breath. Faced him more fully, curving a knee against the cushion. "Look, there's no right or wrong way. The most important thing is that you're sincere. You and Ambyr are...friends...at least, right?"

Felt like a safe question—somewhat. Weirdly, the words still seemed like eggshells. Wasn't like I wanted the intimate details about their relationship, but maybe he'd disclose a few key details to work with.

"Friends." He repeated it like learning a word in a new language. "Hmmm. Yes. I suppose that will suffice."

I forced composure into my face. If I didn't, I'd surely laugh. Or cry. I wasn't sure which. *That will suffice?* He was going there because of the language difference, right? Surely, even if the union with Ambyr was being induced by Arcadia's current politics, the woman had to be more than "sufficient" in his life.

A long moment passed as I waited for more. Kernels, even a few, of something I could use to help him with this dilemma.

The silence stretched on. Thick...then awkward.

Finally, I heaved a harsh sigh. "Okay, and what else?"

The man stared like I really was speaking another language. "What else...what?"

"Sheez." Another long breath. Carefully in, not so patiently back out. "Shiraz. You've spent at least a little time with this woman, right?"

"Yes," he snapped, adding a *duh* face. "Of course. I have escorted her to three palais dinners and the annual fencing tournament. She also went with me to—"

"Don't need the Wikipedia entry." I flung up a hand. "So you've dated, and—"

"No." His eyes turned stormy. "Those weren't *dates*."

I struggled to stifle a smirk. Success. Wasn't so winning with staving my follow-up question. "Errrm. What's your idea of a date?"

He grunted. "Not what I did with Ambyr."

I wanted to push more, if only to interact with this oddly cute side of him. By now, the only reminders of the imposing corporate hunk from this afternoon were the formal loafers on his feet and the styling product in his hair.

"All right, then," I murmured. "So you've been to some events and parties together. Had some pleasant times. Probably a good night kiss or two..." I watched him carefully while letting that one linger. *There.* His shoulders stiffened against his shirt. "Or more than good night kisses?"

More intent observation, especially when he didn't deny it. Well, shit. Maybe my reading on Ambyr and him was all wrong—an admission instantly twinging my chest...and worse, making me scramble for ways to finish this conversation without helping him one damn bit. If he'd been able to stick his dick into the girl, what the hell was he doing in the guest suite of a stranger, asking for advice on how to propose to her?

"What if...I have not even kissed her?"

A stranger now feeling like twenty kinds of a bitch.

And forty kinds of elated.

And sixty kinds of holy-shit-what-do-I-do-with-*this*?

"Wait." I pointed at him. Flummoxed, let my hand drop. "You're going to propose marriage to this woman, but you haven't even kissed her?"

His shoulders hunched, even more huge with embarrassment. "That is...weird, I suppose?" He glanced over, lips twisting. "Wrong?"

"No." Before I could think to stop, I leaned and grabbed the shoulder closest to me. *Fuck.* Nothing met my touch but stone-hard sinew. "No," I blurted again, trying to squeeze him in reassurance. "It's sweet. And sexy. And kind of cool. And it also answers your question about how to begin the proposal."

Awareness dawned in his eyes. "Kiss her?"

"Uh-huh." So much for getting enjoying my shoulder feel-up. Not cool to be sizing up a man's arms while discussing his first kiss with his potential bride.

"How?"

"What do you mean, how?"

"How should I kiss her?"

I shoved out my chin. Hit him with a major stare of *are you serious*. Wasn't computing with the dork, and his open expression said so. He was just as lost as the moment he'd knocked on the door.

"Well. How do you think she wants to be kissed?"

Gah. Was I really doing this? With *him?*

He's the client. Return to that *preset. You'd be able to do this if he was still the client. Only now, instead of leaving this place with a deposit check, you be leaving with karma points.*

Which, at this point, was nearly better than a check—considering how much karma was going to owe me.

"Kissing." He peered around the room again, seeking his unseen angel or devil. His jaw jutted, a fascinating sight due to his dark stubble. "It is...like artwork, yes? Disgusting or stunning, depending on who wields the brush."

Just like that, the knot in my gut fell loose. A sound fell out of me. I recognized it, bizarrely, as a laugh. "That's a damn good way of looking at it."

After my laughter, I let a smile linger.

Felt it drop as he dipped his gaze back toward me.

Then pierced it all the way through me.

Blue-bright glass, edged in a silver sheen of something I could no longer ignore or deny...

...as he leaned over, closer and closer...

And cupped my face with his long, firm fingers. Touched me with his sure, steady intent.

"Tell me, Lucina...how *you* like to be painted."

CHAPTER EIGHT

Star shine. Sun glow. Lightning streaks. Electric jolts. At least a thousand more of the comparisons shot through me, evoking everything and anything I knew that was bright and bold and blinding and amazing, as he threaded fingertips into my hair... and filled everything above my shoulders with perfect heat.

God...*no.*

God...*yes.*

"Sh-Shiraz—"

"Tell me." He curled his grip in, yanking me tighter toward him. His voice was guttural and rough. "Tell me how you like it."

"I... I don't think..."

His gaze swept down, zeroing in on my mouth. "Or maybe you should just show me."

I took a breath. I'd pass out if I didn't. Or was that just the force of his power over me? And did it matter once his sharp, sexy scent filled my nostrils...once his heady, swirling heat wrapped around the rest of my body?

"Oh *God*," I whispered. "This...ummm...well, this is a good start..."

His lush mouth swirled up in a pleased smile. The couch crunched as he adjusted his weight, molding himself closer. "But what happens next?"

"Errmm." If I wasn't so busy remembering how to breathe, I likely would've laughed. I hadn't stammered my way through a conversation this much since Shari Pearson and I had run into Justin Timberlake at Amoeba Records in Hollywood one Sunday afternoon. Ditching Catechism had never been so much fun. "Well, uhhh..." Fun. Oh, yeah. This was fun too...right? No. *No*. This wasn't like harmless flirting with JT between the 80s Punk and Classic R&B sections. But my body wasn't listening. My mouth *sure* as hell wasn't, opening and offering, "Wh-What you'd d-do next would be..."

"Soft and slow?" he provided instead. "Like...this?"

He gently dropped his head. Let his sublime lips brush in and then down, flowing over mine like a feather on the wind. I tried to breathe, but only a squeak came out. The sound was obnoxious, but I was past caring. The currents he zapped through my body, from head to toe, were like a lightning storm from a sci-fi movie.

Dear, fucking God...

"Th-That's good too," I finally rasped.

A growl rumbled from deep in his chest. Though it was one of the most incredible sounds I'd ever heard, I couldn't figure out what had generated it. Was he aroused? Unsettled? Maybe both? Was that even possible?

"Good?" he finally echoed.

"Oh, yeah." I managed a hurried nod. "*Very* good."

"But not the best."

"I don't think you have to worry about that." Nervous laugh. "Honestly. You're—dear God, you're—"

I whimpered once more as he stole the rest of it, sweeping his mouth down again. No sweet little pressure this time, but no full-blown assault either—though by the time he finished, plying my lips with tantalizing thrusts and teases, I was practically begging for the assault. My blood thrummed with need. My senses boiled with lust. And my sex...

So much pressure. So much desire. My hips bucked from it. My body tightened into a hot, eager wire. Air rushed up my throat and out of my parted, panting lips—every breath consumed by the man strung as tautly next to me.

Ready...*for what?*

This wasn't going any further. This *couldn't* go any further.

Too bad fate forgot to give *him* that memo.

"I am *what?*" Shiraz demanded in a terse husk. "Is this still just...'good'?" He nipped the curve of my chin, breathing moist fire into my skin, before parting his lips more, using the edges of his teeth along the column of my neck.

"Holy...shit." My head fell back as my arms curled up, hands twisting into the luxurious mess of his hair. My muscles tightened as I poised for him, ready for him, longing for the descent of that delicious heat into my cleavage and then across my breasts. Thank God for V-neck T-shirts—and my proclivity of taking my bra off whenever I possibly could. My nipples were painful points now, stabbing into the cotton, ample evidence of the rest of my reply for him.

"That is not an answer."

Like that was going to stop him from demanding one.

Damn it to hell.

"Lucina?" He halted, hovering his face less than an inch above my sternum.

"*What?*" I snapped it without thinking, battling to force him back down. He fought me, aligning our gazes in a fiery, feral clash.

Nothing had ever turned me on more.

He grabbed one of my wrists. Pulled it up and away from his head. Released a quiet wildcat snarl...as he lowered it next to my head. The move shifted our positions. He had me flattened against the couch's back, with him kneeling over me. It was utterly sexual, altogether inappropriate, fully unreal...

A full fucking turn-on.

"Perhaps I need to repeat the question."

The phrase came with mixed messages. His tone was a sultry flirt, but his gaze was a definite challenge. Every molecule of my being wanted to take him up on both, but how? Reality was just a sliver of light in my consciousness, despite how desperately I reached for it.

"Maybe you need to *change* the question."

"And if I do?"

"Shiraz." I swallowed hard. Jabbed my gaze up at him. "Change. The. Question."

He said nothing.

But his frame tensed.

The light in his gaze changed.

Just half a shade, from steel blue to deep cobalt—but it was enough.

Enough to prove he understood me. That he recognized the thin edge upon which we now balanced. That the line, already just a thread between us since the start, could never be redrawn if wiped out.

But maybe it already was.

Our pull was a tangible pain inside me...and I saw that torment in his eyes too. We were careening toward darkness. The shadowed side of our orbiting moons. The nasty beneath our propriety. The connection of souls beneath all the corporate bullshit.

The joining that, to the rest of the world, would be so wrong.

The collision that seemed so damn right.

In every sleek line of his face, I watched the same thoughts—and their ramifications—take hold.

Ramifications. It wasn't a fun word to think, let alone brace for. But the knot of nails in my stomach grew, knowing exactly what waited ahead. Ramifications. Reality. A fiancée for him to claim. New questions for him to phrase.

Not to me.

"Lucina."

His whisper was heavy on the air. And technically not a question, though everything about it beckoned like one. Pulled like one.

Frayed my self-control like one.

"What?"

I spat it like before, shutting my eyes before they could issue a silent apology. I didn't want to be sorry. Not for this.

When I reopened my gaze, I fought to look up at him—but only managed it halfway. My gaze made it as far as his neck. Wasn't exactly doing myself a huge favor. Was there such a thing as neck porn? If so, I had a serious addiction already.

"What happens next?"

Well.

That was one way of lifting my gaze all the way up.

And what I found waiting in *his* stare...

Holy shit.

His sensual surety swelled in me, heated and simmering and straining. Pushed at my mind, which I'd closed so damn tightly since learning he and Ambyr were going to be Arcadia's next golden couple.

I wasn't golden. I was nowhere near it. I'd tried to become that once, yearning to be perfect enough for Ryan and his polo-

wearing, football-loving, missionary-position world, but in the
end, it had all fit as shitty as a wrong-sized bra. Hadn't been
pretty. Or happy.

But the man leaning over me now...

Staring with such intensity now...

He fit.

Damn it, I have no idea how I knew it. But how did flowers
know to open every morning? How did seagulls know how
to drift on the wind? It just was. *He* just was. It was fruitless
to fight it. To even try, in my mortal and meaningless way, to
resist.

Sometimes, heat was meant to burn.

Locks were meant to be released.

Battles were meant to be lost.

And right here, right now, was that such an awful thing?
Did it make me a hideous person? He hadn't given Ambyr a
ring yet. He hadn't given Ambyr a *kiss* yet.

He just wanted to know...

What came next.

And God freaking help me, I wanted to show him.

CHAPTER NINE

"Come here."

Wasn't the first thing I'd wanted to say, but my well of pithy and witty was drained. My senses spun, processing so much inside *and* out. Could I be blamed when a dark demigod hovered over me, driving his blue-fire stare into me? How else was my body supposed to react, except to go up in flames?

I backed the entreaty by sprawling my fingers against the back of his head. Dug my nails into his scalp. Reveled in how he hissed and then dipped toward me. Groaned deep as I pulled him lower, toward the parted hunger of my lips.

On his way down, he grated just one thing.

"Yes, *tupulai.*"

He could have just called me a one-eyed goose and I didn't care. I adored the sensual sibilance of the Arcadian language—who didn't?—but on his lips, the native words became verbal diamonds, spraying my senses with their sparkling facets. I smiled. When he returned the look, I felt nothing near a goose. Once more, I simply rejoiced in his wind on my wings. His sun on my petals. His purpose in being here, if only for the one moment we'd have to recognize this thing between us... whatever this "thing" was.

Did I even want to define it? Analyze it? Why? Wouldn't change the fact that it just *was.* This pull to him—this need to pull *at* him—was like nothing I'd ever let inside the tower of my heart...and for just one moment, I was going to let him climb inside.

I know, I know; it sounded completely crazy. Where had these grand, romantic fireworks come from? I was the girl who only wanted the danger, the burn, the hard-'n'-hot fuck. But maybe that was fate's psyche-out this time. Guys like him—*princes* like him—weren't after women like me. They could ask for, and get, females named Barbie, Jessie...Ambyr. They wanted girls who wore sweater sets at dinner and lacy lingerie sets afterward, who liked screwing with the lights off as they moaned in all the right places. A delicate blow job from time to time was okay too, but that was where the lines got drawn.

Women like me weren't delicate.

Our lines were messy.

Our needs were dirty.

We were...weird.

But maybe, just maybe, Shiraz Cimarron wanted to know what weird felt like for a moment. Maybe even two.

He sure as hell liked it so far—if I interpreted his groan clearly enough. And the growl it turned into as my grip on his hair became demanding, all but forcing him across the last few inches over my open mouth.

Dear...God.

Weird had never felt so good to *me*, and I'd practically invented the word.

No kiss had ever been this messy either. Or this wet and hot and needing and deep—and, even a little painful, as our teeth collided—during our mutual quest to practically devour each other.

Yet again, could I be blamed? The man was a fucking natural at this shit. No. More than that. Shiraz Cimarron was a man destined to do this to a woman. His kiss was an extension of his being, his passion like a beast eating him from the inside out. He rolled his head in, groaning and growling, making me feel like the Andromeda beneath his Cetus...the virgin given to a god for his pleasure alone. Would've been a damn fine analogy, if it wasn't completely twisted around. Virginal and I had said a very pleasant buh-bye at least seven years ago, when a spin-the-bottle game at an after-game party landed me in the closet with Brodie McMullen. I might be one of the weird girls, but I was also smart enough to see a once-in-a-lifetime chance to jump the baseball team captain when it hit me between the eyes.

Though technically, I wasn't doing much of the "jumping" tonight.

And it was...amazing.

Even when he reached up, seized my hand, and then slammed it against the couch, angling my arm just like the other.

Even when he charged in on my lips again, harsher and harder, holding my tongue hostage to the violent sweeps of his.

Even when he shifted so one of his legs was extended, bracing his foot on the floor and leveraging his body over mine.

Sliding against mine...

Fitting very certain parts of him to very certain parts of me.

I gasped.

He groaned. "Creator have mercy."

I gulped, fighting shivers, as the contact of his chest sizzled fire into my breasts. "This...isn't merciful." My tips hardened, jutting into sharp relief beneath my shirt. Alexander Hamilton's proud pose achieved bold new meaning.

Shiraz stiffened. Jerked away a little. "It is not—you do

not like it?"

Weak laugh. But not unwelcomed. A hint of levity was probably what we needed. "Oh, I *like* it plenty." I raised my head, but my gaze stayed hooded, especially when studying the curves of his mouth, now swollen like pillows. *Pillows. Really? You're thinking of this man and anything related to a bed right now?* "It's just...intense."

"Intense is not comfortable for you?"

"Intense is *not* comfortable for me." I was completely honest.

His chin jutted. His eyes darkened. "Oh."

"That's why I really, really like it."

"Oh." Comprehension was a new thread in his tone. *He got it.* Just like that, he simply *knew*. If I had any doubt about it, the fresh force in his grip took care of it. What the man lacked in experience—and at this point, I began wondering about that—he more than reclaimed in enthusiasm. Clamping down on me harder, he monitored every nuance of my reaction—as if masking them was possible. My chest pumped double-time, betraying my hammering heartbeat. My nipples formed stiff moguls in my T-shirt. I was flushed and hot, practically writhing with arousal.

"Fuck." Before I could think of stopping it, the desire rushed out. "Oh...damn!"

A low hum unfurled from him. "I know," he rasped, dipping a heated kiss to my forehead. "Yes, Lucina. I know."

I tilted my head to meet his stare. "You do, don't you?" I didn't disguise my wonderment. "You...just *know*. You're not saying it just to assuage me or to be polite and princely."

His blue-steel gaze pierced through the hair cascading over his forehead, seeming a combination of chastisement and cherishment at once. "Tupulai"—he inserted another defined slide of his hips—"does this feel polite or princely?"

I gasped as his heavy bulge violated more of the space between my thighs. Moaned as I opened wider, helping the friction by another degree. Shiraz slipped back and then rubbed forward again. We stared at each other over the little billow of my T-shirt, the soft cotton yielding to the force of his denim. Even our clothes had the right idea.

"No," I finally got out in answer to his sarcasm. "It feels..." But then hesitated. Should I disclose what I was really thinking?

"Like what?" He emphasized the command with another push of his hips. Well, that did it. Time to suck it up and fully confess shit.

"It feels like a man who knows what he's doing."

His brow furrowed. "And that concerns you?"

"I'm not concerned." It was the truth. "I'm confused."

But so was that—and his bizarre silence of a reaction didn't ease anything. Okay, as silent as a man could possibly be while turning a dry hump into something as intense as the real thing, finally interrupted by his measured pull of breath. But his gaze was still unflinching. While the valleys persisted in his brow, so did that knowing glint in his eyes—that light emanating from the window he alone had carved into my mind...

Making it possible for him to give words speaking straight to my soul.

"For the first time in a long time, I am *not* confused." He let go of my hands to slide his grip around my thighs. He repositioned me, making me open for him in a full-facing missionary. It was wonderful, and I was so damn wet—except for one glitch. Neither of us had taken off a stitch of clothing.

"From the moment I walked out of my office and saw you today...everything simply seemed clearer." He smiled, despite the mutual quivers of our bodies, as he settled himself tighter between my legs. "Better."

"Better?" My incredulity was as naked as my body yearned to be. He lived and worked in a palace on one of the lushest islands on the planet. He was a *prince* of this land.

But hadn't I learned the prime paradigm of the rich and famous by now? Perfection was just redirected perceptions. The grass was always greener when one didn't have to mow it.

But still...I'd brought a sliver of better into his world.

Made his grass a little greener, just by walking across it.

So why was I questioning it? Though he didn't seem surprised that I did. Even flashed a hell-to-the-yes gaze at the chance to answer me.

"You surprised me," he admitted, lips tilting up. "And strange as it seems, I am not surprised by much anymore."

"Why would that seem strange?"

His eyes flared. His mouth quirked. Surprise was one breathtaking look on the man. "Between both my brothers' *betranlis* and the interactions I have on the phone with New York and Los Angeles, I thought I had American females—how do you say it?—'sized up,' yes? Figured out?"

Narrowed eyes. "Come on. We can't be that different from Arcadian girls." I hissed as he rocked harder against me. "Most of...the important stuff...is the same." Through my sarcastic snorts, I managed to emphasize "important."

When he countered that with a growly chuckle, delighted shock joined my lust. "My little surprise party, you have redefined 'the important stuff.'"

I bit my lip, feigning innocence. "Why, what*ever* do you

mean?"

Another sound, low and rumbling, punched from him. It was full of leashed intent, like a predator baiting its prey—until he whipped his hands up again, meshing fingers into mine. Palm-to-palm, he forced my arms all the way up, over my head.

"You know what I mean, tupulai." He grated the hot syllables into my temple, my cheek, my jaw. "You know I mean...exactly this."

I sighed heavily. Being pinned beneath him like this...dear God, *yes...*

His mouth traced over the same path, leaving a wake of fire through my whole body, until igniting the throbbing tissues between my legs. By the time he rose back up, aligning our faces once more, I was a panting mess of arousal.

"Yes," I finally rasped. "I do know."

He curled a knowing grin. "You want to be locked like this, for me. Trapped like this, by me."

"Yes." I could barely choke it now, but his approving growl was all the reinforcement I needed. And oh yeah, there was the effect it had on his cock, swelling and hardening against my cleft. And the musk of his desire. And the spice of sweat along his neck... "*Yes*. Damn!"

He answered with a fervent kiss to my neck. "Now tell it to me again, as you would a man who dared to capture you. And master you."

Fucking. God.

The man didn't just have a window to my soul.

He had a direct-access pass to my most illicit fantasies.

"Yes...Sir." I hardly recognized my own voice and reveled in that. Getting pulled outside myself, commanded to become someone else, was like pulling shackles off my naughtiest desire. As soon as the words were free, my breasts ached, my sex tautened, my clit throbbed—and damn it if Shiraz didn't know all of that by simply raking that hot cobalt stare across my face.

"Perfect." He twisted our hands tighter. His heartbeat thundered in through the pulse in his wrists. As his thrusts intensified, he swept up and over me, taking my mouth in a consuming kiss. Relentlessly, he spread my jaw until it ached. "So *damn* perfect," he grated when we parted.

"Yes!" I prayed he'd order me to say more. The words took me away. Made me reach beyond myself. Helped me fly.

"Yes...what?" he prompted. Thank fuck.

"Yes, Sir."

He snarled softly. "Is that all?"

Screw the direct line to my psyche. He'd just rewired himself to my pussy.

"I...I meant, yes, Sir. It's damn perfect."

His gaze dragged open. He looked down on me, his bronze god features afire and his broad sculpted shoulders coiled, and I understood why sacrificial virgins were paralyzed when offered to the immortals. He could have pulled my heart from my chest and eaten it front of me, and I would have died an ecstatic woman.

Ecstatic.

Damn good word, especially right now.

"Perfect," Shiraz echoed, lunging in so hard, my soaked panties were stretched tight against my intimate center. "Tell me, sweet surprise. Describe it."

I attempted a steadying breath. *Riiigght.* Not happening any time in the next century. "My...my blood is like fire. My skin...feels so tight. And...and my pussy..."

"I feel it." He ground in with more passion, his face defined by harsh lines. He was a work of art, like a lush watercolor and a granite statue mixed into the same incredible masterpiece. "Throbbing now. So hot now. Your clit wants to come for me, yes?"

"Oh, my God!"

"Not a proper answer." He enforced the scolding by backing off on his pressure. My body protested at once, bucking to keep him locked against me.

"Shiraz! Damn it...*please*..."

"Please *what*?"

Please fuck me. The real way. But that wouldn't get me anywhere. I already knew it, sure as the dark control in his gaze and the merciless lock of his hold. That wasn't my call to make right now—and I adored him for it. Might even, in a little while, thank him for it. Right now, I only wanted to seethe at him for it, so I did. The bastard only smirked, relishing every second of my frustration.

"Make my clit come." Fine. If he wanted begging, I'd give him begging. "I... I need to come."

Finally, he shoved his straining bulge back against me. As our bodies slammed, I burst with a rickety moan. He joined me. His thrusts intensified, though his execution turned as rocky as our breaths. He was driven in need but unthinking in form, like a starving beast given a virgin to devour...and deflower. His face was lost in passion, white teeth clenched, noble forehead pursed, as he concentrated on each hard, sliding stroke.

"Beg me again," he ordered. "Beg me...respectfully."

I shivered in force. Dissolved in full.

Suddenly, the direct hack at my fantasies didn't feel like so much of a joke.

How did he know?

How the *hell* did he know what I'd craved for so long? All the dirty, depraved detail of it? And yet, how did he know how to make it all so sound magnificent, so regal...

So exactly like everything he'd craved too?

And at this moment, did I even care?

"Please, Sir. I'm begging you. Please, *please* make me come."

I had my answer as soon as I gave him his "respect." I didn't give a crap how he knew, only that he did—and knew exactly what to do with all of it.

"Make you come...how?"

Yeah. Knew exactly what to do...

Just

like

that.

"With—with your cock."

"Slamming at your pussy, like this?"

"Yes." Shaking gasp. "Yes please. Slamming at my pussy."

"Even if I rub it raw?"

"Yes. Even if you—oh, God!"

"Lucina?"

"*Yes*, damn it. Even if you— *Shit!*"

He rammed harder, making me cry out—and expose myself more. Damn it, he was doing it. Yanking out the Lucy so few had seen, shaking with need, weak with wanting, naked with vulnerability. She looked up at him, was even reflected to me in the bold, blue flames of his eyes—and I silently screamed at her to retreat, to come back inside where it was safe, but the pain made that impossible. It demanded I stay right here, present and aware and marveling at every magical move he made. My bruised pussy demanded I feel every thrust of this fuck—and in a blinding, dazzling burst of lightning, every force of my climax.

Before my scream could hit the air, he devoured the sound with his lips. I emptied my elation into him, surrendering every sated moan and desperate cry, intensifying when he began answering with violent groans of his own—corresponding to the desperate, urgent thrusts of his body. I dragged my eyes open in time to view his passion in full glory, pinching his forehead and clenching his jaw, before it drained into a dazed kind of peace.

He expelled a long breath.

I inhaled a wistful sigh.

Then again. And again.

Then more silent synchronicity.

And sadness? Yeah, perhaps a little, but not for regret of what we'd done. I ached because we'd never be able to do it again, especially the right way. Not that there was a damn thing wrong with *that* way—I sucked in another breath, struggling to remember the last time a sexual experience had been so intense for me—making me wonder, if only for a second, what things could be like if we were truly naked, horizontal, and in a real bed with each other.

"Lucina? What is it?"

Shit. The fervency of his tone made me realize I'd let my longing show through. Hell, had just dropped my guard in general. I bit my cheek to abstain from the obligatory "nothing," since even a prince from a postage-stamp island could see through that bullshit. Instead I answered, "Just spinning down from the high, gorgeous." New curiosity. I went ahead and let him see it. "How do you say *gorgeous* in Arcadian?"

His brows crunched. Bewilderment was another good look for him. On that note, a brown paper bag would be a good look for him. "We do not really have such a word."

"Now you do. It's pronounced *sheeeer-ahhzzz*."

His eyes narrowed. "You should be thrown into the dungeon for that."

"Promises, promises."

He had no idea how close we danced to the truth. *Did he?*

"I enjoy it when you invent names for me in your *own* language."

He backed it up by gently rubbing his nose atop mine. Every inch of me softened all over again. "Why?"

"Because it means you shall really remember me. Now what?" he prompted, as I sneaked in another laugh.

"Gorgeous, you are *not* easily forgotten."

"Oh? And how is that?"

I averted my gaze. The force of his deepened. Time to change the subject. "What was that word *you* just kept using? *Tup*..."

"Tupulai." He corrected my pronunciation in his hotter-than-hell accent, taking the syllables *toop-ah-lie* to the top of my favorites list—sorry, *mar-gahr-ee-tah*. At the same time, his voice thickened and his body shifted, betraying the impact of the memories—just as I'd hoped. My anticipation hadn't included my own heated recall of what we'd just done... not that I was particularly complaining about it. "The closest translation in English is 'little piece of trouble.'"

"Trouble? What the...?" Though my deliberate trail-off, along with a sassy head wag, pretty much validated his point. He said so with a short chuckle before leaning and brushing his lips back over mine.

"It is intended fondly." Another brush, with a tiny slide of his tongue over my bottom lip. "*Very* fondly." Then a growl, not so gentle—utterly perfect. "It fits you well. *Very* well."

Shivers.

Dangerous ones.

Dear hell, what this beautiful, purposeful prince did to me...

And kept doing as he dipped his head even lower. Then lower...before I stopped him with a wriggle of my hips, determined to be cute and girlish about it. This conversation needed to stay light. The reconstruction project on my heart, already begun in earnest, couldn't handle things any other way.

"You know what? That *does* fit," I quipped. "I'm trouble. With a capital T. So be careful if you don't want to get completely corrupted."

Perfect. I'd kept it light but warned him off at the same time. With luck, he'd pick up the snark and run with it. But did I mean that? Weren't his intensity and focus what my body had first reacted to? Wasn't his power, dealt with such deliberation, what had turned me into aroused mush? Like what it did right now...

"Tupulai?"

"Yes, Sir?"

"I am the equivalent of your politicians, yes? So perhaps I already know a few things about corruption."

Forget the shivers.

Now, he brought the fire.

God, I yearned to be burned.

My lips parted, almost begging again for more of those nasty words. He didn't give me the chance, swiftly stuffing the pad of his thumb into my mouth. I opened more, giving him access to darker regions—yet lighting up a thousand other places in my psyche. Naughty, kinky places...

"You feel that?" he charged. "Singed. Searing. On fire. Because of you, Lucina Fava. Because of what you have done to me." He worked the pad of his thumb along the flat of my tongue. "By the Creator, what I still want you to do to me."

My breath hitched. My lungs were pierced as if with needles, struggling to funnel new air to my body. My eyelids dragged, heavy with arousal, but I forced myself to keep looking at him. If I didn't, I'd fantasize about that finger turning into other body parts. Who the hell was I kidding? I'd already gone there. It was clear *he* had too. Our stares locked and glued, bound by the new fantasy. I flicked my tongue to his fingertip. He hissed and then swallowed.

Okay, this shit had to end. Right here.

Through sheer determination, I pulled back. Between the harsh pumps of my breaths, finally got out, "What *Ambyr* should be doing to you."

I backed it with a firm stare, though in the end, couldn't compete with the impact of his—especially when the sea gods conspired with him, sending a gust of wind into the room. The blast flapped the filmy curtains and then lifted his hair, turning him into something worthy of a Peter Jackson epic. Beautiful. Primal. I jotted a mental note. *Lodge official complaint with Mother Nature.* I'd dutifully chosen an earth-saving hybrid over the red Mustang of my dreams and gotten rewarded with a windblown sex god I couldn't touch again?

Okay, not any more than how much I still touched him. Or was *he* touching me? And wasn't that just semantics, considering how our bodies were still positioned? God, how perfect he felt, with his crotch still fitted against mine, his ridged abdomen molded against my belly, his shoulders still blocking most of my view?

Along with his glare.

Oh, yeah. That.

"So that is the way of it now?" He funneled the look into visual form. "I am Ambyr's problem once again?"

Seethe. Then a glower to match his, though infused with my own touches. Pissed-off and bewildered. "Problem? Really? *That's* your takeaway, buddy?"

"Take...away."

And just like that, the windswept god turned into an adorable child mulling a new vocabulary word. Also just like that, I forgot to be irked with him. Instead, I longed to soothe his confusion. And what a lovely wave of fresh conflict *that* jump started...

Shit.

This was *not* going the right way. I supposed to be pulling down the mental menu of tactful post-orgasm buh-byes, not wondering how to ease the furrows pinching his forehead. Though I had to admit, the quotation marks in his flesh simply seemed another facet of his beauty, like his thick eyelashes and straight nose. But while God had put him together so flawlessly, all those aspects had traits of uniqueness. Features I could lie here and explore for hours, given the chance...

Not. Happening.

Pack it up, missy. Pack him *up.*

Good plan.

One I'd carry out—just as soon as I took care of those furrows. *Only* the furrows. I meant it; I really did, no matter how warm and firm his skin was as I lifted fingertips to the space between his eyebrows. I meant it, even as I trailed my touch down, eliciting a shaking breath from him...

Just as I inhaled sharply.

Synched once more.

To each other.

With each other.

No. People didn't just "synch." That bullshit was for things like Merchant & Ivory movies with actresses who tossed "bloody hells" the way I slung the F-word, rocking the corset-and-pantaloons look with their creamy breasts and tiny waists. My breasts had been called a number of things, but never creamy. And the last time my waist and "tiny" were in the same sentence, I was twelve.

But dear God, how I wanted to let out a good "bloody hell" as the man dipped his stare down, all the way to where our bodies were still tangled.

Instead I rasped, "Shiraz..."

He lifted his head. "What, tupulai?"

Bloody fucking hell.

"I'm damn certain Ambyr will consider you the best 'problem' she's ever had."

It was a lob into the unknown. I still wasn't sure exactly where he and Ambyr were at and was damn sure Miss Manners was on the tsk-tsk side of mentioning a man's potential fiancée while he was still lodged between one's legs, dressed or not. But necessity didn't always take stage cues well. The truth of it was symbolized with piercing precision by the stronger gust in the room now.

The blast felt angry—another spot-on parallel, if the cast of Shiraz's face was any proof. Yeah, I'd only met the man hours ago but would stake hard cash his jutted jaw and magma glare were his you-said-the-wrong-damn-thing look.

Which meant I should've been setting off victory flares, right? This was what I'd been after. A way, *some* way, to wrap this up before our cool-off turned into a new heat-up—and we were doing more things that wouldn't be great ideas in anyone's book. Things I wouldn't be able to forget come morning...

Yes. The affirmation should've lightened my mind as he eased away from my body. Instead, as he lurched all the way to his feet, all I felt was heavy, chilled, and alone. On a logical level, the reaction made sense. It'd been too long since my last orgasm from anyone or thing other than Sam—aka *SAMM*, the Sexy-Ass Magic Machine, streamlined with my fantasies about the other Sam, as in Heughan, whom I'd never actually fuck because I'd faint from ecstasy first—and I was beyond jetlagged, meaning my emotional defenses were low. That damn wind didn't help things, rushing in to plaster his T-shirt against the ripples of his torso and his hair against the bold cliffs of his forehead—but none of that was why my pussy throbbed worse than before.

That had everything to do with the wet spot at the front of his jeans.

I know—*ew*—but something about the knowledge that I'd put it there, that he'd been so heated from the *semblance* of fucking me that he'd lost control from it, made me literally dizzy. And so damn horny. Yeah, this fast. Yeah, all over again.

He wheeled away—the sight of his taut ass atop those lean thighs *didn't* help the rebellious clit, thank you very much— and stalked toward the door. If I were lucky, he'd keep going. I had to keep telling myself that. How he'd make it to his own part of the palais rocking that wet spot was *not* my concern. Right now, all this place could be was a facility in which to catch sleep and a shower before the plane left for home. And before all *that*, a quick check-in with Sam to rub out the edge in my blood, courtesy of the prince who couldn't get out of here fast enough.

But he didn't leave.

Instead, scuffed to a stop next to the door, scooped up a phone mounted on the wall next to it, and punched in a pair of numbers to the panel. I'd wondered about the device when walking in, figuring Arcadia's infrastructure was still so new that they still needed land lines, but the way Shiraz spat a few lines in Arcadian made me rethink the premise. An intercom? Whoever he'd called, he absolutely knew—and wasn't afraid to growl at like a bear with an ulcer.

I steeled myself for the same behavior after he turned around, but my lifted chin and challenging gaze had him instantly backing off. Outwardly, at least.

"My valet is bringing fresh clothes." He barely let up on the grump factor. "As soon as he is here, I will most definitely not be your problem anymore."

What the hell?

I told him as much with my glower—and the surge to my own feet. Good thing I obeyed the instinct, since he spun and started stomping toward the kitchenette. I caught him before he got there, spinning him back around by an elbow.

"Hey," I spat.

"What?"

"What do you mean, *what?*" Loud *thwack*s punctuated me. The lightweight curtains, snapped in by the wind. "Why are you pulling the prince of pricks act?"

He jerked all the way around. Pushed back at me, looming now. Dear hell. Had I already forgotten how much he dwarfed me? "The prince of *what?*"

"You heard me." Yeah, but that didn't mean he comprehended me. European universities didn't include automatic enrollment in American trash talk. On the other hand, I hadn't known a single word he'd spoken on the phone—but I'd *understood.* "I'm trying to be cordial here. No, wait. I'm even being *nice,* damn it, and—"

"Nice?"

I would've laughed at his confusion, if it wasn't so effing real. "Nice," I flung. "It's a little expression we have in the real world. It means to be pleasant with one another, especially after episodes of mutually satisfying sexual fun. What?" I challenged at the glare intimating I'd all but barfed on him. "You didn't have fun?"

"Fun." He spat it while stepping back, pushing hands down his thighs—wiping away the barf. "Fun. Certainly. Yes. That is exactly what happened. Fun. A grand, galloping lot of *fun.*"

As he rattled it all off, I watched him carefully. At first, the natural burnish of his skin prevented detection of his flush—and the insight I gained from it.

Oh, my God.

His flinch made me realize I'd blurted it aloud too. The color cranked in my own cheeks. Was it possible? Was Ezra's crazy claim really true? Could this male of jaw-dropping beauty, who'd been created by heaven to tempt all who saw him into hell, whose every damn *step* made a woman ache to be fucked by him, truly be a virgin? Because he sure as hell was acting like one now.

"Shiraz—"

He silenced me by raising a hand. A commanding, obey-me-now, very *non*-virgin hand.

What the hell did that mean? And what the hell did that make me?

His effing yo-yo, of course.

I hated yo-yos.

"The subject is finished, Lucina. And soon, your *problem* will be, as well."

Annnnd here came the butt-hurt virgin again.

Meaning the yo-yo should've taken her cue and bounced clear.

Instead, I was already yanked back up and reeled back in, my temper in the palm of his hand.

"Baby Jesus in a high chair." I rushed across the room, hands shooting up, not stopping until I'd landed a solid shove to the center of his chest. And yeah, I reveled in his backward stumble—though damn it, he made *that* all ballroom graceful too—before adding a seething snap. "Are you *even* serious right now?"

His lips parted. His chest pumped. "As 'serious' as you."

"No." I jabbed a finger. "No fucking way do you get to air quote me, prince of pricks. Nor do you get to make me the bad guy here, just because you can't deal with what just happened between us."

"Oh, I know what happened," he snarled. "You made it abundantly clear. Fun. We had *fun*. Rah-rah-woo, take the pom-poms too, this shit is bananas, ladies and fellas."

For the record, he melted me in about a million new ways. Holy crap, the power of an exotic accent on a bunch of hip-hop.

But for the record, part two, he enraged me more. I felt the enamel scraping off my teeth as I clenched them.

"It was fun because we *can't* make it more." And just like that, as I raised hands to touch him with gentler intent, my wrath dissolved. As the heartbeat under my fingers strengthened, I even tried to smile. "If we could, we'd call it what it was, okay?"

He formed a hand over one of mine. Pressed it harder against his sternum. "And what would we call it?"

Wider smile, brought on by the quickening of my own pulse. "Awesome," I supplied. "Not even that. Incredible. Maybe even...epic."

"Oh." His gaze flared as he drew out the word. "Epic?"

I thumped him with my free hand. "But we don't get to run with that. Not in this lifetime."

He inhaled sharply. Nodded with just as much determination. "You are right."

"So why are you crying in your damn cereal?" I turned my hand over, clasping it into his. Used the hold to slide my body closer to his. There were only a few more minutes I could be this tawdry, and no way would they be wasted. "Where I come from, cereal isn't wasted. You eat it even if you cry in it."

More thunder rolled in his chest as he settled me tighter against it. "That does not sound appetizing."

"Isn't," I concurred, basking in the new warmth of his gaze. "Unless you're talking about Frosted Cheerios. But then, it's a moot point. Who would cry with Frosted Cheerios in front of them?"

"Who would cry with *you* in front of them?"

Fucking. Sigh.

Letting go of his hand so I could wrap mine around his neck, I raised on tiptoes, lifted my head, and let desire drive the rest.

And him.

Shit, he was a good driver. Our deep, wet, lingering,

longing kiss went on and on and on—and I let myself rejoice in every surrendering, quivering, perfect moment of it.

And yeah, let myself moan softly in protest when he tenderly tugged away—but not too far. It was simple to slide my other hand from his chest to his cheek, now raspy with incoming stubble. The contrast of the sharp hairs with his sleek beauty had me dealing with a new clench in my sex, especially with this renewed pressure against his. When his cock answered with a pulse of its own, I knew the faucets needed a crank to cold again.

But not yet.

Just one more moment...

"I'm glad you came." Tiny quirk of lips, to show him how thoroughly I meant the double entendre.

His own, swollen from our contact, parted to show his white, perfect teeth. "I am glad too."

I released a little sigh.

As he pulled in a resigned breath.

It was all we needed to draw back together again. Bound. Magnetized.

Our lips never met.

Rapid raps at the door accompanied another blast of wind.

We dragged apart, each swearing in our own language.

"Probably Adym." Shiraz clawed a hand through his hair, not helping my battle to lay one last smack on him. "My valet. With fresh clothes."

"Yeah." Under normal circumstances, I'd add a quip to that about how "valet" meant only one thing in LA, and it usually meant getting a whole car instead of new pants. But nothing about me felt normal right now. My body, my senses, and sure as hell not my mind.

So much for thinking I'd get a minute of sleep in the cloud bed tonight.

And thank God I always carried replacement batteries for SAMM.

And thank God, times two, I was able to sneak in a full breath before Shiraz yanked open the door.

Because it wasn't Adym who'd knocked.

Unless Adym was a superior drag queen and had transformed himself into a perfect fusion of Tinkerbell and Morticia, complete with the wide lemur stare.

"Crista." Shiraz's own confusion drenched the tone. "Where is—"

"Adym paged me, Your Highness." The woman wasn't slow. Her gaze worked fast, instantly absorbing our mutual fresh-fucked hair, kiss-swollen lips, and—oh yeah—the dark spot at the front of Shiraz's jeans. If I thought she'd missed it, the woman's fresh blush set me straight. "He is frantic, trying to help with locking down the apartments in the royal wing."

If Shiraz noticed the same thing, he gave no indication. He faced her fully, not a hint of apology on his face, accepting the wad of clothes she thrust out. "Lock down?" he demanded. "From what?" His face hardened. "Is there a fresh threat from Kavill?"

"Fuck." While I kept it mostly beneath my breath, my fear was real. Rune Kavill was human smegma. He'd been taken down in a blaze of glory by Samsyn Cimarron, who'd displayed legendary restraint by sparing the dickwad after Kavill captured and injured Brooke. Syn had banked on the bigger bounty of making Kavill stand trial, but that had never come to pass. Suggestions abounded across the globe that the

ANGEL PAYNE

criminal had made a pact with the devil to get out of Censhyr Prison, a story not difficult to believe once someone actually comprehended what a fortress Censhyr was.

"No, Your Highness." The new care in Crista's voice wasn't hard to interpret. I used the same tone when trying to explain to a bride that ninety percent chance of rain meant inside ceremony options needed to be considered. "We are locking down because of the storm."

"The...storm?" It blurted out of me as facts began rushing at me—and making more sense. The wind, gusting in angrier bursts. The crash of the waves outside, seeming more and more violent. And now, the eerie cast of clouds over the sea, visible because of the lightning flashing between them. "Wait. Don't you guys get stuff like this all the time?" Okay, it was about as lame as I could get, but a habitat as green as this needed lots of rain. A girl from ever-brown Southern California should know.

My answer came clearly enough through the new intensity in Shiraz's gaze, stabbed out the window like a steel blade. "Rain?" he returned. "Yes. But not...this."

"Not what?" More of the lame...but his trepidation started freaking me out.

"What is the status?" He directed the command at Crista as if I hadn't spoken. At the same time, accepted a smart pad she offered, its screen filled with an image. A map of the Mediterranean, with Arcadia's location marked by a red inverted teardrop. I actually felt my eyes widen at the thick white sworl off to its right. Yeah, I was a native Cali girl but had planned enough weddings on the East Coast to know what that image meant.

"The upgrade is expected within the hour," Crista answered him softly.

"Fuck," he muttered.

"The upgrade to what?" I interjected.

Crista looked over, her gaze seeming rueful. She bit her lower lip before explaining, "The storm. The Mediterranean Weather Service shall likely declare it a medicane soon."

"A medi *what?*"

"A medicane." Shiraz pulled his focus from the sea back to me, his mouth now a firm line, his cheekbones stark with tension. "Our version of a hurricane. And it is tracking directly for us."

CHAPTER TEN

I'd be a rich woman if I got a dollar every time someone called me crazy for living in a state known for earthquakes. In the moments after a six-plus shaker on the Richter scale, I had a tendency to believe them.

Not anymore.

That wasn't crazy.

This was crazy.

Crista's prediction had come true. Shiraz had barely finished changing into his new jeans when his phone buzzed with text after text. As he'd paused to answer them all, fingers flying over the keys, I'd jammed into a cotton hoodie, a pair of leggings, and my trusty Doc Martens—though the outfit might as well have been a Spicy Cheeto costume, judging by Shiraz's stunned reaction.

"What are you doing?" he'd barked.

"You think I'm staying up here?" I'd swung a hand at the room—and its sweeping fourth-floor view. "With a freaking hurricane on the way?" As if on cue, the wind had whipped the cushions free from the deck chairs and toppled over my remaining nectar. *Gah.* That had made it personal.

I was willing to release the grudge when Shiraz conceded, "Valid point." But reclaimed it twice as hard when he continued, "Gather your valuables, then. I shall escort you to the palais shelter before joining Samsyn and the emergency task force."

"The hell you will."

Crista's bugged eyes alerted me about *that* faux pas before her boss's glare had kicked in. Not that I cared. He was no longer a potential client, or even a hot and memorable—*really* memorable—fling. In short, I was free to faux pas all over his stubborn ass—maybe a good thing when a man needed help with getting shitloads of people to safety in a short amount of time and refused to see the help being freely offered.

"The matter is not up for discussion, Miss Fava."

"Damn straight it isn't." He wanted to play know-it-all dictator? I could match that game. "You need people who know how to move large numbers of other people. Guess what I've been damn good at for the last year and a half?"

For a second, he'd looked like I whacked him with a two-by-four. "You...wish to assist with our evacuations?"

His shock had been so genuine, it yanked at a weird place in my chest. "Is that so hard to believe?"

"Yes." Such tender sincerity. "And I will not allow it."

Concluded by utter assholeness.

Yeah, he had me torqued enough to be inventing new words.

Even now, a handful of hours later, I had yet another fresh one.

Prickitude.

As I sat with Crista somewhere in the palais's underground with a hundred court employees and their families, there was plenty of time to compose the whole dictionary listing for it too.

Prickitude
1: Attitude affected by that of being a prick, shown by overbearing disposition, churlish ways, and disregard for logical

sources of assistance in dire emergencies.

2: The state of being such a prick, all common sense is ignored.

3: Movement led by Prince Shiraz Cimarron, Kingdom of Arcadia.

I was tempted to add a picture along with the mental heading but wasn't ready to take the edge off my rage—a given if I envisioned even part of the man's face. Or hair. Or shoulders. Or chest. Or other body parts I'd only felt through clothing but sure as hell could fill in the blanks on...

"Damn it." I spat it to no one in particular, keeping my voice low out of respect for the small kids playing nearby. The group was a secret blessing to my nerves, with their sense of wide-eyed adventure. To them, the storm surge was an excuse for potential puddle stomping, the wind howling through the palais tunnels a new beast to befriend. Their delight was oddly calming—to an extent. I was too stressed to relax all the way.

Hanging on to my anger also meant I didn't have to face my fear.

That a storm raged so hard above us, I could hear its effects through layers of solid stone.

That said storm was going to blow over the whole damn castle, entombing us beneath it.

Worse, that the ramparts wouldn't hold against the surge and we'd drown.

And I'd be helpless to do anything about it.

I didn't do helplessness very well.

Who the hell was I kidding?

I didn't do it at all.

So why was I subjecting myself to it now?

"Because you're crazy?"

Like I said before...

My mumble inspired an empathetic look from Crista, her wide eyes even more pronounced with her hair yanked away from her face. Tendrils of the stuff were webbed across her cheeks and neck as she gazed at the kids too. "Crazy," she echoed, her voice wistful. "That is a funny word. I believe I like it."

I leaned my head against the tunnel wall. We sat next to each other on the damp stone floor, our phones side-by-side between us. A lot of good that did, since the thick walls and rain soup all but ensured we wouldn't have decent signals for a while. "It's a sturdy one," I returned. "Serves a variety of uses."

"Especially when a male of a certain royal family drives one to pull her hair out?"

I snickered but stopped, turning my side-eye into an astonished stare. "Holy shit. *Crista.*" Barely held back from face-palming myself.

"Holy shit what?"

Despite how adorable as she was, blurting the profanity through her formal accent, my shock was unfazed. "You have a jones for him, don't you?"

"A what?" Then the context slammed her. "Wait. For who? For...*His Highness?*"

"I'm sorry. I should have realized sooner. And oh my *God*, you're the only one who knows what I did to him! I mean, not what I did *to* him—I mean, *with* him—but not even in *that* way—"

"Oh, dear Creator." She giggled softly. "No. *No*, Lucy. He is my—how do you say it?—my direct employer. My..."

"Boss?"

"Yes. My boss." She jerked another inch upright, face twisting with the squick factor. "I mean, His Highness Shiraz is certainly lovely to gaze upon and has that Cimarron air that makes everyone nervous and fidgety..."

Nervous. Fidgety. Not exactly the two words I would've picked, but they sure did apply. "But...?" I prompted into the clear pause she provided.

"But," she repeated before sheepishly shrugging. "I mean...well..."

"Ew?" I finally supplied.

"Yes." She beamed. "Ew." Tilted her head, murmuring the word one more time beneath her breath. "I like that American word too."

I didn't have the heart to tell her it wasn't really a word. Didn't matter anyway, especially with the issue I still attempted drilling down on. "So if Shiraz is an 'ew,' and you can't be referring to Evrest or Samsyn..."

Her face turned ashen. "No! They are also fine men, but—" Her nose crinkled. "They are taken and mated and—" A rapid shake of her head became a shudder. "Just...no."

I scrunched my brows. I was tired but not *that* tired. She'd brought up "that Cimarron air," as if she'd had firsthand experience with the subject, but—

Wait.

A flash hit. Part of my first conversation with Shiraz.

A pair of my father's finest advisors...were joined by my cousin...

"Tytan." The memory helped fill it in. As soon as the name left my lips, Crista's gaze flew everywhere, and her lips kneaded each other to a pulp. "Hmmm. Tytan," I repeated knowingly. "Your own maddening Cimarron, hmmm?"

Her face darkened. "Not mine." She gazed longingly at the children, as if beholding an idyll she'd never know. "No. Not mine. I—we—" A short huff. "I mean, even if our statuses were closer, it would not be...suitable."

"Statuses? Suitable?" I let my own gaze gain a few shadows. "Is that even a thing here anymore?" My perusal roamed the crowd, a human mixture as diverse as what I'd first seen in the palais offices. "Your country is changing, Crista. At a very fast pace."

She grimaced. Traced a striation in the floor with one finger. "Only some things, Lucina."

"Lucy," I corrected. "Or Luce. I don't care." We were huddled in a storm shelter, sharing protein bars and water rations. Formalities were for the business offices and marble hallways above us.

"Lucy." Her dutiful echo was negated by a sullen shrug. "The point is the same. Even if his last name was Smythe, it would be useless. Ty and I are...quite different."

Ty? I refrained from smirking fully. "Sometimes that's good."

So maybe waiting out a hurricane in a shelter *wasn't* insanity. The conversation, one I didn't see happening anywhere in the real world above, had taken a turn toward interesting—in more than a few ways. I mean, I'd just surprised myself. Okay, perhaps even shocked myself. I was the queen of the wedding pragmatists, not a matrimony groupie. That was still a good thing, right? Okay, maybe there was a little relief involved, a residual ecstasy after learning she wasn't interested in Shiraz. But why would I try to keep pushing the situation?

Not worth dissecting. So I didn't, instead following up with: "Opposites really do attract, girlfriend. More than you know."

This time, her adamant head shake meant whipping her shoulders with her own ponytail. "Opposites, yes. But two people as far apart as the poles themselves?" She stared through the crowd, sighing wistfully. "I want...all *this*, Lucy. A crowd of children running around. Family togetherness, even in adversity. Sharing the hard times and the good...and all of the crazy." Her lips inched up, trying out the word in her own syntax. My mouth emulated the look.

"That all sounds damn good to me."

"I was raised with it." She checked the reception on her phone, like I'd done every ten minutes since we got down here. And just like the last time I'd checked, not even half a bar appeared. "I am the oldest of six."

"Whoa."

She laughed. "A word my parents are clearly *not* familiar with."

"No shit." It deserved a hearty laugh. "Most of my life, it was just my mom and me. I always had a friend or two hanging out on the weekends, but six at a time, *all* the time?" Shudder. "Yeeps."

"It was certainly...busy." She pulled up her knees and rested her chin atop them. "And loud. And loving. And full. Abundantly full."

I softly squeezed her shoulder. "Nothing wrong with that."

Her smile faded. "Unless one wants it with Tytan Cimarron."

"Why?" If Tytan was half as magnetic as his cousin, I didn't blame her for pining for the guy. On the other hand, maybe Tytan faced the same marital obligations as Shiraz... "Oh, yikes. Does he already belong to someone else?"

Her eyes slid shut. "No."

"Just obligated, then?"

"No."

"Married?" Shit. *That* wasn't a mess worth screwing with.

"No."

Thank God. I was too beat to get out the whipping stick about married men—not that Crista Noble struck me as "that type" for a single second.

She finally rasped, "Tytan Cimarron belongs to no one, Lucy."

"*Psssshhh.*" I waved a hand. "Maybe he says that now. But—"

"No. Not ever." She nearly bit the words out. "He is—how do you say it?—the permanent bachelor. Yes?"

I snorted. Hard. "That's what they said about Kanye and Clooney."

"Who?"

"Not important." I pushed off the wall and into a full crisscross position. It did nothing to help the strain on my backside but got my stare in position to challenge her more directly. "C'mon. Tell me more about him." Evil grin. "More importantly, why he turns you into a puddle of goo."

She spurted a giggle. Cut it short by burying her face against her knees. "He does not turn me into a puddle of *anything*."

"Hmmm."

She glanced back up. "Hmmm?"

"Nothing. It's just that...I hadn't realized what pretty brown eyes you had."

"Huh?" Her head jerked higher. "I have green eyes."

"Ohhhh." I tapped a finger to my lips, drawing the word

out. "So you really *are* that full of shit, then."

She jerked away from the wall herself. Drew a sizable breath, clearly winding up a line drive of a retort. I almost grinned. This was going to be fun.

The breath left her in a single whoosh—without a single word joining it.

As she stared, dumbstruck, right over my shoulder.

As a discernible wave of energy rustled through the crowd.

The excited murmurings, accompanied by most people lurching to their feet and bowing, were definitely due to a new arrival in the shelter. A woman. For many moments, I had trouble understanding the fuss. The petite thing resembled a porcelain doll with her big sparkling eyes, shiny black curls, and high cheekbones. She seemed familiar, but I couldn't place my finger on why...

Until I *did* realize why.

She was at least eighteen inches shorter than her three brothers. Evrest, Samsyn, and Shiraz.

Didn't stop Jayd Cimarron from exuding the same force-of-nature vibe, even dressed in dull brown puddle stompers, faded blue jeans, a dark T-shirt, and a bright-orange jacket. Water poured off the neon nylon as the princess rushed through the crowd, greeting people but still clearly in search of someone. A pair of guards flanked her but weren't one damn bit happy about the pell-mell path she cut through the shelter...

Until her face flooded with relief.

As soon as she laid eyes on Crista.

"Thank the Creator," Jayd exclaimed, breaking into a little run.

"Damn it," the larger of her guards gritted. Not only did he catch my attention because of his reddish-blond Highlander mane, but with that raspy quality in his voice and that take-no-shit swagger? *Hello, superhero audition.*

"Settle your feathers, Jagger Fox," Jayd groused at superhero before crushing Crista with a hug. "We found her, and I am allowed to be relieved about it."

"Your Highness Jayd?" Crista, clearly stunned, didn't hug the princess back. "Errrm...what are you..."

"Shiraz sent me," Jayd cut in—though her expression sobered so tightly, I began to understand the bigger guard's tension. *Jagger.* His name fit. The only smooth thing about him were his eyes, the color of buttered caramel.

"His H-Highness...s-s-sent you?" The words went parrot mode on Crista's lips, mostly because her chin was violently trembling. My gut twisted as I watched it get worse, but I couldn't very well tell her to chill. With her distress so tangible, I surged forward and grabbed one of her hands. The action startled her enough to stammer, "Creator's mercy. My deplorable manners. Your Highness Jayd, this is—"

"Yes. I know." Like her brothers, Jayd was no stranger to taking charge of a situation. "Miss Fava." She nodded, though the move was more friendly than formal. "Brooke and Cam told me about their meeting with you outside 'Raz's office. I wish we were meeting under better circumstances."

"What is happening? *What* circumstances?" Crista struggled to be polite about it, but the spike in her stress was transparent. Since I'd never met Jayd before, having only read she was the most outgoing of the Cimarron siblings, I had to assume this tight tension wasn't the norm for the woman. I also had to assume this was more about Crista, not Shiraz. If this was about him, he'd not send his little sister all the way to the shelter to fetch his assistant, especially after all but commanding Crista and me to stay down here until the security team's "all clear."

He was okay. He had to be. He *would* be, unless he wanted me to kick his very fine ass into next Tuesday.

"Crista." Jayd stepped forward again, pushing her hands together like a petite prayer angel.

"*Rahmié Créacu.*" Crista sagged against me. "No, *no*. What happened? Is it my *maimanne*? My *paipanne*? Tell me!"

Jayd rushed in, embracing her tight "*Dinné*, they are both fine. I promise." But as she moved away, she kept both hands cupped to the other woman's delicate shoulders. "But we do need you to be strong, *arkami*, because—"

"Because...*why*?" Crista didn't stand on ceremony anymore, for which I would've been supremely grateful, if not for her distress. A whimper escaped her defying words, the kind that stabbed the gut of anyone within earshot—because it was a sound of raw fear.

Jayd took in a visible breath. "It is Forryst and Fawna—"

"*What?*"

"Crista, I need you to stay calm and—"

"Calm?" She pushed the princess away, lurching past even Jagger. "By the mercy of the Creator!"

Jayd spun around, flicking a help-me glance my way as she did. "They are not dead, dinné." Another look back gave me a silent addendum. *Not yet.*

As I followed the princess, I tugged on Jagger's sleeve and whispered, "They who? Forryst? Fawna?" Sounded like a couple of characters from a Peter Jackson film—but a lot of Arcadian names did.

"Crista's youngest siblings," Jagger explained. "A boy and a girl. Twins. Just six years of age."

My mouth turned into a huge *O*. "Holy shit."

His jaw tautened. "Perhaps the *un* holy shit, as well."

Crista stopped. Paced a full, frantic circle. Returned our direction. Stopped again. Her arms fell to her sides, balling into fists. "Not dead," she repeated. "All right, all right. They are not dead. What *are* they, then?"

Jayd straightened. Her posture was so formidable and her presence so certain, I forgot all about the hard numbers missing from her height. "Not what," she replied. "But *where*."

Crista grimaced. "So they are missing?"

Jagger squared his massive shoulders. "Officially, as of an hour ago."

"The little *preesh*es likely sneaked off again," Crista gritted. "When they are together, they think there is some kind of a force field keeping them safe. They should be disciplined, but Forryst knows exactly how to play Maimanne, and Fawna has Paipanne wrapped around her little finger."

"They cannot be far," Jayd assured. "And Shiraz is heading the search party himself—but he told us you might be able to help with specific information. You have relayed stories to him before, of how the kids enjoy going to Parryss Landing...?"

"On the river. Yes."

Crista added a nod, but it was jerky and scared. I couldn't blame her. Not right now. *The river.* In Sancti, that could only mean the Mousselayan, which was as wide as the Mississippi on low days and predicted to become a lake-sized hazard in this storm. I remembered at least that much from the chatter on the walkie-talkie Shiraz had grabbed while delivering us down here. The situation was turned into a double whammy of disaster when considering all the structures now erected for the Grand Sancti Bridge reconstruction project. Once the violent waters knocked them loose, there wouldn't be just normal debris to worry about. The torrent would likely contain spare wood, nails, and sheet metal.

The same thought clearly struck Crista. Her manic combination of laughter and tears was followed with a rapid-fire explanation. "The water has always fascinated them. They enjoy watching the ships go by. They even dug out a little cave in one of the banks as their 'lookout fort.'" Her throat convulsed as the sobs threatened to win the battle. "The little preeshes. As soon as they heard about the hurricane and the flood, they probably hatched a secret scheme to get there." A full moan broke free, making her wrap both arms around her middle. "If anything happens to them, I shall—"

"*Nothing* is going to happen to them." I was the one who said it this time, going shoulder-to-shoulder with Jayd for the effort.

"Especially if you can help us with *any* more information," she added, grabbing one of Crista's elbows. "Please, Crista. Anything at all..."

The small touch carried a galvanizing effect. Crista's shoulder's straightened. Her head shot up. Though tears rimmed her dark-brown eyes, her reply was underlined in pure determination. "We have to get to the river. *Now*."

Jayd nodded. "Excellent idea."

"*We?*" Jagger cocked his head, watching like an intense buzzard as Crista crouched and started stuffing her shit back into her duffel. When he straightened, it was to slice the same look back at Jayd. "Yes," he leveled, "*We*, as in Shai and me." He seesawed a finger between himself and the other guard, who stayed carefully silent, despite a startling green gaze that missed absolutely nothing—

Especially every steady inch of Crista's rise back up. And the sharp resolve in her own eyes. "You only get the information if I go too." She daggered that determination into both the men. "They are *my* brother and sister. They must already be so terrified"—her voice caught on a quaver—"and when we find them—and we *will* find them—I can help calm them."

"And we can help calm *her*." I stepped into the space between Crista and Jayd, forming us into a chain by linking our elbows.

Jayd grinned and gave me a fast wink. I swore to God, despite the situation, I almost laughed. Only one person on the face of the earth could've taught her that cocky smirk.

The man who was out there right now, risking his generous, gorgeous hide to find those two kids...

And what had I expected he'd be doing? Sitting around in some command center, playing solitaire with the radio dispatchers?

Holy Mary, full of grace—what the hell; I was already in practice—*please keep that man safe, or I'll have to break his beautiful face.* Practice being relative.

"No. Everyone wait." Shockingly, Crista issued the mandate—as she looked at me with wide, questioning eyes. "*Lucy.*" Stepped around, grabbing both my hands. "This is not what you came to Arcadia to do. And I cannot ask you to—"

"Whoa." I jerked free from her, only because getting both my hands to my hips was the more important statement at the moment. "Not what I *came to do*?" With the pose came the full channeling of my inner Ezra, as well. "What the hell part of that statement is relevant here, missy? Timing my trip perfectly with a rare Mediterranean hurricane thing? Having to deal with the subsequent freak-out in the palais basement?

Or actually putting my stress to good use by helping to find two adorable kids?"

Crista's face crunched, trying to deal with scowling and laughing at me at once. Finally, tearfully, she simply hauled me into a hug. "Adorable? You have never even met them."

"They're *your* kid sibs, right? How could they be anything less than beautiful?"

As we pulled apart, another meaningful look passed between us. There was one more thing I hadn't come to the island to do—namely, her boss—a secret I knew she'd keep, no matter what I decided right now. I sent her an equally determined regard in return, driving home the point that my decision had nothing to do with that. Two children were in danger here—more than Jagger and Shai even wanted to let on. Dealing with hundreds of wedding days in all kinds of conditions, I'd learned to spot when huger secrets were being kept from people "for their own good."

"It is settled, then." Jayd pivoted, squaring off with Jagger, once more making me think of a bad-ass fantasy heroine in leather and spiked boots instead of her durable storm gear. "*We* shall be going to the riverfront—as in all five of us."

Jagger's nostrils flared. "Damn it."

She imitated the look. "Your stance on the matter is noted, Mr. Fox."

His nostrils calmed—only because the tension shot out to every other part of his body. Still, I had to bite back a smile. Unless my instincts had been screwed to hell by now, it was totally clear Jagger battled the craving to throw Jayd over his knee—and then into his bed.

He compensated by all but snarling his retaliation. "Do you even understand what is going on out there right now? The river has surged by six feet already. Do you know how bloody dangerous—"

"I *know* that two children are still missing." Jayd marched in on him, placing their chests just inches apart. The princess clearly couldn't spot a spanking in a man's stare, even when it seared into her. "And that you are wasting precious minutes of search time, being an overbearing ape."

"Your Highness Jayd." Wow. Shai did have a voice—and it was as rich as the *café au lait* his skin matched. "With all due respect, the *ape* has a point." He swung his bright-green gaze to all three of us—though it rested the longest on Crista. "Directive or not, Shiraz will turn primal if we make a call that endangers you. *Any* of you."

I didn't know what to make of his last three words but related to the rest of his statement. I'd seen the primal side of Shiraz Cimarron—in the sensual sense of the word. It'd been scary. I'd been in heaven. But seeing him go caveman in *this* situation? No freaking thank you.

Nevertheless, I caught Shai's gaze with the determination of my own. "*We'll* worry about Shiraz. You guys take care of getting us to Parryss Landing." I tugged Crista close again. "We've got a family to reunite, and we've got to do it now."

For another moment longer, Shai gazed at the woman in my arms—openly longing to trade places with me. Wow. That look. I didn't know anything about Tytan Cimarron beyond what Crista had just relayed, but if the guy stared at her with half this intensity, no wonder she was smitten.

Shai knocked himself out of the reverie by shaking his head, muttering a frustrated oath in Arcadian, and then dashing a look back over at Jagger. "Perhaps we can plead temporary insanity?"

Jagger shot back his answer with his glare glued on Jayd. "It would not even be a lie."

Jayd had the girl balls to smile in triumph. "Very well. Let us hurry, then."

We sprinted from the shelter.

Raced a storm.

Hoped like hell we made it in time to a riverfront that was, by now, very likely a lakefront—where a pair of six-year-olds had wandered, filled with impossible dreams.

Holy Mary, full of grace...

This time, I prayed it sincerely.

Please, please, don't let us be too late.

CHAPTER ELEVEN

Some experiences you couldn't compare to anything in a movie.

Not that I could even think of movies right now. Or a single thing beyond surviving the next moment. Hopefully. Then the one after that. *Hopefully.*

God, I wished how the mental italics weren't necessary. But they were. A layer of boldface would have been appropriate too.

As we drove—hydro glided?—our way through Sancti's near-empty streets, I contemplated yet another *Hail Mary* reprise. Forget air turbulence; careening through a hurricane took home the award for best holy-shit-am-I-going-to-live moment from this trip. Or any other.

Despite the insane conditions, Captain Storm—yes, that was really Shai's last name, and no, I didn't go one inch near the snarky possibilities for it—handled the big SUV with the same quiet focus he directed at everything else, especially Crista. No time for playing matchmaker right now, though. Had I just called the conditions insane? No. Impossible fit so much better. Beyond the front windshield, the wind had turned the rain into sideways slashes, and water wasn't the only thing getting hurled. Items like wood crates, whole bushes, and a pair of bicycles blew past the car. Jayd, Crista, and I were death-gripping each other by the time Shai braked the vehicle on a rise overlooking tempestuous waters.

I did *not* want to get out.

The river looked like the Nile in *The Ten Commandments*—the epic Cecil B. Demille version, not the lame remake. The violent currents, filled with enough construction debris to confirm part of the bridge construction had indeed given out, were bisected by rows of trees and structures that must've lined the river's shore a few hours ago. Now, the trees resembled decorative parsley and the roofs poked from the flood like broken teeth of a giant zipper—or so it seemed when I could see anything through the sheet-like rain.

Shit was officially insane.

A standpoint Crista clearly argued—and put her money where her mouth was too.

We'd barely stopped before the woman clicked free from her seat belt, scrambled for the door, and then tumbled out. Jayd was right behind her. At once, a huge gust slammed them back against the car, and they gripped the car handles for purchase. While I gasped, gaping like a numb dork, Jagger and Shai went into action. With powerful efficiency, they swooped out. Jagger flattened himself against Jayd, and Shai imitated the move for Crista—though she sure as hell wasn't happy about it. Instantly she fought the confinement, flailing like crazy, but Shai tucked his head against her neck, barking forceful orders into her ear. I couldn't understand the Arcadian, but I understood the tone. He wasn't going to be disobeyed. Luckily, she came to the same conclusion and stilled.

Poor Jagger wasn't having such an easy go with the princess. She gave back the yells as swiftly as he bellowed them and batted away the rain poncho he offered with a few words I *could* make out, like "bossy ape," "useless poncho," and "not a little girl anymore." Even under the circumstances, I almost broke out giggling. After this whole thing was over, Jagger was either going to murder her or screw her silly. After watching the way that warrior moved, I hoped Jayd was in for the latter.

They all turned, obviously preparing to descend the slope.

And I was still sitting in here, creating the mental Vegas odds pool about a Jagger-Jayd hookup.

My ass had to move, no matter how freaking scared that made me.

"Cheese and rice," I berated in a mutter. "Come *on*, Luce. You've got this, damn it." For the sake of helping two innocents out on their own in this shit without a Shai or Jagger of their own.

Right now, I was damn glad for the ones *we* had—explaining why I crawled across the seat and exited the SUV through the same door Crista and Jayd had used. The two of them would have to be happy sharing the guys for human anchor services.

Nothing could have been more true as soon as I was hit by the barrage.

It seemed the only appropriate word for everything that hit me next—literally. The rain stung like BB pellets. The wind threatened to scalp me. The combined noise from both had me wondering where Mother Nature had hidden her subwoofers. The whomp against my ears was more deafening than the newest superhero movie in equally super stereo.

Without shame, I accepted the poncho Jayd had dissed. Somehow, I managed to get the thing over my shoulders and my arms stabbed into the draping holes. Instantly, I understood the princess's disdain. This thing was freaking useless. I was soaked in seconds.

Jagger inched toward the SUV's hood, using the car for

cover, his massive thighs bunching beneath his wet black combat pants. He angled one arm back, stabbing that forefinger toward the ground, and Shai backed up the order, yelling, "Get down! Stay low!"

Not a problem, buddy.

Unbelievably, Jayd joined me in complying with that—though the direction was as good as a flip-the-bird for Crista. She inched forward in Jagger's wake, pushing up next to him and peering over the SUV's hood. I made out the shadow of his glare as he looked down to her intent profile.

"Do you see anything?" she yelled—though the tempest already provided the answer. Well, lack of one. As far as we could see, the landscape was the same. Water. Mud. Rubble. Water.

Lots and lots and *lots* of water.

And nothing else—except for brief lulls in the wind allowing for glimpses up the river, where the higher banks existed. Flashes of lightning helped illuminate the skeletons of scaffolding that were still standing, battered over and over by the waves until relenting another chunk into the drink, making my own gut plummet with a strange, drowning foreboding.

No. No, damn it.

The kids had to be alive.

Children were resourceful—and a lot smarter than people usually gave them credit for. I wasn't a mom but had vast experience with the subject, having thwarted thousands of little hands swiping at wedding cakes, chocolate fountains, and gift tables over the years. If the intelligence of their big sister was any clue, those twins would have found a way to stay safe. Somehow...

"There!" Shai shouted, pointing at a roof a little taller

than the others. "That's the top of the Parryss Boathouse. To the right of that is where the dock usually begins. Those poles, painted white at the top—"

"Are the pilings securing the end of the dock." Jayd pressed a hand to the base of her throat as her gaze extended across the white-capped waves. "Where the twins might have gone to get a better view of the storm."

"Yes," Shai said with quiet finality.

"Shit," Jayd and I muttered at the same time. Jagger layered another oath atop them, in gritted Arcadian.

Our reactions were like fingers on a trigger—on a gun named Crista. She bolted from the truck, spraying mud in her wake, manic with fear. "*No!* They are safe. I can feel it. I *know* it!"

"Crista!" Jayd and I screamed it together—before sprinting out as well. But while Jayd was yanked short, caught around the waist by a cursing Jagger, I went over the side of the hill—where my foot hit a slick spot of mud at once. I went down for the count, careening down the slope on my butt.

"Lucina!" Jayd again.

"Fuck." A snarling Jagger.

But not a single sound from Shai—fully explained the next second, as he vaulted past me, chasing after Crista.

"Thank God," I rasped, drenched in relieved warmth, replaced nearly at once by an overall chill. The rain and mud had started seeping under my clothes in force. The storm was by no means a chilled front, but I was a thin-skinned California girl down to the helix of my DNA. Mud in the cooch was *not* my gig. On the other hand, my brain's frantic orders to move were wholly ignored by my quivering body. My limbs felt dipped in chilled glue. I was frozen in place, terrified for Crista but even more fearful of following her.

I managed to lurch to my feet and stumble back up the hill, helped the last few feet by an equally muddy Jayd. Once we struggled back to the truck, the wind had a temper tantrum again, and we had to grip the truck's wheel well to stay upright. I turned my head, trying to locate Crista and Shai, but the world had turned into a Jackson Pollock painting. The mud, the hill, the river, and the sky were splattered everywhere, mashing into a wild palette of brown, gray, green, and black. I yearned to close my eyes just to right my balance but didn't dare. What if another bicycle materialized from the mist—or worse? And what the hell would "worse" look like?

And wasn't *that* enough to take my mind on a new horror ride of possibilities?

Especially as I spotted Crista and Shai again.

Jayd's cry of shock joined my own.

"What the hell?" The shout came from Jagger—as he sloshed down the hill toward them, apparently to help Shai out with a still-struggling Crista. Not that it was going to do any good. The men, bigger and stronger than the fairy-sized woman, were also bogged down by heavier clothing and holsters full of equipment. Shai also had a loop of heavy rope draped across his torso. Crista rocked nothing but skinny jeans, a T-shirt, and a hard finger on the giant panic button.

"By the Creator," Jayd blurted. "The little *imbezak* is going to get herself into serious trouble."

I nodded agreement but finished the action with bobbing my head toward the river. Correction. The freaking *lake.* "We have to help somehow!"

"Agreed," she answered, to my relief. But no sooner had we pushed away from the SUV and started down the hill than we skidded and stopped, stunned by a new object rushing from the storm mists.

No. Not an object.

A sight that *did* answer the question about what "worse" would look like.

Like a soaked, stalking, glowering Shiraz Cimarron.

Who, as he stomped closer, sure as fuck took care of the chill in my bones. And heated up a whole lot of everything else from his bad-ass presence.

Who, despite looking like he yearned to tear my head off, ripped me with the longing to kiss his *face* off.

Who, despite the glory of his dripping hair, search-and-rescue uniform, and combat boots, rocked banners of bloodshot in his eyes rivaling the neon orange of his jacket. His steps were mighty but heavy. The weight of a thousand kingdoms dragged on his shoulders.

"What the *fuck* are you doing out here?"

"Lovely to see you too, brother."

"I still know where you keep your favorite shoes, Jayd."

"Ass," she groused.

"Get back in the truck," he countered. "And while doing so, tell Fox a temporary insanity plea isn't going to work this time."

Jayd's feet made slurping plops as she planted them and folded her arms. "I will do nothing of the sort."

In solidarity, I braced next to her. "Neither will I."

Shiraz scrubbed a hand up his face. Continued it all the way over his head. Like that prevented more water and mud from streaming back down. "I have not even started with *you* yet." As he glared at me—*through* me—a sole refrain beat through my system as an appropriate riposte.

Oh, please start with me. Then on me. Then inside me.

Instead I managed, "Nice to see you too."

"Nice is not a term you want to bring up with me right now, Miss Fava."

And just like that, the darker glare. The prowling, possessive, addiction-worthy energy—just like the shit he'd pulled last night before jumping on me, only amplified by one hell of an insane situation.

Sheeez-usss.

Between the adrenaline from the storm and the adrenaline from him, it was a miracle I didn't suffer a coronary there in the mud.

No time for coronaries now. First—and much more important—things first.

"Have you eaten at all?" I demanded him. "Or even rested?" A lot of hours had passed since he'd taken Crista and me to the shelter. Dawn had to be near, though I highly doubted the sky would look much different than now.

"Questions are not your privilege right now either, Lucina."

"How convenient for you," Jayd sneered. "Just as it shall be so convenient when you drop over from exhaustion."

His jaw steeled. I hoped to hell Jayd didn't notice how my breath snagged. Couldn't be helped. His ticked-off look was seriously one of his sexiest. "We have had just a few items on the task list tonight."

His dry irony didn't go unnoticed, and I would've shown a little more appreciation, except that some subjects needed to be front burner right now. "Like finding a pair of runaway twins?"

His brows crashed down. "Not yet." He snapped his

gaze to where Crista and Shai still grappled. "We are doing everything we can."

Again, he latched a breath right out of my throat—as he melted my heart a little more. He cared about those kids—because he cared deeply for the woman who worked for him. But there was more. He was a prince deeply connected to his country, beyond just the required royal patriotism.

"Crista thought the twins would have come here," Jayd stated.

Shiraz nodded. "Logical." His comment sealed another speculation as fact. Parryss Landing was to the Sancti kids what Santa Monica had been to my friends and me. Water, sun, and adventure, though on a smaller and safer scale. Just not today. Just not now.

Definitely not in the next moment, exploding with Crista's hysterical scream. Then her fight against Shai's grip, resembling a panicked cat clawing its captor. Once I tracked the line of her attention, out into and then across the water, I deciphered her insta-tigress mode.

Weirdly—miraculously—one buoy in the river hadn't been torn off its moorings. It bobbed wildly on the waves, clinging to position despite the force of the wind and the beating of the water...

And the two figures huddled together atop its base.

A small boy and a small girl.

"Forryst!" Crista shrieked. "Fawna! Hang on! Hang *on!*"

"Holy hell," I rasped. Next to me, Shiraz voiced the same thought in a guttural Arcadian oath.

"Crista!" he bellowed. "You are ordered to stand down. *Stay. There.*" He bounded toward her and Shai, each step sending up a powerful splash. "Captain Storm, keep her secured!"

"Trying!" Shai gritted—only to join his filthy Arcadian to Shiraz's, grabbing at the eye Crista had nearly scratched out and the balls to which she'd landed a solid knee. With a loud moan, the soldier sank to his knees...

As Crista tore free and ran like a madwoman into the river.

A madwoman with a damn death wish.

CHAPTER TWELVE

"Creator's fucking mercy."

It spewed from Shiraz as he chased Crista. Jagger yelled the same thing while sprinting down the hill. He quickly bypassed Shiraz, who halted to snap a walkie-talkie off his belt and yell into it. By then, Jayd and I had caught up with him. Since most of his orders were in fluent Arcadian, I only discerned every fourth or fifth word. The important stuff was noticeable, like *kod rouge*—code red—*priorlik*—priority—and *chenklars.*

Children.

I watched his profile, ashamed to admit how every other heartbeat in my chest—and there were a lot of those, considering the adrenaline had really kicked in—was still dedicated to utter fascination with his profile. Meshing the dirt-spattered warrior before me now with the sleek corporate machine of a man I'd met yesterday... "Head trip" was getting a fun mental rewrite.

As if I wasn't preoccupied enough, trying to keep the man out of any wet dreams he *hadn't* infiltrated. There were very few left. Only the hot 'n' sweaty tattooed guy ones. If the man had tatts, I didn't want to know about—

Shit.

One second of distraction, and fate gleefully kicked me in the ass for it.

Forcing me to watch, my mouth parting like a hooked fish,

as he stripped away his jacket, utility belt, and T-shirt—down to the splendor of his muscle-upon-muscle torso.

And the pair of stunning tattoos dominating the planes of his chest.

There was one on each huge pectoral, both in black with red shading: a hawk across the left, a dove taking flight on the right. They were beautiful, and so was he—a wonderfully shallow thought, one I should have grabbed with all my might as he shoved his clothes and the radio into my arms—but instead, I let my mind plummet to deeper places. Scarier shadows.

He was going to join Jagger and Shai—and jump in after Crista.

And he might never get back out alive.

The conclusions collided, launching a shrill cry from my throat.

"Shiraz!"

He was already two strides into the drink. He halted, sending up a bigger spray, and hurried back to stand in front of me. Tall. Magnificent. Strong. But would the river be stronger?

Enough selfishness. Unbelievably, Crista was already halfway to the buoy, Shai and Jagger right behind her, but that meant nothing. Anything could still happen. That knowledge was stamped across Shiraz's face—and now, in my agonized heart.

An agony I fully showed him while twisting a hand into his hair, desperately pulling him down. Our lips crashed clumsily but passionately. Close enough for a code red. I wasted no time jamming my tongue against his, needing to mark his taste, his scent, and his heat on me, inside me. Well, as much as the situation allowed.

In three seconds, it was over.

But I greedily grabbed three more. Through them, I kept him close. Speared him with the urgent grit of my gaze before stabbing him with you-*will*-listen-to-me syllables.

"Be. Careful."

He nodded. Once. There was no time for sap, as much as I longed for it. I could only watch, blistered I couldn't do anything more than stand there with his sister and watch him dive into the teeming shit fest.

Jayd pushed up next to me. Hooked our elbows once more. "He is a strong swimmer."

I pulled the little princess tighter. Clenched his clothes harder. Attempted to nod. Failed abysmally. "Okay," I practically gasped. "Th-That's good. Yeah."

"I wager he will be even better after that kiss," she said, for my ears only.

Despite the tempest, my face flushed. "Heat of the moment. I'm sorry."

"I certainly am not."

Even through the howling wind, I heard the smile in her voice. And endured the deeper blush across my cheeks.

Her brother wasted no time in proving her claim—*not* the one about our kiss. Shiraz's arms cut the waves like a pair of curved copper scissors in a bunch of rippling silk—and I tried not to think how flood waters really were like that slippery fabric. Unpredictable as hell.

Miraculously, the wind abated for a few minutes—a long enough window for Crista, Shai, Jagger, and Shiraz to make it successfully to the buoy. I watched, heart swelling, as the kids riveted their attention on their prince, giving frightened nods to questions he shouted. But even from this distance, I could practically read their little minds. *Prince Shiraz is here. Everything is going to be fine.*

They listened even more intently as Shiraz jabbed an arm at the sky. Had one of his orders into the radio been a call for helicopter involvement? How the hell that was going to happen in this storm, I had no idea—but if anyone could make it so via the sheer intensity of their belief, that person had to be him.

My chest expanded even more.

Maybe more than that.

Watching him take command of the situation, calming those kids in the middle of a dangerous crisis like this, bizarrely made me yearn to jump into the damn water myself, simply to be closer to him. Just like that, my mind flashed to the moments I *had* been that close, sharing passion and breath and orgasms with him—and suddenly, sharply, desiring it all over again.

No. Craving even more.

Without shame, I let the hot stings in my eyes blend with the chilled rain on my cheeks. I fought to rationalize it away, the magnitude of the situation taking over me, but my gut knew better. My *soul* knew better. It was him—and the fact that it was going to take a long fucking time to forget about him.

I forced more air down. Focused on bringing more of my senses back online again. Smelling the tangy salt in the water. *Ew*ing at the inch of wet sand my shoes had somehow collected. Concentrating on *anything* except how long it was taking for that damn helicopter to get here.

Especially as the storm intensified again.

"No!" I uttered, falling to the hillside next to Jayd. No way in hell was I wussing out by returning to the truck. Shiraz, Shai, Crista, and those kids had to stick this out, and I would too—despite how hard Shiraz glared at me for the decision.

Yeah, I actually felt the intensity of his eyes across the waves. And yeah, I was tempted to flip him off for it from here.

Saved by the radio.

I forgot my rashness when the handset, still pressed to my chest along with Shiraz's clothes, suddenly squawked.

"Savage to Driver. Driver, come in. Savage to Driver."

I rolled over, huddling my back over the radio. The wind was really starting to howl, so I hunched low and tight against the hill and then pushed the fattest button on the side of the device, hoping I remembered enough about this from military movies. As if I'd ever focused on the damn radio when Channing Tatum was on screen.

"H-Hello?"

Long pause. I shook the handset, wondering if I'd broken the whole thing. But finally, a voice barked, "Who is this?"

Okay, the button functioned. So did my temper. "Who the hell is *this*?"

Jayd yanked the radio from me. "Samsyn, it is Jayd. I am here with—"

"*Jayd?* What the fuck are you—"

"*Calmay.* There is no time!"

"The hell there is not. What in Creator's name—"

"She's right," I barked into the device, newly seized back from the princess. "There's no damn time." At least not enough to referee a brother-sister spat. Besides, Samsyn sounded enough like Shiraz that I was strangely comforted. "My name is Lucina Fava. When are you guys sending the helicopter for those kids?"

Another pause. "Lucina Fava? The wedding planner?"

"Not the damn Queen of England," Jayd muttered.

"Yes." I gritted my teeth to keep it calm.

"What the fuck are *you* doing out there?"

So much for gritted teeth. Or being civil. "I'll update my social media when I get a second, okay? For now, you want to give me an ETA on that helicopter, because Shai Storm, Crista Noble, Jagger Fox, and your little brother are hanging on a buoy in the middle of the Mousselayan, trying to keep a pair of six-year-olds safe!"

It only took a few seconds for the radio to crackle this time—imagine that—though it sounded like Samsyn had used the gap to swear his brains out. I caught the end of an English-Arcadian profanity mash-up before he yelled, "ETA on the helo is two minutes. Can you tell them that?"

"I... I don't know." The wind had abated, but that was because the rain had intensified. As I ducked my head to protect the radio again, the sides of my neck became dual waterfalls. "We'll try."

"Outstanding."

I flung myself to a sitting position, spitting water as I did. Jayd was sputtering full streams of the stuff.

For a second, I couldn't locate the buoy. "Shit, shit, shit. Can you see them anymore?"

"No," she answered.

It came out as frantic rasps. "Where the hell—"

There.

They were still there, thank God—though I could barely see them through the curtains of water. Damn, this crap was crazy. The rare times we got thunderstorms in LA, Mom told me it was the angels bowling, the rain their tears of laughter. Well, this was the angels laughing, sweating, and pissing at once, and I planned on having a chat with God about teaching them some manners. Thankfully, despite the fresh torrents, the buoy was still upright and everyone had managed to hang on...

Until a chunk of the far riverbank suddenly went under.

"Damn it," I breathed. One second, there was an outcropping of trees, bushes, boulders, and even a couple of quaint wrought-iron benches; the next, the scenic lookout was gone. Totally. Swallowed whole by the ravenous swell, its appetite barely sated by the park it had just devoured.

It wanted a new snack.

And the buoy was prime for the taking.

I gasped. Then screamed.

Unbelievably, the buoy held—but listed. Hard.

The jolt tossed Forryst and Fawna off.

Jayd and I shrieked, though I was positive I heard Crista's outcry at the same time. She was loud enough to catch the angels' attention though; they took a break from the pissing match to send one of the kids into Shai's waiting grip. Jagger instantly latched on to Shai's other arm, in order to keep him secured to the buoy...

As the other child was carried away by the current.

No wail from Crista now. She didn't waste the time—not while pushing off the buoy and swimming after her little sibling.

"Fuck," I croaked.

"Rahmié Créacu," Jayd exclaimed.

I paced now, every step frantically bouncing, like a lunatic wind-up toy. I was helpless, useless, and probably a little mindless, my brain refusing to accept what I *knew* Shiraz was about to do.

I really hated it when I was right.

Sure enough, in he went. Right after Crista and the kid.

"Save them." My tear-wracked plea was heard only by the wind and the rain, due to the deafening *thwop*s of the helicopter on the air. As the aircraft hovered lower, dropping a rescue basket thingie toward Shai, Jagger, and the other child, I dropped to my knees, clenched hands together in my lap, and choked out once more, "Save them. *Please*. Save them, and I'll even let the angels have a bye on their shitty manners today."

CHAPTER THIRTEEN

I still felt a lot like the stupid wind-up toy, despite the travertine tiles beneath my feet instead of a muddy hillside. Though there was an inch of warm slipper foam cushioning my toes instead of soaked sand, I'd refused to change the rest of my clothes. I'd also shunned the cup of hot tea brought by the palais rescue center volunteers. It sat on the floor next to where I'd positioned myself three hours ago, in the hallway reserved for people brought in by the search-and-rescue teams.

A couple of hours ago, they'd carried in a soaked and scared Forryst, reunited with his sister in a flood of tears and cheers from all—but my manic stares down the hall in their wake, expecting to see Shiraz drag in with Crista any moment, were answered only by a grubby trio of rescue guys, trying to be tactful about the story they relayed.

His Highness passed the child up to us...
Rotor wash caused waves...
Woman was unable to hang on...
Shiraz swam after her...
Refused to come with us...

The worst part about the memory gutted me all over again. The way they'd finished the story, assuring me other crews were out combing the river upon orders from Prince Samsyn and that none of them would give up until Shiraz and Crista were found...

All of it meant to be reassuring.

None of it easing my agony at all.

None of it helping the damn confusion that flowed in right after, gobbling my sanity exactly as the river had eaten that whole park.

You are keeping vigil for a man who was barely a client. Who isn't even a full lover.

Who sure as hell will never be yours.

I hitched an elbow on a knee and slammed my forehead into my palm.

Like that was going to jar the insanity free from my mind. Or even budge me one inch from this wet, hard lookout.

Maybe logic would be appeased if I bargained with it. "Only long enough to know he and Crista are okay," I reasoned in a whisper. "Then I'll pack up and get the hell out of here."

As soon as I *could* get out of here. Though heavy wooden doors guarded the end of the hall, they were opened and closed enough to give elemental updates about the storm. The worst had seemed to pass, though the weather was still damp and blustery. Now the cleanup would begin, and God only knew what that meant for the strip of asphalt Arcadia called an airport. *If* the runway was even there anymore...

That track of thought looped my memory back to the disappearance of the park. Then the surge that had toppled the buoy—and set all the horror into motion.

I flattened my palm against my temple. Squeezed my eyes shut, fighting and losing against the recall of those moments. Twisting fingers into my hair as winces escaped me and the images assaulted me. Children toppled into the water. Screaming along with Crista. Watching her tear into the water.

Watching Shiraz go after her...

An explosion of shrieks blasted my eyes back open. Jolted

fully back to the present, all senses firing, I shot to my feet. One of them had fallen asleep, making me stumble a little—a blessing in disguise, for it gave the seconds needed to identify the joy beneath the cries and the exact source of that jubilance.

Queen Mother Xaria appeared in the hall. I recognized her from the wedding research. She was a petite but regal woman, even without makeup or formalwear. She reminded me of an older Audrey Hepburn mixed with one of the Kennedys, dressed in a basic black turtleneck paired with burgundy pencil capris and black kitten heels. Yeah, kitten heels. *Here.* But she was the damn queen.

While many in the hall bowed to her, she clearly wasn't paying attention. Like anyone blamed her, with her son stomping in, wet and weary, from the opposite end of the hall.

"Merderim va Créacu," the woman cried.

"Thanks be to the Creator!" yelled Jayd, rushing in behind her.

"Look what the cat dragged in!" The cheer came from the man behind them, inciting my dorky grin in lieu of what I should've been doing: bowing to His Majesty Ardent, Arcadia's king father. But if the angels had shit on their manners today, so could I—and the occasion needed some unscripted joy.

Shiraz was back.

Soaked, muddy, and even bearing a few bruises—but here and alive.

Alive.

"Thank you." I rasped it to my own version of the big dude in heaven, gulping hard as Jayd hauled Shiraz into a ruthless hug. Somebody had found another jacket for him, but her embrace knocked it partway down his shoulder, exposing a perfect stretch of coiled, soaked sinew.

I openly gawked, only to be cut off after a few seconds. Ambyr Stratiss, poofing into existence from seemingly nowhere, rushed up in a cloud of breathy Arcadian. Wasn't a damn diss I had for that, either. Given the same permission to grope the man, even sounding all Marilyn Monroe about it, I would have done the exact same thing.

Right now, I was ecstatic just to see him. Walking. *Breathing.* Engulfed in a family lovefest, with no noticeable damage except a few cuts and nicks. While I'd never known the completion of such a moment, I imagined he was just as joyful and...

Shit.

The stare he lifted, boring into mine, was full of nothing but grief.

That was when a huge recognition impaled me.

Punching two anguished words out of me.

"Where's Crista?"

CHAPTER FOURTEEN

"Shiraz, darling, you *have* to eat. Just one tiny bite."

Not for the first time in the last hour, I chomped ice out of sheer frustration. Yeah yeah, it was like taking a pickax to my tooth enamel, but it beat taking a pickax to Ambyr Stratiss's throat—the same one producing the Betty Boop coo while she pushed another strawberry at Shiraz's lips.

When I heard my crunch being emulated, I looked up. Directly across the long wooden table in the palais's rescue center, King Evrest Cimarron dug into the cubes from his own drink. His sea-green eyes were sharp and glittery, his jaw hardened to the same texture.

Shiver. If that look was directed at me, I'd be scared.

But the woman to whom it *was* directed was *not* scared—basically because she was oblivious. Yeah, to everyone except Shiraz. Was a little hard to believe, since the crowd at the table included the two people she wanted to be naming as in-laws soon, but it was Ambyr's ring finger to burn, not mine.

"'*Raz*," she exhorted again. "Come, now. You have always loved strawberries, dear."

The Kewpie Doll voice was gone, though she still used that strange nickname. From my position at the end of the table, I could only glimpse part of Shiraz's face—though the jump in his tension, along with everyone else's, was palpable. Next to me sat Jayd, who looked ready to throat punch someone. The queen mother and king father filled out our bench. Evrest shared his side of the table with Camellia, Ambyr, and then Shiraz.

"Thank you," Shiraz managed in a tight but civil tone. "But no, Ambyr."

"But—"

"I said *no*." When she acceded to his snarl, he released an apologetic grunt. "Désonnum, Ambyr. You are only trying to help."

"Nice of you to notice." Her tone was a mix of sugar and acid, causing new squirms around the table.

Time to chomp ice again.

Once more, Evrest joined me.

As we commiserated, Shiraz exhaled heavily. "I cannot think of food until they bring back Crista."

"*If* they bring back Crista."

That gut-wrencher was delivered by His Majesty Ardent, who didn't flinch when Shiraz lurched from the table—and then pounded a fist to it. "Fuck!"

"Shiraz Noir," Xaria fumed. "*The children.*"

Shiraz threw back a vicious growl. Tore off the blanket around his shoulders with matching fury. Paced across the room, over to where floor-to-ceiling windows overlooked the storm-ravaged streets of Sancti. Though most of the city had fared all right, some outlying areas still clearly dealt with some flooding issues—but the scariest sight of all was still the swollen, muddy mess of the Mousselayan, almost looking like a hot chocolate spill if one squinted their eyes. Debris from the decimated bridge project, along with parts of trees and bushes and boats, littered both sides of the liquid barrage. From up here, the sight was practically peaceful—but I knew differently, and the enlightenment scared me all over again, only worse.

Way worse. This time, my trepidation wasn't wasted on a girl with skills like doll voices and making up cute nicknames for the boyfriend-who-wasn't-a-boyfriend. It was wrapped around real fear for a woman who'd risked her life for her kid brother and sister.

Risked her life...

Perhaps lost her life.

Oh, God.

"I should be out there." Shiraz's snarl was barely audible, especially past the rage that all but sizzled off his form. From the damp waves on his head to the soaked darkness of his boots, he visibly vibrated with the tension. "I should be out there, helping..." He skittered fingertips atop his thighs. "Stubborn, impetuous woman! She has no regard for her own safety or boundaries. First falling for my filthy *éslik* of a cousin, now jumping into the river without so much as a backward—"

"All right. Sssshhh." Ambyr rose and went to him, dragging her touch down his taut arm. I watched, jealous—of course, I wasn't going to lie—but also warmed by her tender gesture.

Until she murmured the follow-up.

"No need to make a scene, dearest."

So much for acting like the impartial bystander.

The truth was, I *wasn't* impartial. Not after everything that had happened today. Not with this weight of anguish for a woman with whom I shared brief but tight ties, bonded in the unique ways of disaster. Not with the connections to Shiraz I could no longer write off as simply sex—the conduit we'd had even in a damn hurricane...

The electricity arcing and sizzling between us, even now.

The fire I had to snuff out.

My lurch up from the table wasn't nearly as graceful as his.

166

At this point, I didn't care. Fury and urgency made me clumsy and jerky but at least lent me the fortitude to stand. "I... I think I'm a little tired," I stammered. "Thank you all for—errmm—having me, but I'm not very hungry either, and I—" *Need to get the hell out of here before I drop-kick Bettie Boop into the chocolate river myself.* "I think I need some rest."

"Of course, dear." Xaria's face was full of compassion, but her voice rang strangely hollow. On the other hand, I *was* so tired, *everything* sounded hollow.

"Miss Fava."

Except for him.

The fullness of his baritone. The sensual pull of his accent. Most of all, the command underlying it all, compelling me to stop. All but ordering me to lift my head and look back at him. Damn it, whether I wanted to or not. Because I definitely did not.

No matter how much my racing heart, sizzling blood, and tight throat said otherwise.

None of it would negate what my soul already knew—and my heart tried to forget.

I could no longer write off our connection as first-meeting chemistry or one instance rubbing out the hot-and-hornies. This wasn't just a case of insta-fangirl over a prince who rearranged the air as if that were his kingdom too.

This was one of *those* bonds. A click of utterly right, happening at the completely wrong time. The guy who met me, saw me, just *knew* me—and wanted me anyway. He was the Ron to my Hermione. The Mr. Big who knew how to smirk at my Carrie. The Navarre doomed as the wolf to my Isabeau.

Hell.

One more second down this fucking path, and I'd be

borrowing his dagger to stab myself in the tomb with him.

Sometimes, shit timing was just shit timing.

This was one of those times.

Next.

I pulled in a deep breath. Pushed out a brave smile at all of them once more. "I'm sure they'll find Crista soon. Can someone send an update to my room?"

"Of course," Evrest supplied as his little brother moved forward—setting my nerves on alert all over again.

"I will escort you back to your suite."

I glared at the elbow Shiraz offered, as if it were a tree branch on fire. Hell if it didn't already have the texture of an oak—not that I was visiting those damn memories anymore.

"I know the way," I added in a mutter, letting him see my pointed glance in Ambyr's direction. "But thank you anyway."

"*I* can escort her."

For some reason, Ardent's offer clanged even more inner alarms. Xaria's indifference about it provided weird validation for the feeling. "No," I all but snapped. "Really, Your Majesty Ardent, I *do* know the way. Merderim and bon *sonar.*"

With everyone in the room handled, especially the prince who studied every inch of movement I dared, I spun on my heel.

First goal, only goal: the sanctuary of my suite.

There was only one problem with that plan.

I really didn't know the way.

Shit.

It was on the fourth level of the guest wing, right? Or was that the fifth? And wasn't it just past the bend in the hall, after the first atrium? Had there *been* an atrium?

Double shit.

Every wrong turn and misstep took me deeper into a labyrinth starting to feel like a cosmic joke with me as the punchline. I imagined some room full of Arcadian internet geeks, training their hidden cameras on the cute American rat in their maze, laughing their asses off while downing Doritos and Triple Jolt cola.

Just when I debated making their day by pulling out my more colorful profanity, I finally plodded up to the entrance arch of my suite.

And how, exactly, did I know that fate had at last beamed down its favor? There'd been no time to tie a ribbon on the door or even memorize the damn number cascading down the entrance arch. To be honest, I might have even walked past here already...

Which meant I should've been damn grateful for the dark, dirt-encrusted demigod who leaned against the portal...

From his stance inside the room.

Who danced his sleek eyebrows as I trudged forward, unfiltered about the intent of my steady glare.

Who lifted just one side of his elegant mouth in a new, knowing look—ensuring my glower wouldn't be put away anytime soon.

"Knew your way back, hmm?"

CHAPTER FIFTEEN

I pushed past him into the room. Made my way straight to the bar, where I grabbed a bottle of water and then the whole bottle of tequila. I'd so kill for a plate of chili nachos and a Gervase triple special with a wedge of pineapple. The Patrón would have to do for now. At least it was the good stuff.

I poured myself a generous shot and downed the thing—watching with narrowed eyes as Shiraz approached on quiet steps. Let my gaze widen as he scooped up the bottle and downed as much as I just had.

"You trying to be impressive?" I quipped it as he took his second swig. Tried, and failed, to disregard the warmth of the alcohol through my muscles and the heat of *him* through my veins. He'd shucked the search-and-rescue jacket, so a lot more of his body was on display in just his black, skintight T-shirt and those alpha-guy cargo pants. Gone as well were his shit kicker boots, replaced by a pair of back slip-ons closely resembling the comfortable Vans preferred by surfers back home.

Sheez. We could almost be just chilling at Ez's place in Venice Beach, the waves of the Pacific pounding the shore beyond the balcony. He could almost just be some hottie surfer-slash-model I'd met at The Whaler and wanted to know better...

Almost.

But not really.

"Maybe," he answered me at last, adding such a graceful shrug, I went back to the hottie surfer image. "Probably." His gaze roamed everywhere but finally settled back over me.

Ohhhh, sheez.

He simply wasn't going to give me quarter from this, was he? The clutched breath. The sizzling bloodstream. The altered atmosphere that happened each time he was near. Everything so much sharper. Hotter. Needier. Pushing back to that edge between lust and craving, fantasy and reality, wanting and doing...

So painful.

So perfect.

So not happening.

There was too much to lose now, even with the bid for the wedding stricken from the picture. In a way, this risk was even more dangerous. The valley of my psyche was on the line. The cliff dive after Ryan was bone-crushing enough—and I'd had a parachute of common sense to help brace the fall. Deep inside, I'd known Ryan and I were headed for the crash, but Shiraz Noir Cimarron was a ride I wanted to take into the stars themselves...

A ride I wasn't destined to take.

As stupid as it sounded, his country needed him now more than ever. Fate owed Arcadia a fucking break, and his marriage to Ambyr would be the beacon to guide them there. With a true Arcadian bride in the mix, even the purists would be mollified, making it easier for everyone to accept Camellia and Brooke as well.

So Ambyr got to take the ride.

Which meant I was doomed to take the fall.

Best to get off the rocket now, when the plummet wouldn't

hurt so damn much.

"Why are you here, Shiraz?" I made the subtext clear. *Why are you in here, putting us both in this goddamn position, when you should be with your family and fiancée?*

Not his fiancée. Not yet.

Not a fact that should've given my bloodstream a drop of glory-glory-hallelujah—

But did.

Damn it.

He leaned both elbows on the bar. Stroked the sides of the Patrón with his damnably long fingers, clearly contemplating another douse. With a heavy huff, denied himself. "They found Crista."

His lead tone fisted the middle of my chest. "Shit." Made me struggle for air. "And she's—"

"Alive."

"*Shit.*" I clutched his forearm. Dug in tighter when nothing changed about the cloud over his composure. "That's awesome, right?"

He nodded. Sort of. "She is alive," he clarified, "for now."

"For...now?"

"The river carried her far." His face darkened. "*Very* far."

"But they found her before the falls?" I knew he got my reference to Atlavoler Falls, one of the island's most breathtaking natural sights. The waterfall, fifty feet across, had a drop three times that much down. If they'd found Crista south of the site, even "alive" might be a relative term.

Shiraz pushed out another long breath and supplied, "Yes. Before the falls. She managed to swim her way into a small ravine before the drop."

"Oh." It was as much exclamation as reaction. "Thank

fuck. So what's the problem?"

There *was* a problem. It was still stamped in harsh lines all over his face. He confirmed it by wheeling away and pacing across the room, stabbing a hand through his hair. "Samsyn does not know what kind of condition she is in. He told me she waved at them, so they know she is alive, though she seems to be wedged between some rocks. She is trapped, injured, or both." With hands still locked at the back of his head, he pivoted back. "The whole situation is—" he grunted "—fucked all to hell."

I strolled out from behind the counter, hitching a hip to the small service counter surrounding it. Examined his chiseled profile—not a bad assignment—while attempting to connect the beginning of his statement to its ending conclusion, a considerably harder one.

As a matter of fact, it was outright impossible.

"Does not compute, hard drive," I finally confessed. "It's fucked all to hell...why?"

"Because, damn it! Because—" He threw his hands akimbo, keeping them splayed as he stalked deeper into the room. "Never mind. Fuck it."

There. As his voice broke apart on a disgusted mutter, it let me see all the way into him. Shit. It was now so obvious. "Because...you want to be out there helping to rescue her."

"I *need* to be out there!" He spun back around. "I can help, damn it. I know that terrain, Lucina. I have trained parkour across every mile of it—"

"And you're the only one who has?" I managed to sift the snark from it. Making light of his frustration wasn't my intention—but nor was making light of his *life*. Samsyn hadn't told him to stay back to deny him a training session or keep him "out of the fun" of things. Maybe he just needed to hear that.

"What they're doing out there isn't going to be easy, Shiraz."

"Which is why Syn needs every pair of experienced hands he can get," he snapped. "That ravine is tight as hell. It will take an army of many to get to her, perhaps assist with lifting the boulders—"

"And maybe your brother already has that army in place." An instant confirmation that I really was a glutton for punishment, considering the glare I received in return.

"I am *not* his slobbering lap dog!" He stuck the glower in by sweeping a harsh finger. "I will not be commanded to just 'sit' and 'stay' here, when one of my people needs help! When *I* can be helping to rescue her!"

His fury slammed through the room like a brand-new hurricane. But I knew a lot more about hurricanes now.

And I knew a lot more about *him* now.

"Rescue her," I echoed, nearly under my breath. Yeah, because—*note to self, duh*—rescuing was what a prince did for his people. What a leader did for his followers. What a hero did for his team. What this man had grown up watching his brothers do, Evrest as king of the nation and Samsyn as commander of its army, and had yearned to do himself, likely countless of times before this...

And how many of those times had he been sidelined, just like this? Burning to make a difference, to be the protector he was born to be, only to be held back?

My gut confirmed it as truth—as my heart dealt with an odd mix of reaction. Why didn't his family see this? Couldn't they see he wasn't still their kid brother, pestering to be in on the adventures? He was a man, as fit and formidable as the rest of them, with a spirit hungering to give back to his kingdom. To make a difference...

But there was a flip side to the coin. While the Cimarrons weren't ruling royals in the purest sense of the word, their word carried huge sway with the Arcadian High Council. They were also important symbols to the kingdom's citizens. If even one of them was killed rescue-roping down a canyon, it'd gouge the national psyche. In this case, Samsyn was clearly that risk— and hopefully, the royal who made it back alive.

It made sense on paper.

Watching it tear this man up was another thing.

Letting it stretch *me* apart too? There was a zinger I hadn't prepared for—but what was one more on the list for this trip?—a deliberation that must've made its way to my face, for his accusing finger swept up once more.

"Do *not* start the lecture," Shiraz charged. "I can recite the talking points backward. The Cimarrons are 'vital to the country's morale and patriotism.' Our lives are not 'just about us.' We must 'look at the entire picture' with every decision we make and 'put the people first.'" He dropped his hand, clenching it at his side as he crossed the room in three wide stomps. Without stopping, he mounted the two steps leading to the bedroom area. "Creator's cock, is that *not* what I am fighting to do?"

I took a step forward. Stopped to let him watch me take calming breath. "Look, I get it—"

His bitter laugh cut me short. "You 'get it.' Is that so?"

My hands shot to my hips. "Yeah, prince of pricks, it is."

He stayed silent. Watching. Assessing. Perhaps finally acknowledging I'd meant what I said...and that I really did get it. That I saw him, felt him. That I recognized his frustration beyond just a weight on the air. It was a detonation inside me too, forming a full-on canyon in my chest, blown wider by the second, as more understanding set in.

Shiraz Cimarron didn't do anything halfway.

And he was definitely all-in on this shit.

In his heart, "reign" was the same word as "service." The birds on his chest weren't just for the cool patriotism factor. His birthright had made him a prince, but his heart had made him a leader, and neither role was ever far from his psyche— leading to the electricity everyone felt the moment he entered a room. What *I'd* felt and still did. Most people wrote off that buzz to the power of his beauty, but when one looked beneath that surface and saw the deeper truths about him...

That the resplendence on the outside was only the beginning.

That the magic of him...*was* him.

It changed things.

It made people yearn for more.

It made *me* crave more.

Much more.

So much that without thinking, I'd crossed the room. Stepped up so I was only a foot from him. Reached out, fitting my hand into his. Lifted my gaze, waiting on the verdict of his.

It was only the clasp of our hands. That was all it had to be.

At least that was what I told myself. Over and over and over and—

"Lucina."

Not a question, though implying one. Underlining it in the new focus of his eyes, the responding pressure of his hold.

"Shiraz." I pivoted enough to face him in full. Slid my fingers against the palm of his other hand. "I really do get it."

Rough inhalation. So damn sexy. "I know."

"And I just want to help."

"I know."

I lifted a heartened smile. He meant that. I felt it in the warmth of his grasp, despite the tightness still governing his face. The bruise on his cheek had darkened, making me feel maternal and primal at the same time, wanting to simultaneously soothe him and fuck him. On the other hand, yearning to fuck him wasn't new. Not by a longshot. Just the other part was new.

Though no less dangerous.

Which had probably made this move a very dumbass choice.

I let my gaze dash to the side. *Not* an easy task. "Sometimes, all you need is a friend to listen." *Leave it there. Leave. It. There.* "But if this *isn't* helping..."

Dumb. Ass. Dumb. Ass.

He let my hands fall. "It is not."

Stupid embarrassment as his definite tone sank in.

But then shocked wonderment—as he filled his grip with my ass instead.

Racing arousal, as he yanked me in, molded me close, and kissed a whole layer of skin off my lips. Sucked every molecule of air out of my lungs. Stole every logical thought straight from my mind. Steamed every sensual, dewy drop in my pussy.

Finally, dragged his head up enough to look at me—though his eyes, full of blue lava lust, stayed riveted on my parted, panting lips.

"*This* is helping."

CHAPTER SIXTEEN

Three seconds.

It was all he gave me before bending his head deeper and then taking my lips again.

Three seconds...to decide.

For both of us.

Restraint, brakes, and an easy but aching coast toward goodbye—or full speed, turbo jets, and a hell of a fireball before the ending credits of this thing?

Fireballs always made the credits so pretty.

At least it was what I told myself as I let him crash all the way down on me. A conviction I let consume me, exactly as his taste and scent and heat did. A thought that even brought weird comfort, as he hitched my thighs around his waist and then turned, carrying me toward the bed.

He needed this.

I was helping him.

Diverting his rage toward something that wouldn't get him killed—though it was sure as hell going to feel like self-impalement to walk away from him now.

But the skewering would be worth it. The pain, so damn sweet.

Who the fuck was I kidding? I wasn't made for sweet. And this time, the pain was going to suck ass—a punishment I'd take like a big girl, once the time came.

Now was not that time.

Right now, slammed to my back and then crushed beneath his body, it was only time to welcome the good pain. The best kind.

The grind of his teeth against mine as he plunged his mouth back down. The bite of his cargo pants zipper as he made room for himself between my thighs, parting them with his own. The rough slide of his hands up my thighs and then my waist, pushing up my shirt, palming my bare skin with his passion-driven hands.

Then impaling me all by himself...with the force of his stare. Cobalt layered with flint, daggering me, driving every beat of my heart before slicing straight to my throbbing core. Harsh, hot, ruthless. Gleaming with all the angry edges of his own pain. The control he needed to feel. The power he needed to give. The passion he needed to share.

The escape he needed to take.

I got it.

I saw it.

I showed him so.

I reached up, skating both hands along his jaw and then up higher, until I'd twined the dark luxury of his hair around my fingers. Twisted in more as I wrapped my legs tighter around him, a husky hiss escaping as his bulge slotted against my crotch. He made a sound too, a mix of breath and sound I couldn't exactly define but was all the more turned on for. So many things about this man kept surprising me...I gasped again, amazed by the magnitude of it all. While I saw so much about the landscape of who he was, the nuances of that world still delighted me at every new step.

And every shared breath...

And every twine of heartbeats...

And every degree of lust...

God, *yes*. Especially that.

"Lucina..."

"Hmmm?" It sounded as dreamy as I felt. Despite how every pore of my skin felt opened and electrified at once—maybe because of that—my mind already spun, blissful and wild, somewhere between truth and fantasy. His new kiss intensified the sensation. God, how good he felt. His lips molded mine, commanding every degree of my desire. His tongue, wet and fierce, drowned me in more perfect, shivering, shaking need.

"Creator's mercy, you are beautiful."

I sighed once more, lips parting as he trailed his mouth along my jawline, down my neck. New tremors. Hotter blood. Delicious desire. And shit, we were still completely dressed.

I let a hand trail to his nape. Turned my head enough to watch my fingers play at the ends of his hair, still damp against his neck. "You've gotta stop stealing my lines, mister."

He snorted. "That would be like *me* telling *you* not to be so much trouble."

I scowled. And meant it. "Trouble? What the hell?"

"Leaving the shelter with Crista, in the middle of the storm—" His jaw tensed. I felt it back to the muscles beneath my fingers. "It was foolhardy, Lucy."

"Foolhardy?" A laugh spurted before I could control it. "Ohhhh, my. Of course." Then a nod, full of pseudo sobriety. "Foolhardy."

"Do you prefer *completely stupid*?" In contrast, he wasn't pseudo anything. Well, damn. Then *damn*, as he angled up long enough to grab my hand and slam it back down to the bed, next to my head. "Perhaps a *shit-for-brains-move*?" he spat. "How about just *dipstick dumb*?"

"All right," I snapped. "I got it, I got it." But when I jerked against his hold, his grip was as tight as double padlocks. Instantly, my system reacted by declaring war on itself. While my sex pulsed and clenched, at once recognizing its kinky temptation, my brain fantasized about getting free and smacking him. "It wasn't like I had a choice—"

"You *had* a choice, Lucina."

"I had *no* choice!"

"So Crista and Jayd pointed a gun and ordered you to help out?"

"That's not fair."

"Just like what you did was without a fucking brain cell."

Walloping him seemed a better option by the second. "So *you* would've stayed behind? Let them go out on their own?"

"Not a relevant question."

"Excuse the hell out of me?"

"Jayd is my sister, and Crista might as well be. I have known her for seven years and employed her for the last three. I attended Forryst and Fawna's *vaftême*. Their christening," he responded to my furrowed brow before matching the look. "Those twins are like extended family to me."

"But they aren't to me." I flung it as accusation and wasn't one bit sorry. "And *that's* your reasoning why I should've sat there on my ass and watched Crista *fight her own fight*?"

His jawline turned to steel. "You are twisting my intention."

"Seriously?" Bitter shrug. "Seems crystal clear to me."

"Lucina..." It edged on a growl. Undoubtedly, he felt the answering quivers of my pussy. I couldn't control those, but I *could* keep up the pissed glare. Easily.

"Just calling this show like I see it, *Your Highness*."

He arched a brow. "And how is that?"

"That you're actually upset that I helped Crista out." Hearing it out loud only honed my anger about it. "That even though I've known her only seven hours instead of seven years, you're pissed that I actually gave a damn. That I actually—"

His hard kiss cut me off. But did the dickwad think it would make me all melty-silent? I grunted hard and then groaned harder, clarifying what he could do with that presumption. The bastard turned the moment into full advantage, sweeping his tongue in past my parted lips and then stabbing it against mine. Ravaging me without apology or mercy or leniency.

By the time he was done, I *was* melted.

Actually wondered if I'd have to re-learn how to speak again.

"I am not 'upset,' tupulai." He rolled his hips, mashing his throbbing bulge against all the most sensitive parts of me. "Your heart...its unspeakable generosity..." Another thrust, more adamant than before. "It makes me hard in ways you cannot fathom."

"Oh." Okay, at least I managed *that*. Maybe there was hope for the rest of my vocabulary. "Well. I actually think I *can* fathom—ahhh!"

My yelp cracked the air as he rammed me even more roughly. The treatment was almost punishment, confirmed by the new lightning in his eyes—and the unflinching command in his tone.

"But you also do not fathom how seriously, permanently you could have been hurt." He dug that in with quiet brutality, watching without a blink as I winced, mentally gored by the tangibility of *his* pain. "You could have died, Lucina," he gritted. "Things could have gone very differently this afternoon. Even up on that rise, you were not safe. A few more inches of rain, and that river might have swept you away too—and I would not have been there for you. Nobody would have been. And then—"

Abruptly, he released me. Shoved up and then completely off the bed. Spun away like a man possessed, hands knotting at his sides. "*Damn it.*"

For a long moment, I was motionless. Just lay there, pushed up on my elbows, chest heaving, weathering the force of his fury on the air—a little stunned by it.

Maybe a little more than a little.

Sheez.

Was this the reason why he was still taut as a grenade with half the pin out?

Because of...me?

He had to knock that shit off. Right now.

"Shiraz." I rose too. "Hey. That didn't happen, did it?" I stepped around so we faced each other once more. "Look. I'm right here, and everything's f—"

I gulped as soon as he looked up again. Damn. Blue Fire wasn't just the name of my favorite cocktail at the Santa Monica pier dive bar anymore. The blaze in his eyes...

"Everything is *not* fine, Lucina."

As my hands lifted to my hips, my brows jumped for my hairline. "Why?" I fired. "Because *you* say so, lord and master?"

Just as rapidly, his demeanor changed again. Drastically. Seriously, I almost wondered who'd punched the special-effects button on his side of the room—the button marked *Boost the intense-and-interested stare.*

And the newly braced stance.

And the quietly commanding mouth lift. Just at the corners. Just enough to make me think of the thoughts behind the move...

Shit. Did he *practice* that? It was too damned unnerving to just be natural...

"Hmm. That has a nice ring to it."

On the other hand, rehearsed or not, I'd take it—with a side of that new, silky dessert thing in his voice too. Cream and butter and even whipped chocolate had nothing on that tone. It slid over my whole body, warm and smooth and invasive, making me think of dessert kind of things...like licking. And sucking. And savoring...

I gave my head a fast shake. No. I was still irked with him for the caveman melodrama, for which he wasn't getting off the hook that damn easily.

I screwed my hands tighter on my hips. "Everything's not fine *why*?"

The blue fire ceded to the Bowie knife gray again. He dipped his head in, just enough to lend menace to his look, before he stated, "Because I am concerned about what will happen if you do it again."

Double-take. Could I be blamed? "Do it...*again*?" I reined in a full giggle by biting my lip. "You mean break out of a storm shelter to help a friend find her six-year-old siblings? Because unless you have another medicane waiting on the horizon, mister, I think we're squared up."

I had another small laugh teed up, ready to finish in style, but he sneaked a finger beneath my chin, yanking it up. Worse, he shifted even closer, filling my gaze with nothing but him as he responded.

"I *mean* what will happen if you defy my wishes again."

"Defy your—" I ran the risk of seeming a stuttering idiot, but at the risk of redundancy, *blame me, anyone*? I banked on the sentiment to carry me through the next open-jawed moment and the next.

Even as he leveled me with his next shocker.

By angling his hand up and then sliding his thumb into my mouth.

Holy.

Shit.

Right in, scraping the pad over my bottom teeth, before pressing his flesh on the flat of my tongue.

What...the...

A thought my traitorous body didn't let me finish. My bloodstream burst into so many flames of response, I instantly gave up on putting *any* out.

Gave up. Then gave in.

Closed my lips over his warm, firm flesh and rolled my tongue around it. Tried not to think of how my sex vibrated from every note of his answering growl.

Tried. Failed.

Especially when thinking this lord and master thing *was* going to happen.

Hoped. Prayed.

Yeah, despite how he still pissed me off. Maybe, like the good little deviant I was, because of it. All at once, recasting him in my head as the dominant, distant ruler and me as the loving, serving slave girl...

Oh, dear God.

The temperature in my blood now.

The hunger in my nerves.

The need in my sex...

"Do you think about my wishes, Lucina?" His voice was rust on steel. His thumb was incessant pressure. He lifted his other hand, bracing fingers around the back of my jaw. Used the hold to pull me forward and then back again, forward and then back, working my mouth back and forth on his finger. "Are my wishes important to you? My...needs?"

Well...hell.

He didn't snap free the padlock. He took a sledgehammer to the thing, shattering it. Immediately my mind surged into the breech—to a space I showed to nearly nobody, because nearly nobody understood it. But this man, this prince with the face of a god and the soul of a hero and now, it seemed, with the dominant hunger of a lion, had shined his incredible light on that special space. Yanked me into the stuff of my most incredible fantasies...

But did I obey? Did I dare?

We'd only ever have the next few hours. Once the Sancti airport was back online, I'd be on a plane and this would all be an aching, magical memory. But wasn't everything about this man going to be that anyway? Wasn't I going to be *that woman* from every star-crossed love story ever put on film—except *Romeo and Juliet,* which didn't really count—face reflected in a rain-drenched plane window, watching clouds superimposed with memories of his face? This was reckless and mindless and headed for such an obvious disaster of a conclusion, we were fools to ignore the clichés.

Except that we couldn't ignore all the stuff that *wasn't* a cliché.

This.

Us.

The connection that meshed us. The spell that bound us. The sight into each other, framing us. Remolding us. Redefining what we would be to each other even now.

We could be a different kind of movie.

Flutes and guitars, blended by synthesizers, began playing in my head. The soundtrack of a mini movie. Duran Duran's "Save A Prayer."

Some people call it a one-night stand, but we can call it paradise.

Paradise.

Yes.

"Yes." I had to set his finger free to voice it aloud, but if I read the look on his face right, that thumb was just the prelude of what he wanted in my mouth. "Yes, Your Highness. Your wishes *are* important to me."

Somebody punched that special-effects button again—only this time, his fierce focus was layered with absolute command. His gaze, sharp as blue lasers, sliced into me. His hand, still wrapped against the back curve of my jaw, squeezed in just a little tighter. Compelled me forward, my body liquid and obedient, until our mouths nearly touched.

I gasped up at him. Breathed every harsh, heavy, consuming breath as an offering to him...an open entreaty to him. *God, yes. Kiss me...please...*

The corners of his lips curled again.

Holy *shit*, that look again.

"'Master' will be fine for now, tupulai."

Not a kiss.

Even better.

"Yes, Master," I whispered, letting the magic settle in thicker. "Whatever you wish."

I leaned a little closer, craving his harder grip, but he slipped his hand free, gliding it out to my shoulder. He cupped a hand around my other shoulder before saying anything again.

"What I wish...is to be inside you, Lucina." His touch turned heavy, pushing me down. "Beginning with how you'll take me from your knees."

Oh...

damn...

yes.

The ecstasy wrapped around me as sensual need engulfed me. The need to do exactly this for him. To be completely claimed by him, controlled by him, guided by him—points emphasized as he caught handfuls of my shirt during my descent. With efficient tugs, he removed it completely from me. One more twist, and he'd opened the clasp of my bra, setting my bare breasts free.

My tingling, aching, completely erect breasts.

"Fuck." He nudged one with one of his calves, making my nipple stand up even harder. Did the same with his other leg, resulting in my pensive moan. Before I could help it, my hips bucked, a desperate attempt to give my clenching core a little relief.

The temptation was ripped away when Shiraz cupped my chin, forcing my head back up. In his dilated pupils, I beheld my own reflection. Kiss-swollen lips. Nipples at full attention, centered in puckered, dusky areolas. Eyes glassy with unthinking lust.

But there were just seconds to process all of that before the curious tilt of his head claimed my attention.

"Fuckkkk." He drew it out this time. "You really *do* want this."

I dared the smallest of nods. "Yes, Master. I do."

He snarled. Just for a moment. Shifted his hold from my chin, sliding that hand into a possessive clench across the back of my head. "Then you shall have what you crave. Serve me, tupulai—with your mouth."

I smiled. Just a little. "It will be my pleasure, Master."

And God, how it was.

No. It was better than pleasure. It was heaven.

Unbuckling his pants.

Unzipping his fly.

Dipping my head in to breathe his musk...and then savoring my first taste of his hard flesh. A low rumble emanated from him as I licked the base of his shaft, wanting to remember this feeling. The way I made him swell. The way I made him sound. The wonderful, primal things that were all male about him...calling to everything that was female in me.

"Damn it," he finally husked. "*Enough.*" With his free hand, pushed down the fabric still trapping his cock, springing more of the shaft free. His erection was more beautiful than I'd imagined—and I *had* imagined—with a nest of dark hair supporting a penis the color of polished copper. Veins stood out against his skin, pulsing burgundy with his blood, his life. The crown was a shade darker, throbbing with arousal and topped with a milky drop I couldn't wait to get my mouth on.

A good thing, considering what he did next.

Slid his hand forward until he could squeeze the juncture of my jaw. Used that same grip to force my mouth to his glistening tip. "Suck it off. Then take the rest of me."

He tasted perfect.

I'd no more savored the salty precome than he fed me the rest of his length. I nearly couldn't take him all on the first thrust, being rusty at best on this since Ryan had some hang-up that only sluts really liked blowing their men, but the memory of this joy returned quickly.

Thank God.

Wasn't the only thing I was grateful for.

As a matter of fact, I started to wonder if blood cells could function on nothing but bliss, since the certainty hit that every inch of me flowed with the stuff. To be wrapped around him like this, so connected to his center of him like this...nurturing the part of him coursing with life itself...I'd never been happier. Felt more powerful. Felt more needed by, or worthy of, a man.

And there it was. The nucleus of everything. The deepest, darkest reason I needed this as well.

Because if I'd known how to make Ryan need me more, he wouldn't have said goodbye.

If I'd known how to be more worthy, God wouldn't have taken Dad from us.

Things would be different. *I'd* be different. Not such a deviant, strange, stupid mess. Wouldn't want things like pain to take me away...

from the bigger pain.

It only took seconds for all of it to collide inside, hitting like a cosmic jolt—and driving the tears to my eyes. I hated them as soon as they came, longing to reach up and make them disappear, but dissolving into a weepy mess simply wasn't an option right now. Not with Shiraz's flesh filling me, commanding me. Not with his growls vibrating through me, his lust empowering me...

And his thumbs, wiping at my cheeks?

Huh?

I looked up. Was pierced all over again by his face, awash in a new expression. His eyes, so intense. His nose, flared with lust. His lips, curled with—what? I couldn't discern the emotion behind the subtle smile, only to know what feelings it spiked higher in me. The need to please him more. To take him even deeper.

"Damn, tupulai," he hissed. "Yes. Deeper. Take me. Open to me. Give it all to me."

I had no choice but to obey. To offer him every inch of my mouth and every corner of my heart. It should have terrified me. I should be wondering and worrying about how much this was going to hurt later, when I couldn't have this anymore— but there was no room for that. No space for anything but the vortex of energy with this incredible man. The unbroken connection to this perfect prince.

Ended all too soon as he pulled back from me with a gritted curse in Arcadian.

"Wh-What is it?" I finally stammered. "What's wrong?"

"Wrong?" He actually laughed while dropping to his knees next to me. "Creator's mercy, Lucina. Not a fucking thing." He pulled on both sides of my face, holding me still for a hard kiss. "You have me ready to burst. But I—"

He cut himself off with another gruff sound. I ran a hand atop one of his. "But you...what?"

He dipped that hand to the side of my neck. Locked my gaze with his. "I do not want to come in your mouth." Swallowed hard. "I... I want to—"

"You want to come inside me...somewhere else?"

I smiled a little wider at the confirming look of lust—and terror—on his face. I'd never forget that expression, with his gleaming eyes and gritted teeth, for as long as I lived. Holy shit. The Mediterranean prince with the made-for-sin body really was a virgin. *Nasty and Naughty or Virgin in Hiding?*

What about both?

I didn't need four strawberry margaritas to figure out that

answer.

"I want that too...Master."

He gulped again. A huge breath left him. "You do?"

Now *I* was tempted to laugh. Holy hell, if he only knew how much...

Maybe showing him was simply a better idea.

With our gazes still entwined, I wrapped a hand around one of his wrists. Pulled until he ceded, making sure his fingers brushed the sharp point of my nipple, before pushing his hand beneath my leggings...and then between my legs.

From there, the man really knew what to do.

Dear...fuck.

I let it spill out loud as his long, perfect fingers dipped between my soaked folds, exploring and spreading, sliding and enticing, finally lunging...and finding. I cried out then, ignited by the ecstasy of his touch along my intimate sheath—instantly craving more. *More...*

"Shiraz!"

He reacted by plunging even deeper. His moan mixed with my own. "Wet," he uttered, amazement lacing his growl. "Tight. And so perfect..."

"Because of you," I whispered. "*For* you."

He lowered his other hand, using it to push my leggings to my knees. His movements were jerky and fevered, only adding to my heat. I needed him with the same hot urgency, though he seemed to need the knowledge for himself, testing deeper parts of me with harsher thrusts of his finger.

"For me to claim?" he finally demanded.

"Yes." What his words did to me. How his lust consumed me.

"With my cock?"

"God, yes!"

For a virgin, he was fucking good at this—especially at the whole edging thing, damn him. Three seconds more of that dirty verbal foreplay, along with the thorough finger fucking, and I would have been tumbling into one of the best climaxes of my existence—but the bastard withdrew, rising on his haunches, though keeping me riveted to him with a stare belonging more on a medieval gladiator.

Or a master about to shackle his slave.

"Then take these off." He yanked at one ankle of my leggings. Let it snap back before stripping his shirt in one sweep and nearly making me swallow my tongue. Baby Jesus in a play mobile, the man was really like something out of a movie. Thor, Wolverine, and all 1800 abdominal ridges of *The 300* weren't enough comparison for his defined, muscled glory, especially with a torso punctuated by that long, perfect cock—

And given to a man who knew exactly how I liked my foreplay.

Erotic. Explicit.

"Lucina?" He stressed the bark with both raised brows. "The leggings?"

"Right," I managed. "Sorry, I—"

"No explanations." The sleek surety was back in every note of his voice, every inch of his actions. "Just actions. I want you nude and spread, Lucina. Now."

Thank God I only had two inches of the leggings left by that point. By the time I'd recovered enough to murmur a fast, "Yes, Master," all I had to do was lie down, shivering a little from the travertine tile against my bare back, and part my legs for him.

Opening myself to him...

Freeing myself for him...

Burning for the exact stare he raked over my nudity as he stretched one hand over the length of his own.

"Holy fuck," he rasped, and I nearly echoed the words. Had he just manifested a condom from thin air? A glance to the open nightstand drawer answered my silent question— how a tiny island palais stocked shit like *that* in guest rooms was beyond my understanding—and chose to simply be grateful for it. I'd started birth-control pills for the first time in my life when Ryan asked me to but tossed them in rebellion when things went sideways. On a kinkier note, it was a definite panty-soaker to watch a demigod squeeze his balls, to withhold coming just from the sight of one's spread crotch—*if* there were any panties on hand to drench.

Snark wasn't going to get me out of *that* larger point.

That all my juices had nowhere to go but out—fully exposed to his searing gaze. That with tears still tracking my face, I had nowhere to hide from this man—nothing to do but accept him into my arms as he shifted, angling himself over me...

Then surging into me.

Groaning as I gasped.

Shuddering as I sighed.

Plunging his tongue down my throat as he drove his body deep inside mine. Moaning again, harder and longer, as he held himself there, locking his hips to still us both as he grew, pushing at my walls, filling all my corners.

Joining himself to me...as no man ever had.

And yeah, I was going to get Biblical again. But never had *flesh of my flesh* had more effortless, flawless meaning— or been more significant in the depths of my heart and soul.

Denying it wasn't an option. Trivializing *him* was no longer an option. I realized it as soon as he pulled up enough to gaze at me, now moving with slow, steady purpose inside me. With hands cupped at my temples, brushing back the hair from my face, his gaze swept over me, alive and alight, looking as if he'd just been given the secret of the damn cosmos.

Before I could gulp it back, a new burn attacked the backs of my eyes. I dug fingers into his back, hanging on as the emotion washed over me. Even more seeped out with every new lunge of his cock, and I no longer cared. I wanted him to see—to understand that this meant as much to me as him.

And he did see.

And he did get it.

Beyond how I even hoped he would.

An understanding he not only grasped but acted on— when his hands delved back, tangling in my hair and then pulling the strands taut. Hard. Until I shrieked from it—right before clenching my sex tighter around him for it.

Yes.

Please.

Yes.

He yanked more ruthlessly. Another scream escaped as my head jacked backward. He dug his teeth into the column of my neck. I clawed my nails into the column of his spine.

"Hot...sweet...woman," he husked against my ear.

I could only whisper two words in return. "My Master."

He bit into the shell beneath my three pierced studs. "I want to rip you apart."

Ragged sigh. Grabbing his ass. Forcing him deeper. "Do it."

His cock expanded. His hips strained. "Going to...fuck

you..."

"Yes."

"Deep..."

"Yes!"

"Hard."

"Yes, yessssss..."

I was lost.

To his brutal thrusts. To my answering screams. To the gasps replacing them when he shifted his hold to my waist, in order to ram my body harder down on his stalk. My torso lifted, my hair rasping along the floor, as he pounded me like a machine on high gear, a beast beyond control—a prince fucking his concubine.

For those few perfect minutes, it was all I had to be.

His body for the using. His pussy for the conquering. His woman for the possessing. Filled with all the pain—and pleasure—he had to give.

I surrendered to the fantasy, riding the erotic, frenetic wave through every heated lunge of his cock and every filthy Arcadian word he growled, until he shocked me in another sweep of sudden movement. I was on my back again, my legs lifted and wrapped around his waist, as Shiraz loomed directly over me once more. One of his hands smacked down to the floor next to my head. The other he clamped around my jaw again—the front part now, holding my head rigidly in place.

"Show it to me," he ordered, his teeth barely parting for the words. "You will come, tupulai—and you will show it to me!"

A breath. A shiver. A moment's worth of wondering how he knew that was all I needed, before abandoning even that—

To give him exactly what he commanded.

To let my body give in and my senses implode.

To let the fire of sweet, hot oblivion sweep in, devouring me. And just letting it, no longer holding back the deep, perfect pulses that torched everything between my legs—before gripping him, milking him, enflaming him—

To give me the same.

His hand slipped away as his entire body clutched, coiled in masculine magnificence, ripping his climax through every striation of his muscles and finally into his harsh bellow.

"By the...fucking...Creator!"

His orgasm was so full and hot, I wondered if the condom would hold. I had to pray the Arcadians bought their sexual supplies like their patio furniture, by going for the best. The wish intensified as, unbelievably, Shiraz's orgasm did. With another groan, he powered into a second release, his body shaking from the effort. Silent with amazement, I clutched him close, letting the passion work its way completely through him, before slackening my grip.

"No."

His quiet dictate made me jolt a little.

"Do not let go," he clarified, burrowing his face to the crook of my neck. "Not yet."

More astonishment—though it was the best kind, as I circled my arms around him once more. Treasured the feel of him against me, his warmth still permeating me. Listened intently as our heartbeats evened out together.

So soon, *too* soon, the respite was over. He slipped out of me, resting on his heels while peeling the latex from his cock. I scooted up too, shoulders hunching as my brain hurried to throw a force field over my heart.

Why did it feel like trying to put on a dress three sizes too small?

Get over it.

I knew this drill, damn it. Forward, backward, and from half a dozen different other angles. After the jollies got had, the feels got ditched. Granted, I'd gotten a little bonus time due to the honor of being the royal cherry popper, but no way in hell did I think—or could I think—that earned me extra court time from a man about to sign another woman in the fiancée first draft.

It was time to take my ball and go home.

On my own terms.

With at least a little of my dignity intact.

The man would allow me at least that much, especially since I'd turned into a weepy mess on him. No guy alive wanted *more* time with a woman who'd gone sappy on him, especially during the hot-and-naked part of the night's fun. And maybe that had happened for the best too. Gave us both an excuse to declare our hornies officially satisfied for each other and now move the hell on.

There was only one flaw to that thinking.

A pretty huge one.

I was even more horny for Shiraz Cimarron now than I had been an hour ago.

And...*shit.*

It looked like he couldn't be more a fan of that thinking, as he returned from tossing the condom, his half-hard erection already leading the way. This time, though, he headed straight for the bed—but turned when he got there, looking expectantly back at me.

"You want to come over here on your own, or shall I order you to it, sweetheart?"

CHAPTER SEVENTEEN

As enticed as I was to see if he'd really do it—and what fun activities he'd add to the decree—I decided not to tempt fate in that moment. God only knew when I'd need to call in on that favor later, especially with the way he waited for me beneath the covers, head leaning on the tripod of his raised hand and bent elbow.

Donning the demure—since he likely wasn't going to let me wear much else—I slid in, settled my head against the pillows, and dutifully closed my eyes.

Who the hell was I kidding? Duty had nothing to do it. Nerves had everything to do with it. We'd "been together" twice now, with tiffs as the ice breaker. I racked my brain for a reason to start another. Locking horns with him meant I could focus on...well, his *horns*...and not other things.

Like...nearly everything.

His carved shoulders. His elegant fingers. His intense energy. Everything about him that was much too close now. Much too naked now. Much too ready for me now. Yeah, I'd stolen a tiny glance as I'd gotten in—at the arousal that wasn't "tiny" at all. What was I supposed to do with that, other than the obvious? Come *on*. Wouldn't any other female think the same thing?

Thoughts receiving *no* help at containment, as the rogue let out a savoring growl—while grabbing me by the waist and rolling me nearly atop him. I pushed back, only to be ordered back into place with a sharp smack on my left ass cheek.

"Ow!" But damn it if the protest didn't spill out more as a moan—an encouraging one at that.

As my cheeks blazed, Shiraz chuckled. "My little piece of trouble. You shall stay right where you are, hmm?"

Snort. "If I'm the little piece of trouble, you're the big piece of— *Ow!*"

At least my bottom would be a nice matched set of pink. His slow smile indicated the same conclusion.

"You are most welcome," he murmured.

"I didn't say—"

"Your eyes did." He'd continued to cup my right cheek. Gave it a firm squeeze while finishing, "But you can say it with your lips as well. Use Arcadian, if you please. *Merderim, my Master* rolls out beautifully, yes?"

I rolled my eyes. Because no way did he get to see the hundred ways that turned me to fresh goo. "Oh, my God."

"Do you not mean, 'Oh my Master'?"

"Oh, my *God.*" I openly laughed. Loud and hard. Not only did the release feel damn good, but it was reassuring to watch his lips quirk, joining in a little, proving he didn't take himself *that* seriously—which, of course, melted me for him more.

Made me want to give him a sweet surprise in return...

So I put melty into action. Softened in his arms, letting my body contour along his. My breasts cushioned along his ribs. My thigh slid into his crotch. The answering jerk of his cock ensured the melty made its way to my voice as well.

"Merderim, my Master."

His rumble was like smoke, curling through us both. "Fuck." His free hand, raising to my hair, was like the matching blaze. "My little tupulai."

Then his kiss...

Forest fire.

Wild, rampant, invading, pervading. Such a sudden, furious flare, it stole every breath I had, every rational thought of survival...and I didn't care. Not one damn bit.

Trouble.

Until now, it had been a cute joke.

Only now, my heart wasn't.

I was officially in it with this man. Deep and hot and intense, like the scary lightning hell realm from *Raiders of the Lost Ark*, only I was on the wrong side this time. I was one of the cocky scientists who'd thought I could play with fate and get away with it.

Fine. If I was a bad guy, then might as well commit myself to the cause.

Bad could be fun.

And addicting.

And wonderful.

They were the last thoughts I let myself acknowledge before opening for his ravaging tongue. Moaning encouragement for his hurting grip. Plunging full-on into the fire of his assault. Long minutes later, when we finally had to drag apart for air, I clung to numb lust, letting my gaze fill with his dark, sculpted beauty.

Shiraz lifted a lopsided smile, teeth gleaming against his bronze skin. He drifted his hand from my hair to my shoulder and left it there, tracing circles on my skin with enough force to communicate a silent message. I was to stay put. Not that he'd get any protest now.

"Ssshh, tupulai." He snickered when I shot back a Scooby Doo-like *hhnnnh*. "I can hear you thinking," he clarified.

"News to me." Snort. "I was doing my best *not* to think."

"Probably why I heard you."

I matched his lazy strokes on my arm by exploring the amazing contours of his chest. Damn. Even the dip in his sternum was sexy as fuck. I loved exploring the oval disks of his nipples too—but most fascinating of all were the intricate lines of his tattoos.

"These are incredible," I finally murmured.

He released a soft hum. "I am glad they are pleasurable to you."

I indulged a secret smile. *Pleasurable* was probably an understatement, but his formal phrasing made me feel as treasured as a true princess.

"Did you have them done here, on Arcadia?"

"No," he answered. "In Helsinki. During my university years."

When Ambyr went to visit him a lot...

Not a subject I wanted to go diving into right now. The woman was going to have the rest of her life with him. I had this tiny bubble, and I was going to hog it with questions *I* wanted answered.

"Did you attend college in Europe because Evrest did?"

He tossed down a what-the-hell glance. "Point for your end of the mat. I did not guess you were thinking *that*."

I flattened a hand over his inked eagle and rested my chin atop that. "Just trying to figure out why you don't feel like you measure up—to him *or* Samsyn."

He hitched up on one elbow. "What the hell gave you that impression?"

I popped my stare wider. "Ummm...the full fuse you blew when we first got here? Something about not being Samsyn's 'lap dog'? I paged Dr. Freud from there and figured Evrest was wrapped up in that baggage too."

A pulse ticked in his jaw. "They are my big brothers, Lucina. Family, baggage...they go together, you see?"

"No." I ducked my head when his stare turned probing. *Note to self. Don't go getting curious about hot princey's cushy upbringing again.* "I mean...sorry...no, I *don't* see." I picked at imaginary lint on the sheet. "I was an only child. It was basically just my mom and me."

"Why?" He huffed and dragged a hand through his hair. "I apologize. Please do not answer if you do not want—"

"My dad was killed when I was twelve."

I had no damn idea why I blurted it—except that it felt important for him to know. Why the hell *that* was, I had no idea. Even with Ezra, it had taken me a good three or four months to come clean about Dad. "He was a cop." I went ahead and let that little jewel pop out too. "He was...a hero."

Shiraz reached up. Brushed strands of hair off my face. "Of course he was."

I looked up as his fingers sifted back across my scalp. For a second, my breath caught at what I saw in the depths of his gaze. He'd meant it. Every syllable. I knew it inside an instant—and gave him the most honest answer of my heart in response. "Thank you."

He closed his eyes briefly, a regal version of a nod. His fingers kept twirling in my hair, slowly caressing down to the ends. His gaze, open again, serenely followed each new descent.

"My brothers are my heroes."

"Aha."

As I teased it, he fell to his back once more, hands raised.

"Guilty as charged."

I wiggled my shoulders in a saucy preen. "Okay, hot shot. What am I thinking *now*?"

His half grin became a quiet smirk. "Oh, it is easy this time."

"That so?"

"Hmmm. Yes."

The thick heat in his gaze recaptured my attention—in my mind *and* my pussy. "Oh, great mind reader Shiraz, please impart me with your wisdom, then."

He rolled to his side and then pulled me down to mine. When we fully faced each other. his stare turned to azure smoke. "That you...liked having to obey my orders tonight."

A smile grew across my lips. "Well. You may be a mind reader after all."

"That is not all of it."

I pressed closer to him. "Interested. Go on."

His stare turned even darker. "You are definitely hoping more reward is coming for it."

He emphasized "reward" with a buck of his hips that, tried by any other guy, might have been dorky. But with the way *this* man could roll *those* hips with *that* erection, my scoffing laugh became an aroused sigh. Damn. His cock was like a baton against my thigh. I'd taken baton once. I was damn good at it.

I rubbed light fingers at the base of his...stick. "Mr. Cimarron?"

He grunted. Let out a shaky breath. But growled with force, "Yes, Miss Fava?"

"You're one cocky sonofabitch."

"So I have been...informed." He husked out the last of it as I fondled the two globes in his sack.

"I bet you'll be insufferable now, having given your goods for a girl and all."

He unleashed a growl—a whole snarl, actually—while rearing up and over, flattening me to my back. My responding squeal was stolen by his hard punch of a kiss. "My goods, hmmm? I suppose that will do." He did that lush hip roll again, giving my other thigh a workout with his impressive length. There was a slick of moisture this time, making my stare go wide. He really *was* ready to go again.

Maybe I'd been mistaken, and this wasn't lightning strike hell.

It was heaven, with a lover missing nothing except angel's wings.

Point proven the very next moment, with the new light in his gaze and the measured concentration in his strokes to my hair. To be honest, the intensity almost scared me. This wasn't I'm-going-to-fuck-you-raw focus. This was I-want-to-see-*into*-you attention.

"What?" I valiantly went for levity anyway. "You don't like 'the goods'? But they *are* good, gorgeous." Bitten lip. Cutie-flirty smile. "Very, *very* good."

No change in his face. But no change to his cock, either, which kept stirring fond baton lesson memories. A good sign that maybe he *could* be distracted...

"There is not a single man back in LA who wants to do this with you regularly?"

Okay. Scratch the "good sign." But was it a *bad* sign? That he was clearly, genuinely puzzled by why I didn't have a steady someone back home? That he wanted to know more about the intricacies of my life?

Except that was what they were. Intricacies. Cracks. The

telltale signs of why I wasn't "Miss Right" for anyone. Why I should just stay in his lane of "Miss Right *Now*," period.

"*Unnnhhh.*" I flopped both arms to the pillow, crisscrossing wrists over my head. "That's a really complicated question."

Translation: back off now and save us both the trouble.

But if I'd learned anything about the man in the last two days, it was how he and "back off" weren't on speaking terms. Like, ever.

His hand scooted down from my hair. Settled against the side of my face just like he rearranged his body at my side, with firm determination. Caressed my temple, just beyond the corner of my eye, with knowing swirls of his thumb.

"I manage operations and finances for an entire kingdom, tupulai. I think I can handle 'complicated.'"

I opened my eyes. Grabbed his hand, that magical thumb included, and pushed it away. "And what if I just don't want to be 'handled'?"

He stilled. I mean, to the point of it getting weird. My heart pounded the crap out of my ribs. A roaring panther was a reason for anxiety, but a silent panther was a reason for terror.

"What was his name?"

Pounce. *Fuck.*

"His name, Lucina." His tone was quiet but sharp. Not pissed-off, but definitely not okay with my be-still-and-hope-the-panther-walks-by thing.

"His name who?"

"The one who made you afraid of what you are." Pounce number two, this time the real kind. Inside two seconds, he had both my wrists locked beneath his hand. "Of what you need."

I huffed. Shook my head. Like I said about him and backing off...

"I'm not afraid of anything, okay? Wait. Maybe bad sitcom reboots and certain kinds of sushi, but—"

My breath caught—and my pussy trembled—as his hold screwed tighter and his face loomed closer. "You *are* afraid," he uttered. "It scares you, how much you like this. Of how your senses want to take off again, even as I do just this to you. But you hold back. You stop yourself, Lucy. Why?"

How the hell was he getting all that just by looking at me? Then again, *I* wasn't the one looking at me, with the thrumming pulse in my throat, the shallow cadence of my breath, and pupils likely dilated to super marble status with arousal...

Holy *shit*, such arousal.

I slammed my eyes shut. At least that cut off one of his supply lines—and my own. Thinking straight with the man in the same *room* was damn near impossible, let alone when he hovered just inches away. And now he pulled the dark and dangerous panther thing...

Think.

Think!

"Damn it, Shiraz." It was a start. "It's not that easy to explain." It was also the truth.

"Of course it is," he retorted. "I just want to know his name so I do not have to keep replacing it in my head with things like *soldask* and *kimfuk.*"

The Arcadian profanities—I'd be shocked if they weren't—made me laugh. "God forbid you have to do *that.*" I dared another glance into his piercing blues. "Besides, you'd need a lot more than two substitutes." I didn't give him too long to dig into that one. "But before you skewer half the state of California, let's get one thing clear. I'm pretty good friends with most of my exes, and there's a reason for that."

"This is supposed to *assure* me?"

"Would you let me finish?"

"If it gets us past the subject of your exes."

"A subject *you* introduced?"

He glowered. I huffed. "Continue," he finally growled, scarily calm about it. Added in an annoyed mutter, "Please."

Deep breath. He *had* said please. "All right, so...you aren't going to believe this, but you have to." I ignored his jerk of a brow. "In the past, *I've* actually been the scary one in the relationship. I *said* you had to believe me!"

"*Lucina.*"

"Shiraz," I countered—though damn him, yanked at more threads in my soul by lowering a soft kiss to the end of my nose. "Just...listen." *Don't make this shit harder than it already is.*

"Lucina," he repeated. Gazed at me through the dark cinnamon hair toppled over his forehead. "You are many things." Trailed his lips up, landing another kiss between my eyebrows. "Passionate and obstinate. Creative and addictive..."

"Damn it—"

"Not finished." He brushed his mouth back down. "Beautiful," he whispered. "Especially that." Pressed in a little more, tasting the seam of my lips with the tip of his tongue. "As I said, so many things. But *none* of them scary."

He rose back up. His gaze was mixed with reflections of mine. The chestnut flecks were a stunning contrast to his ocean blue. I went liquid again, just gazing into those gorgeous depths. For the first time, I wished my hands were free so I could reach up and touch him. I needed to know he was real.

Damn. Would he ever *not* do this to me? Would I ever be certain I wasn't having a super long, incredible dream? Maybe on the flight home—in which case, I'd just beg to fall back asleep.

"Shiraz"—he needed to hear this as the guy still with stars in his eyes, not the master with his cock on my thigh—"you've known me for barely two days—"

"And attempting to know you better."

"*A* for that effort," I countered. "So turn down the violins and hear me on this."

I dealt with the mixture of ache and acceptance as he quietly nodded and then released my wrists. For the moment, Master Cimarron was slipped to the back shelf. I already missed him.

Another long breath—and then I just gave it to him without sugar coating. "I can be...intense." Nervous laugh. "Yeah, I know that's a real mind-bender, but—"

"Intense."

His perplexed scowl stopped me as much as his borderline question. "Yes," I said slowly, sensing he needed to hear the emphasis. "Look, I know you get it in the professional sense, but on the personal front, it's not such a great character trait."

His frown deepened. "Why is it a matter of character at all?"

"Huh?" Good thing I'd decided to leave my hands where they were. I was able to tug my hair as a calculated distraction. Yeah, calculated. Yeah, because I needed it. It was no small feat to keep thinking logically with this man near, especially skin to skin—but also because we'd dropped the shields of sarcasm. The thrum he'd first brought to my blood was now a full-blown throb, not entirely due to our physical chemistry. *That* part could be easily appeased. But emotional dissection? *Gah.*

Shiraz shrugged. *Shrugged,* as if we merely discussed the merits of pizza toppings. "Character is a matter of choice," he stated. "It is the sum of the ways you have chosen to live, whether in respect and love and honor for yourself and others or not. It is the path we all pick for ourselves, having hopefully been brought up to respect the importance of those choices by parents and other mentors, so we select the right path even when it is not the easiest way."

Tug. Tug. A little harder now. "All right," I answered, drawing the words out. "Following you so far. I think."

"Your character, Lucina, is already clear to me. I saw a great deal of it before we even met, in the details of your proposal for the wedding. Nobody directed you to weave in so many of our country's traditions to the theme of the ceremony and reception, but your ideas conveyed your careful thought and respect for our family's deep ties to Arcadia. 'Twas not just the kingdom you honored but the land it rests on. This jewel the sea has given us... You had never even been here when you conveyed your ideas, but you comprehended that importance already. You just...got it."

"Shit." Tug. *Really* hard. I gulped, struggling to stuff the sting behind my eyes back past the lump in my throat. "You actually read it."

He stroked a thumb across my cheek. "Of course. Every word."

"No. I mean, *you* read it. You didn't throw it at some fancy-poo assistant and then just ask for the highlights to review."

"Some 'fancy-poo assistant'—like Crista?"

"Errrr..." I laughed. "Yeah."

"The same woman you risked your own hide for, just about twelve hours ago?"

Colliding brows. "What's your point?"

He leaned in again. "That your character is fucking

beautiful to me." A pause, as he pulled in a long breath. "And that what you need in bed—or on the couch, or on the floor, or anywhere else you would have it—has nothing to do with any 'character flaw.'"

Major huff. "Fine. So it's not a damn *character* flaw."

He shoved up. Pushed all the way back until he knelt, muscled quads jutted at me, rippled torso rising over me. "It is not a flaw at all!" His nostrils flared. "By the Creator, Lucy. It is simply you. *Perfectly* you. And it enrages me that some small-minded imbezak—actually, it seems, a number of them—have led you to believe otherwise!"

For another long second, I simply stared. "I don't understand." Not a lie.

His fingers visibly dug into his thighs, *not* helping my effort to avoid staring at what was between them. "Let us talk about Ezra."

"Now I *really* don't understand."

"Your superior?" he countered. "Ezra Lowe?"

"I know who he is, damn it. But why do you want to talk about—"

"He is also your friend, yes?"

Snort. "Most of the time." A sobering look, when seeing he didn't—or chose not to—get it. "Yes. He's also my friend."

"And he also is gay?"

"Yes. But what the hell does that have to—"

"And you accept him that way?"

Now I straightened, pushing up until my back rammed the headboard. "What the hell kind of a question is that?"

"An honest one." His posture stayed so straight, I almost imagined him in one of those fancy conference rooms in the other wing, serenely pacing the room—while eviscerating a business associate. "You accept Ezra Lowe as a leader and as a friend, as well as the fact that he is gay, right?"

Glower. It felt more than justified. "I don't just 'accept' Ezra. I love him. He's a little nuts around the edges"—subject matter for a different time and place—"but he wouldn't be *him* without all of that. He's talented, funny, creative, challenging, honest—"

"And gay."

I pushed into the same position as him. The move made the sheet slip down. My breasts spilled out like a pair of plumped muffins, making him glance down. Good. I hope he'd gotten a huge eyeful—because right now, the lord and master wasn't getting these goods.

"What the hell is your point?" I bit out. "Ezra's actually bi, if you really need to know, but you don't. Not really. It's nobody's business except his lovers."

Well. Nothing wrong with my verbal diarrhea tonight. As soon as the spew was finished, a blush invaded my face— exacerbated by the man's cocky head tilt and boardroom arrogance. Yeah, even now. Yeah, even buck naked and beautiful in front of me.

"Hmmm. Bisexual," he murmured. "That is even more interesting."

"And your point is what?" I shot back.

"Just that it is interesting."

He was baiting me. I could feel it—but the burn in my psyche made it impossible not to jump at the lure. "But why does it have to be *interesting*? Why does it have to be anything?"

"Why indeed?"

"He's bisexual, Shiraz. It's just another facet to him, like he has green eyes, a shellfish allergy, and the ability to score

ANGEL PAYNE

the best tan during the first week of summer." Which always
turned *me* three shades of envious, but we all had crosses to
bear. "Why you're fixating on it is beyond me."

He cocked his head the other direction. "So qualifying
someone on their preference for certain...passions...is not
right?"

"No!" I volleyed. "Passions are passions. People are just
wired the way they're wired, and—" I literally choked myself
to a stop. Fell back against the headboard with a cushioned
whump. "Shit." Blinked once. Twice.

Before the tears burst up and then overflowed.

"Shit," I repeated.

"Tupulai," he sighed.

"Shit!" I gasped as he surged over, tucking me against his
chest. Even with that amazing anchor of muscle and warmth,
my psyche tilted and then slid as if Tilda Swinton in swami
clothes had just punched me into a glowing astral plane and
altered my gravity, my reality, my sanity.

Shiraz just kept holding me. His silent strength kept me
grounded, threading me back to reality a little at a time, until
I sniffed back snot with embarrassing volume. There was
nothing to be done with the remaining wetness on my cheeks,
though—especially when he tugged gently on the back of my
head, all but ordering my face to lift.

His gaze was waiting, brilliant and perfect as the morning
sea, before his thick lashes lowered and he dipped toward me...

But not to kiss my lips.

To wick the rest of the salty drops from my skin. One by
one, he tenderly took them away, at last licking them from his
lips with a swipe of his tongue so slow and intent, it became
carnal. Or maybe it was just me. The new, mind-blown me.

The me slowly beginning to realize that maybe I wasn't the "too intense," "too passionate," "too crazy," "too needy" one. That maybe there was nothing "too *anything*" about me at all.

That maybe I'd just not met anyone *enough* for *me*.

That maybe, I finally had.

The connection was a burst of right in my brain—and a bolt of wrong in my heart. *Through* my heart. *Fate is cruel.* The genius who coined that one must have also been like swami Tilda, possessing the ability to see through time and peg this moment as the perfect example. My soul had never expanded with such joy, only to be deluged by such grief. The mix turned me into a mute, confused mess...

As I clutched at the only person on the planet who could make it better.

The one person I should have been shoving away.

The man I kissed with fevered desperation...and open surrender.

Who moaned into me, his lips crushing me harder, his tongue invading me deeper.

Who growled even harder as I pulled back and started licking my way down the rippled ladder of his abdomen.

Who tangled both his elegant hands into my hair, slicking the strands back to watch with dark lust as I worked my tongue into the weeping slit atop his hard stalk.

"Va cock de Créacu," he grated. Hitched his hips forward so a little more of his flesh slid between my lips. A half inch of movement, awakening every nerve ending in my body...and shard of gratitude in my soul.

I needed to show it to him. In the most elemental, primal, perfect way I could imagine.

"Master..."

He growled low. "Yes, sweet one?"

"May I worship you with my mouth?"

"I expect nothing less, tupulai."

He pushed his cock down my throat.

I took his essence into my soul.

I couldn't have him forever. But I was sure as hell going to take whatever moments the grace of fate now gifted to us.

Because sometimes, a moment was all it took to change things.

To change everything.

CHAPTER EIGHTEEN

"Baby Jesus in a windstorm."

It wasn't a cute turn of phrase this time, only I wished it was. Staring at the tarmac where I'd taken my first step on Arcadia just three days ago—well, what was left of it—drilled a truth into my head with brand-new clarity.

You can call the wind Mariah, but don't ever call her gutless.

The airstrip was located about thirty minutes from Sancti, on Arcadia's southwest side, flanked on two sides by thick groves of banana trees. Well, they *had* been groves. About half the trees, sitting in rain-drenched soil, had been blown right out of the ground and then decided on an orgy in the middle of the runway. Piles of the trunks, twenty and thirty deep, could inspire revisions to the *Kama Sutra*. Their tattered fronds were strewn everywhere, almost forming a leafy carpet as I walked along the asphalt with Prince Samsyn, King Father Ardent, and Jagger Foxx.

When we got to the middle of the strip, Arden paused, locked hands at his back, and made a slow circle. I studied his profile for a second, noting that in So-Cal, he'd likely be a hot commodity on the market. Lots of older women with dirty minds in LA-LA Land, ready and willing to tap that lean, plus-fifty ass, despite the weathered skin speaking to tobacco use. Like I said, an easy negative to overlook for the full package. Ardent, standing nearly as tall as Samsyn, also wore his hair on the longer side. The style lent him a roguish air, though today, also like Syn, he'd tied it back with a thick leather band.

"It is a *désorlik*, to be certain," the man finally muttered.

Samsyn dipped a precise nod. "Indeed, Majesty."

Hmmm.

Majesty.

Samysn didn't call him *Father*, like Shiraz, Evrest, and Jayd did. The difference struck me as odd, but maybe it wasn't, considering Samsyn's status as the military commander for the island. The formality was probably an "Arcadian thing."

"So getting aerial aid is out for now." Ardent's eyes were hidden by spectator shades, though I glimpsed the hardened creases at their corners. Clearly, Samsyn did too. So I wasn't imagining it. There were cords of tension between the two men. Ardent's implied disappointment. Samsyn's answering energy, filled with the same damn thing.

Thank God Jagger had tagged along. Back home, he'd be a solid entry in the category of Sizzling Surfer Sex God, with those whiskey-colored waves to his shoulders and those significant shoulder bulges. Right now, I was just glad he wanted to play affable peacemaker.

"We have two search-and-rescue helicopters on loan from the Hellenic Air Force, Majesty," he asserted. "They are bringing first aid and temporary housing provisions and will remain to help with evacuations, rescues, and rebuilding efforts where needed. Cyprus has offered two more helos on top of that, but ground support is not available yet."

"We had to let some of the men rest." Samsyn's addendum carried an edge, and his glare at Ardent practically filled in the remaining implication. *Like you care, asshole.*

Well, sheez.

No more time for me to ponder that mystery much further, once Syn pivoted toward me. "As you can see, Miss Fava—"

"Lucina," I interjected. "Please, Your Highness. We're standing in the middle of *Jurassic Park*, post T-Rex escape." And for hours last night, in between ravaging his brother's body as nastily as I could, I'd heard all about his fondness for orange smoothies, his boyhood collection of plastic army men, and how he volunteered to be Jayd's "makeup model" until she turned sixteen and Xaria let her finally wear the stuff.

Thoughts I could *not* betray to the man now, so I stepped away and dropped my gaze. Not that the action helped. Holy shit. The banana frond carpeting was at least three or four layers thick.

"And yeah," I said then, looking back up the decimated tarmac. "I guess I *do* see." No flights were getting in or out of here for days. I hadn't believed Samsyn when he'd first broken the news at breakfast this morning. I sure as hell did now.

Samsyn, pacing over to stand next to me, dug a toe into the mess. "You did ask to see it for yourself."

"I did." Wry chuff. "And I am."

Which introduced a new dilemma. It *was* a dilemma, no matter how many giddy streamers my heart unfurled because of it.

I wasn't leaving Arcadia today. Or probably tomorrow, or the next day. This was an island principality where tractors were barely used in the fields and Wi-Fi was "that newfangled shit" they only carried in the palais. No heavy-duty equipment was on its way to help clean up this mess. It would be done the old-fashioned way.

Which meant being on the same chunk of real estate as Shiraz Cimarron.

Sleeping in the same building.

Knowing *he* knew I was still here...

Wondering what he'd do about it.

Trying to forget I'd even just thought all that.

"Miss Fava?"

"Huh?" I exited the daydream, straight into backhanding Samsyn's massive shoulder. "Hey! What'd I say about that 'Miss Fava' shit?"

He smirked, as amused as if a butterfly had struck him. "I was saying, if you need to get a flight out right away, I can possibly get you to Athens. I shall pull one of the SAR helicopters out of duty here, and—"

"The hell you will." I whacked him harder. And once I backed Ferdinanda out of *that* china shop, determinedly went on, "It won't be necessary, Your Highness. Really. My schedule has been cleared for the week." While it made us both squirm for different reasons, it was still the truth. Ezra had cleared my week based on the hope of staying here to finalize the contract for the wedding. "Please use the helos for the people who need the help. I even promise not to highjack Shiraz's radio and tell you where to fly them."

His smirk widened into a grin. "Deal."

I curled a hand and then held it up sideways, preparing to seal that shit with a proper fist bump but dropped it before Samsyn could make contact. "Wait. Maybe we don't." I cocked a contemplative look. "Not yet."

"The fuck?"

For a second, with his hair pulled back and the post-storm light darkening his eyes, he looked just like Shiraz. I took the resemblance as a good sign—but inhaled for composure anyway.

"You know how much your little brother looks up to you, right?"

He gave a bull's snort. "'Raz?"

"You have another little brother?"

His lips twisted. "None that I know about."

Okaaayyy.

Deciding to steer clear of that one, I went on. "He worships you, Samsyn. You have to know that much."

Apparently, he didn't—or was fantastic at faking it. "*Pssshhh.*"

I rocked my head back. Folded my arms. "You saying I'm a liar?"

"I am saying you are ill-informed."

I knocked my head back into place. Took another huge breath. Came to a crazy decision. What the hell; I was leaving in a few days and would never see him again. "Did you know he's memorized the details of every military op you've ever led?"

Deep canyons developed across his brow. His expression was menacing enough to land him in the *300* front line with Shiraz. "He what? Never mind," he answered himself, clearly deciding my assertion made weird sense, before another scowl crunched his features. "How the hell do you know that?"

Because he kept me up half the night, bragging about you.

"I just do, okay?"

Rough grunt. "So what about it?"

I took a turn at toeing the leaves, hiding my new smirk. The expression wasn't native for him, though the words carried Brooke's bold influence. "You'd be making a dozen of his fantasies come true if you included him in the fun sometime, yeah?"

"If I *what*?"

His retort yanked my head up, challenging stare already in place. "He's not a kid anymore. Did you know he can parkour the Astralle Canyon in under fifteen minutes? And that he can reassemble an M16 in two and a half minutes?"

No more *300* references. Now Syn was a seething ork from one of those CGI fantasy movies. "Where the *fuck* is he getting his hands on an M16? And why?"

"You're missing the point."

"I believe I am perceiving the point just fine!"

I dropped my arms. Breathed hard again, trying to stay away from the mental space of a four-year-old-backed-into-time-out. "I'm not talking about dragging him on some midnight raid or bomb deactivation. But even if you did, he'd hold his own—and maybe he just wants the chance to prove that to you."

He leaned sharply at me, gaze back to being the color of hard ice. "He proves himself every fucking day. He keeps this kingdom on an even financial keel. *Every day* he makes decisions affecting tens of thousands of people throughout this land. *Important* decisions. Now he wants to lose a limb, as well? Maybe more than that?"

I arched both brows. "Are you that sure that he would?"

"Are *you* that sure he would not?"

"Damn straight I am." I held firm to my stance, despite feeling like a mouse to his roaring dragon. Shit. The Cimarron men were formidable when the firing pins were pulled from their temper.

After a long minute of the stare-down, his lips finally twisted. A soft snort pushed from his nostrils. "He really remembered *all* my missions?"

I canted my head, giving him a sardonic side-eye. "Does about three hours' worth of stories sound about right?" Added enough of a smile that he knew I wasn't complaining—but hopefully couldn't infer anything else. Like the fact that I'd savored every minute of those three hours, since nothing beat Shiraz Noir Cimarron in naked storytelling mode.

"Hmmph." Whether that meant he believed me or not was anyone's guess—though a silvery twinkle entered his gaze. "Fine. I shall consider your request." Whipped up a finger, countering the fist I pumped skyward. "I said *consider*."

"Acceptable." I swung over, bumping his elbow with my shoulder. "Ferris Bueller, you're my hero."

"Fair is *what*?"

"Never mind." I laughed and then mumbled, "But as soon as you and your little bro have saved a few kittens and knocked back a few gallons of nectar, he needs to get this place on Netflix premium."

"Huh?"

"Not important," I reassured. "Really, Your Highness."

He held up both hands in good-natured surrender. "Oh, I do believe you." When I shot back a quizzical glance at his emphasizing chuckle, he explained, "Something tells me I will know it when a matter is important to you."

A blush warmed my cheeks, but I replied, "Something tells me you're probably right."

And he was...

With one glaring exception.

The man could never know how achingly important his brother had become to me. Nobody could. Not even Shiraz himself.

I just had to keep up the ruse for a few more days.

CHAPTER NINETEEN

"So tell me the royal codpiece is wet in more ways than one."

I should have known better than to take a swig of water during my first contact in two days with Ezra. As soon as I chugged, the shit came back up on a giggling choke. It spattered into the soft sand next to the Endigoh Beach palm tree under which I enjoyed a break from helping with the storm cleanup efforts. Nearby, the seven other women from my task crew also lolled in the sand and chatted, though a few eyed my reaction with open curiosity.

"'Gee, Luce, how are you?'" I emphasized the razz in my tone, since the island's touch-and-go cell reception made a video call impossible. "'So nice to know you're still alive, darling, after surviving the first hurricane of your life. I was sick with worry, my little Ferdinanda. Haven't slept in days, wondering if you were alive or dead.'"

For a second, silence. Then the distinct sound of him sipping on something. Since it was close to midnight in LA, I assumed he was sucking down a martini. "Well, I could say it, but I'd be lying. Wait," Ez cut in before I could fume, "it would *not* have been a lie, had the Prince of Hotness not reached out like he did."

"The Prince of—" My turn for the self-interruption thing. "*Who* did *what?*"

"Oooo. Coy girl," he drawled. "New one for you, but I like

it."

"What the hell?" Coy, my ass. This was genuine vexation. And confusion. And probably the beginnings of agitation, though I couldn't explain why. I rose, needing to take the conversation beyond earshot of my posse. Though every one of the women was a gem, and we'd cleared *a lot* of debris together in the last two days, none of them needed to take home a little extra gossip today too.

Especially because said "scoop" would be unfounded.

I hadn't seen Shiraz since he left my suite yesterday morning, before I left myself to tour the tarmac with his brother. After that, I'd asked Samsyn where I could best help with getting the island cleaned up—though I had to admit, stepping foot onto this shoreline, I'd wondered who'd received the better part of the deal. Even half-destroyed by a hurricane, Arcadia's coast looked damn near CGIed. This kind of beauty, with trees this lush, sand this white, and water this stunning, simply couldn't be real.

I'd stayed on the beach for as long as I could, meaning I was an exhausted heap by the time I returned to the suite. Shiraz's text had pinged during the five minutes of consciousness between showering and sleeping.

Cannot see you tonight—but you already know that, yes?

"I already know *what?*" I'd groused at the display, fighting a roiling stomach at my first logical—and horrible—conclusion. Clearly, he'd decided to go to Ambyr. To patch up their tension from the storm shelter....perhaps to even use the détente as an excuse to propose to her...

Oh, God.

But something about that scenario hadn't fit. Because I hadn't wanted it to? Or because there was a "tone" in his message, as well? Something in the way my head replayed the words, hearing them spoken in his silk-over-steel voice...and hearing the overture of accusation in them. A teasing thing but impossible to miss.

And hopeless to interpret.

"Now you're the prince of obscure too?"

I'd told him that with my answer, sending him a purple kitty with a confused frown, along with three question marks.

His response was more mystifying than its predecessor.

We WILL discuss this tomorrow.

Forget obscure.

He got the crown of totally confusing.

Words I'd have typed back if I'd been certain to continue the conversation, but that blue moon wasn't happening in the cosmos of my exhaustion. Though more rested today, I'd managed to keep the bafflement at bay—until now. Ez was talking with the same odd overture Shiraz had used in those damn texts. *You know what I'm talking about—it's just up to you to run through my little maze and figure it out.*

"Ezra."

"Hmmm?"

"I'm too tired for mazes."

"*Huh?*"

A look back at the posse. I'd walked far enough away that they wouldn't hear my huff. "Let's just go for straight-up. What the hell are you talking about?"

Another pointed sip. "You mean the Prince of Hotness himself wasn't clear enough?"

"Ssshhh." I tucked next to a palm tree, instinct driving my shoulders into a hunch. Just this morning, a couple of the women behind me had been chattering about what a beautiful betranli Ambyr was going to make for Shiraz. If they knew what *another* American hussy had been doing night before last with *their* sweet Cimarron boy...

Yikes.

Melted over a casserole of *ohhhhh crap.*

"Ssshhh?" Ez volleyed. "But all I said was..."

"I *know* what you said. Just tell me why." After ten seconds of his thick silence stretched into fifteen, I persisted, "Ez?"

"Still here."

Though now his voice rattled with the same anxiety prickling my chest, betraying how much he almost wished that wasn't true. If we got lucky, the connection would poop out now and he wouldn't have to utter what he did next.

No such luck.

Damn it.

"Fuck me, Luce. Please tell me you're going all secret spy voice on me because five guys in black trench coats are tailing you—not because you cracked that boy's virgin bat."

I crouched lower over my phone. "I don't think anyone on this island owns a trench coat, Ez."

"Holy. Shit."

Pissy huff. *Really* pissy. "Seriously? *This?* After sending me a thousand gawk-and-stalk pictures of the man before I left LA? After all the wet codpiece jokes once I *was* here?"

He sighed. Muttered dismally, "At least you waited until after Expectation was dead on the vine anyway."

"*Stop,*" I bit out. "We're *not* dead." Burrowed my toes into the sand, drawing strength from the grainy warmth against my toes. "Not yet."

"Sure. Because you stand a chance of landing that wedding contract now, after grabbing Shiraz's cherry for your fruit bowl?"

"After *you* kept telling me to push the bowl at him?"

"Because that's the kind of shit I *always* say—and then you always ignore."

"You're going with that one too?"

"Sounds better than 'I couldn't resist his gorgeous Arcadian cock, Ez.'"

I swung my gaze toward the water. Silently asked the sea for even a fraction of its azure serenity, but my fury was too intense. "Was that fucking necessary?"

Ezra grunted. "Was fucking *him* necessary?"

"Maybe it was." I knocked the side of my fist into the tree, bracing for more of his tirade. When it didn't come, and the line was only filled with his weird, sad silence, I braced even harder. Even got a little afraid.

"Luce?"

I let my butt slide down the palm. Plunked into the sand, hitting with heavy resignation. "Yeah?"

"You're not even sorry for it, are you?"

I inhaled. Exhaled. Let him hear both breaths. Gazed again toward the water. Identified at once with a massive knot of kelp, newly dumped on the shore. "I'd do it again in a heartbeat."

I'd do it again with *all* my heartbeats.

With every fiber of the body only Shiraz awakened so well. Every neuron of the mind he challenged. Every part of the soul he just...knew.

"I was really afraid of that," Ez muttered.

I jabbed a foot deeper into the sand. Huffed defensively. "Untwist the knickers, bucky. My eyes are wide open here."

"Yeah. Along with other things."

"Okay, *stop*." I pushed back to my feet, needing to pace. "Why are you doing this?"

"What?"

"Dragging this down. Turning it into a bunch of slut jokes." No way was I backing off on the conviction. I refused to banter about Shiraz—about the magic I'd shared with him—as if he were simply another great fuck.

"Sorry, Luce." His mutter was an incision of accusation. "I had no idea you hated it so much in my little gutter."

"Damn it, Ez." I turned and walked deeper into the shade of the palm grove. The seven stares behind me were a tangible weight down my spine. "That's not what I meant, and you know it. I just—" Gave in to a heated huff. Another plunk down, this time using a fallen tree as a seat. "*He's* just—"

"I know."

His voice, thick with compassion, buzz-sawed my composure. "No," I snapped past thick tears, "you *don't* know. How could you know, when *I* don't even know?"

Ezra sighed. Just like before, it was omniscience and sorrow blended into a weird oneness. "I just do, Betty Stepford. I just do."

I broke into a growl—which sounded dorky through my tears.

"I'm sorry I smutted it all up. He's a good guy. In a different stratosphere."

I sniffed. "I didn't say that."

"Your heart did."

And Ez had been listening. Because, damn him, that's

what he listened to when my mouth was being too damn stupid for common sense.

"Well, my heart needs to shut up," I muttered.

"Wouldn't matter," Ez contested. "Because Prince Hottie-McHottie has already made the case for himself, loud and clear."

"Huh?" I jerked up my head, probably looking like an ostrich who'd been forced into the sun. Good analogy, since Ez's laugh suffused the line with his special kind of warmth.

"Shiraz really didn't tell you, did he?"

"Contrary to what you're probably thinking, I haven't seen the man in nearly thirty-six hours." Which had been about thirty-five hours too long—but Ez didn't need to know that. He was having too much fun with his I've-got-a-secret hum, anyhow.

"Well," he finally dove in with dramatic relish, "it seems His Highness carved out at least a little time in his schedule last night to find *some* kind of working phone line on Arcadia— and then use it to call both your mom and me."

Stunned silences seemed to be the new trend. I took a crack at it now myself, letting my mouth pop wide as my head ostrich-cocked. "He..."

"Called us," Ez repeated.

"Why?" No pretense on that. I was genuinely curious about the answer. Though it seemed obvious, I needed to hear it.

"Well, he didn't take time to shoot the shit, if that's what you're wondering."

"Of course not." Now I fibbed. I *was* wondering. Why would Shiraz hassle to find a satellite line, since those had been the only functioning communication modes on the island until an hour ago, and then burn the valuable time for *two* calls to the US?

"He was pretty straightforward." Ez hummed again. "I was pretty bummed about that. Melted cheese on a breadstick, girl. That man's *voice*."

"Tangent for a different time." I gave it enough humor to let him know it was a promise. At some point in the future, long after I could talk about Shiraz's voice without fighting the instant pressure between my thighs, we'd have that discussion. For now, I had to stick to the facts. *Strictly* the facts. "Just tell me what he said to you and Mom."

"Practically the same thing." He emulated my matter-of-fact tone. "Like I said, he didn't linger. Just explained cell service was still down across the island, but he knew we'd be worried about your safety. He assured us you were secure and well and said that as soon as safe transport off the island is available, he'll personally make sure you're on it. Errr...Luce? You still with me?"

His hail was founded on my thick silence, spent in a tangle worthy of a dozen seaweed balls. *As soon as safe transport off the island is available.* How long would that be? And why did I both dread and anticipate the answer?

More importantly, why did it feel important that I avoid Shiraz until then?

Our goodbye of yesterday morning had been a perfect way to wrap things up. A few hours of solid sleep. Another hot, heated trip to fuck-me-like-there's-no-tomorrow land. A passionate kiss that never strayed into melancholy, since he had a country to run and I had a life to unstick from the hold button. Or was it still on play, with me longing to loop the scene over and over?

And weren't they the same damn thing?

"Yeah." I uttered it with dawning comprehension, though Ez took it as his response, as well.

"So..." he started again. "Guess you're having a little more island fun whether you like it or not, darling."

Soft laugh. Ezra knew how to drag me out of my head, even if I went kicking and screaming. "I'm actually helping with the cleanup. You'd be stunned what this thing did in just a few hours."

"Oy," he muttered before audibly brightening. "Hey! Did you get to ride in one of those cool motorized raft things?"

Spurting giggle. "No."

"See any cars in trees?"

"Errr...no."

"Boats having sex?"

"The *hell*?"

"Hmmm. You're right. Take that one back. If the boats are having sex, they probably don't want anyone finding them."

Another laugh, much fuller. "Just when I think *I'm* the biggest dork on the planet..."

"I was actually just looking for a smooth transition slide."

My humor faded. "Uh-oh."

"Oh, come *on*," he lobbed. "You knew it was coming." A knowing grunt. "You don't drop a bomb like 'I rode the royal scepter' and then *not* expect the Ezra Lowe inquisition."

"The royal scepter?" I shook my head. "Did you really just go there?"

"Hey. Be thankful I chose 'inquisition' instead of 'probe.'"

"Oh, my God."

"Hmmm. That one rolled off quite nicely," he pushed on, unapologetic. "But inquiring minds need to know how many times it got screamed in your bed." A scandalous gasp. "Or was it *his*? Oh, tell me it was. The royal *beaudoir*. God, I'll bet it was gorgeous. What's the thread count on the sheets? Were they like sleeping on butter? Did you sneak any snaps?"

"*Stop.*" I didn't know whether to laugh or groan, so I mushed them into one.

"Sorry," he relented. "You're right."

Whooshing sigh. "Thank you."

"I mean, who cares about the sheets? It's what happened between them. And do *not* skimp the details, woman. Is he an animal? I'll bet he's an animal. And do you think you'll do it again, with your indefinite delay there?"

"Sheez-ussss, Ez."

"Hey," he slung back. "Fair question!"

"Oh yeah?" I pushed to my feet, stretching the kinks in my back. Two days of clearing trash, palm fronds, and driftwood were a much different workout than Zumba class at The Beach Burn. "And how's that?"

"Hmmm." It was shockingly thoughtful, in light of his more recent tracks toward sheets and wildlife. "Intuition, I suppose. But while the man said all but fifty words to me yesterday, there was something in his voice..."

I stopped in the middle of the clearing. Was grateful the wind kicked up, blowing hair into my face, giving a real distraction from the painful skip in my pulse. "Something like what?"

He made a little ticking noise.

I knew that sound.

It always came with a grimace, like he was on a ladder but still stretching for his answer. "The way he spoke your name," he said slowly. "I think that was it. And it was more than the accent or the formality—though I have to say, he turns 'Lucina' into an art form."

"Yeah." I bit my lower lip. Like a freaking thirteen-year-old. And didn't care one damn bit. "He does, doesn't he?"

"Another topic, another time." His voice carried a warning, for which I was thankful. The tangent of Shiraz's magical voice would've had us skipping down a path populated by everyone from Bowie and Axl to Cumberbatch and Banderas and beyond. "For now, let's just leave it at the obvious."

I bit the other side of my lip, this time in a weird surge of trepidation. "Which is what?"

He cleared his throat—all but confirming my apprehension. "He practically prowls around the subject of you, Luce." He attempted a self-deprecating chuckle. "I know that sounds strange, but I can't think of a better way to say it. The entire time we were talking, I imagined him pacing the room like a lion or a panther or something, ready to bite someone's hand off for coming near its food."

I turned. Let the wind hit me full in the face, needing the blast. The moment I thought of a pacing Shiraz, pounding a room's floorboards with his single-minded stride, every blood cell in my body lit signal fires of arousal. But that was no excuse for not getting out my reply. "Was he...violent?"

"Huh?" A choking laugh. "God, *no*. Just growly. And protective. Like a mash-up of Firth as Darcy, Craig as Bond, and that Daryl guy from *The Walking Dead*, only without the crossbow. Or maybe Cimarron has one of those too." He snickered again. "Maybe he's *really* good with a crossbow and a certain someone's just being stingy with the details about it."

I groaned. "It's not stingy, okay? It's just—"

"What?" he prompted into my deliberate pause.

"Confusion."

I knew how ridiculous it sounded. How the hell was I confused about a guy I'd met three days ago, with whom I'd slept with once? Once and a half, if technical details were applicable. And granted, there had been pillow talk—the usual sharing of little life stories, acceptable in the aftermath of rocking world-class orgasms together—but nothing I hadn't disclosed to other lovers, for the sake of smoothly escaping back to real life after the passion.

And there was where the reasoning fell apart.

Shiraz Cimarron hadn't been just another lover. Avoiding that fact was as useless as avoiding the sun through the trees or the wind on my face.

Equal truth: I hadn't given my stories to him as a damn "escape."

I'd shared myself with him, as a gift.

I'd wanted nothing in return because I hadn't expected anything else. But that was because I never expected to ever see him again. Because I was supposed to be back in LA by now.

Walls of defense that were all but rubble now—especially as the words of his last text seared themselves again on my brain.

We WILL discuss this...tomorrow.

Today was that tomorrow.

"Confusion?"

Ezra's echo made me focus on verbalizing this shit. Like *that* was going to happen easily. But I had to try. "Yeah. About... him. About what happened between us. I feel kind of caged wildcat about it too, Ez. Maybe it was just because of what we'd been through first, with the storm and rescuing those kids

234

and..."

I let my thundering heartbeat conquer even the words for a second—thankful Ez filled them in.

"Thinking about your own mortality?"

"Yeah," I got out after a lengthy pause. Another lap around the clearing had me flattening a hand over my head, wondering how far to take the revelation. "So things got...intense."

Ez hummed again—this time, communicating a smile. "But in the Book of Lucy, intense is usually good."

"In the Book of Lucy, intense is *very* good." I stopped. Swallowed hard. "But Shiraz Cimarron..."

"Rewrites the book?"

"If you were here, I'd punch you for that."

"Which means I'm right."

"In more ways than I want to give you credit for." I slumped against another tree. "Which wouldn't be a problem at all, if the Sancti airport hadn't been turned back into a jungle."

"And now?"

Weighted sigh. "Now, I don't know what to do. What to think..."

"Then maybe you shouldn't."

"Shouldn't what?" I countered. "*Think?*"

His huff held up to mine. "It's called raw instinct, Luce. And sometimes, indulging it is better than fighting it."

I let a sound burst out, scoffing and gagging at once. "You're kidding, right?"

"Best way to kill a star is to let it go supernova," he rebutted at once—my first clue that he really *wasn't* kidding. "So speed up the process. Feed the explosion."

"Fine idea, Galileo," I cracked. "Only there's a huge fly on the telescope, and her name is Ambyr Stratiss. Remember her?

The woman who's going to be wearing the man's engagement ring any day now?"

"But not yet." He sang the last word, modulating it like a celebratory aria. "Anything can happen, my darling. You know it as well as I do." He *tsk*ed with grand emphasis. "*Now* aren't you happy about all the reality TV binges?"

I raised him by a cluck, tossing in a brutal growl. "This isn't TV, damn it."

"Which only makes it more romantic." He had the nerve to sigh the words. Even bigger balls to add, "True princesses start in the magic of the heart. And let's face it. 'Princess Lucina' has a damn nice ring—"

"*No.*" I didn't just cut him off. I snarled him into silence, using the vehemence to mask the truth crashing through me, the terror threatening to crush me.

Princess Lucina.

No fucking way.

Yeah, okay; like every little girl, I'd once dreamed of being a princess—for five seconds. That was before I grew up and realized the truth about princesses. They wore big dresses to keep the world at arm's length. They wore white gloves because they weren't allowed to get dirty. Palace balls were another word for scripted boredom, and castles were another word for gilded cages.

The angels hadn't crafted me to be a princess.

I liked dirty dancing and dirtier words. Leather skirts and fingerless gloves, both in black. Ballroom floors were my playground only when I orchestrated someone *else's* happy-ever-after, and that was just the way I liked it. Being on the periphery of the fairy tale meant one didn't have to live it—or explain why their version of it started in the castle's dungeon.

Arcadia needed a real princess, to stand at the side of its new hero—a knight with a spirit as stunning as his face and with courage as boundless as his passion. A leader who could rely on a *normal* princess. A woman who—

"Lucina."

Who didn't turn at the sound of his voice and instantly yearn to drop to her knees for him.

Then dream of having him drag her into the forest with him. Naked.

Then shake so badly from that desire, she dropped her phone into the dirt—and left it there. Then stood like a mute idiot, watching as he scooped the thing up and pressed it to his ear.

"Bon sonar?" Shiraz's face warmed by just a degree. His lips—holy shit, how had I forgotten the incredible curves of his lips?—tilted up at the edges. "Ah, Mr. Lowe. It is indeed nice to speak with you again. Merderim for your concern; all is well." The light in his eyes began to rival the sun on the waves for gleaming brilliance, especially as Ez went on longer about something. I strained to pick up even snippets of words, but Shiraz kept the thing tightly pressed against his ear.

Damn it, Ezra. You'd better be sharing nothing with the man but a great recipe for guacamole. Nothing, across every chiseled inch of Shiraz's face, told me differently. He looked like any other demigod prince shooting the shit on the phone with a friend. In the middle of a lush palm tree forest lining a postcard-perfect beach. In the wake of a rare Mediterranean hurricane. In front of the woman he'd screwed into half a dozen incredible orgasms the night before last...

The woman whose heartbeat surely registered on the decibel scale as he ended the call with Ez.

Who watched every move he made now, tongue working over her lips, as he turned off the device and then secured it into a pocket of his cargo pants. Who noticed he was still wearing cargo pants instead of his high-fashion office threads, topped by a Henley in a color matching his eyes. Whose heart tripped several beats as those eyes darkened, fastening to her with deliberate intent...

Who then stammered lamely, "Uh...hey."

He didn't move. Just regarded me like a gorgeous hunk of coastal rock, letting my words soak around him before finally stating, "Hello, tupulai."

I gulped.

He watched.

Tupulai. Why did I feel like he meant it in the original form of the word and not as an endearment?

Trouble.

No. Ridiculous. I hadn't done anything to earn it.

But then he paced directly toward me. At the last minute, stepped around me.

And as he kept going, ducking off the main path between the thick ferns, juniper, and oleander, clasped my hand tight against his.

"*Whoa.*" I jerked stumbled to keep up with his wide strides. "Where the hell are we—"

"Did you receive my texts?"

Tight huff. "You know I did."

"And what did they say?"

I tried twisting my hand free. No way was his iron grip letting that happen. "I'm not four," I snapped.

He barked a laugh. "Thank fuck."

"What the hell is your point?" I finally yanked hard

enough to at least slow him. "Did you come all the way out here just to rub it in that you finally proposed to Ambyr?"

He stopped.

We both skidded hard.

Until he wheeled, pinning me between his unyielding body and a tall cypress trunk.

We were a good twenty feet deeper into the grove, invisible to anyone on the main path, and his new move made that even more true. With his arms stretched out, grabbing a pair of low-lying branches over my head, I was trapped in a Cimarron-style cage.

"You truly thought I was with Ambyr?"

"Well, what the hell else was I supposed to—"

"I was not with Ambyr."

"Okay, okay." I squirmed. Couldn't help it. The reawakened bursts of energy through my body, just because he was close enough to smell, to touch, to absorb once more, were...incredible. "But do you blame me for—"

"I was *not* with Ambyr."

"*Shit.* All right."

He pressed forward. Surrounded everything I could see, only with his startling beauty and his potent ire. "You believe me."

Definitely not a question.

I breathed deep and then quietly murmured, "Yes."

"Then say it."

My teeth locked. The *balls* he possessed, going all demigod dictator on me—

Damn it.

As if he already knew how my body would respond...

Opening to every note of his command.

Heating, sizzling, awakening, craving.

Savoring every damn second of the fantasies he brought to life for me...

Again.

"I believe you."

He came even closer, fitting his body to mine with a sweep of graceful confidence. Heated my hair with his exhalation, compelling my head to rock back, just in time to drag my eyes open for his quiet, brash smile.

Holy God, he was breathtaking.

"Shiraz." It escaped in a rasp as both my hands slid up his chest, molding over the incredible mounds of his pecs and shoulders. "You feel so... God, just let me..."

Thunder flowed up his throat. "Not until you tell me... what did my texts say?"

I raised my hands around his neck. Swallowed hard as he caressed his mouth to my jaw, flowing his power over the air itself...over *me*. Pulling me away from myself, from the anxiety over everything in the talk with Ezra, even from the awareness about where we were in relation to seven potential sources of scandalized gossip. He took it all away. He took the damn world away.

"That—that you'd have to be gone," I managed to whisper. "And that I knew why." A whimper spilled out. "But I *don't* know why. I thought you were with—"

"Yes," he snarled. "We have been over *that* part." He rolled his hips, jolting me back to obeisance. "Focus on the rest, Lucina. *Focus.*"

How the hell he expected full compliance, with his hips finding their way to the perfect position between mine, made him a mad dictator indeed—not that I didn't mind a little madness sometimes.

"I—you—oh *shit*, shit that feels—"

"What *else*, Lucina?"

"You—ummm—you said that we would discuss things..."

At last, the approving hum I was waiting for—though I sensed the man didn't plan on ceasing this torment anytime soon.

"Very good," he said against my neck. "That is correct. And we are officially beginning that discussion. Right now."

CHAPTER TWENTY

Sure thing, buddy. Let's get right on that.

When the only thing I could think of "getting on" was the thick, long rod he ground ruthlessly against my cleft through his thick pants...

When the only thing I could comprehend "discussing" was how fast we could make it to a bed...

When the command on his face transformed into the lust through my body, and I wondered if we'd even *need* a bed...

But his dictate hadn't been a suave "suggestion." He expected one answer only. The response I'd be more than happy to give, if one whopper of a challenge didn't still stand in the way.

"Ummm...Master?" He hadn't demanded that one yet— but no way did his proper name feel right with a tree trunk at my back and his body surrounding me from the front.

"Yes?"

"What the hell are we even discussing?"

He stilled. It helped my tension—a little. While the friction was no longer a torment, the pressure of his cock, so full and hard, still was. His stare was an equal force, wrapping around me like the midnight it resembled. When one side of his mouth kicked up by half an inch, tweaking his look with a roguish combo of Captain Hook and Indiana Jones, that midnight was suddenly burst apart—by an explosion of curiosity.

Not all the good kind.

"Shiraz?" Master would have to deal with that. Bulging cock or not, that smirk couldn't be ignored. "What the hell *have* you been up to?"

He tilted his head the other way—looking full of astonishment to match my own. "You really do not know? Samsyn did not keep you...filled in on the scoop?"

If his hold wasn't so relentless, I would have wrenched free. I let my glare say as much. "On what scoop? From *Samsyn*?"

His brows arched. His jaw ticked. But while those tells communicated ire, his eyes twinkled like a giddy Vin Diesel en route to race a car off a cliff. What the hell? "Did you think I would not draw all the lines of logic, tupulai?"

Growly huff. It was better than the shoulder punch I originally considered. "About *what*?"

He rolled his eyes. Yeah, him. And yeah, it was damn sexy—except for the fact that I was still so irked, the shoulder punch still wasn't out of the question.

Finally, he clarified, "About the fact that I spent the night with you, carrying on like a lunatic about my brother's heroic feats—"

"You weren't a lunatic."

"Followed by the morning you spent with him at the air strip," he continued, slamming the mute button to my interjection. "Followed by Syn ordering me back to the rescue center so I could 'help him out' on airlifting some horses stranded on the Asuman cliffs."

My eyes bugged. A good thing. That explained the rough-and-ready wardrobe. Another good thing. Best of all, it clarified why he looked a little wind-chapped and a lot happy. Two *really* good things.

"Wow!" I exclaimed. "Really?"

His answering look was puzzling. Though his gaze still gleamed, his lips pursed. "Yes," he finally replied. "Really. Though I thought you would be the first to be filled in."

My own lips twisted. "Why?"

"Because you were the reason it happened."

The man did snarky as well as he did eye rolls—though this wasn't sexy at all. This was outright accusation, and it was beginning to tick me off. "Is that what Samsyn told you?"

"Of course not." He frowned. "He had some story about being down on men because people needed to rotate out due to exhaustion. Said the horses were thoroughbreds and would have to be counted as collateral damage from the storm if a crew did not get to them."

I glowered harder. "He had 'some story,' huh? And then he went and parked a bunch of expensive thoroughbreds on a cliff too? And told a bunch of men, who'd been working around the clock, to go *pretend* they were exhausted and asleep—all just for you? All because I talked to him?"

His mouth contorted. He parked a hand against the tree trunk, drumming his fingers against the wood. *Good. Fidget away, asshole.*

"I talked to him simply to enlighten him, Shiraz—to make him see that he had a damn good asset of an extra man sitting in front of him but that perhaps he was missing something because that guy's usually hidden under a three-piece suit, attending to a schedule full of important decisions."

The drumming stopped. His head dropped in a jerk of surprise. "*Important* decisions?"

"His words, not mine." I caressed fingertips through his heavy stubble. "Though I have to agree with them. You *are* important around here—even if you need to go gallivanting around on the cliffs, in the middle of the night, to prove it to yourself."

He pushed his face against my hand, though his eyes stayed open and ardent the whole time. "Not to prove it...to you?"

My fingertips curled in, fighting the new arousal from his soft growl. Dear God, what he could do to me with one look and half a dozen words. "I don't care if you rescue one horse or a hundred...if you're the prince of a hundred thousand cats, or a hundred thousand people. None of it matters, gorgeous. The man you are, the *person* you are, is all that matters to me."

He turned his head. Pressed his lips to the center of my palm. "And you are the only person who has ever said that... whom I believe."

I flattened my hand against his cheek, hoping to share the magic of his kiss with him. His lids lowered, turning his stare sultry, making me think the mission had been a success. He exhaled in shaky spurts. I inhaled in matching measure. More energy sparked and arced between us, throbbing on the air itself now and giving me courage to dare a little jibe.

"You mean others have called you the prince of cats?"

A rough purr exuded from him. "That one *was* a first."

My own breath turned shaky. "A wildcat, maybe." Especially with the way he started rocking against me once more. "One of those black jaguars, with all the interesting patterns across their body." I swirled fingertips across one of his pecs, envisioning the exotic tattoo across that muscled slab. "A creature only capable of snarls and hisses, instead of phone calls to Los Angeles, talking to the other kitties' *mothers* and *bosses* without them knowing about it."

He lowered his arms. Used his powerful grip to palm my thighs and then hike them around his waist. Locked me to the tree again as he readjusted our bodies, notching his hardness into my valley with even more throbbing insistence. "You mean properly looking after the other kitties?" he rumbled. "Making sure their mothers and friends do not go mad with worry about their safety in a strange land, after a huge storm?"

"And distributing untrue impressions about the cat prince's intentions?"

That would sure as hell sober him up.

Or so I'd thought.

Apparently, stupidly.

The man looked as if he'd expected every word I flung. Might even be proud of them. As I wrestled with the storm that blasted my psyche from *that* observation, he finally responded.

"Hmmm."

If I cared to qualify that as a "response." Not that he looked open to giving me any more options.

"Hmmm?" No more pectoral caresses for him. This time he got a full smack, enforced by my narrowed stare—answered by the sultry weight of his own. But noticing it didn't seal me off from the effects of it, molten and mesmerizing in my blood... especially as he leaned even tighter over me, shoulders flexing as if he craved to crawl right into me...

"Do you have issues with 'hmmm,' little tupulai?"

I managed to jog my chin up. Shot him a glare that I mostly meant. "That depends."

"On what?"

"On what it means."

"Ah." His lids got even heavier...as his stare descended to my lips. "Perhaps it means a great many things."

Shit. The way he could even speak things...

Could reach inside me with their lush magic, touching me with more than just the sensuality of his voice. He threaded the very fibers of my body with his command, until my blood and tendons sang for him...my inhalations and exhalations sang with need for him...

"Things like...what?"

He let his lips hover over mine. "Like how I should be exercising my...princely rights."

"Oh?" I let him see my open amusement at that. "Your princely rights to *what*?"

His brows pushed together. "To punish you, of course."

Well, that did it. The full laugh escaped now. "Oh, yeah. Of *course*. Because that makes sense...not one fucking bit."

He pushed in harder. My hips could no longer move. Secured his hands around my waist, digging into my skin—readily accepting my challenge, as if that were his purpose all along. "I should not discipline you for interceding with my brother?"

My teeth grinded. His grip hurt, pissing me off—but one second of reengaging his gaze, and I knew *that* was part of the plan too.

Well.

Two could play this game.

And would enjoy the hell out of it too.

I scraped my hand from his chest to his neck, twisting my fingers into the ends of his hair...and then pulling brutally. "And *I* shouldn't discipline *you* for interceding with my mother?"

My retort was backed by his long hiss. He tore free from my grip, his head snapping forward, bumping his nose to mine. Within a second, he snapped a hand to my scalp too, locking me in place, forcing my lips to accept the fierce, wet plunge of his mouth.

I opened for him at once.

It was heaven.

I whimpered, digging my hands into his thick, silken strands again, tearing and tangling and hurting him just as he sliced new daggers of pain through me. My heartbeat sped. My senses opened. I was an addict given a taste of my own special crack, and he was my incredible, beautiful supplier.

And I wanted more.

Of all of it.

Of him.

"No," he finally grated. "No way. You have dealt your punishment already."

I torqued my hold tighter. "What the hell?"

"Seeing you, back there in the glade...even having to get through one damn minute of not touching you, kissing you..." He gritted his teeth harder. They were blinding white past the contrast of his burnished lips. "It was like being flogged. Having my flesh torn open and then being unable to do anything about it."

Hard gulp—to fight the new sprint of my heart. "You're a melodramatic dork," I managed to choke, yanking him for a new, slamming kiss. "But there'd better be more where that came from."

His lips kicked up, making him too resplendent to resist for another kiss—only this one lasted longer and twirled deeper, our tongues unable to get enough of each other's, our heat and lust crushing and crashing until we fell to the ground in a pile of panting breaths and groping hands. A huge pile of downed palm fronds formed an impromptu bed, granting me my wish in a primitive kind of way. A *perfect* kind of way—especially if his next words were what I hoped they'd be.

Sure enough, after releasing me with a sharp jerk, he locked his hard gaze to mine. Issued in a deep snarl, "You shall take your punishment in whatever way I want to give it, woman."

I wet my lips before rasping back, "Y-Yes, Master."

Please, Master.

We'd landed at a funny diagonal, letting us both get at least one hand at the bare skin of the other. During another fierce kiss, I clawed at his back as he slid a hand up and over my bra, pinching my nipple hard—though he shoved even that aside, making me moan harder as he tugged at my bare tip with his knowing fingers.

"Oh, my God." It spilled out atop a gasp, heavy with desire and thick with surrender. His answering groan was an equal turn-on—doubled as he flattened me fully to the ground, grinding his body against the apex of mine once more. Just as violently, he reclaimed my mouth again. Invaded me with force that stole my breath, seized my heart, dominated my body...

Made all my fantasies come true.

In return, I scored him deeper with my nails. Opened myself to the beautiful brutality of his passion—and gave back as good as I got. I buried my other hand back in his hair, pulling tighter at the luxurious lengths, even as I snarled into his throat and bit into his lip. He hissed, pulling back and stabbing me with his stare as he ran his tongue gingerly over the nick.

His brows knitted.

As his cock grew.

Before he dropped back onto me, impaling me deeper with his tongue, making me taste the metal of his blood, the heat of his passion, the force of his need. I groaned and writhed, hooking my ankles behind the perfect globes of his ass, notching the center of his body to the center of mine, knowing neither of us could last long like this—but also realizing I couldn't let him stroll back out the beach with a massive spot at the front of his pants. Crista, still recovering in the palais infirmary, wouldn't be at our rescue with a change of clothes this time.

But holy shit, how I wanted to career into nothingness with him. My lungs pumped. My blood sizzled. My pussy throbbed in time to the frantic race of my heart. I burned. Needed. Craved. The point of no return approached fast, like a broken bridge in front of a speeding train...

Until suddenly, it didn't.

"Fuck."

Shiraz tore away from me. Burned a stare at me through the tumble of his hair before raking it back with a hand as he reared back on his haunches.

"By the Creator, Lucina. What the *fuck* are you doing to me?"

I gulped again.

Harder.

So much harder.

My dry throat resisted the moisture, as if letting that in also meant I had to address the sting behind my eyes. I pushed up on my hands, the tree line tilting, skewed by my shot-to-hell equilibrium.

"I...understand." I was shocked I got it out, considering how hard my heart started squeezing, trying to keep its edges together. I promised the thing it could shatter in full later, when he wasn't around to witness the carnage. When nobody was.

Which, in and of itself, had to be the most ridiculous concept of the week.

The week in which I'd only just met the man.

Whom, just two minutes ago, I was exalting as the fulfillment of my fantasies.

Freaking. Hell.

When had I become *that* nutcase of a woman? That desperate whacko, thinking I'd really land on a remote island, meet the prince, and find out—*by the magic of the unicorn!*—he was actually my soul mate waiting to be found? My kinky other half?

Life did *not* go like that.

Soul mates didn't exist for weirdos like me.

"I understand." I had to repeat it, as much for me now. "I'll...um... I can go back to the beach and distract the other women so they don't see you leaving with me, and—"

The horizon cartwheeled again—as he laid me out with another consuming kiss. No. That wasn't even the word for it. His mouth was on assault mode, full of driving anger and imperious intent. I was so stunned, I didn't even know what to do with the new onslaught of arousal it brought on.

As if he was going to give me half a breath to process even that. "You shall do no such thing," he dictated lowly, scooping a hand back beneath my shirt and going straight for the clasp at the front of my bra. One masterful twist later, my bare nipples stabbed the air, awakening to the cobalt flames in his gaze. "You shall stay *right* here and take your full punishment, woman."

I sat up as he did, naturally doing so as he yanked the shirt off the rest of the way. The bra fell to the ground behind me. "Yes, Sir," I said, almost sensing it was expected but utterly unsure what *I* was supposed to do next.

"You shall accept it...naked."

That was sure as hell an answer.

A dangerous one.

All right, we weren't just right off the walking path anymore—but we weren't a mile deep into the middle of the palm grove either. Anyone coming through the grove from the beach might stand a chance of seeing us. Which would mean what, exactly? At this exact moment, he was still a man who could have anyone he wanted—and thank this island's really awesome Creator, he wanted me.

And holy hell, how I wanted him.

How, despite my cynical mope, he was checking off more of my deepest, wildest fantasies by the minute.

Especially as he stood, unsnapped, and then unzipped, setting his erection fully free.

Especially as he took that dark, swollen length in hand, starting to stroke as he firmly ordered, "Stand up, tupulai. And strip."

CHAPTER TWENTY-ONE

I wasn't sure I'd ever taken off my pants faster.

And was damn proud of myself for doing it without tripping over my own two feet.

Ha fucking ha; great joke to laugh at—until one had to match the will of their brain to the actions of their body, with *that* part of Shiraz Cimarron's anatomy just a few feet ahead. I didn't want to take my eyes off him, even wondering for a moment if this was all one hell of an incredible dream. If it wasn't, I knew the sight of his elegant fingers around his stiff, proud cock were going to be actually featured in a few dreams now...

But at the moment, I was a long, lonnnggg way from thinking of sleep.

At all.

The salty breeze filtered through the grove, making the trees whisper and my skin tingle, as I stepped before him, nude and vulnerable. I shivered again as his gaze touched every inch of me, noticeably pausing at my puckered nipples...and the pussy that clenched in anticipation of his cock conquering me there.

Dear *God*, I hoped that was part of this punishment shit.

His lips parted, but for a long moment, he said nothing. His stare, like his penis, just got darker and thicker.

Finally, he uttered, "By the Creator, Lucina. You are... something from my dreams. Like a siren from the sea."

His voice poured over me like a wave, weakening my knees and throbbing my pulse. "I'm not *that* wet...yet." And the attempt to one-liner myself back to composure was a soggy mess on the air—until he lasered it to pieces with the intensity of his attention, the command in his stance.

"*I* will be the arbiter of how wet you get, woman."

Yes, please.

"Of course," I murmured.

"Of course...what?"

"Of course, Master."

"How you please me." His voice rode the wind, wrapping warmth around me and then inside me. He spread his legs, bracketing his stance, continuing to taunt me with the sight of his hard-veined length, the crimson head now kissed with the milky evidence of his lust. How I wanted to fall to my knees before him and taste that cream. Take it from him, as he commanded more of my thoughts, my will, the very drops of my desire. But I didn't dare move toward him on my own. I didn't even want to. I wanted everything masculine in him to take—and rule—everything female in me. Use it. Transform it into his special, sexual putty...

The thoughts lent me enough mettle to look back to his face. His jaw was firm, his neck corded with tension. Nobody gave better neck porn than Shiraz Noir Cimarron.

"How can I please you even more, Master?"

He inhaled, as if my words were the perfect perfume for him, before he directed a nod toward our palm frond bed.

"Get back down there for me. On your hands and knees. I am going to take you like an animal."

"Yes, Master." Though I came very, very close to not complying—due to my melting blood and knees gone to mush.

Dear God. Did this man actually possess the power to reach into my psyche, learning every damn hot button I had?

Hot being relative.

Meaning it needed an instant superlative, nearly from the second I sank to the ground once more...and he lowered directly behind me.

Raked his touch up the front of my body.

Scratched his fingernails back down my spine.

Rose up, letting his cock rest on the small of my back, as he smacked one side of my ass and then the other.

Hard.

"Fuck!" I gasped—and then writhed as my intimate channel dripped and pulsed and yearned for him...

"Yes?" he growled—spanking both cheeks together now.

"Yes," I whispered back, my head dropping, my shoulders sagging...

Until he hunched over, jerking my head up with a hand in my hair and using the angle to sink his teeth into the base of my neck.

The pain jolted me even stronger. Fed my need even deeper. Made me moan and buck back against him—a good thing, since his other hand dipped in, seeking the hottest place between my soaked folds. He lunged a finger into me. A second.

I keened.

He purred. "Yes."

"Y-Yes," I finally stammered as he worked in a third finger. Stretching me. Pumping into me. "*Damn.* Yes!"

He nipped his mouth up to my ear. "It will be my cock next."

I nodded feebly. "Yes, Master."

"Tell me you want it, Lucina. Use my name this time.

I need to hear you say it with desire on your tongue and my touch on your pussy."

I struggled to summon the words, simply because he was making them impossible. He was making thought itself impossible. "I... I want your cock, Shiraz Cimarron. I want it inside me...filling me...punishing me."

And maybe the words weren't so hard after all.

Hard being relative.

Because holy shit, did the man's cock give the word new meaning.

A quick crinkle of foil, a slick of latex over his skin—and another turn-on, thinking he'd come looking for me, already thinking of doing this to me—and he was spreading my sensitive lips, making room for his length down there...

Then filling me down there.

Dominating every inch of my sex.

Pushing deeper, thrusting longer, fucking harder...

Showing no mercy.

Taking me to heaven.

I spiraled up fast and furiously, my clit already primed and aching for his touch. When he slid his fingers from my channel to that hot little ridge, it instantly quaked and throbbed, so ready to burst...

And it did.

A blinding, beautiful cataclysm, taking me to the tips of the treetops and then back again on the wings of its perfect bliss...

But my eyes had barely uncrossed from the first orgasm when he began coaxing me toward the next. Correction: dictating me to it. Literally.

"Such a sweet, wet clit. Rahmié Créacu, woman...how

you tremble for my fingers. How you come alive beneath my touch..."

"Holy...shit," I panted. His velvet words...his long, knowing fingers...his thrusting, relentless cock... He wove a perfect lover's witchcraft over my helpless, submissive senses and my rejoicing, ecstatic soul. Inside, I begged that the paradise would never end...

Though the rest of me insisted otherwise.

My clit tremored and ached. My intimate walls were collections of clenching need. While I dreaded the explosion about to come, I also prayed like a frantic schoolgirl for it.

"Oh God."

Perhaps even screamed for it.

"Oh God, oh God, oh—"

Smack.

He stole the rest of it from me with a spank. I yelped, wondering if the impact would leave a mark and then praying for *that* part too. I'd have something even better than a signed contract to take home with me from Arcadia...

"Not. Him." Forget the spanking. Now I just wanted a recording of those two words, gritted exactly like that, from this man. Like he was going to even let me have *that* thought either. "Not him," he repeated, dragging both syllables across razor blade beds. "You will beg *me* for it, tupulai."

I didn't dare not answer.

I didn't dare not pick any other words.

"Yes...Master."

With one whoosh, he twisted me around until I was on my back. In another, he was back inside me, shuttling his beautiful cock up into me, ramming everywhere inside me.

"Beg."

He pounded.

"Me."

He thrusted.

"Master."

He stilled.

"Please!"

He throbbed.

"*Fuck.*"

We came.

Detonating in tandem. Screaming in silence. Intensity so complete, it shook us in spasms that surely must have bubbled the air itself, causing time to stop and the world to tilt.

Through it all, we stared at each other. Took in all the straining, stunning, ugly, unreal, unfiltered beauty of orgasms transcending physical bursts or even emotional connections. In those wild, weird moments, something happened to us... beyond the chemical. Surpassing the sexual. Something transforming my cells...from the sheer force of my spirit.

Something metaphysical.

Something magical.

Something that was going change me.

Forever.

Thank freaking God the recognition fled as fast as it had hit.

And thank everything else for the incessant vibrations of Shiraz's phone, still tucked in his back pocket, still in the cargo pants covering most of his ass. The pulses radiated through both our crotches, inciting us to shared spurts of laughter, resulting in the sad but inevitable slide of his body out of mine. But even as he rolled to his back, he didn't let me go. With one arm, he kept me tucked close. After peeling off the condom, he used the opposite hand to hook my free leg across his middle. His cock, still warm and firm, indented my inner thigh. I smiled through a few blissful minutes of I-am-Eve-hear-me-roar. For just a little while longer, I could choose to believe the world was nothing but the distant surf, the kiss of the wind, and this man in my arms, lost in our private Eden.

The light swirls he made against my leg turned into an inquisitive squeeze. "What are you thinking?"

Tiny grunt. A kiss to the heartbeat beneath my ear. "That's a dangerous question, mister."

"More dangerous than sprawling in the open with my cock hanging out, after catching a gorgeous forest nymph?"

He had a point. And had expressed it with swoon-worthy effectiveness. "I'm thinking that if that was your idea of punishment, I've got to think of more ways to be bad."

The hand he'd gripped to my shoulder trailed down to my breast. "I am already filled with *those* kind of ideas, tupulai..."

He dipped his lips to finish that with a kiss—

But uttered an Arcadian oath instead, thanks to the new buzz of his phone.

"Somebody needs you." I teased the subtext to that with a little buck of my hips. "More than me. If *that's* possible."

He dug out the phone, scowled at the screen, and then rammed the device to his ear while jabbing a thumb in to open the line. "Adym. I left instructions not to be—" His features bugged in shock. He bolted to a sitting position. "When?" He swiveled around, glaring in the direction of the beach. "You are certain?" By the time he looked back to me, my clothes were already in his other hand. "Understood," he barked, pushing the garments at me. "Merderim, Adym."

His voice emphasized the thanks. A lot.

Did I dare ask him what for?

"One of the women on the beach saw me entering the grove," he muttered as I climbed back into my T-shirt.

The second my head emerged, I flashed a curious stare. "And called Adym about it?"

"No." His face tightened as he stood and zipped up. "Called *Ambyr* about it."

That sure as hell explained things.

"Holy shit." I hurried back into my jeans—mentally bashing myself at the same time. Officially, there was nothing here to be holy-shitting about. On paper, Shiraz was still an unclaimed man—though that wasn't a valid argument either. "On paper" didn't mean crap when it came to people's hearts and minds. *On paper*, I'd been Ryan's committed girl. *On paper.* Dad was a bad-ass detective, out to catch bad guys. The descriptions hadn't stopped Ryan from leaving or a criminal from putting a bullet through Dad's brain.

On paper wouldn't stop everyone in this kingdom, and possibly the world, from branding me as the skank who'd been Shiraz Cimarron's fuck buddy before he settled down with the nice island girl.

Not the lover he'd taken to the damn moon and back.

Not the woman he'd led back a special part of herself with his dominance.

Not the person who was never going to be the same, after knowing the perfection of his passion...

Moroseness for another time. A *much* later time.

Right now, I had to find my damn shoe.

The black boot magically appeared—clutched in long fingers I was doing my best to forget. "Thank you." I accepted it without looking up. Adding his eyes atop the temptation of his fingers was a definite no-go at this moment.

Though the beautiful bastard himself had other ideas.

"Lucina."

Much different ideas than getting out of here—with those fingers now sifting into my hair, his breath mingling with my own, and his head tucking lower, making me watch how he bit into his bottom lip. Yeah, right into the part *I'd* taken a nick out of.

"The thanks, tupulai, is mine."

I didn't want to answer him with such a swoony smile. I *should* have been giggling at him and that clichéd line, not angling a stare so enamored, I could *feel* the stars going twirly-sparkly in my eyes. Shiraz smirked in return, knowing how his sultry utterance would unravel my resistance...melt the marrow in my bones...fry the damn blood cells in my veins.

He knew it would tear down all my walls again, making it possible to take me in his arms for another long, toe-curling kiss.

And yeah, every one of my toes coiled in. As I sighed into him.

As he moaned back—and then pushed in more. Parted me. Invaded me. Reduced me...

And in the doing, reimagined me.

Once more, I wasn't anyone or anything. Gone was the little girl who'd had to grow up so fast, as well as the woman she grew up into. And the woman who just wanted to be that loved little girl again. And the woman who recognized those issues, knew she'd been escaping them with sex and didn't care.

But gone as well was the wedding planner who always scoffed at the concepts of soul mates, colliding stars, and the sacrifice of true love.

Who'd become a woman *in* love.

The lightning hit me so hard, I jolted backward. Slammed fingertips to my lips, as if they'd burst with the words if I didn't keep them pushed inside.

Only there was the fucking rub. The lightning burning my brain. Pushing at my lips.

I love him.

"Tupulai? What is it?"

I love you.

No.

I didn't.

I couldn't.

I wouldn't.

I took another step back. As I did, I literally imagined that part of me—that burning, bright, ball of completion and joy I'd allowed myself to acknowledge, even if just for those few seconds—now left behind, plopped on the ground between us. If the orb had been real, it would've left a burn on the ground. Would have branded that small part of the world...

The same way he'd changed mine.

Had changed *me.*

I couldn't fight the acknowledgment any longer. Couldn't deny I'd be leaving Arcadia a much different woman, a much different *person* than I was just a few days ago. But renouncing that new Lucy was like shitting on the man who'd given her to me in the first place. Shown me the truth of who I was...

And how beautiful that truth could really be.

Me.

Just like this. Snarky, smartass, silly, passionate, kinky, weird little me.

She was pretty fucking cool.

And now, I even believed it too.

Shiraz Cimarron had given me so much—but most of all, he'd given me that.

And somehow, I'd find a way to keep honoring him...by cherishing her.

Starting now.

Forcing my lips into a soft smile, I took one more step back. For some reason, this one was harder than the first. Could've had something to do with how Shiraz watched me do it. Like I took *his* legs with me.

Damn it.

"Lucina?"

Damn it.

"I have to go now, gorgeous." I let him reach for my hand. Even let him take it—though when he tugged to draw me closer, I resisted. "I have to go."

For a second, he grimaced like I'd taken his legs *and* broken his nose. Yep. He'd gotten my meaning, all right.

I swallowed a lump the size of this whole island.

He gripped me tighter.

The lump grew, pressing up my throat. Swelled against the back of my skull and then at the backs of my eyes, shoving tears forward. I trembled, fighting them back.

Stupid. This was so damn stupid. Every time we'd touched, every time we'd kissed, every time we'd fucked, we knew it would come to this. I'd have to go back to my world. He'd have to go back to his. I'd plan happy-ever-afters, and he'd pretend to live one.

No.

I refused to think of it that way, and I swore he wouldn't, either.

"I'll be okay, Shiraz. And you will be too."

He let my hand drop. "With all due respect, Miss Fava, fuck the hell off."

Good thing I had the hand back. Made it easier to ball it up, along with the other one, and then drive both into the stubborn slabs of his chest. "With all due respect, get the fuck over *yourself.*" I stood my ground, despite the scary fire in his retaliating glower. "This is how it has to finish, Shiraz. What the hell did you expect? We don't get to do *Casablanca.* We don't get to do *The Bridges of Madison County.* Nobody gets to pass the Kleenex and rewind the playback so they can keep bawling for us—which means we don't get to do it for ourselves." *Deep breath, deep breath.* Wasn't happening. I swallowed the goddamn lump and pushed on. "This kingdom needs a new fairy tale, and you're up in the casting rotation, buddy. And you're going to do it right—with the woman who's on her way here right now."

He wheeled away. "Who had me tracked here!"

"Probably because she was *worried* about you?" I backed off that one as soon as his skeptical glare stabbed me. "All right, maybe not worried in the traditional sense of the word..."

Which meant Ambyr's concern had started running to other things.

Things that would lead to me becoming that public skank now. And wouldn't *that* be just dandy for so many aspects of both our lives. Him, having to stay and deal with the PR fallout—and Ambyr's wrath. Me, having to confront the clown costume for months of kids' birthday parties—and *Ezra's* wrath.

Shiraz's mind clearly hadn't gotten that far. He dug hands into his hair, yanking it back from his Italian fresco face. His eyes glimmered with sharp cobalt pain. "This is *not* acceptable."

My hands curled at my sides. I focused on the stabs of my fingernails into my palms to avoid rushing into his arms and kissing away his torment. "My prince of perfection, life rarely *is* acceptable."

He pushed out a bitter chuff. "Make this easier. Just call me the prince of pricks."

Here came the lump again. The pressure, too great now, knocking all the tears loose. "No. You're the prince of my dreams."

He locked his hands at the back of his head. As his arms flexed in flawless striations, his face crumpled in visible pain. "That helps even less, my princess."

My princess.

He might as well have clocked me.

I actually wondered how I stayed upright instead of ass-down in the dirt but thanked my feet for keeping it that way. The rest of my body sure as hell wasn't helping. My extremities sizzled. My lungs pounded. My mind reeled.

My princess.

The echo didn't make it any easier. I doubted a thousand echoes would. But the recognition of it brought at least one blessing in disguise. The acceptance, sudden and sure, of the most merciful response I could give him...before turning my back on him for the last time. *God please, for the last time.*

"Yeah, yeah. Fuck you too."

CHAPTER TWENTY-TWO

"And then he held your hand during the whole flight back here?"

As soon as Jayd sighed out the question to Crista, I had to suppress a giggle. I was the same age as the princess, but in many ways it seemed like years separated us. Had her sheltered upbringing made her that much younger, or had life hardened me into someone older? Maybe a combination.

Maybe I just didn't want to know.

I was getting good at that mental shutoff thing lately— especially when it came to not thinking about the three days that had passed since stepping away from Shiraz in the palm grove. This private room in the palais infirmary wasn't anywhere close to that setting, but those last moments, buffeted by the wind and speared through by his pain, were as sharp and agonizing as if they'd happened three *minutes* ago...

The biggest part of the problem wasn't hard to pinpoint.

I was still here, damn it.

Wasn't like I hadn't tried to rectify the situation, even a few hours after the "my princess" bombshell, but the status at Sancti airport had become the plot of a damn disaster movie. Bad went from worse to shitty to we're-just-fucked. After the debris had been cleared from the tarmac, they'd prepped King Evrest's private Cessna to run through a trial takeoff, as a retest for the communications equipment. The plane never hit the air—after its wheels sank into the runway deep enough to flip the plane over. Though the three crew members were unhurt, nobody was happy to learn about the swath of asphalt that'd been compromised by the storm's torrential rains. Now, a couple of helicopters had to be pulled off rescue duties for simply transporting the necessary repair materials from Athens.

In short, my departure from Arcadia had been moved waaaayy down on the priority list.

I'd been too tired to go the snarky bitch route in reaction. Would it have altered anyone's stress factor one skitch? Besides, this glass-half-full approach was kind of cool, as long as it didn't brim into totally cheesy. For starters, I was able to add some cheer to Crista's healing process. Even met her whole family too. Holy crap, I'd been to Dodgers games with less of a crowd—though Forryst and Fawna, who looked like Mini Mes of their big sister, stole the show with a little song about their "medicane adventure."

Second, the weather had turned epic—this time in all the good ways. Days of golden sun gave way to nights filled with fragrant breezes, moon-dappled seas, and skies full of stars. I began to understand why so many movie production companies wanted to film here, and I'd only seen the ten-mile radius surrounding Sancti.

Third—and best of all—Shiraz made it a definite point to keep his distance.

Significantly.

Thoroughly.

Damn near creepily.

But it was still a good thing. No. The best thing.

I just had to keep telling myself that.

Despite everything—*everything*—that wanted to keep

pounding me with the opposite.

The daily delivery of sunny flowers to Crista's room from him. The hint of Creed cologne I'd catch on the air, even in empty palais hallways. That sparkling, sizzling feeling I'd get out of nowhere, pulse racing and neck hairs tingling, for no damn reason...followed by that feeling, somehow, of being watched...

And damn it, how I'd always tried to watch back.

Only to peer into empty shadows, empty corners...

The emptiness of my heart, without him near.

No.

Don't go there again.

I let the mandate kick my consciousness back to the present—and listening in real happiness to the black-haired fairy in the bed. Crista had been thrilled about this surprise visit from Jayd, and seeing her happy did the same for me, no matter how torturous it was not to steer Jayd toward even a fly-by mention of her brother. Just so I knew he was doing all right...

No.

Because even knowing that would recatapult my thoughts into a Mach five flight full of lust—and he was still too close to resist.

Because maybe I didn't want to know the scarier answer. That he was doing just fine by now, thank you very much...

"Shai insisted on being in the helicopter crew that lifted me out of the ravine," Crista explained to her wide-eyed princess. "They did not know if they could even fit the rescue basket into the space I was wedged in, so he came down on a rope and got me."

Both Jayd's hands flew to her cheeks. "Like Tarzan? Or

Captain Blood?"

There was no helping my laugh now. Fortunately, Crista broke out into a simultaneous one—though probably not because the princess had just invoked a pirate from a 70-year-old movie. A classic, but still...

"No, arkami," she chided good-naturedly. "He was in a harness. It was rather business-like, actually."

Jayd bounced in her chair. "But he saved your life!"

Crista's mirth turned mysterious. "Well, the *whole* experience was not like that."

"Ah." More bouncing, though Jayd kept it to a dull roar now. The infirmary walls were modern drywall, not the thick stone and stucco we could count on in many other parts of the palais. "Yes, yes," she eagerly prodded. "The hand holding! Get to that part."

"And...the parts *after* that too?" Crista's grin turned kittenish.

"There were *after* parts?" That one actually came from me. This was getting even more interesting, perhaps even a chance to forget the-Cimarron-who-would-not-be-named. "I've been here visiting for the last three days. You never said anything about an 'after' part."

"Désonnum, my friend," Crista murmured, coloring a little. The blush was great to see, since she'd been so pale until this morning. Hypothermia, three cracked ribs, one broken leg, and immeasurable exhaustion had an odd way of doing that to a person. "I was waiting for my mind to clear from all the medication, just to be certain it was not a dream."

I lowered one thigh to the bed and nodded my head like an approving professor. "That good, hrrmm?"

Crista's lips twitched. "Perhaps. Yes. Probably."

"Well, tie me *up* and make me *scream*." Jayd's joyous gasp had my jaw plunked so hard to the floor, I barely noticed the choirgirl handclasp with which she finished. "Captain Shai Storm. Who knew? We probably all *should* have known. The reserved ones are always the hottest ones. Milord gentleman on the outside, devil with a dick on the inside."

"Devil with a—" I laughed but let my stare go wide. "And he had time to get out the pitchfork...when?"

"*Pssshh.*" Jayd waved an impatient hand. Brought it down to take up the ends of Crista's fingers. "All right, dinné, we *will* hear this entire tale now. No details spared. I am assuming lips met? And tongues too? Did Shai try to...*hold you*...anywhere else?"

I laughed harder. "She was in a lot of pain!"

Crista giggled. "Not enough pain to ignore *that*."

"Aha!" Jayd went bouncy toy again. "There *was* tongue!"

"I beg your pardon?"

Four words—ice bucketing all four corners of the room, in a voice just as chilled. As soon as I joined Jayd and Crista, whipping my head toward the door to determine the source, the rest of the space turned icy tundra on us too.

How appropriate, then, that Ambyr Stratiss wore a dress in icicle blue, with a svelte silhouette to match. Her demure V neckline was accessorized by one strand of pearls. Her fitted skirt ended below the knees, finished by dyed-to-match shoes. Flats. Pointy toes. Of course.

"Miss Stratiss." Disgusting, that the person in the hospital bed had the stones to speak first. "Uhhmm...bon *sabah*." Crista's greeting was damn near a question, but that was okay. A fast glance at Jayd confirmed my belief about us *all* wondering why Ambyr was here.

"Bon sabah to you as well, Crista—but if you call me Miss Stratiss once more, I may have to just turn tail and leave."

Do it, Crista. Please.

Too late. Before Crista could reply, Ambyr stepped forward, dropping into a short but graceful bow, murmuring. "Your Highness Jayd. How lovely to see you here. And Miss Fava." The Cleopatra in her gaze jetted to the North Pole upon regarding me. "What is it that they say in your country? *Great minds think alike?*"

I let my eyes give up a little shrug. "They do say that."

Ambyr rang the red courtesy phone of smiles. Once. For a second. "Well, then. I brought some cheer." Directing her attention back to Crista also had her clacking across the floor in order to set down a large vase of flowers—next to the container bursting with Shiraz's blooms. Her arrangement, a dazzling display of orange and blue, looked perfect next to the shades of gold and yellow in his. I fought—and failed—not to take that as a great-smelling sign from the universe. *They're already a beautiful couple.*

"Merderim," Crista said to Ambyr. "They are lovely."

Ambyr's lips curled up. "And look. They are perfect next to His Highness's."

Way to rub it in, lady.

The slight narrowing of Jayd's gaze didn't escape my attention—or my ego. I noted the development with a secret and shameless glee. Let it grow a little as Jayd issued with a tight smile, "What brings you this way, Ambyr? Deciding to slum it in the infirmary?"

Crista burst with the beginning of a giggle. Quickly bit it short. "Deepest *déssonum.*" She lifted her taped-up arm. "They pulled out the IV but an hour ago. The drugs must still be—" Another laugh spurted. "Yes, well. The drugs."

"Of course." Ambyr shifted, clasping hands in front like one of the Von Trapp family kids about to ask for more champagne. "I do apologize as well, Crista, for not stopping in on you sooner. I assumed you needed your rest, of course—"

"Of course." Jayd's interjection took the terse up a notch.

"—and have been, perhaps, just a bit...distracted."

If she'd strip-teased out of the icicle dress and revealed a body bomb underneath, we all wouldn't have been more stunned. Crista noticeably frowned. Jayd openly glowered. I wasn't able to monitor what my face did, since the exploding grenade in my chest was a bit of an attention hog.

"Distracted?" Thank God for Jayd and her royal ability to put a veneer of propriety atop a mountain of suspicion. "By what?"

Or whom?

I forced aside my mind's auto-add. There was no damn validation for it. If Shiraz had rebounded from my fuck-off by fucking *in* to Ambyr, I had nobody to blame but the girl in the mirror. He'd sure as hell not made it official yet, since she didn't make it a point to flash her ring finger with every other word— but my belly knotted with a strange certainty that it was a foregone conclusion now. There was something about Ambyr's energy, oddly confirming exactly that. The regal upturn to her chin. The way she coyly brushed a toe on the floor. The return of Dolores Umbridge to the edges of her smile.

"I have been working on...a secret project." The woman's eyes gave away the mental trumpets she'd inserted into the middle of it—quashed by Jayd's unimpressed answer.

"Oh. A project." If her tone were any flatter, we'd have to peel it off the floor like a wet pancake. "How...nice. Like what?"

The toe swishing stopped. Tough to swish when a girl was busy bouncing on that toe instead. "A party." Ambyr beamed at the other two women. It hadn't escaped my attention that after her initial hello, she'd all but dismissed my presence. "A celebration of romance, to give our people hope and cheer!"

Jayd rose. Her ebony curls brushed her shoulder as she cocked her head. "A...*what?*"

Ambyr blinked, clearly bewildered. "A party, Your Highness. Taking place this Saturday night."

"This Saturday night." Crista's echo carried the fog of someone who'd slept through a lot of the last few days. "Errr... when is that?

"Three days from now," Jayd supplied, gritting it hard.

"Whoa," I kicked in, beneath my breath.

"It shall be an engagement party, Your Highness." Ambyr beamed. "To celebrate the love your brothers have found—"

"*Two* of my brothers," Jayd injected.

"Yes. Of course. For now." The woman had to be given credit for turning catty into an art form—as well as redirecting the spotlight of a conversation in seconds. "It is going to be... spectacular!" She fanned her arms, fingers outspread. "The Altor Ballroom is being prepared as we speak!"

"The Altor Ballroom?" Both Jayd's arms dropped to her sides. Her fingers twitched, as if craving to form into fists. "That is...impressive, indeed."

Ambyr practically preened. "I know."

"There is a *full staff* preparing it?" Jayd pressed. "Polishing the gold inlays? And buffing that huge floor?"

Ambyr nodded. "Happily so, Your Highness."

Jayd's lips thinned. "Does His Majesty Evrest know about this?"

"The queen mother and king father do." It was better than a yes, and we all knew it. Even as an outsider, I knew Evrest capitulated to his parents about social events, with the understanding that the kingdom's government, military, and operations were his jurisdiction.

"The entire evening will be broadcast live to the whole country," Ambyr went on excitedly. "Several entertainment shows from around the world will also be carrying the feed. It shall show off the best of the best about Arcadia!"

A blast of breath burst out of Jayd, visibly startling Ambyr but not Crista or myself. To be cliché but accurate, the fuse had been smoldering for at least five minutes. "I would think, at this juncture, that would be our ability to get the internet working, the homeless sheltered, and the streets dry."

Ambyr blinked. Then again. The blast zone had finally stretched into her brain. "They also need to know we will not be this way forever. Seeing their monarchs happy and in love—"

"And pressured to propose by a public-relations stunt?" Jayd volleyed.

Ambyr flattened a hand to the base of her throat. Blinked with huge, hurt eyes. "With all due respect, Your Highness...I did not think, for one moment—"

"No, Miss Stratiss." Jayd stiffened, the opalescence of her own gaze glimmering with ire. "You did *not* think, and that is why—"

I stepped forward, damn near desperately. "With all due respect of my own"—a peacekeeper was necessary, right this second—"Ambyr has some good points." If only said diplomat didn't feel like the gladiator thrown to the lionesses. "Seeing you and your brothers in fully shiny mode, making Arcadia look great to the world, will make everyone feel more secure and ready to move on from all this mess." I turned from Jayd's silent pout to confront Ambyr's preening one. "And if you want this thing to score a few more points on the citizens' approval scale, invite a few of them up the hill for the night, to rub shoulders with the Cimarrons in person. Have Camellia give them a walking tour of the palais. It'll be like what Jackie O did for America in the 60s, only a lot more fun."

A blink-blink from Jayd.

Another set from Ambyr.

An excited spatter of applause—from the woman in the bed.

"Oh, Lucy. I love all those ideas!" Crista jabbed an awkward thumb in the air, wincing a little as all the medical tape pulled at her arm hair. "Kick *ass*!"

I openly laughed. The woman's stabs at my slang were worth another round of blink-blinks from the others, though those never came. Apparently, the lionesses were still circling and hungry for blood.

Perhaps it was time to just get the hell out of the ring.

"Right now, it's time to kick my little ass into the ladies' room." I stood, giving Crista an encouraging hand squeeze. "I'll be right back. Maybe I'll find that cute doctor and ask him where the hell your discharge papers are."

Crista flashed a Christmas-is-coming grin. "Kicking ass yet again, Miss Fava."

★ ★ ★

My excuse hadn't been a lie. The morning's coffee had caught up, so I was grateful to find the restroom down the hall and take care of business...

Only to finish up and have my business given back to me.

More correctly, shoved so hard against the wall, my breath escaped in an astonished gust.

I was so stunned I looked down first, instead of up...

At the hand with the flawless manicure, still pinning me like a butterfly to a science board. Several feet below that, a pair of ice-blue flats were planted on the tile.

I jerked my head up, narrowing a what-the-fuck glare.

Ambyr didn't give me the chance to utter a syllable of it.

"Follow. Me." The seethe in her tone brooked no dissention—not that I would've allowed her to rip me apart here, less than ten feet from people recuperating from the various traumas courtesy of a six-feet-plus storm surge. When we were private, she could tear away. I shook my head, saddened that I already expected no less.

At the end of a short breezeway, the building opened up to a small courtyard. The major debris had been cleared from the benches and tables, but most of the planters would need to be dug up and repotted. The flowers and shrubs had been decimated. If I were picking out a new look, I'd think of installing an herb garden. The space looked like it'd get plenty of afternoon sunshine, and—

But that choice wasn't mine. And never would be.

Filling me with even deeper sadness.

Which, maybe not so weirdly, I channeled into a fresh sense of peace as Ambyr led the way across the flagstones.

Finally, she spun back around. *Clack. Clack.* Planted her stance, ready for confrontation, just as she had back in the hallway. Her stare had bypassed lioness, going straight for she-dragon. Her lips were a twist of deep crimson. Her chest was furiously pumping up and down against the confines of her tailored blue linen.

"Miss Stratiss." I spread my arms. "What can I do for you?"

"Do? For me?" For a second, I wondered if she'd go full catty-whomper bitch with it, splicing in a cackling laugh, but pushed the mental delete as soon as it occurred. Ambyr wasn't a cackler. She took her shit seriously. It might only be glued onto construction paper pages, but every damn corner was sealed and secured. "What you can *do* is not *do* anything else, Miss Fava," she finally added. "Most especially the man who will be proposing to me this Saturday night."

CHAPTER TWENTY-THREE

It didn't completely shock me.

But my mouth popped open enough to make her happy. Or whatever Ambyr Stratiss's version of "happy" was. As established, the woman took serious to a new level of dedication.

That being said, she tapped her foot—actually waiting for me to answer. Must've been prewritten in her mind's eye for this scene. No way in hell did I risk taking her off-script now.

"Okay...Ambyr...listen—"

"Shut. Up." Right on schedule, along with the acidic huff of punctuation. "Excuses are futile. I may dress like a fashion doll, but I assure you, I am not one."

I lowered to a bench, hoping the motion would signify respect. "That's been clear from the start, I assure you."

"Good. So you must know that *I* know by now." She moved only to raise up her spine, regarding me with a new infusion of haughty. "I have eleven years of history with Shiraz Cimarron, in which I have studied nearly every nuance of his moods, masks, and miens. The one he presented at breakfast the morning after the storm..."

The morning after he and I had finally fucked.

No.

Made love.

I forced myself to make the private confession, despite carefully hiding it from her. Yeah, I'd loved him, even that night. From the moment he'd exposed my darkest fantasies... and then boldly accepted them...and then made so many of them come true with such blinding, brilliant magic...

Goner. Me.

His goner.

"Was what?" I filled in Ambyr's extended silence, forcing myself to go gently. Her hands were raised in front of her waist again, though now they were restless twists instead of choirgirl serenity.

"He was...different," she finally murmured—only to jolt herself from the troubled trance, as if remembering she wasn't confessing to a friend but confronting an adversary. "Yes," she spat. "Different...in that way a man gets when he has been... slaked."

"Slaked." I dove at it like trying out an exotic food in a foreign land, because when would the opportunity ever roll around again? Had to admit, it wasn't as gross as munching on crickets. Barely. "You mean...he was happy?"

She laughed then. An honest-to-God giggle. But instead of enhancing her natural beauty, it harshened the sharp angles of her face. "Go ahead and gloat, salpu. Even throw a parade that you had him all that night, and then again in the dirt at Endigoh Beach, and Creator-knows-where after *that*. For all I know, Samsyn even covered for the two of you with that tale about rescuing horses out at Asuman." She struck a pose, one hand raised and the opposite toe pointed, fashion plate haughty on bitch steroids. "For all of that, I am actually grateful. You broke him in, so I did not have to."

Blink.

Blink.

Well...fuck.

I replayed the callous words and her carefree tone—still coming up with zilch on a definitive conclusion. What the hell had the woman just confessed? Did I really want to know? Was it really any of my business?

"I beg your pardon?"

Guess I did. Guess it was.

Because after everything was said, done, celebrated, and settled—this conversation, Saturday night's party, the kingdom's recovery, the weddings, the births, and years after that—the only damn thing that mattered to me was Shiraz Cimarron's happiness.

Ultimately, that meant serving his people.

With a worthy woman by his side.

"Oh, you do not have to beg it of me," Ambyr replied breezily. "You have my pardon, Lucina." She hitched a penciled eyebrow. "Indeed, you have my *thanks.*"

I pushed to the edge of the bench seat. Balled both hands atop my pressed knees. Talk about the universe's kick in the head. I'd sat just like this, on the edge of Shiraz's office couch, less than a week ago—minus the fists. And the cosmic shift in my heart.

"I don't understand." No having to sugarcoat that one. Her thanks? For "breaking him in"? What was she saying? What the *hell* was Shiraz getting into? My heart thudded, spinning the possibilities to the realm of the bizarre. Was he going to end up the sex slave of some sado-crazy dominatrix? Or cuckold of a woman who *really* believed in adhering to the traditions of the old court—including playing musical beds with her courtiers? Like either of those would go over well with a man like Shiraz.

Ambyr acknowledge my move with another flighty hand

wave. "Of course you don't understand. You probably *liked* what he did to you."

You mean what we did together? But I wasn't about to point that out. Not here Not now. Not *ever* with her.

Ruminations that didn't lead to any kind of a tactful reply, so I didn't render one. Thankfully, didn't need to. The ice princess rendered a rolling shiver that spoke volumes. "Yes, yes," she muttered. "You American salpus...you all enjoy that sort of thing, don't you?" Another delicate flinch. "The sweat. The strain. The...bodily fluids."

My fists unraveled. I dipped my head quickly so she didn't catch my smirk. "Don't knock it till you've tried it, sister."

She stumbled backward by a step. Bobbed her head to the side, as if my words were a slap. "We are *not* 'sisters,' Lucina Fava. Nowhere near it." Her head came back up, stiffening until the cords were like cable ropes beneath her skin. "In that regard, I am going to be completely clear about your 'help' for *my* event on Saturday night. It is not needed or wanted—and neither are you. While it is my sincere hope Samsyn finds a way to get you completely off Arcadia by then, I must be realistic about the challenges we face in logistics, with getting the key members of the press over here for the festivities."

I only nodded. The woman didn't want to hear that I was likely on a first-name basis with many of the celebrity beat reporters and could coach them to live feed locales showing off the palais at its best. She also didn't want to hear that even before now, every additional hour I spent on this island was like another damn stake in my heart. She was running her own script, shooting her own movie, and I hoped it wouldn't end up as everyone's punchline in the next news cycle.

"To that end, Miss Fava, I must fiercely urge your absence

from the celebration." She adopted a new pose, hands joined together atop one of her hips, feet scooted into a ballet third position. "If you eschew my mandate, I will have no choice but to hail Arcadian security forces to assist you out of the ballroom."

Screw the secret smirk. I was *so* tempted to. It'd be fun, just laughing in the priss's face, but no way could I let her have even that satisfaction. If I was being openly blackballed, then she was truly scared—in itself a curious thing, if she really believed me to be Shiraz's "trite little slake"—but I bypassed the snub in favor of the bigger picture. The *much* bigger picture.

And because of that, the much bigger fear I planned on throwing down.

Starting. This. Second.

Two steps took me back over the gap between her and me. Two more beats committed, just to be certain she saw the resolution in my gaze and felt the fire of my energy. Done and done...

And now, time to do this.

"I'll honor your *mandate*, Miss Stratiss—but only because I have one of my own."

Her lips twinged, spilling with a delicate chuff. "Oh? Is that so?"

One more step. One more moment of letting her see I wasn't kidding about this. Not. One. Fucking. Bit.

"The universe is giving you a damn good man, Ambyr. A gift from the angels. He deserves the very best in return, including the woman on his arm, in his bed, and in his life."

For a tiny moment, I took a huge risk. Let the walls drop, shedding all the shields of snarky, sarcastic, and cynical from my face...letting her see through to the woman beneath.

The adversary now handing her the full victory—and the nonnegotiable challenge.

"Vow to be that woman. Ambyr. Lift yourself higher...for him. Be *better*...for him. Because I'll promise you this. I *will* be watching."

CHAPTER TWENTY-FOUR

This was *so* not a great idea.

It was Saturday night. And I was *not* parked on the terrace of my suite, with a paperback in hand, where I'd vowed—and made very clear to *everyone*, down to the girl from food services who'd brought my dinner—that I'd be remaining. *All night.* As in, not moving. Butt on the mattress. Nose parked in the newest Steve Berry book. He was a great alternative to my normal steamy romances, which were *not* a wise choice for the night. No melty panties tonight. No *thinking* of melty panties tonight. I'd been good on every damn front.

Except that now...I wasn't.

"Shit, shit, shit," I rasped while hurrying as fast as I could down the hallway in the palais's south wing. Yeah, that south wing. The one containing all the royal family's apartments.

The apartments located directly over the Altor Ballroom.

I yanked off my flip-flops and attempted deep Zen breaths. Okay, *attempted.* That shit never worked for me even *in* yoga class, and this stress far outweighed whether I'd accomplish tree pose without falling over.

Fifteen minutes. That was all it'd taken for all my good to get scrapped in this pot of crazy. Fifteen damn minutes.

As the night had begun, with media helicopters circling the palais for their aerial shots, I'd practically felt my spirit in the skies with them. It had been a damn good week, at least for staying busy and dodging two bullets named Shiraz and

Crista. Not that I hadn't been grazed, especially during an afternoon visit to Crista's cottage. One minute the two of us were chatting, the next Shiraz's advance security team had swept in, announcing the prince was on his way for a "quick stop" on his way to checking the repair progress at the tarmac. I'd successfully slipped free the second he'd arrived, climbing into the Mini Cooper on loan from the court auto pool as he'd climbed out of his royal Bentley.

Not before he'd gotten in a good, long, skewer of a stare across the road. A thunderstorm inside an instant...a look confirming exactly what my heart already dreaded and my soul already knew.

Our "goodbye" at Endigoh hadn't been the finish. For either of us.

But looking for that ending was also useless.

The two of us would never be finished.

Meaning I really needed to do what I came over here to do and then get the freaking hell out.

The urgency needed no enforcement but got one anyway. From the ballroom below, the strains of an orchestra surged into the air. It wasn't standard dancing fare. The Arcadian national anthem, majestic and official, swelled through the whole building.

Freaking great.

I wasn't just going to get caught this close to the "forbidden" party, dressed in nothing but my sleep tank and a pair of drawstring shorts. That bombast of a song alone was going to turn my apprehending soldiers into bloody national heroes.

"What the hell. Go big or go home."

Why had it sounded so much better in my head?

And how much farther until I got to Jayd's damn apartment?

I didn't want to stop but did. My sense of direction in this small city of a building had already been established—at next-to-nil. Quickly, I keyed in a message at the bottom of the thread, fifteen minutes old, between Jayd and me.

I'm here. Where are you?

Thank God for her three bouncing dots, appearing immediately.

Still in the ballroom. I cannot get free yet. This dress is going to pop any second!

As she'd already told me, in shouty-caps texts above.

With her seamstress on loan to Ambyr, as she'd also relayed above.

Meaning she needed someone to sew her back into the dress. Perhaps someone who'd done the same thing for half a dozen brides before...?

Hence, the reason I was here, trembling like an escaped convict from Alcatraz, fingers shaking as I managed to respond.

I'm directly over the ballroom. How much farther to your rooms?

No comforting trio of dots now.

While waiting, I kept moving, keeping my back flattened to the wall. Like that was going to help for cover if a battalion of red-and-golds suddenly rushed up the hallway. I had the comfort factor, at least—and right now, I'd take what I could get.

"Come on, Jayd," I gritted, now practically padding on the balls of my feet. *"Come on."*

My screen remained blank.

Shit.

But around one more curve in the hallway: a set of broad double doors. Guarded, as Jayd had promised, by only one man in uniform. Jagger Fox. Behind him, carved into the left panel, was an ornate hawk. A dove dominated the other.

I'd seen those images before. In ink, across Shiraz's biceps.

Yesssss.

Jagger spotted me. Urged me forward by lifting a hand and ninja-tapping his fingers. No further clarification needed. I sprinted for the doors and let him shut me in. Only then did I expel a huge breath of relief, my back still against the door.

The chance to breathe easy was too awesome to pass up. I did it again, letting my lungs fill, before finally checking out Jayd's digs. Well, what I could see of them. With the lights dimmed in the whole apartment, I could only make out the stuff in the main living room—and even then, only basic shapes. I smelled leather, though. And fresh wood oil on the floor. And, damn it, a distinct hint of currant and bergamot cologne.

Or maybe I was just doomed to smell Shiraz on the air, no matter where I went from now on. Which wasn't such a horrible thing...

"His Highness, Prince Shiraz Noir!"

Okay, the court crier accompaniment might get to be a drag.

Only that part happened to be reality at work, confirmed by the thunder of a cheering crowd from outside.

Outside?

"What the hell?" I added to that beneath my breath while

padding across the room. Just before clearing the couch, I stealthily slipped my shoes and phone to the cushions. Not that anyone in that throng—I stuck in the assumption, based on the volume level—was going to hear a damn thing I did.

On cautious steps, I sneaked closer and closer to the terrace. Halted a few inches inside the partly open sliders. If I took another step forward, it'd mean the risk of getting hit by the floodlights. And yeah, it *was* floodlights, cranked so high the lawn looked like it had time-warped from ten at night to ten in the morning.

"What the *hell*?" I repeated in a rasp.

A drop to my knees became a quick crawl across the terrace, to a shadowed corner enabling me to peek out. Glimpsing the TV reporters and cameras was a blatant explanation for the extra wattage. The cameras needed the illumination for the best shots out here. What I didn't know was *why out here*? The party itself was supposed to be contained to the ballroom—or so Ezra had told me, during his last update on what he liked calling "the daily juice on bitch honey's soiree."

The official name for the events was the *Fête de Yan*, an expression loosely meaning "Celebrate the New" in Arcadian, and Ambyr had more than accomplished her goal of making it the hottest story of the week for American celebrity media. According to Ez, all reports were that everything would take place in the ballroom, with the exception of a private reception for the "Citizen VIPs" in Evrest and Camellia's private garden, followed by a tour of the palais from Camellia and Brooke. Imagine *that*.

Finally, after civil unrest, a royal abduction, bridge bombs, and a raging medicane, Arcadia had scored a win. Ambyr Stratiss had to be several galaxies over the moon by now.

Though no one would know it, beholding the woman's face.

I let a gape take over my own as I studied her, standing to the side of a red-carpeted riser, around which the formal-attired crowd had gathered. A podium was placed in the center of the stage, decorated with a drape displaying the Arcadian country crest: a dove with sunbeams as wings. At the back corners, giant urns brimmed with red and gold flowers. Everything was regal and luxurious, everything Ambyr had hoped for, but her expression was pinched and impatient, her skin paler than the shimmery ivory sheath draping her elegant Grecian figure. It didn't make sense. This was the night she'd waited for. She should be glowing and hopeful, the kingdom's next perfect princess, just minutes away from taking her place on that stage...

Maybe she was just nervous. I sure as hell related to that one. If that was me down there, waiting to have a ring slammed on my finger, a crown rammed on my head, and expectations shoved down my throat...

But it wasn't me, thank God, so I could tell the cold sweat to go away now.

The herald finished presenting the royal family. Seemed they were going with the "countdown of importance" thing, so Shiraz had followed Jayd, who took each step with pronounced caution. I winced, hoping her satin and chiffon production of a gown held together until after this ceremony—or whatever the hell it was. After Shiraz, Samsyn and Brooke were introduced and then the queen mother and king father, Evrest and Camellia took the stage, buffeted by the longest and loudest cheers of the night.

As the ovation grew louder, my smile stretched wider.

"Shit," I whispered, even swallowing against a telltale burn behind my eyes. How was this possible? How could I be battling tears at the sound of those Arcadian cheers and chants? How had just a week in this country equated into this swelling pride on its behalf?

But the truth was a medicane blast in my brain—and just as impossible to ignore. This island had spun its magic around me, nearly as completely as its mystery prince.

No.

He was a mystery no longer.

He was the clearest, brightest part of my heart. The most indelible light in my soul.

The best thing that had ever happened to me.

Thoughts I forced myself to stow as the crowd fell into sudden silence. Another peek, and I saw why. Evrest had stepped to the podium, arms raised in stately welcome. Holy shit. The serene and commanding thing certainly ran in the DNA. The man was, from his head to his toes, every inch a king...

Surpassed in hotness only by his youngest brother.

To be fair, all the Cimarron men were stunning tonight, clad in the modernized brocade doublets befitting their status, paired with tailored black trousers tucked into gleaming Hessian boots. But Ardent, Evrest, and Samsyn came nowhere close to filling their regal wear like Shiraz. He was beauty and masculinity, elegance but confidence, serenity meshed with strength. As his long fingers rested against his black-clad thighs, my mind surged with a parade of items around which they'd wrap perfectly. The stem of a wine glass. The hilt of a sword. Both my erect nipples.

My breath snagged painfully.

Not just because of the fantasy.

Because the second it slammed me, it slammed him.

No. It was a thorough coincidence, even a careless slip, that I'd been so fixated on him, my head had risen beyond the "just peeking" position—and that in the same second he'd looked up, burning his stare at the very spot I crouched in.

Total coincidence. Nothing more.

And everything more.

As our gazes latched. Held. Connected.

Grieved.

Even then, I couldn't stop looking. Despite the pain... perhaps because of it. Needing the jolt, to remind me of the reality. It hadn't all been just a fantasy. It had all really happened.

He'd really happened.

I'd fallen for him this hard.

We were forced back to reality when Evrest's voice flowed out through the loud speakers.

"Ladies and gentlemen of the foreign press, my fellow Arcadian Court and High Council, and of course, my honored guests of island citizenry...karsivoir en Arcadia."

A milder spatter of applause had the king pausing and smiling.

And again, Shiraz lifting...and staring.

"Those words are the highest welcome of our land," Evrest went on, "extended to all of you, as our honored guests at the Palais Arcadia this evening—a night in which we rededicate ourselves to putting aside the challenges of our past, to celebrate the shining hope of our future. I am happy to announce that the first step of that future commences construction in two days: a new, modern air terminal, supporting our new, operational plane tarmac."

He lifted his voice on the last syllable, to compete with the motorized roar suddenly splitting the sky. Everyone looked up, breaking into exhilarated yells once more, as the Cimarron Cessna dipped over the lawn, the crew members tossing handfuls of shiny confetti.

The crowd cheered louder.

Red and gold danced on the air.

I saw only cobalt blue, pierced into me once more. For minutes this time. Long, wonderful, agonizing minutes.

When the confetti finally settled, Evrest continued.

"It is a bright future—but not one without lessons we have learned from the past—most importantly, that we are part of the world's community now. With that community, we must also respect and revere our national security. We can no longer expect the western world to do it for us"—the king straightened and jerked back his shoulders—"which is why we shall go to the western world to teach us."

An audible murmur sprinkled through the crowd along with the dissipating confetti. I focused on the puzzled faces below as an excuse not to acknowledge the one already staring at mine. *Again.*

"I have spoken with the leaders of several major countries, the United States and Great Britain included, about clearing select members of the Arcadian armed forces to join *their* special operations teams, to learn better ways of protecting our beautiful land in hands-on training situations. This process will take approximately six to eight months and only involve select members of our military." Evrest cocked a brow toward the cameras and reporters, pressing in for dramatic effect as they live-fed the announcement to the world. "I promise you all a formal press conference tomorrow morning, with more details forthcoming then—but tonight, we are focused on celebrating our future. On all the new, incredible things in that future."

He reached backward then, beckoning for Camellia. A nod brought Brooke to her feet, dragging a grumbling Samsyn with her. Obviously, the big warrior enjoyed the spotlight as much as he would a root canal.

"Last year, as most of you know, I worked to dissolve the tradition of the Distinct in Arcadia," Evrest pressed on, sliding a hand against the curve of Camellia's waist, which was hidden beneath a Roman-style gown in ivory chiffon. "My reason for doing so is not a secret to anyone. She is here beside me, the woman the Creator truly destined for me, the keeper of my heart and the love of my soul." His smile grew. "She stands here next to the sister of *her* heart, the warrioress who has, unbelievably, turned my brother into a tolerable person at times."

As the crowd snickered, Samsyn groused, "Do *not* push it, *rerda.*"

Brooke, dressed in a more contemporary gown of black-accented ivory, gently nudged her man in the ribs. "You *like* being pushed."

While Samsyn ducked his head toward Brooke's ear, growling something only she could hear, Evrest turned his attention away from the familial ribbing and back to the crowd. A long breath expanded his chest. Defined portent sharpened his tourmaline gaze.

The biggest announcement of the night was on its way.

A disgusting truth confirmed—as I looked to where Shiraz stood...and beheld only empty space.

I didn't look for where he'd gone. I couldn't.

I didn't search for him next to Ambyr. I wouldn't.

I didn't wait to watch him grasping her hand, gently tugging her toward the stage, opposite hand already digging in his pocket for the engagement ring there. He'd have made sure the stone was what she wanted. In short, it would be the size of Half Dome.

Didn't care.

Couldn't care.

I crawled back into the shadows of Jayd's apartment. Huddled myself against the back of her couch, digging fingernails into my curled knees and funneling my attention on one desperate, urgent mantra.

Don't you dare fucking cry.

The crowd settled into expectant silence.

Don't you dare fucking cry.

Evrest cleared his throat.

Don't you dare fucking cry.

"Now, it is my inexplicable joy to announce..."

The tears gushed, heavy and hard and silent.

"...that six months hence, Camellia shall be your queen in the fullest sense of the word. As we speak, Arcadia's next sovereign has begun to grow in her womb."

CHAPTER TWENTY-FIVE

For a second, I couldn't breathe.

Mostly because I didn't know whether to keep sobbing or not.

In a knot of twisted-up tension, hands now bunched into fists between my knees, I listened to the hugest explosion from the crowd so far. Damn accurate description. If a stranger entered the palais right now, they'd think the night was ending in a full-on rock concert.

Complete with the pyrotechnics.

Voilà. The enigma of the location shift to the lawn was made clear, in the bursts of lush color consuming the sky over the sea. It took me a second to realize the fireworks were synched to a soundtrack—the alt-rock song "Change," by Moon Taxi, was one of the best choices I could imagine—and the uplifting strains of the song helped me at least struggle to my feet again.

For a few seconds, I let the magic of the scene bring a smile back to my lips. And yeah, it *was* magical. No snark this time. Just inwardly joining a few *ooohs* and *aahhhs* of my own to those of the crowd, thankful for the realizations of the last tumultuous minute.

Arcadia wasn't just going to have a new princess. They were going have a baby—a new life. Because of the latter, maybe I'd get lucky and not have to hear the former come to pass. Maybe Shiraz had dragged Ambyr off to a secluded shadow, choosing to start their story with a moment of private romance. She wouldn't be completely happy about that but still had a few hours to make up for it, flashing the engagement rock to everyone at the party.

Shit I didn't have to witness.

Which left taking care of Jayd and then getting the hell out of this wing.

Then tomorrow, with the air strip functional again, I could finally get the hell off this island too.

I watched as more rockets shot into the sky. The crowd gasped and clapped, totally entranced. If Jayd was smart, and I knew she was, she'd use the distraction to scoot her hiney up here for the wardrobe repair. I could be done with the gown and gone before the show even—

"Lucina."

—ended.

I spun around. On a rush of wild breath, blurted, "Shit."

Before saying goodbye to the air in my body again.

Perhaps for good.

Dear, holy hell. He looked even more incredible from just ten feet away, with his presence altering the air, his height more magnificent and majestic. From here, I could also see the fine blue threads worked into the black brocade of his doublet. The shade was perfect, as brilliant as the fireworks bursting against the stars but as rich as the new intensity of his gaze.

Way more intense than it had been from the distance of the stage.

What a difference twenty yards made.

Shit, shit, *shit.*

"Tupul—"

I stopped him with a slash of a hand. Not that, goddamnit.

Anything but that. "Wh-Where's Jayd?"

"Lucina—"

"I'm waiting for her. She'll be here any second, Shiraz. She had a problem with her gown. Ambyr's using her seamstress, so she called me." Though my snark was still on vacation, seemed the inner Chatty Cathy was still ready to rock. "*Ambyr*," I stressed, as that oh-so-special revelation took hold. "Where's Ambyr?"

Shiraz stepped toward one end of the couch. "I have no idea."

I rushed toward the other end. "Why don't you know? And why aren't you with her right now? Proposing with Half Dome in your hand?"

He shook his head. Let out a combination of laugh and sigh. *Fuck.* That soft, sultry sound, on the rolling hills of his incredible lips... I was so close to letting it undo me. And damn it if that didn't look like he intended exactly that.

No. *No.*

"What the hell?" I was finally able to get out. "How did you even know I was—" Logic began tapping, incessant and alarming, at the edges of my psyche. "Where the *hell* is Jayd?"

"She is not coming." Shiraz released a measured breath. "This is my apartment, tupulai, not hers."

"Huh?" I darted a glance around. Well, shit. That explained some things—elements I should have pieced together, if I hadn't walked in here skittish of my own shadow. The decidedly masculine furniture. The splay of guy-tastic video games on the end table. And the air, filled with his confident, decadent scent—even stronger now.

I needed to be pissed about this. And I was. Maybe. A little.

Why wasn't I more pissed about this?

"She never was." He turned back the way he'd come. Damn man, with his shadows-and-smoke moves. He infuriated me. He mesmerized me. "Her dress is fine. She sent those texts because I asked her to."

"*What?*" I shuffled backward—only to realize my shoes and phone were still on the cushions halfway between us. *Damn it.* "And...and Jagger—"

"Helped as well."

"*Why?*"

"Would you have come if I openly asked to see you?"

"Damn good point." I managed to snag the phone. The flip-flops, lying closer to him, might just have to be collateral damage for the greater good. Translation: getting out of here without succumbing to touching him. A harder exertion by the second...

"I'm not proposing to Ambyr."

I froze. I had to. It meant conceding some space to him, but hiding the utter elation from my face took significant priority—

Until logic stepped in.

"Okay, wait." I sliced a hand, palm down, on the air. "Not proposing *tonight*, right? Because of the announcement about the baby?"

"Lucina—"

"That's really sweet, mister." I folded my arms—as he kicked up the speed on his re-approach. "But in the end, it changes nothing."

"Damn it, Lucina." He rumbled it from a place inside, a part of him matching the dark granite of his face. More colors burst in the sky, illuminating those bold angles, firing into the brilliant depths of his eyes. For a moment, I could do nothing but stare, praying his stark beauty was scorched on my memory forever...

Before forcing myself to move again.

Bolting for the door.

For freedom from the perfection of him.

For escape from the pain of him.

From the heat in my throat, the fire in my veins...and ohhh fuck, the pressure in my sex. The need, crawling through me like electrical lines hit by that damn lightning, sparking and sizzling, wild and out of control...

Then captured.

Trapped against the wall between his guy-tastic video gamer set-up and the door that would have been my freedom.

Freedom I no longer wanted—or cared about.

Yeah, just like that.

Yeah, just that perfectly.

This. I just wanted this. Being caged by his big body against my back, his arms against the wall, and his hot, heavy breaths against my neck...

Yeah, just like my best fantasies.

"Do you still not understand?" he grated into the shell of my ear. "Everything has changed. Everything *was* changed, from the moment I first saw you." He dragged a hand along the front of my body, fingers spread. "And touched you..."

As he came back up, it was skin to skin, fingers searching beneath my tank. He squeezed both aching swells of my breasts, tugging at the taut nipples until I moaned, before splaying fingers across my sternum.

"We—we still can't do this. Oh, *God*." That, choked out as he shifted his hold up by a few inches...enough to brace around just the bottom of my throat. Just when I thought he wouldn't uncover any more of my most illicit dreams...

"We...can't..."

I tried. So hard. Struggled for just one breath free of his scent, his energy, his power...

Not to be.

As thunder dominated the sky and the sea, his desire boomed through the very fiber of my muscles, the cells in my blood, the essence of my senses.

"I have thought of nothing *but* this." His lips serrated my ear. His body throbbed bigger and harder and tighter against me. His chest heaved at my shoulders. His abs tautened against my torso. His cock swelled into the crack of my ass.

"Damn." I gasped it when he reached down, locked both hands around my wrists, and then slammed them to the wall. As he leaned over me, our bodies fitted together. Our breaths billowed on the air, desperate huffs of mounting desire.

Another long moan curled out of me. Resisting him. Wanting him. Craving him...so damn badly. "Oh, damn it, damn it, damn it!"

The luxury of his hair cascaded over the back of my neck as he pressed in, openly biting the curve of my ear. "Tell me," he growled, "you have not thought of it too—at least a thousand times a day. A *million* times a day." He rolled his hips with that power so unique to him, making me groan again, before he offered, "Tell me, tupulai, that you have not thought of me, of *this*, and I shall set you free this moment."

But I didn't want to be set free. He knew it, and so did I.

I let one desperate sob spill out...just before my confession did. "I've thought of you every fucking second."

His sigh flooded my neck. "*Lucina.*"

Fireworks and music filled the night. The space around us turned into an otherworldly kaleidoscope.

Baby, we're not gonna stop...

"*Shiraz.*" It was still a protest, though I already accepted its utter futility. We were already a launched rocket, destined to burst no matter where the ashes fell. It was going to happen— he'd be inside me, and I'd welcome every inch of him— and yet I had to vocalize the protest however I still could, hoping it wove even threads of strength to the shields of my heart.

Who the hell was I kidding?

When it came to this man, my heart had no more borders left. It would give itself to him the same way my body did. Thoroughly. Openly. Knowing in the end, we'd both be nothing but detonated, wasted shells. Weak cinders in the sky.

Knowing it would be worth it.

If not...praying it would just kill us.

"Tell me again." His rasp warmed my hair as he moved my hands together on the wall, locking them beneath one of his. "Tell me how often you have thought of me. Needed me."

I jerked my head up, attempting a challenging glare, but he forced me forward with his jaw at my temple, his free hand at my waist. His fingers clenched hard, his grip a command... turning me to putty. I was nothing against his physical power, and I loved it. Surrounded by his dark, forceful scent and craving it. Even my clothes were flimsy barriers compared to his, cotton and lace battling his brocade and boots—

A point he proved the very next moment.

In a pair of sharp jerks, he pushed my shorts all the way to my ankles. They slipped off fully as he kicked my legs apart.

I turned to butter.

In another motion, he shoved my shirt up over my head,

stretching it across my shoulders to form a tight seal across my eyes. The cotton only reached the top of my nose, so I was free to gasp and moan for him as I pleased.

I was liquid.

My pussy took care of demonstrating that one. Wet...I'd never been so damn wet. I seeped with arousal, the drops tickling as they descended my channel. My musky scent bathed the air around us as my filthy prince, my unerring master, taunted me further with the sensual rolls of his body. As he tormented me further, I writhed harder. Brazenly campaigned for more contact with his huge, incredible body...

"Yes," I finally rasped. "I've thought of exactly this. Every minute, every hour. *This. You. Yesssss.*"

"Fuck." It was a rumble from his chest, twisted from the lock of his teeth, pouring over me like a spell. "You have consumed me too, tupulai." Wrapped his mastery tighter around me as he took down his fly in an urgent grind. "Made me think of nothing but this. Nothing but having you like this." He grunted softly, guiding his taut, hot tip closer to my pouting, soaked pussy.

I wasn't even liquid anymore. I was smoke. *His* smoke. Dipping and twisting, gossamer beneath his touch, blending with the air itself...everything but the tissues between my legs, which had become a furnace of ruthless, determined lust.

Despite that demand, I had more words of confession for him. Things that needed to be said, while I still had the shred of a mind left to form them.

"You know me."

And for the first time in my life, knew complete freedom.

"You see me."

And for the first time in my life, knew complete self-forgiveness.

"And yet, you still want me."

He slipped his free hand from my waist. Caressed it all the way up to my neck again—only this time, continued on until gripping into the back of my scalp. He scraped in deep, twisting until snapping my head back, exposing me for the ravishment of his deep but surprisingly soft kiss.

"See you," he echoed, thick and somber against my lips.

"Want you," he also repeated.

Then, just when I thought he'd invade me with another kiss, gave me something more devastating.

"Because I love you."

CHAPTER TWENTY-SIX

"I love you too. God help me...I do."

The tears were as impossible to fight as the words, unlocking even more shackles from my spirit, as he rewarded me for them by kissing me again. Deeper than before. Longer than before. And yes, oh yes, harder than before. As if restraints had been unlocked from him too.

A lot of restraints.

As our kiss lengthened, the change was even more evident. A new force moved through us and then between us, shock waves emanating from the perfect bomb of our new bond...our brilliant freedom. As Shiraz groaned, every inch of his giant body shuddered. As I answered, letting high-pitches of need twirl up my throat, every pore of my skin popped open, shivering for him. Surrendering to him.

Wild for him.

"Shiraz!" I panted, my muscles nearly spasming, my desire fully burning...my sex clenching, aching, needing. "Please!" I pushed back, reveling in the slick friction between our fitted forms but needing more. So much more.

Craving what he'd do if every single leash could be yanked off.

His hand, still coiled in my hair, jerked tight again. Against the column of my neck, he commanded, "Not the right way to ask, my sweet."

Hell.

He did see me.

Knew me.

Loved me.

Really, really loved me.

"Please," I repeated, a whisper my only capable sound now. "Please, Master..."

"Yessss," he hissed, moving with nips of lips and teeth down to my shoulder. The scrape of his stubble and the caress of his hair were nearly enough to bring my first orgasm. He had me that wound up. That hot inside. That wet and quivering for him.

"I... I— Master!"

"Yes, tupulai?"

Okay, he loved me. But he also knew exactly how to turn me into a babbling lunatic, using that lush, teasing voice while sluicing his cock along my weeping cleft. Appropriate, since I hadn't stopped crying—only now my sobs were a mix of adoration, vexation...frustration.

"*Please*, Master."

"Please what, sweet one?"

I tried to simply show him by bucking backward, angling my pussy for his invasion—but I was his complete prisoner, locked by the clamps of his hands and the firm brace of his legs.

"I... I need you...to...to..."

His sandpaper hum in my ear flowed along the energy of his body, turning him into a human power station. If the force of his electricity could be harnessed, the whole island would never have to worry about outages ever again.

"To what?" he prompted, each word charged with the same sizzling command. "Tell me, Lucina." He angled out, trailing the drops of his precome into the crack of my ass. "*Beg me.*"

And here I was, fantasizing about unlatching his final tethers—only to find that joke *so* turned on me. Again.

And treasuring my gratitude for the trick. Again.

The locks of my brain unclicked. Flew off into the kaleidoscope, incinerated by my lust...because I knew they were safe in his keeping. They fell away, making room for all the words he'd mandated. The confessions of every filthy craving he'd elicited in me, now pounding and throbbing and screaming from inside me...

"Fuck me," I moaned. "Damn it, Shiraz. I need you so deep inside me. Hard and deep and—" The grind of my own teeth was my interruption, rejoicing in the sound of ripping foil and unraveling latex. But as soon as he stretched the condom on, his hands were back on my body, fingers stabbing into my hips, bruising in their passion.

"Do not stop," he commanded from his own clenched teeth. "Beg me, little tupulai. Give me every fucking word."

I nodded, though it took me another moment to realize he wanted more than that. Had dictated it. He delivered a blatant reminder with a bold slap to my ass, making me jolt sharply—and mewl hard.

As he surged the first inch of his perfect penis into me.

"Yes," I groaned. "Oh yes, Master. More, please. More of your cock. I need it all. I need it fucking me"—a high, elated cry, as he filled me with the rest of that hard, pulsing stalk—"like that! *Please*...just like that..."

His guttural groan blended with my elated gasps. For several thrusts, and then several more, we were both wordless, weightless, mindless...lost to another dimension, the creation of space and time known only to our souls. It was fire and fury, surrender and salvation, an honesty of my body and mind I'd once written off as the stuff of pure fantasy—the kind of connection the universe would never gift to a strange, snarky, kinky creation like me. I'd been simply resigned to exist as a freak, never hoping to find any others like me. Sure as hell not expecting to find that soul mate inside a prince with the body of a Greek Olympian and the face of a Roman god.

Yet again, the joke was sure as fuck on me.

Yet again, I wept with pure joy about it.

As the lover of my wildest dreams delivered an even harsher smack to my other ass cheek.

"Spread your hands wider on the wall, my sweet. You shall need the leverage."

"Yes, Master."

I was even grateful for how he pushed my upper body down, letting my head drop between my shoulders. My grateful tears could splash freely to the floor—and I let them as he drew my senses even further outside my body, yanking my hips back with brutal tugs.

"Such a beautiful cunt." He reangled his cock, driving it down into me. "Beg me to ride it hard, tupulai. Use all the words so I am harder for you."

Shit, shit, shit.

Yes, yes, yes.

"Please...ride me, Master," I husked. "Fuck my cunt with your hard, huge dick."

He grunted ruthlessly. As his cock surged bigger against my walls.

"Beg me to hurt you with it."

"Yes. Please. Stab it into me until I scream. I need it. I need—"

"Say it, Lucina. I shall keep it safe. *Say it.*"

The tears worked into sobs, as the words were freed from my soul. "I need the pain. Give it to me. Take it *from* me..."

"Yes." He thundered into me, filling the room with the brutal smacks of his flesh upon mine, turning my body and my mind and my soul into the willing, wanton instruments of his desire...of *our* desire. Taking my lust and turning it into pure fire. Taking my surrender and turning it into his power—the life force he gave right back to me, burning and strong, in the form of every savage plunge into my hot, tight tunnel.

"My good—"

Thrusts and pain.

"—sweet—"

Desire and deliverance.

"—fuck!"

And then...transcendence.

The explosion of everything. The funneling of my senses, my sex, my essence, my world, into the words he growled out next, while going completely still inside me.

"Beg me again, Lucina." His breaths came heavy and fast on my neck. His chest heaved and pushed at my back. His hands came together, almost in prayer, as he rubbed both thumbs along the pulsing button at my core. "Beg me for my come."

"Yes!" I screamed it, beyond caring who heard, even over the revelry of the crowd and the ongoing booms of the fireworks. "Give it to me, Master. Give it all to me!"

A ferocious sound gripped him, pummeling his body as he penetrated me...and then poured into me. He pumped and pumped and pumped, his cock bursting and his fingers stroking, spiraling my own desire until I could do nothing but detonate, my knees giving out as my sex became a perfect, throbbing star. As the orgasm went on, Shiraz wrapped me tight against him, one arm supporting my weight as the other hand adored my clit, coaxing me toward another wash of incredible implosion.

"M-Master...oh, God...I can't..."

He turned me around—but only so he could press me back against the wall, letting my tank fall back into place, replacing that submissive darkness with an even stricter dominion: his midnight-colored stare.

"You can," he snarled. "And you will. Tell me you understand."

"Y-Yes," I sighed. "I... I understand."

The edges of his eyes creased a little, but that was his only sign of approval. I had no idea what his intention was, even as he withdrew his hand from my pussy in order to rip the condom off his cock, still beautiful and semihard.

"Keep your thighs spread, sweet one."

"Yes, Massss...*oh!*"

He angled his thigh in, replacing his hand with the fullness of his bulging quadricep. Because he was still mostly dressed, my clit had instant, extra abrasion from his pants. Arousal rushed in all over again, searing and pulsing and overwhelming, especially when he dipped his head to fully take my mouth beneath his.

At once, our bodies lurched toward each other. Pressed like power magnets, our seal interrupted only by the heat of his cock—unbelievably, jerking with fresh blood again. I reached down, savoring that heated flesh beneath my fingers, massaging the length of him in time to the rhythm he set for my pussy along his thigh.

"Va cock de Créacu." His whole body undulated, though

he stayed back far enough to keep our gazes locked. His face, set in beautiful lines of pure resolve, was changed by the fireworks from angel to demon and then back again. I watched, fascinated by the changes. I didn't care if we were in heaven or hell, as long as I could hold him like this...worship his magnificent dick like this. "That is...good, tupulai. So fucking good."

With my free hand, I gripped the bulge of his shoulder, conscious yet again of his royal formality and my near nudity. I was so turned on, there was probably a massive streak of my cream on his thigh now—but that consequence was on him. I'd only come in here to fix a friend's evening gown. Not that I complained one damn bit now, as my body raced toward its next shattering climax...

"Squeeze me harder, Lucina. *Fuck*...yessss...near the tip. I have more for you. Make me come again."

Well, hell. Now he was fulfilling fantasies I didn't know I had. But I could definitely go with the flow, especially when it involved attacking him like this. Making him growl at me like this.

"Like this, Master?"

"Yes. *Fuck*, yes." His voice was a sparse grate as he forced my body up and down on his leg. I gripped him tighter, fingers digging into his arm and stroking around his cock, as our lust climbed together...and our hearts collided once again.

We came in a rush, him then me, the hot spurt of his essence coating my fingers before the warm rush of mine drenched his leg. Colors cascaded over us, flashing in his eyes as we found the completion of our passion...the union of our hearts.

Still rocking our bodies in rhythmic sensuality, Shiraz

gazed down through the tumble of his hair, curling up one side of his lip. He was so replete with roguish satisfaction, my heart flipped three more times. We stayed locked like that, spinning down from our ecstasy as the last of the fireworks fizzled in the night. The crowd started strolling back inside, drawn by the promise of dancing and dessert service.

Shit-eating grin still plastered across his face, the prince of perfection finally extracted his thigh from my crotch. I couldn't help but glance down—and then let out a giggle. I was, after all, still me.

"Sure hope you have a discreet dry cleaners around here." In LA, I had a tidy list of recommendations.

Frown. A small and fast one, but as intense as if I'd jabbed myself. Hard.

LA. Even my brain had called it that.

Not *home.*

Not even a place I was looking forward to seeing inside the next twenty-four hours. Okay, yeah; I missed Mom and Ezra and margaritas and bobas—and perhaps, a little, the nice lady who really did rock my dry cleaning—but with the idea of going home, there came the inevitability of leaving Arcadia.

Of leaving...him.

Reactions tumbled around my senses, disjointed and uneven, as Shiraz bent to help me step back into my shorts. Sorrow. Longing. Loss. Aching. All the same stupid shit that'd bombarded during our moony stares across the lawn at each other, only worse. The conflict, and my anger about it, were only worsened by his silent tenderness about covering me again. *What the hell?* I'd been ready for this for days—but not anymore. This last hurrah fuck had changed everything, turning my heart back into a tomato in a pinball machine.

When he was done, he stood, preparing to turn—but still didn't leave well enough alone. One second I was still plastered to the wall, barely keeping my legs from crumbling beneath me; the next I was cradled against his brocaded chest, being hauled off to—

Where?

And why was I so panicked about it?

"Shiraz—"

"Ssshhh, tupulai."

Wasn't going to happen. Tomato. Pinball paddles. End of story.

Only it wasn't.

But how the hell was this different then the conflict I'd already been dealing with? Correction. *Had already dealt with.* I'd taken care of all this, damn it—especially after the "friendly little chat" with Ambyr at the infirmary. If I'd had any doubt regarding the last act of this screenplay, Miss Stratiss had handled the script notes and set me straight. She would be the Sandy in the flying car with his Danny. The Julia Roberts on the fire escape, wooed by his Richard Gere. The Baby having the time of her life on a dance floor with his Patrick Swayze. Shit. I bet Shiraz did those *Dirty Dancing* moves really well...

With *that* helpful thought consuming my mind, I was tossed onto one of the most luxurious beds on the planet. Comforter like a cloud. Pillows that swallowed my head. Best of all, his scent in all one thousand of the threads surely making up the linens. *Damn it.* In any other case, I'd be amenable to the not-so-subtle sleepover invitation. But right here and now, with the woman he had yet to hit with the engagement ring, likely searching for his spectacular ass this second?

"Shiraz—" I attempted again.

"Sssshhh," he ordered again—before tapping a light switch to reveal a walk-in closet more stunning than the bed. *Oh, my God.* It was an *amazing* closet. Cedar paneling. Backlit shoe racks. An automated tie tree.

The subject. Your brain. Now.

"Okay, come on." My spine straightened a little. Well, listen to that. I sounded calm. Even reasonable. Not freaking bad, considering the orgasming banshee I'd been fifteen minutes ago. "Seriously. Come *on*." A little more desperate, but I couldn't be blamed, considering how he shucked the boots and trousers before I could blink. "We can't do this. *Why* are you pushing this?"

No more playing coy, because he didn't. With one *thwick* of a side zipper from neck to waist, he freed himself from the doublet too—officially taking this conversation into the not-fucking-fair zone. "Pushing it" didn't come close to the weapon he'd just wielded in the form of his nudity. If Evrest and Samsyn wanted a real advantage over Arcadia's enemies, they could seriously look no further than their little brother's inked chest, perfect arms, etched abs, and flawless legs.

And that cock.

No woman—hell, probably not a lot of men either—would be able to ignore that virile masterpiece of a cock. I sure as hell couldn't...

Until he forced me to.

With another collection of efficient movements, he sheathed his long legs in a pair of black silk pajama bottoms. I'd never seen the look outside *Saturday Night Live* parodies of Hugh Hefner, but the Prince of Hotness redefined it in thirty seconds—the same way he took my expectations for this postcoital showdown in another direction I hadn't anticipated.

"You are here because I want you to be." He stated it while hitching a knee to the bed. Then the other. He scooted both forward until he was close enough to take my hands in his. "And because you cannot run out as fast from here."

Nervousness prompted my laugh.

He didn't join his own to it. Didn't even smile. Just kept staring, his hands around mine, both his thumbs rubbing my knuckles. He engulfed me with a midnight gaze and an energy I'd never felt from him before.

"I've never run from you, Shiraz." I gulped hard. *Shit.* Why was the Rock of Gibraltar back in my throat? Hadn't I wasted my allotment of tears for the whole year in one night? "Baby Jesus in a romper, I probably should have. But there you were, from the moment we met—"

"What?" It was a rough push of sound, honing my gaze once more on his lush lips. "What *was* I, Lucina?"

More tears pushed out. Guess I'd be overdrawn on the allotment.

"You were...everything." The wet heat trailed down my face. "All that I'd thought I'd never find or given up hope of knowing." A shrug lifted my shoulders as a watery smile broke past my lips. "A bad-ass prince who liked my jokes, knew all my fantasies..."

"And fell in love you anyway."

I pulled one hand free, pressing it to the plane of his jaw. "And made me fall in love with him."

It didn't spill out as I intended. It sounded like a damn murder confession, when regret wasn't what I felt at all. Exposing my heart to him had forced me to reopen to *myself.* To let him accept me and cherish me, I'd had to look in the mirror and do it for myself. I had to become better to *be* better...

for him.

Because of it, I'd never forget him.

Or let my heart stop thanking him.

But telling him that...

Why was it so impossible?

Because I never wanted him to stop looking at me...exactly like this. To form his hand over mine, meshing his fingers into mine, as he drenched me in both perfect oceans of his stare. To surround me with the force of his adoration and the strength of his affirmation for a week that had changed both of us. A week we'd turn into magic for two lifetimes...because that was our only damn choice.

He leaned a little closer. Looked a little deeper, as if he'd lost something and my face was the only place he'd find it. "By the Creator," he rasped. "You really do love me."

His declaration was everything I hadn't been capable of. Fervent. Real. Dripping with the honesty of his heart. Incredible man. Perfect prince. Already my hero.

I kissed him with my thanks. Just once. Very softly. "Yeah, gorgeous. I do."

He engulfed both my hands tightly again. Moved those clasps down to the tiny space between our knees as he dipped his head toward mine, directly lining up our gazes.

"Then marry me."

CHAPTER TWENTY-SEVEN

I almost laughed.

But holy shit...he wasn't kidding.

Not in this reality or any dimension beyond it.

"You—you're—" I sent a wad of lead back down my throat in order to finish "—you're serious."

His lips parted. Lifted a little, hesitant but persistent, before he pushed forward, pressing them to mine. He only pulled back by an inch—too far but not far enough—before answering, "Yes, *raismette*. I am."

Raismette.

Fuck.

Literally translated, it meant *reason*. But the bigger context...

Was huge.

As in, the kind of shit an Arcadian man reserved for his life mate. The woman he considered his partner, his best friend.

His wife.

Everything was real but surreal. My heart throbbed in time to the rush of the waves outside but felt just as far away. My lungs pumped air in slices blazing hot and then arctic cold. My eyes studied the devastating man before me but, through the perspective of my heart, saw much more. The heart he was offering in return. The life he was offering. The future by his side...

Shit.

Shit.

No.

"No."

He flinched as if I'd struck him. I didn't blame him. At the same time, I was damn glad for the distance. Or was I? It didn't help the strange chill that coursed over my whole body, brought on by complete shock. No. Complete terror.

But I didn't tell him that. Damn it, I couldn't. What woman in their right mind willingly said no when a man—*a prince*—like Shiraz Noir Cimarron proposed?

A woman who *wasn't* in their right mind.

A person who planned everyone else's happy-ever-after because she was too messed up to ever get *hers* right. Who had no idea how a real relationship even worked, because she needed to be spanked and tamed before getting off. Who had built up so many walls of snark and sarcasm to guard her spirit, she'd even written herself off as a crazy-ass little brat.

She wasn't wife material.

She wouldn't ever be.

"Shiraz"—despite his fuck-you jolt, I kept one of his hands trapped in both of mine—"I love you. *I do.* But I can't—sheez, *we* just can't..." Lightbulbs flared in my brain. A whole bank of them, forming one word. "Ambyr." I let his hand drop. "This is the part you reserved for Ambyr, remember?"

"*Fuck.*" He shot off the bed like an F-18 launched off a battle carrier. Glared at me with rocket-hot eyes. "This is the part, damn it, where I remind *you* what I said earlier."

I forced in a forbearing breath. "That you're not proposing to her."

With a hand in his hair, he exhaled. "Yes."

"Not tonight."

"Not *ever*."

The jets re-ignited in his eyes. A matching fire, of pure confusion, blazed through my psyche. "No," I finally blurted. "That's not the deal."

Crazily, he laughed. Just a short spurt, as both his hands locked to those sinewy hips, but it threw me even more off-keel as he drawled, "The...deal?"

Huff. Not a pleasant one. Did he really need this all spelled out? "The deal where you finally get to make the difference. Where you stop being the damn lap dog."

Hell. He wasn't making this easy, still silently challenging me by canting his head to one side. With neck *and* hair porn added to the given temptation of his torso and that happy trail into his pants, it was a wonder I could still speak. But I did, damn it—and meant every word that rasped out.

"You've been waiting for this chance, Shiraz. You deserve it. Finally, everyone in Arcadia will recognize you as the hero you are...when you make one of their own your princess."

His head came back up. As it did, fresh sharpness took over his face—something close to another laugh but not getting there.

"Is that what you think I want?" he charged softly. "To be 'recognized' as a hero?"

Confusion rockets, re-engage. "Isn't it?"

Deep valleys formed across his forehead. His lower lip jutted, as an inner dilemma racked him. He looked ready to either put his head into the wall or between my thighs. For the sake of my sanity, I hoped he did neither.

"I never gave a flying fuck about being publicly hailed as a 'hero,' Lucina. I simply wanted to do something worthy of the word—to give back, in some meaningful way, to my people."

The bafflement burners were at full power now. "And you didn't think you were doing that by successfully running the business of the country?"

"That was my job," he explained. "Not my sacrifice."

"And marrying Ambyr would have been that sacrifice."

The tension in his face radiated down his body. "Yes," he bit out.

My follow-up brimmed right to the surface. I didn't want to ask it. I couldn't *not* ask it.

"So what changed?"

Just like that, all the tautness left him. His hands slipped from his waist as an adoring smile lifted his lips—and impaled its brilliance into me.

"You got here."

Heart soaring and then tumbling. Soul rejoicing...and then weeping. This still changed *nothing*. "So...the sacrifice thing is now old news?"

He shook his head slowly. "No. It simply changed."

I forced out a soft laugh. Something had to balance out the weirdness of his energy. Not only because of its sobriety. It was his new *serenity*...

"Changed...to what?"

He began his answer with a backward step. Right into his closet. As I looked on, letting my puzzlement show, he pulled out a square of neatly folded clothing. Plunked it onto the bed in front of me. Only after a long scrutiny did I finally comprehend what I gawked at. That tangled pattern of tan, brown, and olive...

It was military camouflage.

"Our forces going for the special operations training with the Americans..."

It was my turn to jolt. As in a holy-freaking-God *jolt*. "Wh-What?"

"They need more technical specialists," he went on, as if simply telling me the plot of some new book he'd read instead of a nuclear freaking bomb of information. "Personnel who can take data from multiple sources and then swiftly process it into productive action for a huge team of operatives." He crossed his arms, flashing a proud grin. "Sort of like M16 and James Bond, only with better gadgets."

"Gadgets." It spat out before I could help it, though I was stunned coherent words were even a thing for me right now. It was as ambushed as my heart and my soul. I splashed through the goo of another dimension, like Neo struggling to make sense of a new reality in *The Matrix*. Trouble was, the man I loved was still strolling around on the other side of the truth, gleefully talking about James fucking Bond.

"Quite a few, actually. There has been a great deal of preprogram reading to get through."

All right, so he didn't sound gleeful. He was pragmatic to the point of sexy, his posture hoisted by new professionalism, his gaze resolute and committed.

In short, exactly how he'd been when I first met him.

Only tomorrow, he wouldn't be putting on a three-piece suit and then walking to his office in the next building.

Tomorrow, he'd be getting dressed in all this soldier shit— and going God knew where in the world to put his skills put to the test.

To lay his life on the line for his country.

The thought was a brand-new mortar shell in my psyche, cratering me wider. Mortifying me deeper.

And pissing me the hell off.

Which finally gave me back my voice.

"You're fuckingkiddingme." The sound of my incensement brought extra fortitude. It highlighted how crazy *he* sounded. "Right? That's it, isn't it? You're kidding about this shit, just so I'll say yes to your crazy proposal."

Shiraz gave me another swami of serenity look. *Shit*...as if he'd expected exactly what I'd say. Glaring proof? He reached to the camo pile, yanking at the garment on top. It was a basic military uniform jacket, with an imprinted nametag attached over the front pocket.

CIMARRON

"Damn it," I rasped.

"So will you say yes to my crazy proposal?"

I struggled to catch my breath.

I struggled to catch my *thoughts*.

I struggled to grasp every damn corner my senses had turned in the last freaking hour.

He'd tricked me. Made love to me. Proposed to me. Then terrified the living crap out of me.

But was that the real truth?

I spun away. From the question...from him. And God, if I could have done so, even from myself.

As soon as my legs dangled over the edge of the bed, I dropped my head between them. Fought to pull in cleansing air, easing the acid in my gut at least so I wouldn't hurl on his Turkish rug.

In the center of my vision, a pair of hands appeared. Strong and forceful, with fingers beckoning me to hang on— even now. God help me, especially now.

"Luci—"

I slapped a feeble hand over his lips, forcing him to stop. "Shiraz. Please." Spread my fingers across the carved beauty of his jaw. His stubble stabbed my palm, a strange but welcome anchor to reality.

To the reality I had to give him.

For which I already hated myself.

I let my head drop lower.

"Tupulai." His whisper was a plea, stumbling out of him.

I hated myself even more.

"Shiraz." *Just do it. Just get it over with.* "I'm...I'm scared. Too scared. I...I can't do this. I can't—"

"Sssshhh." He scooted closer. "Breathe, sweet one." Then even closer, with his knees against my feet, his arms around my shoulders, and his lips pressed deep in my hair. "It is only for six months, Lucina," he murmured, his tone so steadfast, thinking he was actually helping. "Only six months, all right? And it is only missions for training. It will be over before we know it."

It killed—it *more* than killed—but I forced my head back up, tilting my face to bring his gaze direct with mine. I owed him that.

God. I owed him so much *more* than that. But this was what I could give. Perhaps all I'd ever be able to give. The truth, even this brutal and bitter, wasn't just what he required as a prince or needed as a man. It was what he deserved—as a person. The individual of honesty, bravery, and reality who had captured my heart and soul like none other.

I wouldn't be able to lessen the blow but tried anyway, pushing a smile through my new tears...pressing a hand to the space between the dove and the hawk, where I could feel the beat of his amazing heart beyond the layers of taut muscle.

"Listen to me, Shiraz Noir." My voice shook, but at least my hand didn't. "Those bastards would be lucky to have you for six days, let alone six months. You have got this shit—and you're going to be amazing at it."

As I suspected, that hardly touched his concern—or the flood of my tears. I was beyond trying to stop myself. Beyond trying to pretend the next truth I gave him wasn't one whopper of pain—for us both.

"Then why are you crying again, sweet one?" He wrapped his hand around mine, lifting it to his lips. "Why are you so frightened, Lucina?"

Shit, shit, shit.

"Because I've been frightened since the second you proposed."

CHAPTER TWENTY-EIGHT

Note to self. Drinking a salted-caramel boba in the park beats sweating in the gym every time, all the time.

As notes went, it was okay—but it sure as hell beat the other note. Yeah, the one that'd been pinned to the top of the stack for so long, it should have been worn and yellow, even in the gray matter, by now. It had been nearly four months since I'd put it in—the day I'd gotten back to LA from Arcadia, tired and lonely and hating what I'd done to the man I'd claimed to love.

Fraud.

There was no other word for what I still felt like, even now, for what I'd done to him that night. For what I'd said, even if every word had been the complete truth.

I can't be your princess. I would barely know how to be your damn wife.

We've been living in a fantasy. An amazing one. But marriage isn't a fantasy.

I don't know how to be there for you. I can barely be there for myself.

You deserve a woman who will serve you and Arcadia. Who won't put her entire foot in her mouth at some state dinner, before salads are even cleared.

You need a woman you can be proud of.

You need a woman who knows what family really means...

My stomach fought the boba as the memories hit like

punches—of how I'd pummeled him with every damn syllable. Of how he'd pulled away a little more with every line I'd sobbed, his checks gaunt and his gaze steely, having to accept the truth I already had. Another melodramatic oldie was right on the money.

Sometimes love just ain't enough.

As the refrain haunted my head, my four-month-old note fluttered to the top of the stack once more.

Note to self. This really sucks.

"You're going to stay there for a good long time, huh?"

My mind only answered with more of that damn song.

But there's a danger in loving somebody too much...and it's bad when you know it's your heart you can't trust...there's a reason why people don't stay where they are...

"Baby, sometimes love just ain't enough."

I sang the last of it in a whisper—vowing not to mix tears into my boba. The thing was salted already, damn it—and by the time I got done repaying the bank of self-pity, I'd be an old woman.

Determined huff. "Get your act together, Lucina Louise. You came here to enjoy the day, so fucking enjoy it."

There was a lot to help with that. Mid-April in Ocean View Park was nothing short of awesome. The grass was fragrant, the Pacific air crisp, and there was even a bunch of kids on spring break, tossing Frisbees and flying kites on the rolling hills. Across the street and the beach, out on the ocean, a handful of surfers sat on their boards, waiting for the last sets of the morning.

I pulled in air through my nose. Released it slowly through my mouth. I could do this. I could look out on the waves and not ache for the oceans in Shiraz's eyes. I could enjoy the breeze in my hair and not yearn for it to be his long, confident fingers. I could watch a red and gold kite dance on the air and not be reminded of palais banners.

I could sit for more than five minutes and not wish for a damn transporter switch, coordinates keyed in for Arcadia.

God, how I missed it.

All of it.

Every part of the fantasy, sometimes seeming just a taunting dream now, dangling out of my reach. The island that gave me so much. The week that had changed me for good.

Never to be again.

I set the boba down with a slam, scooping up my cell instead. Like an addict needing a hit, I went for the text messages. None from any unidentified numbers, born from the distant hope Shiraz would get lonely on his training adventures and reach out, but plenty from Crista and Jayd. Thank God. They were my willing suppliers, feeding my hunger for all images Arcadia. I stored everything carefully, according to categories—even some for parts of the island I'd never seen. The breathtaking cliffs and coves of Asuman. The majestic mountain vistas of Tahreuse. The sprawling ranches of the central valley and Faisant Township. And then my two favorites: springtime shots from the Palais Arcadia and Endigoh Beach.

Each image seemed more extraordinary than the last. It was a travelogue of Technicolor flowers, cerulean waters, sweeping skies, and joy-filled people...

Except for one.

The one not in any pictures because he'd left Arcadia the same day I did. Cast me a stare the texture of stone as our paths had crossed on the new Sancti tarmac—his leading to a waiting troop helicopter, mine to the twelve-passenger plane which would at last fly me to Athens.

Then he'd disappeared...into my dreams.

And every other thought I possessed. And every other breath in my lungs.

And *every* damn pang in my heart.

I darkened the screen. Swiped two more drops off my cheeks, making the boo-hoo bankers rejoice. Damn glad someone was.

This would get better, damn it.

It had to.

In the meantime, I was content to suck back the boba... and wallow.

"Yes, I may have hurt you," I whisper-sung. "But I did not desert y—"

I stopped, half-puzzled and half-alarmed, as a shadow fell over the bench. The shade from a really big man, judging from the size fourteens filling out the lime-green flip-flops stepping into my view. My stare climbed tree trunk legs attached to those feet, clad in green and pink board shorts. Then a massive torso on top of *that*, covered in a white wife beater. Prominent lips in the man's bold Roman face released a distinct baritone.

"Any more seats left at this weep-fest?"

"Oh, my *God.*" I leapt up so fast, tackle hugging and boba drowning him in one elated surge. "Samsyn. Holy *shit*, how did you—why are you—*what* are you doing here?"

"Wearing your drink, apparently," the prince grumbled while sitting down. Good thing the bench was bolted to the ground, since his weight creaked and shook the boards of the little wooden structure.

"Sorry, sorry, sorry." I yanked a packet of tissues from my purse and shoved them at him.

Samsyn shrugged. "It smells nice, at least."

"By the Creator, I'm just so excited to—" My own gasp cut it short. I pressed fingertips to my lips, stunned as if I'd invented a fun new profanity. Samsyn, even covered from hip to ankle in salted-caramel boba, join me in the laugh.

"Excited little dinné," he rumbled good-naturedly. "Check *that* box."

As rapidly as my elation had hit, it drained away. I gaped at him, literally shivering in the warm morning. "Wait a second. *Should* I be excited?" My gaze narrowed. "Why *are* you here?" I gulped hard. "Shit. Is it...Shiraz? What happened?"

"Okay, chill the hissy, little *wahine*."

"Huh?"

"Your broheim Ezra gave me the skinny on finding you here. Says you like checking out the scene. He says it is off the Richter."

"*Huh?*"

He jerked his head at the parking lot that paralleled the water. "Was just hanging with some surfers and picked up the vibe. Ripping cool, eh, beach bunny?"

I pretended there was something on my nose. "Yeah." I hid my grin behind my hand. "That's...ummm...special, Syn."

I didn't have the heart to break the news that surfer slang and a giant Arcadian in a wife beater weren't a "ripping cool" mix. *Later*, I promised the universe. Right now, I needed him focused on the only subject that mattered here. *Shiraz*. At least if Samsyn was cutting loose with the *hang tens* and *let's shreds*, I took heart that his little brother wasn't lying in a ditch somewhere, mortally wounded.

"So...Shiraz is okay, then," I finally prompted—only to endure another shiver as Samsyn's features crunched into a guarded frown.

After pulling in a long breath, he murmured. "Define 'okay.'"

I kept my ass perched on the edge of the seat. Coiled my hands in my lap, working them nervously into each other. "Define '*not* okay.'"

A pair of Ray-Bans were hiked up behind his ears, holding back his dark-chestnut mane. The thick stuff tumbled free as he dropped the shades over his eyes, fixing his regard out toward the ocean. Weirdly, he reminded me of Tom Skerritt in *Top Gun*, giving a paternal pep talk to Tom Cruise's wigged-out Maverick. Hmm. I'd always wanted a bomber jacket.

"Operationally, Shiraz is one of the best comm techs I have ever seen in the field. He is a born natural for the task and has earned the respect and admiration of everyone who works with him. I am fucking proud of him, as his commander and as his brother, and damn glad we shall be able to call on him during times of crisis in Arcadia." He touched a forefinger to the space between his brows and then lifted it above his head and circled it twice. "Which, the Creator willing, shall *not* be often."

"That all...sounds good." I dipped my head, openly questioning him with my stare. "So what's the problem?"

Samsyn's nostrils flared. He leaned his head back a little, exposing the tension of his jaw to the full light of the sun. "The man can guide a team of snipers down the side of a volcano and through a village full of hostiles, but his own heart is as lost as a glass shard in a lake." Up went the sunglasses again—as he turned the full power of his silver-blue gaze on me. "And I have been told, by some helpful little birds back home, that *you* might be that very special glass."

Openly, I fidgeted. Privately, I tried to breathe away the wild thunder in my chest. No good. With tight teeth, I dealt with the tumult. Finally muttered, offering him a wad of tissues from my purse, "Helpful little birds, my ass."

"Jayd and Crista are as worried about him as I am," he rebutted. "We all are—except, perhaps, for my parents." His expression discernibly tightened, though I couldn't tell if the cause was the subject of his parents or the mess along his leg. "Sometimes, leaving them out of this kind of shit is better for all concerned."

Okay, it *was* about Ardent and Xaria. "And sometimes, maybe they can help." I jerked a little at the new intensity in his stare—bordering now on a glare—but squared my shoulders a little higher. "Maybe you should enlist the queen mother and king father to help talk some sense into your hopeless romantic of a sibling."

Inside an instant, the Syn scowl was gone—overtaken by a laugh so hard, his head fell back. "Ohhhh, Lucina. That made up for turning me into a walking sweet stick." He cocked a broad smile back my way. "Over the years, we have used many words with which to identify Shiraz Noir. *Hopeless* has never been one of them—and neither has *romantic*."

"Then perhaps you all need to remind him of that?" I arched peeved brows. "Because he sure as hell wouldn't hear it from me." Recognizing I'd all but admitted to what happened with Shiraz now, I lunged to my feet, needing to pace out my frustration. The warrior had gotten me started; he was sure as hell going to hear *my* side of the story now. "We shared...moments, okay? And they were amazing, incredible, astounding..."

I stopped, watching a flurry of dandelion stars swirl by on

the breeze. One of the stems stopped, caught on a crosswind.

Suspended...in a moment.

"Perfect," I rasped before the wisp as well my senses tumbled back to terra firma. "Anyway." I cleared my throat. "You get the idea, yeah?"

Samsyn huffed out a laugh. "To be honest, Lucina, I do not." He answered my scowl with a slow shake of his head. "Moments," he repeated, chuckling again. "Are you certain it was actually my brother Shiraz with you? A little leaner and prettier than me? Dark-blue eyes, smells fairly nice?"

He had to remind me.

And confuse me.

I plunked back down. Flattened my lips. "You're missing the fucking point."

"Which is?"

"That they were just moments, Samsyn—and no matter how axis-altering they were, we can't spin them into anything more." I gazed out toward the sea, wishing the clarification for all of this would just get farted across the sky in wisps out the back of a skywriting plane. "I'm not right for him, damn it." *Just. Say. It.* "I'm...not good enough."

He let me sit with that disgusting tidbit as he rose and walked the tissue to a trash can. When he returned, he didn't sit again. Faced the bench with both hands jammed into his pockets, stance deceptively casual. His gaze studied every person in the park. "That was a sincere admission," he offered. "Thank you."

"You're welcome."

"Now I shall ask for another."

My hands twisted together again. "Go for it."

He tilted his head so our gazes fully met. "Do you love

him?"

Half a second—if that—clicked before my reply. "With all my heart and soul, Samsyn."

He looked back toward the grass. "Well, that is bloody good enough for me."

I let a rough sound rush up my throat. "No, damn it." I shoved back to my feet. "It's *not* good enough. Shiraz can't see it, but I need *you* to, okay?" I grabbed him by the sturdy crook of his elbow. "Samsyn, he's a *prince*—"

"That has *not* escaped my attention."

"—and he needs a woman by his side worthy of being called a princess," I powered on, ignoring his sarcasm. "A *princess*, okay? He doesn't get that right now because he's thinking with his dick instead of his brain, but one day, he's going to wake the hell up and remember it—as well as the duty to his people that he holds so high."

Somewhere along the line, the man had cocked a noticeable brow at me. Now the other jumped up, making it a matched set. "And *that* is when you think he will gravitate back to Ambyr Stratiss?"

"Maybe," I murmured, not really meaning it. Picturing Shiraz with the woman, complete with her entitlement issues, brought on a fresh shiver. "Or maybe not. It doesn't have to be her. There are lots of other fish in the Arcadian Sea, right?"

Samsyn pivoted. Planted his feet a little wider apart. Sheez. Even here, a few miles up the coast from Muscle Beach, the guy was a formidable sight when he hit confrontation mode. Nevertheless, his answering tone was mild. "I believe you might be missing the point."

I rocked back, jabbing a finger. "Good try but no dice. *You're* missing *mine*. Time is going to take care of this; you'll see. A couple more months out in the jungle, or wherever the hell you've sent him, and your little brother will come home ready to settle down and think logically about an *acceptable* bride." My dropped gaze fell on my spilled boba cup. As I retrieved it and headed to the trash can myself, I continued, "And this is the part where your parents can be important."

"My *parents*?" His head whipped like I'd said *terrorists*. "Why the hell—" He pinched it off, clearly deciding on a different tack. "My parents have nothing to contribute to this subject."

"Are you kidding? They have *everything* to contribute. What the hell with the glare? You hate saying I'm right?" I refrained from adding *asshole*, but in another minute, he'd be sticking a perfect landing there without my help.

He sat back down, again with a pretense of relaxation. "I am saying you might not have all the facts."

"Facts," I shot back. "Like how Xaria and Ardent are a walking, talking example that prearranged marriage *can* work? That mutual respect and friendship can, over time, become love?"

His pose, with one elbow draped over the back of the bench, hardly shifted. "Who told you that?"

"Shiraz," I supplied. "On the first day I was in Arcadia. There's a photo of your mom and dad on his desk. He told me all about the old tradition of the Distinct and about how the two of them made the situation work." I sat back down too. "They're happy, Samsyn."

"They are a sham, Lucina."

My turn for the snapping head. Not that my glue gun of a stare altered his granite mien. "Excuse the hell out of me?"

He let his elbow drop—all the way to his knee. Parked his

other one the same way and then steepled his fingers. "What I am about to tell you cannot leave this conversation. Not even Shiraz can know."

"Sure. I mean, fine. Okay." Since I'd only see Shiraz again on the covers of gossip mags, that was a no-brainer.

His fingers visibly pressed harder to each other. His jaw tautened. "My mother and father...can barely stand being in the same room together."

"Huh?" Another brainless reaction—though pretty fucking justified.

"They have not slept in the same bed for over ten years," he stated, keeping his voice low. "Perhaps before that. There have even been whispers that Jayd is not truly of my father's seed."

"Shit." My voice was just as soft. "Are...are you sure?"

"About Jayd's heritage?" His nostrils flared. "Of course not. I personally discovered my father's infidelity by accident, when I was eighteen. Not long after that, I learned my mother's own adultery was just as extensive. After that, I was more aware of the court whisperings, but it was several more years before I had knowledge of that particular gem." He pushed his hands fully together, stabbing them against the tense line of his lips. "By then, Jayd was starting college, a young woman, and I was running kingdom security. I could only make sure the gossips were bribed into silence and that any evidence of her illegitimacy was found and then destroyed."

"Did you find any?" I leaned forward to ask it.

"No." The stress in his jaw spread across his face. "But that does not stop me from dreading the day something surfaces."

"Or from dealing with that daily backache." I jerked up half a smile in response to his baffled glance. "From hauling the weight of keeping it from her?" I added, with new revelation, "And Evrest and Shiraz too, right?"

He picked up on the allegation in my voice. "She is their sister through and through, in the fabric of their hearts, just as she is in mine," he explained. "But when secrets fill more ears, they are more at risk of being spilled." He tugged at a caramel-stained corner of his shorts. "Even when the intention is innocent."

I nodded, however reluctantly. One look toward the western foothills, where a collection of white letters spelled out H-O-L-L-Y-W-O-O-D, provided all the backup his statement needed. In this part of the world, no secret was innocent. A lot of intentions weren't, either.

I finally sat back. As I got busy collecting my jaw off the ground, Samsyn had the nerve to grin through a huff. "You look like a woman enlightened."

I rolled my head in a figure eight, going for my mental comfort food of snark. "You could sure as fuck say that."

"Good." His military precision was back in full glory. "Now you have some accurate intel to inform your decision for a change."

I unleashed a new glare on him. "Inform *what* decision? Samsyn, this changes..."

Nothing.

Oh, hell.

It changed everything.

My fade into amazement was filled by his cocky chuckle. "You were saying, Miss Fava?" He waved a regal hand. "Go on. I need to hear this. You were saying, as before then—about not being 'good enough,' even after learning about all the colorful closet skeletons of our family? Was that the part that did not change? Or maybe it was the story about my parents being the walking advertisements for the success of arranged marriage. Do not leave *that* shit out. It is my favorite."

I did it. I really curled up a fist and socked Prince Samsyn of Arcadia in his huge, arrogant shoulder. Didn't matter that it felt like punching a lead pipe or that his whole form shook with his answering snicker. I felt better. A little.

"Well," I finally muttered. "You sure as hell found a good way to pay me back for the boba."

He stood, still smirking, though reestablished his military stance. Even reparked the sunglasses over his eyes. "No," he stated while pulling a crisp white envelope out of his shorts pocket. It was definitely for me. I spotted my name in swooping letters. "*This* is proper payback."

I took it from him—with shaking fingers. "Wh-What is..."

"Just look at it." His tone was back to military mode too. The commanding officer part. "And as you do, know two things."

I arched a brow while sliding a thumb under the flap. "Two things I *want* to know?"

I was pretty sure, beneath the shades, his ice-blue eyes executed a perfect barrel roll. "Number one: I have some meetings up at Hueneme today and will not be leaving from LAX until tomorrow morning."

Okkaaayyy.

Curiosity. Spiked.

"What's number two?"

"The training team is on a few days of leave." He paused before stabbing me with the inevitable conclusion to that. "Shiraz is enjoying it at home, in the palais." He added a blatant grimace. "'Enjoying' being a relative term for my brother right now."

The man actually made that his parting shot.

In a little disbelief, I watched him cover the walk back to the parking lot with wide, sure strides. A group of women in business suits, enjoying an early lunch break in the park, boldly gawked as he strode by. Their faces fell when his wedding ring glinted in the sun. There went another Cimarron man, shattering libidos and hearts in his wake.

The thought would've likely spurred a laugh—if I wasn't so terrified of what this damn envelope contained. I looked down at the expensive vellum inside the flap. My head throbbed. My heart played a drum solo against my ribs. I felt like Bella Swan, splashing across an Italian fountain on the way to her possible doom.

I took a huge, long breath.

Tugged at the paper inside.

"Time to get wet, Luce."

I'd had to say it.

Because the next moment, I turned it into prophecy. New tears burst, drenching my cheeks, as my eyes skimmed down the imprinted text inside and zoomed in on the hand-written note at the bottom.

Lucy:
Please come.
We all need you here.
You are family.
Jayd

Everything mushed together. The words on the page. The sun and the grass and the waves. Hard, stupid crying had that effect on the world, I guess.

So did the power of six dumb little letters, formed into a word that had never meant a thing to me.

And now meant everything.

Family.

CHAPTER TWENTY-NINE

"I'm wondering if I should pinch myself."

It was an honest confession, murmured to the princess with the black curls and opaline eyes, who rewarded me with a soft giggle.

Had it been only three days since my visit to the beach in LA? Seventy-two hours, and my life had careened in a way I'd never expected—or dreamed. Ergo, the whole pinching-myself-as-a-viable-option line, enforced by a brilliant Arcadian afternoon. The sun was golden and warm, the wind salty and bold, the air fragrant with lavender, orange, and eucalyptus.

So maybe the pinching wouldn't be happening—despite the direction I knew this dream was soon going to take.

Oh God, oh God, oh God.

I had no idea what I even prayed for. The guts to see the dream through...or the hope it happened like all my other weird dreams, with a pool full of chocolate, a diving board, and Henry Cavill waiting for me in the shallow end?

Only lately, Henry had taken a hike. For the last four months, it had been Shiraz in the pool.

It was Shiraz...everywhere.

Jayd squeed in delight, joined by an equally effusive Ezra, jolting me back to the moment at hand. Their swoons blended with similar sounds from the group gathered in the private royal garden for Camellia's baby shower. The area, usually a scene of

Renaissance-inspired tranquility, had been turned into a lush jungle for the occasion, in honor of the nursery décor picked out by Evrest and Camellia for Leo, the royal firstborn on his way. A giant prop elephant helped Camellia preside over the event. An aviary of tropical birds was decorated with red and gold bunting. There was even a pair of "rhinos" peeking from the waters of the Elizabethan fountain.

The crowd's enthusiasm was on theme too. Camellia, an image of glowing and healthy pregnancy, held up the latest item she'd unwrapped from the mountain of presents. A baby-sized safari outfit was accompanied by a jungle-themed playmobile.

"Holy shit," Ez murmured. "Cuteness in khaki."

"Right?" Jayd shoulder-bumped him, confirming the instant friendship I'd predicted before Ez and I even disembarked the plane yesterday.

"I'd rock that outfit." Ez bit into a leopard-spotted cake pop. "Just sayin'."

"That settles it." Jayd raised her voice, announcing it to the whole group. "Everyone lock up your daughters. My nephew shall be the hottest-dressed male in the land."

As the crowd laughed, Brooke wagged a saucy finger on the air. "But not the hottest in *other* arenas, sister."

Jayd scowled. "Is this a new entry in the *ew* zone, B?"

"Depends on who you ask."

The new comment made everyone twist around, slamming Brooke's corner of the garden with a flood of feminine interest. That was what happened when one's mountain of a husband appeared on the scene—and then sidled up behind her, nuzzling her ear with brazen intent.

Brooke giggled and then batted at Samsyn. "All right, big guy. Behave."

He grunted. "My ability to...*behave*...was not what you just bragged about, woman."

"Okay," Jayd interjected. "*Now* this is an *ew*."

I would have joined in the new round of laughs at that—except for recognizing, courtesy of the dark bergamot scent on the air, that Syn hadn't crashed the shower alone. I breathed in deeper, just to be sure—and dared a single look back, farther into the shadows of the portico behind Samsyn.

Oh God, oh God, oh God.

It was him.

More perfect, sleek, elegant, and magnificent than even the chocolate dreams had formed of him. And damn it, despite the balmy day, he'd picked black as a fashion statement. He was always breathtaking in black. His long-sleeve polo hugged his torso, more defined by the training missions. His black fatigues were tucked into scuffed, rubber-soled black boots covering up to his calves, undone laces draped over the front of his legs. But that wasn't the finish of the look. That came from his eyes, solemn as ink from Poe's own pen, staring without feeling from atop his angled cheekbones.

Shit. Samsyn hadn't been exaggerating.

Shard of glass. Midnight lake.

I dug my heels into the grass, fighting the longing to run to him.

Stick to the plan.

Samsyn knew what he was doing. He'd delivered as promised, getting his stubborn brother here. I just had to wait until he guided Shiraz over to this side of the party. My chair was on the way to the food table. Wasn't that where the guys ended up at something like this?

"As usual, Jayd has called the play perfectly."

Everyone turned once again—in glaring curiosity. I had to admit, I joined them. The commentary wasn't Samsyn's or Shiraz's—or even that of Jagger Fox, who stepped out from behind Samsyn's far side. The line had come from a fourth man, rocking the long legs and burnished skin of a Cimarron, only with whisky-colored hair and blunter features. He was attractive but not stunning, but maybe that had more to do with his lounge lizard swagger and his shark bite smile.

Fish are friends, buddy, not food.

Thank fuck Jayd clearly shared the conclusion. "Tytan," she issued through tight lips, her nod emulating the energy. "How...gracious...of you to make an appearance in Sancti."

Ezra emitted a soft hum. "Ooooo, honey. Need a little ranch dressing for that bitter subtext?"

"How about some battery acid?" she gritted back. "To toss on his smug face?"

She barely veiled the glare as Tytan Cimarron slither-stepped closer—an event I would have taken more keen notice in, except that it set Shiraz into motion too. In full big brother mode, he followed just steps behind his cousin. Focused protectiveness was stamped across his face.

Until his gaze descended on me.

Locked on me.

Narrowed on me.

Burned into me.

Destroyed me.

One damn second—and time dropped away. One damn second, and we were back in his apartment, clutching each other in the goodbye I'd forced, clinging to my stubborn dictates of "what was best for him." One damn second, and he was back on his knees in front of the bed, rasping harsh pleas into my ear, drenching my face with his heartbroken tears...

One damn second—

I'd made him endure all over again.

He was *not* happy about that. Showed me so by dropping his gaze to my feet—and looking like he might just spit on them. By letting the fists at his side unfurl into long-fingered daggers—with which he mentally impaled me.

By wheeling from me in one fierce sweep and marching his gorgeous ass toward the small semicircle of lawn in front of Camellia.

Mentally, I forecasted the rest of his path. He was headed toward the gate on the other side of the garden, the one leading directly to the palais staff stairwell. Though the flights extended down the cliff and eventually to the beach, they also had landings at every level, with doorways leading inside the building—leaving no mystery about his new plan. Even if I gave chase, he'd lose me after just a couple of turns in the labyrinth of back hallways. With my shitty sense of direction, they'd have to send search-and-rescue dogs after *me* in the maze.

I couldn't let him do it.

I wouldn't.

The entire journey here, I'd agonized about what to actually say when I did. Such stupidity. One moment being near him again, and I already knew. One second seeing his pain, and I was resolved.

One look at him walking away from me, and I was crystal fucking clear.

I never wanted him to do it again.

"Shiraz."

It was doomed to be a sob from the second I opened my mouth, but I didn't care. My anguish cracked the air like a whip, stilling everyone at once. In short, continuing his retreat would scoot him into contender position for World's Biggest Asshole—though I was damn sure he still considered the risk even as he stopped, scuffing into the grass with his sexy untied boots.

As I stepped into the clearing with him, nobody said a word. As I moved even closer, even the wind stilled. It all seemed like a damn movie, but hell if I could name which one. This wasn't even Samsyn's plan—and I owed him *and* Camellia glances of apology for wrecking the plan—but no way was I letting my stare fall now. No way was I deviating from the one thing I'd traveled back here to say.

And, God help me, the love I'd come to save.

So get your shit together, woman—and say it.

"Turn around." Every tremble of my voice was like an airhorn blare in the thick silence. I took a deep breath anyway. Pressed closer to him, so only he could hear, and whispered, "Please, Master. Turn around and look at me."

Shiraz jerked back. But in inches of movement, stiff and fierce, he finally came back to face me. In huffs of breath, harsh and heavy, confronted me.

In one low, ferocious growl, told me exactly how pissed he was about being played. "You and I do not share whispers anymore, Miss Fava," he followed to it. "If you have something to say to me, you shall say it out loud, right here, before my family and friends"—he yanked up his head, throwing a damning look at Samsyn and Jayd—"who shall answer to me later about conveniently 'forgetting' your name was on this party guest list." All too quickly, his glare dropped back to me—and the force of his snarl took over again. "Well?" he prompted. "What the fuck is it?"

Before I could control it, a flinch took over. He nodded tersely, almost as if expecting it, getting halfway through a new whirl before I curled a hand into his shirt, forcing him back. "No!"

He ripped away from me. Spread his arms wide. Leaned in, bellowing, "Then what, Lucy? What the *hell* do you want from me, because there is not a great deal left here!"

I avoided the flinch. Barely. Began shifting from foot to foot instead, trying to focus on the Zen-like squish of my spikes into the grass. *Ladies and gentlemen, Buddha has left the garden.* And had left behind a throbbing headache for me. And muddy shoes.

And the drowning, debilitating force of Shiraz Cimarron's fury.

I didn't care. I *couldn't*. If this came out all wrong, then it just fucking would. If I hiccup-sobbed through it, then I just—

fucking

would.

"Shiraz." I shot up my chin. No more whispering. No more weakness. I was proud of what I had to say. If he wanted me to scream it from the top of the north tower turret then I would. "I... I was wrong. And...I'm sorry." It dissolved into a sob. I still didn't care. "I'm so...fucking...sorry."

He took half a step closer. It was tentative and abrupt—but at last, oh God at last, he was moving in the right direction. "Wrong." He nearly stuttered it out too. His lower lip trembled. The corners of his bleak, beautiful eyes tightened and creased. "Wrong about what?"

"About *what*?" Unbelievably, I laughed—but it wasn't easy because it was real. Sincere. Snark-free. Simply, utterly me. I had no idea who this person was. I didn't know the first thing about being her...about being this naked while still standing here in my clothes. But I wanted to try. God, how I wanted to *try*. "About...all of it, okay? I was...such an idiot. Such an ungrateful bitch, to the universe itself." Another laugh, even more painful, broke free. "And a hypocrite. Oh God, I was a hypocrite even more than a bitch! Did you know I gave Ambyr a speech about becoming a better woman for you? When I should've been looking in the freaking mirror..."

For a moment, the gritty lines on his face succumbed to a full gape. "A speech? To Ambyr? When?"

There'd be time to tell him later. I hoped. Time for talking to him about so much more. *I hoped.* It all came down...

To this.

To what I had to confess to him and mean it.

"I should have been giving *myself* the damn speech," I said through the tears. "I should have been becoming better for you...myself. That means being braver for you. Being here for you. And loving you—by starting with loving myself."

Just saying the words took away some of the fear. Not all of it, but maybe in time, I'd get better at this self-acceptance shit. I'd learn I really *was* good enough. Hell, the biggest part was already handled. I'd fallen head over heels in love with the prince.

I let the courage fill me up—at least enough to reach forward, both my hands wrapping into his—

And letting my heart burst open as he crushed his fingers around mine.

And letting my soul explode as he shoved his big, untied boots against my muddy, four-inch Diors.

And letting my blood race as he dropped his bold, strong forehead right down onto mine. "Fuck," he gritted. "My tupulai." One of his hands slid up, cupping the back of my neck. "Merderim, my sweet woman. Thank you."

My lips lifted. A lot. Got wet all over again as more tears broke free—this time, infused with just a little happy hope. Not a lot. Not yet...

"I love you too, Lucina Louise Fava." He angled his face up in order to press a fervent kiss between my eyebrows. "And I know this is so damn hard for you."

I let out another half-delirious laugh. It was either that or pull a chicken shit on the rest of this plan—and I'd come too far for that now. Across my country. Across an ocean. Past all the cliffs of my own fears. Beyond every boundary of my fantasies.

Into the dream-come-true of loving him.

The man who was going to understand if I had to get a little snarky about this.

"Hard?" I slid out a sideways smirk, while purposefully stepping back a little from him. His face, breathtaking in its perplexity, studied my every move...

As I knelt before him.

With both our hands entwined once more, and my gaze lifted to meet the vast lakes of his gaze, I spoke once more—making each word heard throughout the garden.

"Shiraz Noir Cimarron...you are the destiny I never thought I'd find. The miracle I never thought I'd believe. The fantasy I never knew could be fulfilled. You are the honesty of my soul, the essence of my spirit, the passion of my heart, and the joy in my life."

Salty drops on my face again—this time, rained from above. "*Lucina*. By the Creator...*pahaleur armeau*..."

"Let me finish," I sobbed. "Please. This is the important part."

He laughed now too. "All right."

I took advantage of the moment to get in a deep breath. "I'm not perfect, Shiraz—but damn it, I'm the perfect one for you."

"Halle-fucking-lujah," Ezra exclaimed.

"Creator be praised," Samsyn growled at the same time.

"On *those* special notes," I cracked, slanting my perfect prince an utterly imperfect grin, "what say you, my love, about the idea of...marrying me?"

Shiraz fell silent. But in that silence, I saw absolutely everything. The force of his adoration. The strength of his acceptance. The power of all the passion he offered—now, and for the rest of our lives.

His grip pulled tighter around mine—preparing, I assumed, to bring me back to my feet—only to stun me by being the one to move instead. Sweeping down...to kneel next to me.

Once there, he wasted no time getting his hold on other things. With a hand tunneled in my hair and an arm roped around my waist, he clutched me as close as he could possibly get me...

Before crushing his mouth to mine, in a kiss that gave his answer in a thousand universes of ways.

As applause burst around us—accented by both Ezra and Samsyn's hoots—we kissed and kissed and kissed, our tongues a hot tangle, our bodies pressed and passionate, our hearts pounding wildly against each other. When we pulled part, our breaths still mixed as the crowd still cheered, Shiraz dipped in a little closer, speaking words meant for me alone.

"I accept your proposal, Miss Fava," he murmured. "But you are still getting a ring, you know."

I popped my gaze wide, mocking and coy. "A Half Dome,

gorgeous? For little *moi?*"

"Yes. Soon. But not tonight." The din was so loud, I almost didn't hear the dark growl he inserted before murmuring in my ear, "Tonight...is for the handcuffs."

His words. My blood.

Scorch away, Your Highness.

As those elated cinders tumbled through my psyche, I grabbed the side of his face. Yanked him into another long, hungry, molten, meshing kiss.

"Holy shit," I pulled away long enough to whisper. "You really *can* see all my fantasies."

He smiled softly. Kissed the tip of my nose. Pulled me closer, wrapping me in the heat of his perfect, royal love. "I know."

ALSO BY ANGEL PAYNE

Cimarron Series:
Into His Dark
Into His Command
Into Her Fantasies

The Bolt Saga:
Bolt
Ignite
Pulse
Fuse
Surge
Light

Honor Bound:
Saved
Cuffed
Seduced
Wild
Wet
Hot
Masked
Mastered
Conquered
Ruled

Secrets of Stone Series:
(with Victoria Blue)
No Prince Charming
No More Masquerade
No Perfect Princess
No Magic Moment
No Lucky Number

No Simple Sacrifice
No Broken Bond
No White Knight

Temptation Court:
Naughty Little Gift
Perfect Little Toy
Bold Beautiful Love

**For a full list of Angel's other titles,
visit her at AngelPayne.com**

ACKNOWLEDGMENTS

An incredible, heartfelt thanks to Victoria Blue: You are there to celebrate the good, and you stick like glue through the crazy. You are, and eternally will be, such a precious treasure to me.

For friends I cannot ever thank enough, for the support, day and night, that has been more incredible than you know: Shannon Hunt, Angie Lynch, Theresa Stokes Harrell, and the Smut Book Club, Julie Kenner, Jenna Jacob, Carrie Ann Ryan, Lorraine Gibson, and Tracy Roelle.

Thank you, incredible beta goddesses! This one would NOT have been possible without you and your unflagging honesty: Lisa, Carey, Ceej, Amy.

So many thanks to the gang at Waterhouse Press for loving the Cimarrons as much as I do!

As always...a very special thanks to all the readers who have found this series and celebrate its weirdness. Stay weird, stay wild, stay true to the royalty inside yourself.

This one is also for anyone, anywhere, who feels like they aren't "enough."

You are enough.
You are worth the prince.
You are worth the perfection.

ABOUT ANGEL PAYNE

USA Today bestselling romance author Angel Payne loves to focus on high-heat romance starring memorable alpha men and the women who love them. She has numerous book series to her credit, including the action-packed Bolt Saga and Honor Bound series, Secrets of Stone series (with Victoria Blue), the intertwined Cimarron and Temptation Court series, the Suited for Sin series, and the Lords of Sin historicals, as well as several standalone titles.

Angel is a native Southern Californian, leading to her love of being in the outdoors, where she often reads and writes. She still lives in Southern California with her soul-mate husband and beautiful daughter, to whom she is a proud cosplay/culture con mom. Her passions also include whisky tasting, shoe shopping, and travel.

Visit her at AngelPayne.com